K-9 OUTLAW

A Kelton Jager Adventure
BOOK 1

A novel by

Charles N. Wendt

CHAPTER—1

Baylee Ann let go of Jessie to take off her motorcycle helmet and shake out the wet protruding ends of her dark hair. The muffler hissed from the raindrops rolling off their leather jackets. Her damp tight jeans grabbed as she threw a leg over the bike's seat and she nearly stumbled in the stilettos. She stole a glance at Bambi who was trying to light a cigarette with shivering hands, flicking the lighter without success. The five boys were already unzipping at the concrete columns of the overpass, the oily smell of wet asphalt giving way to the odor of warm urine.

"Watch my boots, Dickhead."

Jackets rustled as someone was shoved.

"Go mark your own tree, Bitch."

Baylee Ann took the lighter from Bambi's numb fingers and made a flame. Her friend's blank eyes showed a soft flicker of gratitude as she leaned in and sucked hard, the orange glow rapidly claiming half an inch of the Marlboro Red. They both leaned against Jessie's bike and shared a drag while the boys hooted in the background over some unheard remark.

"What do you think? Another half hour?" asked Baylee Ann.

Bambi nodded, "With the weather. Boys are lucky. I so have to pee."

"It's getting dark quick with the rain. Maybe you can sneak around the embankment?"

"Only if the rain lets up a little. My cunt's sore enough without getting rubbed by wet panties."

Bambi dropped the butt and coughed, the rattling of phlegm audible over rain pounding the overpass above their heads. She didn't bother to smear it with her foot.

Baylee Ann nodded shivering as drippings from her bangs went between her tattooed boobs. She pulled her thin jacket tighter and looked at the gray divided lanes winding between the cow pastures and scattered woods. Then she saw the figure up ahead walking alongside the road.

She guessed it was male given the broad brimmed slouch hat and the straight gait, but with the failing light she wasn't fully sure. A few more steps, and then yeah, definitely a man given the evident square shoulders despite the dark baggy poncho that hung to just above the hiking boots. There was a dog heeling with him, not big enough to be a German Shepherd, who wore a drab body harness. The dog alerted him and he hesitated a second upon seeing them in the shadows himself. Then they moved quickly across the deserted lanes to the other side of the overpass.

"Who the fuck is that guy?" asked one of the boys in a muffled voice.

Baylee Ann thought it was most probably Grover. He couldn't talk without an F-word in a sentence.

The wanderer weaved around the columns on the far shoulder, and climbed the sloping concrete of the retaining wall. In a few seconds the dog and he had silently disappeared into the darkness of the top corner. The rain slowed some.

Shawn stuck a tongue out of a smiling hairy face and rocked his head side to side. Jessie gave him a playful shove, making his long silver wallet chain jingle. Grover and the others fell in alongside as they formed an informal phalanx and crossed into the median.

Baylee Ann and Bambi huddled closer together without saying a word. They both knew that Shep and Rebel would be pissed at the diversion, but the boys were restless from the long ride down from Richmond and had grown bored of the two of them. The stranger was alone in the wrong place at a very wrong time. Bambi began to reach for another Marlboro, met Baylee Ann's eyes and knowingly pulled out a joint instead. The line of bikers stepped onto the far shoulder.

"That's far enough; I can hear you from there."

It was a commanding voice, with a confident and well measured cadence, despite a tone which indicated a younger man. The forceful challenge made the bikers fumble to an awkward and confused stop.

"We ain't coming to talk," called Jessie.

"We gonna fuck you up!" added Grover to some chuckles.

To her boys, inflicting fear was more fun than inflicting pain. It was probably making Grover's cold clammy dick stir. As Jessie stepped forward, the others followed. Bambi stared blankly at the gravel as her fingers took back the joint, trying to move as little as possible so as not to draw attention.

"Advance at your peril!"

The voice made Baylee Ann look up from Bambi, eyes trying to pierce the darkness above. There was no trace of panic or fear in that voice, the tone and cadence as before and the vocabulary choice a brutal contrast to her socializations near the North Carolina state line. Grover and Jessie exchanged blank looks of knitted eye-brows as their legs raised again.

Baylee Ann's lips began to form "No, wait!" but the inhaled warm smoke choked her voice into a cough. It wouldn't have mattered.

Five shots, so close together they echoed as a single roar. The dazzling muzzle flame of orange and blue licked out like dragon's breath from the shadows. The concussion reflected from the bridge overhead to the asphalt below, rang her ears and crushed her consciousness. Bambi upset the bike as she instinctively turned away, and the two women wound up in a heap on the gravel with high heels in the air.

The boys were dead, all of them. There was no contemplating the end of life while staring at bloody fingers failing to staunch a mortal wound. There was no crawling, vitality draining away, just to see the fading eyes of a fellow comrade. They simply dropped in their black leather jackets like a pile of discarded giant dominoes. She clutched Bambi on the ground, closed her eyes and wailed.

Kelton scanned over the Glock 40, the tritium reflex site glowing as a pale green triangle in the dark. He was sitting with his feet pulled against his butt, using his bent knees as support for his arms and his shins a shield for his vital organs. He switched magazines during the tactical pause to be ready for further action, but no one was moving down below.

"Azrael!"

The Belgian Malinois came bounding back into the darkness under the bridge from where Kelton had sent him outside less than a minute before. There had been no time to dress him in "mutt-muffs" or "doggles". He did a quick pat but the only wetness felt like cool rain water rather than anything warm and sticky and there was no smell of plasma. Ivory fangs glowed white in the low light and the tail repeatedly thumped the concrete as he passed him a Milk-Bone marosnack.

He holstered the gun, pulled off his ear muffs, and chomped several starlight mints as fast as he could. It didn't take long for the adrenaline dump to drop his blood sugar and the shakes to start. He extended his legs and lay down. His head throbbed and he worked on keeping his breathing slow and rhythmical. He wiped sweat away from his burning forehead, but it felt icy cold on his fingers. The world seemed to rush and envelop him as peripheral vision returned and he began to hear crying on the wind. Azrael panted and put a paw on his chest.

Kelton sat up to retrieve the iPhone in his buttoned shirt pocket and turned it on, but returned to scanning below while it booted. The bodies of the five bikers hadn't moved. Across the median and through the concrete columns he could see portions of the motorcycles parked on the far shoulder. It looked as if one or two had maybe fallen over. With the low light and the obstructed view, he was far from certain. He took a deep breath and fingered the keys.

"911 Operator, what is your emergency?" said a man's voice who sounded as if he made that greeting several times an hour.

"I'm at the 615 overpass on Virginia Route 903." Always give them your location first in case the call fails, thought Kelton. Do it just like they taught you at the academy.

"I've been attacked by a group of men and had to fire a pistol in self-defense to save myself. I'm wearing a brown hat and an old military poncho. There is a dog with me."

"Okay, Sir. I'm contacting emergency services to assist you. What's your name?"

"Kelton. Kelton Jager."

"Okay, Kelton. My name is Brett Kissel. Are you in a safe location?"

"No, but I'm hiding under the west end of the bridge. There may be more of them." Of course it's not a safe location he thought looking at the bodies below.

"I need to ask you some more questions, Kelton," insisted Mr. Kissel.

No you don't, he thought. He pushed at the red disconnect button but the call didn't drop.

"Are you injured, Kelton?"

"I'm not sure. I was attacked and I'm not feeling good."

Kelton remembered the old policeman who'd lived next door when he was in school and his advice to never give definitive answers. In nearly every case where someone is convicted of wrongdoing after a defensive shooting the 911 recording is the biggest piece of evidence. Be first to call 911 so you are the victim. Get the emergency services on the way to help you. Establish your self-dense claim. And then, most importantly, shut the hell up!

"How many times did you shoot?"

"I'm not really feeling good; I need to set you down."

"How far away were they when you opened fire?" persisted Brett.

"I think I hear more of them. I've got to hide."

He looked at the time on the phone and shoved it deep into his pocket. More muffled questions came, but he was tearing the wrapper on a power bar. He turned toward Azrael.

"This jerk is going to run our phone battery down."

It took nearly twenty minutes before he could see fast approaching blue flashes with red ones not far behind. Azrael started to howl at the sirens. He petted him, took a swig of water from the CamelBak, and waited.

Sheriff Chandler Fouche leaned forward in his seat, peering through the windshield of the Durango as the 615 bridge quickly came into view. The Rain-X treatment was doing its job so he hardly needed the wipers. Nor did a single bug spot mar the view. A quick glance in the rearview showed Rescue lagging well behind. They weren't brave when shooters were at large, but otherwise were competent and professional.

He stopped short with his high-beams still on, flipped on the auxiliary spot lights, and slowly surveyed from left to right and then bottom to top two times. Everything of note sheltered from the weather under the bridge, the grass embankments and gray concrete yielding nothing of interest. On the right shoulder, two women cowered in the circle of motorcycles like cavalry troopers taking cover behind their dead horses for the final stand at Little Bighorn. On the left shoulder, at the base of the concrete slope, a still line of bodies. Chandler couldn't make out for sure how many. Further up the slope, in the dark corner of the very top, someone turned on a small LED flashlight and gave it a small slow wave.

He pushed his radio's microphone button, "Be advised, Sheriff Fouche is on scene. Better get Buck out here, too. If you can't raise him on the radio, call Dixie's."

St. Albans Control Center came back, "Roger, Sheriff."

He unfastened the seatbelt and got out slowly, placing the pressed smoky bear hat with its clear plastic rain cover on his head despite the slackening drops. A couple steps forward, and then he stopped with hands on his hips to repeat his double scans, left to right and down to up, again. The shoes, pistol belt, and holster were Corfam, with a shiny black finish despite a dusting of rain droplets. His dark brown shirt and khaki trousers were starched, pressed and creased. A little gray showed in his short hair, but he was fit at seventy. No smudges dared infringe upon his brass nameplate or badge.

"Mr. Jager, come down so I can see you."

The voice was commanding, and practiced. Chandler had served as the county sheriff for thirty-five years.

A small light came shuffling down the concrete slope, and he could make out the figure in a poncho holding an iPhone with its flashlight on. The other hand held a web leash to a dog that heeled obediently beside him. Chandler's hand tingled over the magnum stainless-steel revolver. Threat? No Threat?

"I called 911. My name is Kelton Jager, Sir. My sidearm is holstered on my right thigh."

Chandler looked at his face, the vehicle's spotlight illumination dashed with red as well as blue, letting him know without turning around that rescue was on scene behind him.

"I want you to sit down right there at the base of the wall and not move around. Okay?"

"Yes, Sir."

The young man sat and the dog went down beside him. He sat quietly without fidgeting. Chandler could hear the pair of medics trotting up behind, the soft rattle of medical gear in plastic boxes announcing their advance. The sheriff strode forward, eyes still focused on Kelton and his hand at the ready to draw. He circled around behind him, and kneeled to pull the man's gun from the holster on the right thigh.

"Sir, please be advised that my weapon is in a loaded condition," stated Kelton as a matter of fact.

It was a huge automatic with an optic on top and a fat butt that certainly held a double stack magazine.

Chandler stared at Kelton and the dog a few seconds, but neither moved at all. He made a fast judgement, given the limited manpower on scene and the likely urgency of medical attention needed.

He yelled to the medics without moving his head, "The scene is secure. There's men down up ahead by those columns."

Chandler watched as the medics began pulling on latex gloves and kneeling beside the bodies, all sporting jackets of the Lowland Outlaws complete with their own bloody hole. It didn't take long before they knew there would be nothing to do there but stuff body bags after the photos were taken. They then divided forces, one medic crossing the median to the girls and the other returning to Kelton and the sheriff.

"Call me if he moves on you, but I don't think he will. Stay off the road. We haven't stopped traffic on your side yet."

Chandler turned to follow the first medic across the median. His deputy's blue lights became visible to the west on I-85, putting additional help just minutes away.

He recognized the two women, although their names hadn't been worth keeping track of. Young teens, desperate for money, entertained the drivers at the truck stop. Soon they aged out like these two and turned to other nefarious things. In his younger days, Chandler tried to put a stop to it but it was a losing battle. Instead he ticketed the drivers who didn't vote locally, and everyone knew it helped keep downward pressure on rising property taxes.

"Either of you ladies hurt?" began the medic as he kneeled down and flashed a penlight in their eyes. Everyone could smell the lingering pot smoke, but Chandler sized up the motorcycles instead.

They were all older mid-ranged Harleys, who had experienced a lot of time on the road. But beneath the paint chips and small gravel dents, it was clear they were all someone's pride and joy. There was road grime, but not the cake of dirt and bugs that occur in the absence of frequent washes. Plenty of tread showed on the tires. Here and there a new part glowed in comparison to the duller veterans. He unbuckled the straps on a black leather saddlebag.

"Do you have a warrant, Sheriff?" challenged the brunette over the shoulder of the kneeling medic as she sat by the blond girl.

"Does your name appear on the title of this motorcycle, Ma'am?"

Her eyes fell and he flipped the top up. Inside, in a sealed clear plastic pouch, were bales of paper cash. It was heavy duty plastic, like to ship small machine parts. You wouldn't tear at it very long with just your fingers before looking around for a knife. He took a quick picture with his camera phone. There appeared to be many denominations, so he gave a gentle heft holding it in his right hand. Maybe five pounds?

"What's the good word, Boss?" Deputy Buck Garner called from the window of his Chevy Interceptor patrol car. Buck's eyes were intent on the clear plastic bag.

"Back up to the exit so you don't drive through the crime scene and go up and over. Then get across the median and park to block oncoming traffic. There's this guy over there with a dog. Find the drugs on him. This is a deal that went bad."

"Yes, Sir."

Buck put the car in reverse and flew weaving past the Durango and ambulance. A couple of cars parked behind in silent frustration backed up to follow the deputy over the bridge. Another set of headlights approached from that direction, big and blocky, indicating the approach of the county coroner's sedan. Thankfully there were no collisions in the chaos of two-way traffic on one-way lanes.

Chandler advanced on the women, the medic giving a nod of good health to him and tactfully backing away from the interview. The two remained seated on the pavement, backs against the rear tire of the fallen chopper.

"Were you buying or selling?"

The little blond just sat there with blank glassy eyes looking off into space. The tears and wet hair frazzles mixed with the road soot on her face.

"We just stopped because of the rain," said the brunette in a defiant tone.

"Where were you coming from?"

"I don't know, I wasn't driving."

Her eyes gleamed hard.

The sheriff sighed. The two were definitely locals, although their lot lizard days must have ended years ago. He'd send Buck over later to get their witness particulars. That's what deputies were for. He crossed the median a second time, staying on the gravel under the bridge so mud wouldn't foul his shoes, still holding the bag of money in his right hand.

"Did you find the drugs?"

His deputy shook his head slowly, standing easy with hands draped at his side.

"No drugs. I mean other than a small plastic bottle with aspirin, Motrin, and cold medicine."

"What else you got?" asked Chandler posing again with feet shoulder width apart and hands on his hips.

Buck didn't reply to the question as the sheriff scanned the display.

Kelton's poncho had been removed and the contents of the backpack neatly arranged in a few rows on the dry concrete. He had a few pairs of wool army socks and Under Armor synthetic underwear. The damp ones were placed near a net bag. One each shirt and pants. A small gun cleaning kit where the rod and brushes stored in the handle. A couple of three-ounce plastic bottles and a box of baking soda. Some dog equipment including a metal bowl and a pair of rubber Kong toys. A tiny bit of food. There was clearly nothing of value to the bikers worth trading a plastic bag of cash.

"What's in the small bottles?"

"One is bleach with a dropper for treating drinking water. The other laundry soap. He says he washes socks and underwear in the dog bowl and that the synthetics and wool dry quickly in the net bag. When the weather is better anyway," Buck shrugged as if it made sense but not understanding why someone would live this way.

Chandler looked at Kelton's feet. The boots seemed new in that the colors weren't faded, and there was no fraying of the laces. However, there were creases of many miles in the leather and the tread was worn. Dull metal military dog tags were laced into each. Sheriff and Deputy stepped away a few steps and dropped their voices.

"What does he have for identification?"

"He has a current US passport and a laminated DD-214 showing an honorable discharge six weeks ago from the US Army with the rank of captain. No driver's license."

"I had been thinking buyer and seller meet under deserted bridge. Seller leaves product at another location so as not to be ripped off or implicated if a sting. Buyers get pissed he has no product to sell; they go to beat him, and get shot for it. How's that play?"

Buck scratched his chin and shook his head.

"The buyer wants the product and attacking the seller doesn't get them the product. Cold meets generally happen in a parking lot where you can have privacy to talk, but other people are around to curb violence. A deserted venue doesn't go with that. Finally, this guy doesn't really profile as a dealer.

What if we reverse buyer and seller?"

Chandler gave a smirk. They both already knew the answer but they worked by stating the obvious of what they knew.

"Man buys drugs from bikers, and the bikers, after stashing the cash, decide to return and take back drugs we haven't found yet? That's not good for business."

"What's the play, Boss?" Buck blinked his eyes several times as camera flashes from the nearby County Coroner gave him spots.

"Get particulars from our witnesses and give them a ride to where they want to go. I'll secure the cash and take in Mr. Jager."

Buck nodded and walked on. A technician was placing numbered placards by the shell casings on the ground.

"Mr. Jager, I'm going to issue you a notice to appear for late morning tomorrow to give the Commonwealth's Attorney a chance to review preliminary reports and decide how he wants to proceed. I'll keep your gun in the meantime. Can I give you a ride to Ed's Truck Stop? They have a diner and motel rooms."

"Yes, Sir. Thank you. That works for me as long as they take dogs."

"Come on, then. I reckon Miss Doris will just have to put up with it." Best of all, I don't have to do overtime watching you in my holding cell, the old sheriff thought.

Across the street Baylee Ann screeched, "Well if Buck ain't coming for Bambi. Tell me I don't live in the South."

"Shut it, Baylee Ann," snarled the deputy.

CHAPTER—2

Deputy Buck Garner closed his cellphone on Doris, and got into his patrol car to speed up Virginia Route 903. His jaw clinched and his knuckles were white on the steering wheel. In minutes he reached the interchange with I-85, and turned left after the overpass to the onramp that would put him southbound. With no services, the exit didn't rate a cloverleaf. Baylee Ann and Bambi sat together in the middle of the back seat, eyes glaring through the grill and burning up his rearview mirror. A blue sign on the interstate announced diesel, food, and lodging in five miles. There was nothing but black pastures beyond the rusty barbed-wire fences paralleling the road.

"You can drop us off at Ed's," stated Baylee Ann.

"I'm taking both of you to Rebel. Now shut the fuck up, you bitches."

Baylee Ann slapped the grate making it rattle with a snarl on her face, while Bambi sunk lower in the seat. Then she crossed her arms and turned her head to stare out the window. It wasn't just that he was taking them to where they didn't want to go. He'd also gathered up all the marihuana.

He could see the lights of St. Albans, Virginia, the seat of Lowland County, just a mile west of the interstate. It was just a dot of a town in a sliver of a county, mainly floodplains around the Roanoke River. Hopes were high once upon a time as the interstate came through, but things never really took off. The modern rest stops at the North Carolina state line weren't far away. It was flanked on I-85 by the big truck stops of South Hill, Virginia and the 401 interchange in North Carolina. There were no historical markers of some brave general leading his men passing through. The college bound escaped. Young men whose parents didn't own the farms mostly worked the farms or fled to the military. Young women with no marriage prospects spread their legs at Ed's Truck Stop and the skanks in the back were no exception. The Lowland Outlaws motorcycle gang was the only other driver of true crime for a lawman to contend with.

Buck desperately wanted to be sheriff, getting the title on his resume as it were, before the county defaulted and became absorbed by Lunen or Mecklenburg. Lazy, self-absorbed and ancient Chandler Fouche displayed no inclination of vacating the post. The county coffers were empty, fueled only by skyrocketing farm property taxes or traffic fines. However, the small family farms had been losing ground to the big corporate growers and ranchers in the Midwest for decades. There simply wasn't much to tax. The sheriff's office was down to just the two of them now, with personnel slots for other deputies once again unfunded in the county budget.

The county budget didn't contain raises again either. The last one was three years ago, and it was less than 2%. He was never going to get ahead and this Rebel situation was not going to help. He twisted his lips and slapped the steering wheel, making Bambi begin to shake. Baylee Ann held her while he tried to relax himself.

He took the St. Albans' exit, made a right at the bottom of the ramp to head west and immediately passed Ed's Truck Stop on his left. The white cinderblock buildings were peeling paint and black with mildew and diesel soot. Flashing neon signs were missing a letter here and there, but still legible. They boasted of fuel, an all-night diner, cheap coffee, and a small motel. The low-pressure sodium parking lot lights washed a handful of rigs in an orange hue. The diesel island stood deserted. Things definitely had a slow air to them.

Buck noted the parking separation of the rigs. A few were lined up side to side for the shortest possible walk to the diner's entrance. A couple of others were parked in the back of the lot, the farthest they could get from both each other, the road, and the line of trucks close to the buildings despite the wet weather. They'd be his pick for a lizard hunt if Chandler wasn't making him play chauffeur.

After the parking lot it was all overgrown field, with so many bushes and briars it would take a major effort to return it to pasture land. He went thru the flashing yellow light at north-south running Thigpen Road and less than a half mile later he drove among the tired brown brick buildings of downtown with cracking sidewalks, and faded street paint. There were the usual small businesses one sees in a small town: barbershop, bank, cafés, hardware and general merchandisers. A handful of small houses on tiny lots, one of which was Dixie's, mixed in-between. And then, on the right, was the sheriff's office.

It was the last building before the county parking lot and town park, or courthouse square, ended in Lowland Road. In the greenspace stood a bronze civil war soldier standing sentry over a marble tablet listing local casualties amongst the groomed trees; they didn't have a cannon barrel. The north side of the square was bordered by the clinic and rescue squad. Across Lowland Road to the west of the park were the county offices, courthouse and church backing up to the railroad tracks. The Norfolk Southern ran six trains a day and never had reason to stop here. Buck took a left at the stop sign.

Rebel's place was three miles south of town on Lowland Road, a junky garage backing up to those same rails. The guy had only been a year ahead of him in high school, and Buck knew his dad was the old drunk haunting the courthouse square, crippled from when a jack slipped and a tractor crushed his hips. Rebel had taken over the business but had been more into cars than tractors and not into cleanup at all. A scattering of scrub trees relentlessly grew up through the twisted rusty hulks, and Buck wondered if someday the derelicts would be grown from the ground.

Among the cracked shells of Fords and Chevys surrounded by last year's pokeberry weeds, mounds of rusty dented mufflers and rotting tires, and the smears of oil and battery acid was the Gray Ghost herself. Once upon a time it had been a production Dodge Charger before embarking on a career as the local dirt track king. The crowd had roared but the cash prize of production classes didn't cover expenses and no one in this town had money to sponsor. A decade had gone by since her engine had last revved, and the car-hauler trailer upon which she rode had sunk nearly to the axels in the dirt. The faded confederate battle flag and red "4" were hard to read under the layers of pollen despite his high-beams.

A savage bend in the frame ensured she would never be sold for anything but scrap, even if Rebel Tarwick had such inclination.

Buck quickly toggled the siren, setting off various hounds a quarter mile around. He was about to do it again, when he saw the light come on in the greasy shop window. He hit the door release for the back seat instead. Waste oil burned for heat fouled the air that would have otherwise been fresh from spring rain on cedar trees.

Baylee Ann followed Bambi out the passenger side without saying a word. She slammed the door hard and hurried down the dark washed out gravel drive before he had the presence of mind to get out and backhand her. The stilettos gave way in the soft ground and she fell. He floored the accelerator, red clay mud from the churning tires pelting her face, but it wasn't fast enough to race him away from school days.

He'd been a senior when he first noticed the two freshmen girls. The little blond was so precious and innocent. Mouthy Baylee Ann kept getting in his way though, and he'd had no money to buy them nice things like the long-haul truckers. Now, nearly a decade and a half later, he resented having anything to do with them. Buck still wasn't sure how Doris managed to divert Dixie from a similar fate. The thought of Dixie gave him a longing, and he began to drive back toward downtown and her little house. It would give Rebel a chance to cool down over the money before they talked.

Dixie peered into the oval mirror and finished rubbing the cotton ball around her eyes, carefully removing the mascara. Next in her bedtime ritual was the moisturizer, cold upon her fingers, followed by the whitening toothpaste to fight the nicotine stains. She didn't really like to smoke, but Dixie felt staying thin would keep her desirable. Still, the only men who had tried to put a ring on her finger were had-been jocks, dumb fat rednecks, or wore grease-stained blue shirts. Secretly she hoped someone would return from college to visit their parents, they would meet, and she would be whisked away out of here. Realistically though, at twenty-six, Dixie knew she desperately needed another life plan or rapidly be condemned to small town poverty.

A soft knock at the door interrupted her routine and scarlet flushed her cheeks under the silky cream. She wore only the robe of white terrycloth, the chipped nail varnish on her pale toes in full display. Dixie was in no mood for unannounced visitors, but the small house only took a few steps to look through the peephole. Deputy Garner stood on her stoop.

Her mother was always coldly polite to him, but in private was quick to list his shortcomings. When young that would have driven her into his arms, but she seemed to see more eye to eye with mother every year. Sure, she had slept with him a few times in the six months they'd been casually dating. But her attitude toward that was more akin to the unsatisfying chore of changing a car's oil to keep it running.

"Come on, Dixie. Open up," he said.

She did open the door a crack, firm against the unyielding chain, and glowered from around its edge. Her eyes fell upon the rusting wrought iron fence he'd promised a couple of months ago to tend to.

"Let me in, Sweetie," he smiled.

"I'm not accepting visitors, announced or otherwise. Please go away," she said firmly, but softly. There was no reason to make a scene with the neighbors.

Buck scratched the side of his jaw and his shoulders sagged forward. Then his eyes came up to meet hers.

"I just wanted to invite you to an early lunch tomorrow before my shift starts. Say 11:00 at Suzanne's? I think you like their coffee and sandwiches."

The corners of Dixie's mouth turned tense and down, but then softened. She did like their sandwiches and the white linen table cloths. She'd get a respectable public date, without having to fulfill any expectations after.

"Then I will see you there," she said coolly and closed the door. With a quick twist of her hand, the heavy deadbolt slammed into the frame.

Buck rapidly turned to trot down the chipped and worn brick steps and began rubbing his temples as soon as he turned on the sidewalk toward his patrol car. His loins ached in frustration, but his mind was already racing ahead to calling Rebel. If there was going to be an opportunity it would be late morning, but first that man would have to get his cool back and Baylee Ann's bigmouthed disposition wouldn't help. The patrol car started easily and in a quick mile he was past the yellow flasher at Thigpen and making a right into Ed's, its lights glowing lonely by the busy interstate overpass.

He immediately scanned for the young man with the dog upon coming in the door, but only drivers rested at tables taking their time with coffee and newspapers. Doris was working the counter. He grabbed a stool whose red vinyl upholstery was repaired with silver duct tape. She wandered over with a steaming pot and poured without a word.

"What do you think?" he asked without looking up at her.

"What's Rebel have to say?" Doris replied. She never took her eyes from the coffee cup.

"I haven't called him yet, but he knows. I took Baylee Ann to him for that."

She considered, panning the room.

"I think we best lay low. Slow down purchases. There will be an intensive investigation with the shooting and we don't want to raise any additional red flags when there's lots of poking around going on."

"What's your take on the shooter?" asked Buck. He knew she had a really good eye for sizing up people.

Doris shrugged, "A real polite young man. Looks homeless with a dog at first glance, but if you take the time to look you know there's more to him. He's well-spoken and well-kept despite living on the road. You've looked in the eyes of homeless men before. They're dull and distant without any glint of hope. One look in his eyes and you know that not only is a lot going on up there, there's a relaxed confidence that he is exactly where he wants to be. He's not one to trifle with."

"The sooner he wanders up the road the better off we will be," agreed Buck.

He finally took a sip of the black coffee. There was the scorched aftertaste of a pot that spent many long hours on constant duty.

Buck shook his head softly, "But I don't think it's going to go down that way. There will be questioning that will keep him around. And before they are done with him and send him and his mutt packing, Rebel will want the money. I sure as hell want my share."

Doris coldly stared him down, her glare the product of thirty years of low-life interstate travelers.

"If you let anything happen to my Dixie, I mean just a chipped nail, I will drag you down in that pit of hell even if I have to fall down into it with you to do it. You understand me?"

"Yes, Ma'am. I'll get her out of the way. Now bring me the phone."

He tried to act confident and in control, but Rebel Tarwick wasn't someone anyone controlled nor was Doris someone you fooled with an act.

Doris handed it over, the traditional tan keypad supporting the handset on top, with an extra-long and twisted coil cord greasy from being repeatedly dragged across the diner floor. The buttons still made the headset beep as he dialed. The answer came on the ninth ring.

"What?" came Rebel's gruff voice, his breaths coming quick and heavy.

Buck thought he could hear whimpering in the background and looked up at Doris. Her beady gray eyes held him over the tops of her steel wire reading glasses, offering no respite.

"You've got a chance to get the money back. The evidence safe in Chandler's office is a piece of crap. He'll be at Ed's questioning our suspect in the morning. I'm not back on duty till noon and I'm taking Dixie to an early lunch. No one will be there. The alley entrance will be unlocked."

"I'll tell 'em was you who told me where the safe was."

Buck ignored the leverage. It was simply Rebel's way of communicating that they were in this together. They all were, he thought, as he winked at Doris. Her face didn't soften.

"Try not to make a big mess. He won't want to report it missing or a break-in or anything."

The line went dead. He smiled briefly at her as he replaced the headset. She took back the phone and walked her coffee pot to a trucker at the other end of the counter without saying another word to him.

The deputy wiped his sweaty palms along the stripes of his trousers and turned toward the door, leaving the half-empty coffee cup behind. He drove out of the parking lot to a cluster of trees near the exit-ramp shoulder. Buck didn't bother to turn on the radar gun. There were a lot of things that could go wrong tomorrow and he wanted the rest of his shift to ponder them.

CHAPTER—3

Azrael watched Kelton's chest rise and fall under the faded brown blanket. His ears were up and alert, although there hadn't been any concerns to raise his black-masked face off his paws. His coat had dried from last night's bath, and it was all about waiting until his master stirred to get food. There was no reason to worry or to get restless. Food, rest, water, play, and the opportunity to eliminate came with both regularity and flawless reliability. And he enjoyed using his ivory white fangs on any and all whose actions dared infringe upon those basic needs or their provider.

Kelton's dreams of the war were persistent but not unwelcome at night. Those four years deployed were the climactic culmination of adolescent dreams of glory, academy life and many months training at state-side bases. Until a few months ago, it constituted his entire adult life and his subconscious hadn't yet let go.

It was a life hard fought and struggled for. There had been the late nights studying, the long runs and the calisthenics to muscle failure. It was held together with rigid discipline and the suppression of hormones. It rode upon the adventure of training with automatic weapons and rapelling out of helicopters. A life shared with those special type of friends you only make when you are young, magnified by being in an alien world of strange customs, doing things that most dare not dream.

His subconscious didn't concern itself with the proper time and place of faces, or whether or not they still lived. It merely spliced together random fragments of memories, some fantastic like a burning vehicle, and others as mundane as a chow hall line. There were the morning crowds of men commuting in business suits and head scarfs while he walked the sidewalk wearing fatigues and body armor. Honking vehicles were flanked by tan concrete buildings towering over the groomed palm trees. A warm breeze off the heated sands, snaked through the urban canyons, and caressed the skin of his cheeks with its exotic scents of far away.

"Okay, I'm up. You don't have to pant in my face and then act all pleasantly surprised when my eyes open."

Azrael gave a soft whine and thumped his tail expectantly.

"I don't know. Maybe tap me with your paw or something. What time is it?"

Azrael cocked his head to the side at the question. A digital clock-radio unit flashed digits that were obviously incorrect. They were incorrect to Kelton, at least anyway. The iPhone charging next to it said 7:45AM. He pulled the tab on a can of dogfood and banged it out into the stainless-steel bowl. A quick flash of teeth gave way to a licking tongue. Kelton sat down a moment in a rickety chair by the corroded air conditioner and slowly blinked sleep from his eyes. There wasn't any hurry this morning.

The sheets of the bed were threadbare with a tired blanket sporting cigarette burn marks. The concrete block walls were white except where the bed's scarred headboard had battered them in numerous liaisons. No art was wasted on the walls. The carpet was sun faded and showed the trail from bed to the tiny bathroom. Small pebbles and a torn piece of condom wrapper nestled in the corner, out of reach of the superficial vacuuming.

But there were no bugs and it had been much better than being on the ground. Kelton felt good, he decided, and clean. So what if he had killed five more men last night? He stood and stretched away the stiffness from the long sleep. His stomach gave a soft rumble, but he didn't reach for one of his protein bars. He and Azrael had been on the side of the road for several days in damp weather. It was time for a real meal.

With the luxury of power, he made sure the pair of external smart phone batteries had charged properly, and then made a quick check of email and bank statements. With a swipe of the finger he paid his credit card in full. All was as should be, except he kept reaching for his missing gun.

He decided upon another shower and this time he shaved. His towel was still damp from last night, and Azrael had done for the other, but it mostly got the job done. The clothes he'd washed in the sink last night were still a little damp, so he put them in the outside net pockets of his rucksack. He also rinsed out and refilled his CamelBak. Even though it was "city water" he added a drop of bleach anyway. With everything packed, he placed Azrael in harness and laced up his boots.

Kelton did a slow walk around the room for any scattered items saying a mantra to himself "never leave any gear behind as you may not get to come back." He found none. And with that, and a quick detour to a grassy parking lot island where Azrael did his business, he was off to a real breakfast.

The glass door was mud splashed and well fingerprinted, showing not much more than a waitress wanted sign and a tattered "Visa MasterCard accepted here" sticker. There were no hours posted, given the twenty-four hour operations. Old fragments of scotch tape showed where business cards and other advertisements had recently been removed. He entered.

Inside was perhaps a third full, a mix of truckers and travelers. Doris was behind the scarred counter again, even though she had checked him in last night with the sheriff. The counter was "L" shaped, with stools for loners. The register was at the top of the long side on the left, with a gap to get behind the counter where there was a doorway and window to the kitchen. Opposite the counter's long side along the front windows were booths for larger parties. The section by the short side of the counter was a convenience store with soda coolers, racks of bagged snacks, and the restrooms.

"Dogs can't be in the restaurant," she challenged.

People went silent as they looked at the man in drab clothes with the backpack and the dog, before turning away to resume conversation.

He sat down at a booth for four along the front window and sent Azrael up underneath the table to be hidden from view. The menu was on a sheet of paper slid underneath the glass tabletop. Doris came over in a slow stiff walk with her waitress pad.

"I'm sorry. The sheriff says I must stay here and I don't want to leave my dog alone in the room and have him tear it up. I promise he'll be no trouble."

She shrugged, "The health inspector won't like it, but I'm not chasing customers away when Chandler did say that. They haven't given us better than a 'C' in the last five years anyway."

"I'll make it worth your while with steak and eggs, double hash browns with cheese and onions, and a stack of pancakes. Sweet tea to drink, please."

She scribbled with the pen gouging the paper, verified that the meat should be rare and the eggs over easy, and hustled away toward the grill window and then to the coffee pot for a trucker in the corner. Service was decent given the short staffing, and it wasn't long before he relished stuffing himself.

His hands and mouth were on auto-pilot while his mind began to race. He couldn't serve his dog if he was in jail, and even if he'd done nothing wrong that remained a very real outcome for a period of time anyway. Second thoughts about whether he should have called 911 assaulted his mind, beat back by the fact of witnesses and the dim prospect of evading a manhunt on foot and being forever on the run. But not once did he entertain even an iota of regret over taking their lives.

Doris had just refilled his tea glass and carried away the plates when the sheriff's Durango pulled up next to the building. Chandler gave no sign of recognizing him in front of the plate-glass window as he exited the SUV, but it would be hard to excuse even a blind man for not seeing him. The sheriff paused as he entered, feet spread and hands draped at his sides holding a briefcase, and slowly scanned the room a couple of times. His chin stayed high, the Smoky Bear hat rim starched proudly level, giving all plenty of time to note his presence. Then he moved towards Kelton's table.

Kelton stood as he approached, "Good morning, Sheriff."

Chandler extended his hand and Kelton shook it.

"Please sit, Mr. Jager."

Kelton did so and Sheriff Chandler Fouche gracefully sat down opposite, leaning forward so as not to wrinkle his shirt on the booth back. He sat the briefcase on the floor beside his seat.

"I recognize your claim of self-defense, but a couple of factors concern me. The first is the amount of ammunition you were carrying. A total of six magazines, nearly a hundred rounds. It appears as if you were looking for trouble."

"Am I being investigated for the rounds I fired, or the rounds I didn't fire?" challenged Kelton.

Chandler made a slight shrug trying to encourage him to talk. Kelton sat in relaxed silence, which stretched until Doris came with a steaming cup of coffee. Chandler took a sip and waited. Many were uncomfortable with "empty air", but Kelton wasn't concerned. He'd spent years of cadet life not allowed to talk. Finally, Chandler relented, as Kelton knew he would have to.

"Okay, point taken. The other is the distance. They were unarmed and out of arm's reach."

"You ever train the Tueller Drill, Sheriff?"

"Why don't you tell me what that means to you?" asked Chandler.

"The question is, if someone is armed with a contact weapon, like a knife, how close does he have to be before he constitutes an imminent threat? Dennis Tueller was a Utah lawman who attempted to answer that question. He put an armed deputy on the firing line along with a second individual. The second person would take off running away from the berm. This was the cue for the deputy to draw and fire at a target on the berm. When the shot was fired, Tueller noted how far the second person had run. After many trials, the typical distance was found to be around twenty-one feet; a lot further distance than most people think.

What was different for me was I had to shoot four others before I could engage the final target. That would extend the threat distance. Clearly, I was in imminent jeopardy."

The subtle nod of Chandler's head made it clear to Kelton he had heard of Tueller. Most law enforcement who were worth something had. Even if they claimed ignorance, they certainly had been subjected to training based upon it. The sheriff shifted to a more free-form approach of conversation.

"So what are we supposed to do with you?"

Kelton wasn't taking that bait any more than he'd be pressured by silence. There was no reason to share regrets of the soul in the hopes of sympathy or approval. He had no regrets. He didn't need another's validation either; that came from within.

"Return my gun, and send me walking down the road with my dog."

"Maybe," smiled Chandler. "Tell me more about you. Where you headed?"

Kelton shrugged, "Wherever my dog takes me."

"Where you from?"

"Wherever my dog has been."

Sheriff Fouche sat quietly, pouring sugar into the acidic coffee, trying to leverage silence again to encourage Kelton to share more. Kelton touched Safari on his iPhone instead, bringing up the Drudge Report. Chandler cleared his throat in annoyance.

"You have another question, Sheriff?" asked Kelton without looking up.

"How is it you were under that bridge with that much cash money in a saddlebag? I don't know if it was a drug deal or an attempt to setup a tryst with a pair of girls, but it doesn't sound like coincidence to me."

"It wasn't coincidence."

Chandler's eyes widened slightly in surprise. He stared expectantly. Kelton continued.

"It was rain. Good guys or bad, we simply took shelter."

Kelton saw the involuntary eye roll and knew Chandler was on the edge of losing his cool. He'd been insolent enough to put him on the defensive, but didn't want to overdo it and make him mad. Likewise, he knew Sheriff Fouche didn't want to push on him so hard to cause him to lawyer up.

The sheriff pulled the briefcase onto the table by the ketchup, popped the latches, and reached for one of several brown file folders. It contained a stack of photographs which looked to have been hastily printed on office paper rather than sent out for prints. The sheriff's cellphone began to vibrate, but he hit ignore without even looking at it.

"I just need to validate a few things for the record. Many of these have been answered already, either by you or are obvious from the scene. The faster we get through it, the faster we can close this investigation and get you on your way. Okay?"

"Yes, Sir."

The radio on his utility belt crackled, "Deputy Garner entering radio net."

The sheriff reached for his microphone talk button and quickly keyed it two times in acknowledgment before flipping the photo.

"Is this your gun?"

The 8.5" x 11" photograph showed the Glock 40, serial number up, in nearly actual size. Kelton nodded.

"Why such a big one?"

Kelton smirked, "How many survivor interviews indicated they wanted a smaller gun?"

"Right," sighed Chandler, "and it's chambered in 10mm auto?"

Kelton nodded again.

"Your concealed carry permit is a Utah nonresident permit. You don't sound like you are from there?"

"I've never even been there. But their permit has some of the most reciprocity recognition by other states so I applied my mail. But I consider myself to be carrying openly. The holster is in plain view on my right thigh, and my gun is really too large to conceal. However, with my poncho on due to the rain I can see the concealed argument, but since Virginia recognizes my permit that issue would seem moot."

Doris walked over with the lunch menus, and the ticket from breakfast. Kelton pulled out his USAA credit card and handed it to her without looking at the check or taking his eyes from Chandler.

"Okay, moving on. Did you attempt to give any of the victims first aid?"

"Yes, I treated myself for adrenaline overload."

Chandler sighed again.

"I mean the men who were shot," he clarified with strained patience.

The sheriff's phone buzzed again, and again he hit ignore.

"No. I knew there were more of them back at the motorcycles so I thought it prudent to call 911 and stay hidden instead."

"Fine. This is a copy of your identification, which happens to be a passport. Most people we ask for I.D. provide us a driver's license."

"I don't have one. My mom couldn't afford the insurance when I was in high school. Then it was off to West Point and immediately to war. I had a military driver's license so I could operate government vehicles while on post. But frankly, as an officer, I would just grab some private to shuttle me around. The army preferred that, and the young soldiers didn't really mind the light duty."

The sheriff's radio crackled, "Sheriff, this is Doctor Fairborn. Can you pick up your phone please?"

Chandler's eye brows knitted up. Kelton surmised it was highly unusual for a doctor to use the police radio net.

"That's our coroner, Mr. Jager. Please excuse me for a second," he said as he keyed the microphone on his left shoulder. "Sheriff here. I will pick up."

The cellphone vibrated a third time and the sheriff was as good as his word.

"Good morning, Sheriff Fouche."

The volume was turned up to make it easier for the old Sheriff to hear, but it also allowed Kelton to hear the other side of the conversation. Doris wandered over with the coffee pot even though Chandler's cup was mostly full. She poured slowly.

"Chandler, I'm at your office. Came in to drop off my preliminary report to you. Dixie's not here and it looks as if there's been a break-in. Your office safe is open and battered."

Doris stopped pouring the coffee and just froze. Chandler knew she had overheard and keyed his radio.

"Buck, have you seen Dixie this morning?"

The deputy's reply was quick, "We had an early lunch at Suzanne's. She left there, maybe, twenty minutes ago."

Kelton began to relax figuring it was a long walk back or maybe Dixie had some other errands to run while she'd been out anyway. However, Chandler and Doris tensed their shoulders and eyes narrowed.

"Sheriff, you have to find my baby girl."

"Can your dog track?" asked the Sheriff.

"Yes he can, but I'm not sure it would really be my place to get involved. At least until your district attorney clears me."

"Please help find my baby," pleaded Doris.

"Do a good job and I'll make sure he knows of your cooperation. It will support your case about being a 'good guy' under that bridge. Okay?"

"Alright. Let me use the restroom and I'll come with you."

Chandler raised his phone again to the side of his head, "Okay, we will be there in a few minutes."

CHAPTER—4

Kelton appraised the St. Albans Sheriff's Office through the Durango's windshield and decided it looked as if it were built in the twenties. The bricks were weathered and bonded with cracked mortar. Vertical rust stains streaked down from the flat roof's scuppers to half-wild hedges against the base. The windows were caked with mildew and pollen, but had clearly been updated sometime in the last thirty years or so. A couple held air conditioner units whose aluminum was badly oxidized. Ankle high weeds poked from the sidewalk cracks leading to the main entrance and the grass had yet to be mowed this season. In short, most army buildings which dated back to World War II, were in better shape. Kelton also recognized the coroner's vehicle from the night before amongst the others in the city owned lot.

Sheriff Fouche swung out the driver's side and strode on a mission straight toward the sidewalk and the heavy metal doors facing Main Street, but Kelton took his time with Azrael's leash and got a feel for his surroundings. A small hardware and feed store was south across the street, with living space above. A faded painted sign for "Mail Pouch Chewing Tobacco" still loomed on the side of the second floor. The city park to the west and north abutted the parking lot, where the greenery appeared better groomed amongst a few statues. It was surrounded by a knee high stone wall, perhaps a hundred yards on a side. Through a combination of architecture and bits of signage he decided a church, county offices and a few shops faced the west side. He couldn't tell what the buildings to the north were, although one looked "medical" being painted white in contrast to the taller brown brick neighbor on the corner. Chandler was now looking back from the front sidewalk leading to the building's entrance with narrowed eyes.

"Sorry, had to get his leash on. Also left my pack on your back seat on top of that locked ammo can you have on the floor if that's okay."

They went inside without Chandler saying a word, eyes transitioning from the bright light outside to dull fluorescents. Cork bulletin boards displayed wanted and missing person posters mixed around public service announcements featuring McGruff the Crime Dog. The entryway terminated in a front counter which flipped up on one side to walk through to the space behind containing a battleship gray metal desk for the receptionist and several matching file cabinets. All were adorned with magnets holding scraps of paper and the occasional dent. The floor tiles seemed a bit dusty. Old cubicle workstations went around the perimeter, but most looked long unoccupied. Yellow ceiling tiles served as a monument to the once smoking workplace. An old heavyset man in a white lab coat holding a manila folder stood by the water jug just to the right of the back hallway.

"Sorry to keep you waiting, Doug," said the sheriff. "What have you got?"

"Don't you want to know what happened in your office first?" gestured Dr. Doug Fairborn around the corner.

Chandler shook his head, "Nothing was in there for whoever to take. I went home after the scene. This is the first I've been back to the office."

Fairborn looked slightly disappointed, although his bushy drooping eyebrows could hardly fall further than their natural state. Chandler walked over to a bookcase holding several large black binders on top of which was a long black charger holding radio batteries with several LED lights in green and red. He swapped one out with the radio on his belt while Kelton lingered with Azrael in the entryway on the other side of the counter to give them some space. Above the battery charger was a four-foot by six-foot map of the city covered in Plexiglas.

"Well," said Dr. Fairborn with his cheeks drooping like a basset hound, "I wanted to share a couple of my preliminary findings."

His voice was low and muttered, but Kelton could hear him just fine. They stood within arm's reach of each other, the sheriff standing relaxed with his head cocked slightly to one side while the doctor wandered away from the water jug to lean on the side of the receptionist's desk.

"All five of the victims suffered acute coronary and spinal trauma from a single entry wound, and probably bled out in less than a minute after hitting the pavement. All had exit wounds and so far no bullets have been recovered. Given the frontal orientation of the wound channels, I can tell you that none reacted significantly to the assault. First shot to fifth were fired in well under a second, probably closer to half a second, with precision shot placement. Whoever this guy is, he is extremely dangerous with a handgun," finished the doctor, whispering in a low deep tone.

"He's a former army officer who took shelter from the rain. The CA will determine how we proceed, but I think his affirmation defense is strong. We will have to concede the element of disparity of force given it was five to one. Proximity wise, they were certainly close enough to require action on his part if he was in fact facing hostile intent. The only real question is, was he actually under attack?"

"We've two witnesses. What do they have to say?"

"I haven't seen Buck's report, but there would be plenty of room for the defense to challenge their character as well as them having to explain why the victims had moved to the other side of the bridge away from the motorcycles. But that's assuming those women don't collaborate the young man's account. I actually have a suspicion they will."

"Alright. I just do the medical stuff. I will finalize my report by the end of the week," said the old doctor playfully punching him on the arm, "but it is my considered professional opinion that the five motorcycle riders did not die from natural causes."

Azrael's head tracked the doctor and showed a silent fang as he passed the counter and walked down the front hall to the parking lot. Sheriff Fouche held the manila file considering, eyes staring at the empty holster on Kelton's thigh. From down the front hall they heard Doctor Fairborn's voice just before he reached the front doors.

"Good afternoon, Buck."

"Have a good day, Doctor. Hey, Sheriff, what's the scoop?"

Kelton sized up the deputy in the daylight. He was dressed and equipped properly, but his eyes were sunken and his uniform had some fading and fraying. The broad shoulders said he may have been an athlete once, but his stomach was starting to bulge over his utility belt.

"We had a break-in this morning. Mr. Jager and his dog are going to see if we can track the perp who took Dixie."

Kelton saw Buck's eyes flash wide for a second before a poker mask reappeared.

Buck asked, "Okay, so where do we start?"

"Scent trails last for days and since Deputy Dixie is here daily going different directions, I think we should try and track your intruder," advised Kelton.

Buck gave a chuckle.

"What's so funny?"

"Dixie is our receptionist and file girl, Mr. Jager," explained the sheriff with a slight upturn at the corner of his mouth.

"Right. Your office then?"

Sheriff Fouche turned to lead the way down the back hallway with Deputy Garner bringing up the rear. There were a couple of restrooms on the right, one for each traditional gender, flanking a water fountain built-in to the cinderblock walls. It didn't hum with refrigeration equipment and the dry lime deposits indicated it had been replaced by the blue water jug years ago. Beyond the restrooms was an interrogation room with a window to see inside from the hallway. Opposite it and the facilities were a couple of offices occupied by Buck and Chandler. The hallway ended in a glass door, beyond which were three holding cells and a finger printing station. A heavy metal door past the cells and leading to the alley outback was ajar.

Unlike the aged and neglected aspects of the building at large, Chandler's office was neat and tidy. A large black plastic nameplate with white letters, flanked by the Sheriff's Star and the Virginia State Seal, held a couple of black pens. Behind the walnut veneer desk with the green leather top were the American and Virginia State flags, whose colors were new and bright despite being exposed to west sun near the window facing the parking lot. A pair of leather chairs with brass studs waited to make visitors comfortable. Kelton felt it looked more like a photo-studio for making campaign literature, "Re-elect hardworking Sheriff Fouche" as he posed behind his desk, than a real office.

But clearly, it hadn't gone unmolested. The pristine chamber, lacking dust or scratches in woodwork, held a glaring violation of trespass. The polished metal floor safe with its brass dial and lever handle sat on its side, the base sporting twisted lag bolts and anchors with fouled threads. Concrete dust lay near the holes in the carpet. It had been brutally ripped open using a combination of a sledge hammer and a pry bar. It had been a safe more for show than effectiveness, more akin to a personal safe from a hardware store than a bank vault. Inside, a couple boxes of checks and a revolver were askew from the safe's rough handling.

"We should dust for prints," suggested Buck.

"No way. I'm not making a mess with all that dust in here when he probably wore gloves anyway," rebuked Chandler.

"Is anything missing?" asked Kelton.

"No, that looks like everything."

"Okay, the exertion to manually open that safe will give us a strong scent pad to start our track. You smell that boy? You got that?"

Azrael wagged his tail as he circled the area around the safe, nose to floor. Then his body grew tense and his tail became straighter, legs bending like he was ready to pounce.

"Such!," commanded Kelton. It sounded like "Zook". The dog world used German words so the dogs weren't confused by hearing command words used in idle conversation.

The dog exited the office in a rush where Buck stood near the doorway, and took a left toward the cells. Kelton opened the glass hallway door for him, letting the twenty-five foot tracking lead play out before following. By then, Azrael was going through the ajar door into the alley, leading the small posse.

The alley was gravel and narrow for any two-way traffic, but sufficient to keep delivery trucks and unsightly garbage cans off the narrow city streets. Azrael wasn't distracted by the trove of odors available, and stuck to the trail like he was trained to do. He worked steadily, nose down, swaying slightly from side to side with each stride. Azrael turned right, heading east, and Kelton carefully followed, letting the dog move at his own pace, while keeping the lead from fouling and causing a distraction. Sheriff and deputy, also not wanting to interfere, lagged a respectful distance.

Two buildings over Azrael paused, and turned right again down a driveway that exited onto Main Street. He strode out onto the sidewalk, sniffed in an arc from left to right a few times, and then sat down. Kelton slowly approached, coiling the tracking lead as he came closer, with Chandler and Buck on his heels. He looked east and west, up and down the street, noting the occasional parked car and light traffic. There was a barbershop across the street. Turning around he noted that one building was a realtor's office with a sign in the window reading "Out Showing Houses". The other was shuttered with a sheet of plywood across the window, although a painted sign above read "Appliance Repair Parts and Service".

"The trail ends here at the curb," said Kelton as he kneeled to praise Azrael and provide him a marosnack.

"Right. I'll go across the street and see if old Mr. Butler noted anything," said Buck.

He strode across, slowing just enough to check traffic.

"What would happen if I asked you to track Miss Dixie?" asked Chandler.

Kelton remained on one knee rubbing Azrael's chest. The dog's eyes were closed and his nose high in the air as his tongue hung from the left corner of his mouth.

"We would find her trails of the last few days. That's plural. If she walks to work, I will show you her house. I will show you where she walked to lunch if that was her habit. I will show you where her trail ends in the parking lot if she drives.

What I can't do is tell you if she disappeared off of some point of one of those regular tracks, or whether such disappearance was voluntary or not. If there are two trails to lunch, I can't definitively tell you where she went today versus yesterday."

"You've certainly narrowed down the possibilities for us to canvas," said Chandler and then the wise face went dark.

He looked up and down the street and then at the apartment windows above the shops. Kelton stood and brushed off his knee with his hand while Chandler's mental gears turned.

"Our Main Street isn't as busy as most Main Streets in this country, but it's still a lousy place to try and force a young woman into a car if she doesn't want to go," he said as a

Buick station wagon went by. "Can you tell me if Miss Dixie was even here on this sidewalk?"

"Yes, Sir. But I can't tell if its post break-in or from this morning if she walks to work this way."

"I see. Her house is just back up the road there a piece."

Buck came running out of Mr. Butler's barbershop, caused an east bound rusty Ford Bronco to check his brakes, and dashed to join them.

"Mr. Butler said a blue truck was parked here late morning. He didn't see it leave, but he wrote down the license plate. Said he's being nosy about who might buy the old Whirlpool building and fix it up. Doesn't want competition," said Buck with a wink.

"Alright, let's go in and run that plate."

They walked fast down the sidewalk, west toward the city park, rather than retrace their steps in the alley to the back entrance. Once they were through the heavy metal doors, sheriff and deputy raced towards their offices leaving Kelton and Azrael loitering by Dixie's desk.

"Buck, what's that plate so I can put out an A.P.B. with the State Police and neighboring counties?"

The deputy hesitated a quick second, "Give me a minute to boot up this old computer and check if it matches the vehicle described. Mr. Butler's eyes aren't what they used to be and I'd hate to put out bad information."

"Good thinking. I'll be checking email in my office and tidying up. Yell when you have something."

And then they were both gone into their respective office doors, leaving him alone up front.

Kelton looked at the map above the battery charger first. The map wasn't from Rand-McNally, but rather a framed city planner blueprint with scale blotches for the structures. St. Albans was basically a three street town, with Main Street spanning from the railroad tracks on the west side of town to Ed's Truck Stop and then past the interstate. Paralleling Main Street to the north was Smallwood Street, and similarly to the south was Coalson Street. Unlike Main, they both were more residential than commercial. Smallwood Street crossed the tracks and curved off to the northwest. Thigpen Road, running north and south along the interstate connected them on their east ends, and Lowland Road intersected them to the west by the railroad tracks.

Next he wandered over to Dixie's workstation, Azrael heeling obediently on the leash.

"Platz," he commanded and Azrael dropped down to the floor.

He let the leash go slack and turned the sweater covered chair around. A few strands of blond hair lingered on the headrest. The upholstery showed a stain or two from long service, but the sweater looked fashionable and professional in Kelton's limited knowledge of such things. He guessed it lived on the chair for those times the heat struggled or the air conditioning was too much.

The desktop computer hummed with lights, although the monitor was dark, and he reached out and gave the mouse, greasy with hand lotion, a wiggle. He smelled the perfumed lotion on his hand as the screen lit up, showing a log-in page for the Lowland County Sheriff's Department. To the right were the usual office supplies: scissors, paper clips, pens, and rubber bands among others. No light shone on the desk phone to indicate any messages.

Kelton looked over his shoulder down the back hallway, and wondered what was taking so long. No sounds came indicating that either of the two lawmen were imminently leaving their offices. He looked at his dog, and Azrael seemed to smile at him with bright eyes full of boundless energy.

Kelton thought to himself if they weren't going to look for clues, he was going to. He started opening the desk drawers. A couple contained files, or binders with procedures for handling certain types of calls. In the upper left drawer, he found a small clutch purse. He opened the clasp, finding a pair of cigarettes, a tube of lipstick, a tampon, ten dollars, and her driver's license.

Dixie Johnson was twenty-six and lived on Main Street. She was not an organ donor. Her picture looked more like a glamor shot than an I.D. photo with loud mascara, thick lipstick, and her hair styled. There was a resemblance to Doris, but she was much narrower in the face. Judging from the height and weight, if you believe them he thought, she was also taller and slenderer than her mom.

It was as good a scent article as they would find he thought and slipped it into his left side cargo pant pocket. He then turned around, leaned on the desk, and waited staring down the back hallway. Another fifteen minutes passed, and he wondered why he cared to be involved. Old computers from the army would lap these guys several times over. Finally, Buck yelled from his office.

"Okay, I got it. Braxton Greene, he's on Thigpen about three miles south. Also has some misdemeanor drug convictions," Buck stepped into the hallway. "I'll be back with him in half an hour."

"Take Mr. Jager and that dog with you. Tracking might be helpful down in those wilds," instructed the Sheriff from his office.

Buck began, "I'm not sure how good an idea it is to…"

"Can I please have my gun back?" asked Kelton. "Even if just for self-defense purposes?"

The sheriff came to the doorway of his office and declared, "It's evidence."

"Evidence of what? That I most likely shot the bikers because I was found near the bodies and it's my gun? That point is not in dispute.

I'm willing to help you find your receptionist, but we're not approaching known criminals unarmed."

The deputy patted his Colt service revolver and interjected, "We're not, Dog-Boy."

"'We' was referring to Azrael and myself," corrected Kelton. "Besides, having a gun doesn't make you armed any more than having a guitar makes you a musician."

Deputy Garner bristled, "You should be back in one of the cells until the CA makes his decision."

"And just how many qualifying rounds did you fire last year with that?" challenged Kelton.

"Boys, quiet!" ordered Chandler with his hands on his hips.

"I'm returning Mr. Jager's firearm strictly for self-defense. It's in my vehicle. He has no LEO immunity. We need the dog to find Dixie or at least this Braxton character. But get this," the sheriff said with narrowing eyes and voice dropping an octave but not a decibel in volume, "I don't care if you are some West Point war hero. You screw around in my town and I will put you back there in one of those cells until someone else says otherwise. Any questions?"

"Yeah," said Kelton. "What the hell is a LEO?"

Buck sighed in resignation, "Law Enforcement Officer. Come on, let's go. Try not to get hair all over my car."

CHAPTER—5

Dixie squirmed on the floor of the back seat of the crew cab truck not being able to see. She felt tiny bits of gravel dig at her skin and the odor of oily grease filled her nostrils. Her bound hands forced the twisting motion to come from her torso, and a tire iron punished her ribs. The duct tape over her mouth pulled at her skin as her face rubbed against the vinyl seatback, but it caused the old windbreaker tied over her eyes by its sleeves to slip from her head. A gruff voice protested as her knees hit the back of the driver's seat.

"Settle down back there," he ordered.

She could feel the mucous on the back of her throat beginning to interfere with her breathing and she tried to calm herself. She extended her legs to push her head more upright, thumping it against the door panel with a final push from her hands behind her back. She took a slow deep sniffling breath and then violently blew her nose, trying to clear her air passage. The snot sprayed all over the stained white blouse. Breaths came easier and she tried to look around.

"I said to stop moving around," he snarled with added emphasis.

Dixie barely noted his tone. Finally facing upward without the blindfold she could see through the upper part of the truck's windows, but it didn't count for anything but a few treetops and a piece of a billboard. Unfortunately, she didn't recognize it to get a bearing. The roof of the cab was cardboard, the headliner cut away when it had sagged downward. Some remnants of the fabric could be seen in the moldings. On the floor were her high heeled shoes she'd kicked off in the struggle to try and leave behind a clue. He'd been able to gather her up over a shoulder and still kneel down to scoop them up.

She remembered Buck telling her if she was being abducted in a trunk to try and push out one of the taillights. If you could get a foot or a hand outside, no one riding in the vehicle would be able to see it. A "Good Samaritan" cellphone call later and the police would be on their way.

But the floor of the crew cab back seat seemed to offer a lot fewer options. He would hear or feel if she squirmed around too much and no one would see her through the windows if she didn't manage to get higher.

Slowly she extended her legs some more, trying hard not to bump the back of the driver's seat. She got her hips over the hump and began to sit more upright against the rear passenger side door. The fluids in her sinuses and throat drained away some more and breathing became almost normal. She started to lean to her left to be able to see the driver, but thought better of it. If she couldn't see him, he couldn't see her. Dixie hugged the back of the passenger seat instead.

Cocking her head, she looked upward through the corner of her left eye. She hoped someone might see the top of her blond head, but knew it wasn't good enough. It was definitely a full-sized pickup she was riding in, meaning the only people who would see her blond hair would need to be looking down from a tractor-trailer. Anything smaller, even a full size SUV like a Hummer, wouldn't have the angle needed. And frankly, a blond-haired head was unlikely to attract the needed attention. Only the duct tape over her mouth would possibly alarm a passerby.

Dixie decided she needed to go for the door handle. It was an "in the armrest type" that a properly seated passenger would place his hand on the armrest with his four fingers on the vertical lever and pull it toward him. The mechanism would release the catch and the door could then be pushed open. Unfortunately, the cable tie held her hands quite fast and she could feel them and her shoulders beginning to go numb. She decided to try with her face.

She planted her face into the armrest, trying to get her nose behind the lever. She couldn't breathe and backed off for a few breaths before trying again. Dixie thought of the beak on a girl in middle school she had made fun of once and now wished for such a protuberance. Wishes or not, it wasn't working. The right angle of the armrest and the door panel kept her nose from getting anywhere close enough, even if her nose would be strong enough to pull the lever. Cyrano de Bergerac wouldn't be able to do it. It would have to be her hands.

To do that, she would have to climb up onto the seat and attract a strong rebuke from the driver. She'd need to exit as immediately as possible to maximize her chances of getting away. If she didn't, he'd be sure to take other measures that would make the next attempt impossible. She paused to think things through a little more.

With the likely dual rear axle and accompanying wide rear fenders, she'd need to push hard with her legs to launch herself to avoid being run over. That would mean going out the passenger door backward head first and tumbling over to get her legs clear of the truck's rear tires. It would also mean going out blindly. He would likely slam on the brakes and run around the front of the truck to collect her if there weren't too many people around.

Dixie doubted she'd be able to outrun him. Bare feet were not good for running, and she was not athletic. Should she jump back in the truck, and try to lock the doors and hold down the horn? She dismissed it. By the time he stopped the truck, he would be closer to the door than her and she would just be running back into his clutches. The best bet would be to run down the road for all she was worth and hope there was traffic. And the further they drove from St. Albans, the more rural and less busy the roads became.

So she waited for her moment. The big diesel sang for long minutes, but then she felt the automatic transmission down shift as revolutions fell. The truck started to make a right turn, and she felt the centrifugal forces helping her to sit up as she sprang up on to the back seat. With a thrust of her legs, her back was against the door and even with bound hands found the door latch. She started to pull just as he slammed the brakes.

Her body was thrown forward, her neck whiplashing sideways into the passenger headrest. It felt like a punch to her temple, and she dropped like a losing boxer to the mat of the floorboards. She felt the truck speeding up again.

"The child safety locks are on. Now do what I told you and lay there real still."

Dixie's eyes began to well up, and she felt the rumble in her sinuses as she labored to breathe again. She had no further ideas, was powerless and knew it. Her imagination turned from a friend helping her find an ingenious escape, to a creative sadist savoring possibilities which lay ahead. Vibrations from the truck hid the trembling from herself at first, but she couldn't help tuning into her body's physical reaction to the fear.

The wait wasn't long all told. She estimated some thirty minutes of driving, but with several turns and a stretch of gravel road knew they could be anywhere. The last bit was twisty with potholes, and trees were thick in the window tops. Dixie didn't try and get up as the truck stopped, the engine ceased and he got out. A moment later her head fell backward as the rear passenger door opened and he towered over her. The scream came out her nose as he ripped a section of silver duct tape off a large roll and pressed it over her eyes. Dixie tried to scream again, but this time his large hairy hand pinched her nostrils shut. She writhed trying to break free and then heard him laugh as he released while she sneezed and sputtered. She felt his other hand grab her hair on the top of her head and use it to pull her out of the truck, feet dragging behind. He left her shoes.

Through the torn pantyhose she felt the gravel transition to smooth concrete, and a greasy oily smell got stronger. At the same time, she could feel the air transition from sunny breeze to stale cool darkness. She was inside a machine shop or a garage of some sort. The hand let go of her hair, dropping her but she didn't bang her head too hard on the floor. There was a scraping noise of metal on concrete for a second, and then the rumble of an approaching nearby train kept her from hearing anything else.

There wasn't any horn blowing, but the big locomotive gently shook the foundation slab upon which she lay. Then the hand was grabbing her hair again, and she felt an arm around her waist lifting her up. Her feet weren't dragged but a couple yards before she felt them lose contact with the floor and fall beneath her. Then the arm about her waist let go and she was falling.

The handful of hair kept her from dropping and she writhed liked an unfortunate at the gallows. Her legs thrashed every which way as she struggled to find any purchase. Even her gyrating hips, convulsing in fear of the abyss, failed to make contact with any edge or lip of a hole that Dixie knew must be there. Regardless, she couldn't tell if solid ground was feet away or merely inches. She just felt herself sinking lower, her flailing feet not finding bottom, dangling by a giant meaty hand smelling of used engine oil holding tight to the hair on top of her head. Then the hand simply and calmly let go.

She screamed, nostrils spraying again, but she ran out of altitude before she ran out of breath. Her left foot hit first, but off balance, so she twisted backward and sideways to slam her left shoulder and hip on the concrete. Heat and pressure surged about her ankle as she lay on her side, knees drawn up toward her chest as much as bound hands would allow.

She could hear the train continuing, and then become muffled all of a sudden like an exterior door had been closed. Or a cover had been placed upon the pit like a jar's lid with a bug inside. Even muffled, the train was loud enough for her not to hear anything else. Nor could she see with the tape still in place. Tape also sealed taste off from sensation. Smell was overwhelmed with used engine oil, and her fear driven sweat. Only feel spoke to her, the comforting solidarity of the unyielding slab upon which she lay. It was strong and stable and it meant she was somewhere.

Dixie suddenly realized she was not alone, the mental shock destroying any fragment of memory of how she became aware in the first place. Maybe she heard something after the train's departure or felt the stir of breath, warm, fresh and alive. It panicked her, but her wrist's bounds held and the ankle kept her from rising. Before she could do something rash, she felt the grabbing at her cheek.

"Be still, Dimwit. Trying to get this crap off you," the soft voice said. A woman's voice.

Arms gently helped her up into a sitting position, her legs and the throbbing ankle straight out in front of her. The hands slowly and gradually started picking at the tape on her mouth. Despite the sweats of terror, the adhesive maintained a mean grip on her tender skin.

"Stop sniveling. It will be worth it to breathe better, okay? Nod if you can understand me."

Dixie nodded her head so quick those soft hands lost the edge of the tape.

"Hold still so I can get a bit more edge."

Lip and skin pulled away from the side of her mouth, lipstick doing little to blunt the abrasion. A little air began to leak in from the corner, gurgling from her mouthful of saliva. Then her head suddenly jerked to the right as a savage tug tore the tape away, ripping skin and hairs from her face. She screamed as her face burned in agony.

A scream that felt good because she could breathe air again. All the saliva, blood, mucous threatening the breathing she once took for granted, swept away. She gulped in the air, coughed and spit with no regard for being a lady.

"Thank you," she breathed again. "That was terrible."

"Lean forward a bit and I'll get your hands. This might take a while."

"Will you please take the tape off my eyes?" begged Dixie.

"As soon as I free your hands you can do it yourself."

Dixie pleaded, "Please don't cut me then. I'm already so hurt."

A sarcastic chuckle replied, "I've an old fender washer that I've been scraping the edge on the concrete. Those cable ties are tough stuff and its duller than a butter knife. Raise your hands a little so I can get this piece of brick underneath them. It helps to have something hard to press against."

"What's your name?"

"I'm Bambi. My friend Baylee Ann is sleeping on the desk in front of you. She's usually the one who helps people. Even people like you."

"Thank you. I'm Dixie."

"Yeah, we've seen you strutting around, even though you never gave the time of day to us. You're Ed's girl."

The voice was behind her now and Dixie could feel the back and forth rhythm as Bambi sawed at the hard plastic cable tie.

"He'll pay you for helping me. And my boyfriend's a deputy. He'll get us out of this."

"Buck may come to get you out, but he isn't going to do shit for us."

"You know him?"

"This county only got one deputy anymore. Everyone knows Bucky Boy."

"Oh," Dixie considered.

Dixie waited in her darkness as she felt the back and forth scraping of the makeshift tool. Bambi grunted, and drops of sweat fell in the back of Dixie's collar.

"Try and pull your hands apart. I know it won't give yet, it just works better if things are taut."

Dixie pulled until her arms quivered, feeling the broad plastic strap dig into her skin.

"A little lower. Keep it on the brick," she instructed as she sawed away.

Bambi shifted, switching sides to use her other hand. This brought a renewed vigor at first, but it quickly trailed off. Dixie felt the hot breaths on the back of her neck. Years of cigarettes and joints, without teeth brushing, made it quite foul.

"Just a second. Let me get something."

Bambi was back in just a moment like she said.

"Okay, Dixie, pull them tight again," she directed. "Yeah, and push down so the bottom part of the strap is on the brick."

Dixie strained to comply, feeling the girl place the edge of the washer on the strap again but this time not sawing back and forth. Instead came a sharp blow from a second brick, a stone, or maybe just a chunk of left over concrete. More blows came down.

"Ow! That hurt!" Dixie sobbed as the flesh on the edge of her hands was pinched between makeshift hammer and anvil.

"Stop whining, dammit. I think it's almost there."

Another string of blows, with deliberate and focused tapping renewing the assault. And then suddenly, her hands were free.

She brought them immediately around in front of her and rubbed the tortured wrists. Needles of pain shot through her arms and shoulders as circulation returned. She moaned and fell backward into Bambi, splaying out flat on her back. Bambi embraced her gently, and rocked her as Dixie cried just a little.

"Okay, sit up so I can stand up and check on Baylee Ann."

"I thought you said she was sleeping?"

Dixie grabbed at the edges of the tape on her eyes as she heard Bambi move around to the front.

"Passed out would be a better way to put it," explained Bambi.

Dixie took a deep breath and ripped the tape away. Her carefully plucked eyebrows were annihilated, and blood flowed freely as skin around her eyes ripped away. Only her thick makeup kept it from being worse. She rubbed at the gunky adhesive left behind, struggling to get her eyelids open. A small shop light with its dirty bulb initially blinded her, but soon allowed the dingy vault to come into view.

Bambi stood on the far side of a scarred and battered desk, stroking Baylee Ann's dark hair. Baylee Ann's naked form lay upon the desk, head hanging down on the far side. Dixie hobbled over with the genuine concern of a fellow woman. A thin metal strap with small holes down its center, like the bracing for a garage door opener, went over the back of Baylee Ann's neck and had been screwed into the wood of the desktop. The heads of the screws looked stripped, like he had used an electric drill with the torque control set too high. Her bare feet were on the floor, but knees were bent as her hips sagged upon the near side after the strain of countless hours. Angry welts, perhaps inflicted by pinching hands punctuated her bare white buttocks. Dixie averted her eyes downward.

Even with the low light and the black stains of engine repair on the floor, the small pool of blood between Baylee Ann's feet was evident. Dixie tried to resist following to the source with her eyes, but couldn't help tracking the dry bloody streaks. Little trails of crimson snaked up her ankles, arched over her calves and continued up her thighs. The smears were thicker here, and redder with the glisten of sticky wetness. Dixie tried to prepare herself for the sight of the ripped and battered lips of Baylee Ann's sex, and then choked in horror as she realized it was fine. The engorged and torn source of the blood was above it.

CHAPTER—6

Deputy Buck Garner silently seethed, driving around the new partners in his patrol car. He went east on Main Street and, before reaching Ed's Truck Stop and the interstate, took a right at the flashing yellow light to go south on Thigpen Road. Buck stole a peek in the rearview at Azrael panting on the back seat behind the grate. The dog's black face watched the road, not paying him any mind. It was degrading to be playing chauffeur to a dumb animal. It was humiliating to see a homeless man effectively elevated to his status as a deputy after being in town for only a day. And it was outright mortifying not being able to immediately slap down Rebel for taking his frigid bitch girlfriend. The faster this could be resolved the better. He didn't want this drifter getting comfortable in town and deciding he wanted to stick around.

"So who's this Braxton guy?" asked Kelton.

South on Thigpen Road, after passing Coalson Street on the right with its old but well-kept houses, quickly became rural with untamed groves and pasture land. The road's windy direction slowly drifted away from the busy lanes of the interstate to the east.

"A local guy who's been in trouble for weed a few times over the years," Buck said feigning courtesy.

"And he has a blue truck?" pressed Kelton.

"Yeah, just like Mr. Butler said."

"What would he want with your secretary?"

Buck snapped, "What does every man want? And her dad is one of the richest businessmen in town."

Buck took a breath trying to get the annoyance out of his tone, while Kelton nodded thoughtfully. The deputy was shrewd enough to know he wanted to talk as little as possible. The more he said, the more things that could possibly trip him up later. However, he had to play a game of civility or Sheriff Fouche would want to know why. Fortunately, the sharp retort seemed to have headed off more questions and Braxton's place wasn't far. But Kelton's question about motive was one he would have to confront sooner or later.

"Okay partner, it's just up ahead on the left," said Buck reconciling.

They were less than five miles south of Main Street, but there were other ways to measure distance from the kept brown brick buildings of St. Albans. The home looked nearly dilapidated, only a stray splotch of white in an eave indicating it had ever been painted at all. The shrubs and dogwood trees sported wild branches with spring blossoms in a yard choked with saplings and briars. A trace of woodsmoke wafted above the crumbling chimney and a light blue Chevy pickup was parked on the side. No other houses were in view. The small lot nestled into scraggy cow pastures.

Buck turned hard into the drive and keyed his radio mike, "Deputy Garner on scene of primary suspect's residence."

Sheriff Fouche keyed the mike twice in response, but didn't speak.

Azrael whined on the back seat as Buck opened the driver's door.

"Stay here," he ordered.

And then Buck rushed to the front porch with his right hand on the butt of his sidearm.

Kelton watched Deputy Garner bang on the door with his left fist and heard the call of, "Sheriff's Office! Open up!"

However, his eyes were already shifting to the old truck. It was a small thing, maybe an S-10, but Kelton wasn't much into cars. He could barely drive. Clearly it was a working man's vehicle with its racks over the truck's bed holding ladders and assorted pipes. The color was sort of a robin egg blue, with white bottom panels for a two-tone look before the introduction of rusts and dents. The glass seemed to all be intact although a hubcap was missing on the side he could see.

The sound of splintering wood brought Kelton's focus back to the porch where Deputy Garner had assaulted the door. It seemed to be putting up a good fight, but after a few more blows of the shoulder and a kick or two the rotted frame gave and it swung inward. Pistol in the air, the lawman rushed inside. Kelton exited the patrol car, and immediately opened the rear passenger door for Azrael.

The Belgian Shepherd jumped down and immediately took a heel position with bright eyes on Kelton. With multiple trails for Dixie leaving the sheriff's office there was no point in trying to track her so they had gone after the thief. But out here was different. He held out the small purse he'd taken from the desk to his dog's nose.

"Such," he instructed.

Azrael dropped his nose to the ground in excited purpose, rapidly zigzagging across the driveway and the long overgrown yard about the house. Kelton watched for a few moments and then walked over to the blue and white truck. It was unlocked. Various wrenches, heating torches, and other small tools lay loose in the bed. Upon the torn upholstery of the front seat was a cheese splattered microwave. He powered up his iPhone and took a few photographs.

Azrael came back full of energy and a desperate look on his face. He'd found nothing.

"Such," he instructed again and Azrael put nose to the ground and circled the truck.

There were no indications.

"Fuss," Kelton ordered next and fed a treat as soon as Azrael was in the heel position. The command sounded like "Foos". He then started walking toward the front steps of pitted concrete.

Deputy Garner came out with a scraggly old man, short and thin, whose hands were cuffed behind him. His canvas shirt was unbuttoned and hung open to reveal the absence of an undershirt. The man's skin was dark bronze after years of working in the sun, marred with graying hair. The pants were a heavy denim with rips, soils and paint splatters of construction sites or similar work. His eyes looked heavy with sleep.

"I got him. We're going to have a record fast solve. Fuck asking the state police for help!"

"Any sign of the girl?" asked Kelton.

Buck's eyes widened slightly at the question, "I'll get him back to the station and interrogate him. It won't take long to get a confession."

"Sir, can you please tell me which girl you are looking for?" asked Braxton Greene, the old man, in a clear and articulate tone.

"Shut up," ordered Buck as he lifted Braxton's arms behind him to guide him to the car. "We'll play these games back in town."

Braxton didn't resist, but Buck handled him roughly, banging his head while shoving him into the back seat. He slammed the door and turned to Kelton.

"You coming or what?" accused Buck.

"I need to walk my dog," replied Kelton with a shrug. "I guess I'll see you in a couple of hours."

"Suit yourself," Buck said with a could care less smile. In a moment the engine roared, gravel flew, and the patrol car was zooming north on Thigpen Road back toward the flashing light.

Kelton watched them speed off, and wondered if Buck was hopeful that now that he had his gun back he would just wander off. Not likely, with the threat of an indictment hanging over him, he thought; although he would love to leave them to their own devices and focus on his dog. That was all the responsibility that mattered to him anymore. That he hadn't messed up yet, anyway.

But there was something else eating at him, that kept him from washing his hands of it all while waiting for the slow turning wheels of justice. Buck didn't seem that concerned with Dixie's disappearance, only the arrest of the break-in suspect. Kelton didn't know the young lady, but he knew her mother and she'd been civil to Azrael, letting him in the motel room and diner. Also, deeply ingrained in the young male warrior ethos was the moral imperative to rescue damsels in distress. He smiled briefly at an academy memory, where one of his overly popular female classmates was trying to goad him into doing something for her. Kelton had told her that chivalry was only for ladies to which Meghan had replied that chivalry was for everyone. If Buck wasn't looking for her, Kelton would be.

"Okay, what do we know?" asked Kelton as he walked after Buck's car.

Azrael heeled alongside, looking up at Kelton with wide eyes and hanging tongue.

"You're right, Azrael. Dixie was never here."

Azrael barked at him with clear expectation.

"Do you think after he got her out of the truck, he put a microwave in the cab?"

Azrael barked again, his front feet scattering gravel.

"Would you call that truck blue?"

The shepherd's nose and tail came up, feet splayed in all directions.

"Or would you say light blue? Or blue and white?"

"Could that man wrestle a spirited woman down the alley and into his truck? Did he beat open that safe with a pipe wrench?"

The third bark could probably be heard all the way back in town.

Kelton took the rubber Kong toy from his right cargo pocket, swirled it by the foot of rope, and flung it into one of the fields by the road. The dog launched like lightning through the grass and briars to retrieve it as Kelton walked the shoulder on the left side of the road. Normally, it would have been a perfect time to collect thoughts, but the process was continuously interrupted by having to repeat throwing the Kong toy. The one clear thing though was Deputy Gardner was incompetent or not on the up and up.

Braxton Greene blinked his eyes hard, trying to shed their sticky gritty feeling. His head hurt from the deputy banging it and he definitely felt like munching some pretzels or potato chips. And he wanted to use the restroom.

"Mr. Greene, it won't take long to get you back to the sheriff's office," began Buck, "and once that happens I won't have much flexibility to help you out. If that happens you could get accused of all types of bad things. Things like kidnapping and breaking and entering. You probably didn't do it, but it could cost you a lot of time and money until its sorted out.

But if you say your truck was parked across from Mr. Butler's Barbershop this morning, then I can close out an eye witness statement and you can go back to leaky pipes and clogged drains.

What do you say?"

Braxton tried to think, but his head was foggy. There'd been no work today so he'd been up late smoking and strumming his guitar for an upcoming gig at the Outlaw Saloon. Certainly the deputy was no one to trifle with and best avoided. He had no idea who the man with the dog was, or what had brought everyone to his house. Most likely, he never would know.

But he was a principled tradesman who prided himself on honest work. That was always the best play in a small town in the long run. A full day's work for a full day's pay. The corollary was he should be paid for his work.

"What do I get out of this arrangement?" he asked in a simple and even tone.

"You get to avoid being booked, the expense of a lawyer, and I'll throw in being available for work," smiled Buck.

"What about my door?"

Buck's smile faded as his face turned away from the rearview. He pulled a pair of dark glasses from the middle console and slipped them on to his face.

"You needed to replace it anyway. I was just good enough to bring that fact to your attention. But I recognize the hard work may require some 'mellowing' afterward and am prepared to donate an ounce of assorted weeds."

Braxton considered. Part of him wanted to get greedy, but the deputy had already bashed him and his home with relative impunity. Considering Buck would likely be the sheriff one day, Braxton thought it best to cut his losses and get away from the man as quickly and gracefully as he could. An ounce would ease a considerable number of aches and pains over the next several weeks.

"Okay," agreed Braxton.

Buck turned right at the flashing light, and turned into Ed's. For privacy, he weaved through the rigs and found a spot at the back of the parking lot. As soon as he'd put the car into park, he reached under the front seat for the zip-locked plastic bag. He rolled it up, and turned to push it through the divider grate. Braxton grabbed the end of the bag by his teeth and pulled it through.

The deputy exited the car and opened the back seat. Braxton scooted backward upon the seat toward the door, still holding the plastic bag in his mouth. Buck leaned inside to reclaim the handcuffs before stepping back. The old plumber tucked the bag into his shirt pocket before getting out.

"You can walk back. I've got things to do."

"Hey man, you rushed me out before I could get my wallet," complained Braxton with outstretched hands. "Spot me ten bucks for lunch?"

The deputy stepped toward him to give him a shove and tell him to fuck off, but reconsidered before his foot hit the ground. The Jager guy was suspicious, and if Braxton walked home now they couldn't help but pass one another and have a conversation. Braxton could also complain to Chandler and things could quickly fall apart that way, too. His lazy boss wasn't going to chase down any leads, but couldn't ignore credible allegations placed in his lap. He opened his wallet, and lacking the right change, gave him a twenty.

Moments later, Buck was leaving the parking lot. Braxton gave a wave at his back and turned toward the diner, but the deputy barely noticed. He began to take stock of the state of affairs.

Doris meant what she said, but wouldn't act unless something happened to Dixie. Rebel knew that as well and had probably only taken her as mistaken leverage over him. Sure, she was beautiful and he didn't want to lose her. But her lack of enthusiasm toward him wasn't exactly setting him up to miss her forever, either. Chandler merely wanted things to be peaceful and no crime was much better than a solved crime; he wouldn't go looking for trouble. Which left Kelton Jager and that damned dog.

Heading west on Main Street and well past the flashing yellow light he saw Chandler's Durango coming head-on. Buck flashed his lights and the sheriff slowed. They both came to a stop and rolled down their windows.

"Braxton Greene is a possible for the break-in. He could use the money, and has enough construction tools and experience to do the job. I let Mr. Greene go to focus on Dixie and the shooting for now. There was no sign of her there."

"I wonder if Mr. Butler saw what he thought. If he's not cutting hair, he's playing checkers. What did you do with Mr. Jager?" asked Chandler leaning back against his headrest and peering downward to get a better view of the vacant passenger side.

"He wanted to walk his dog," and added thinking fast, "and see if he picked up any trails on the way back."

"Where you off to now?"

A beat-up old pickup with "Farm Use" plates slowly snaked its way around them with wire crates of chickens in the back. Small white feathers floated out onto the road.

"I was going to drop by Dixie's house and see if she was there and then finish my interview with the Outlaw biker women. They were too shaken up last night to give me much."

"Is Dixie really missing?" asked Chandler with suspicious narrow eyes.

Buck took the question head-on, "I don't know. Dixie and I are struggling to define the next phase of our relationship. Lunch was a little… awkward. I was thinking about it on the drive to Mr. Greene's. She may just be avoiding me by going shopping."

"You kids should know," scolded Chandler with a shake of the head, "I won't have any drama in our office. If this goes on, one of you will have to go."

With that, Chandler raised his window and drove away.

Buck watched the rearview carefully as he too crept forward, but was out of sight before noting if the sheriff turned on Thigpen or had gone on to Ed's and the interstate. Had to be Ed's, he thought, to give a report to Doris.

No matter. Things needed to be put in play to neutralize Mr. Jager in case he didn't wander off. The best tool in his arsenal for that was the witness statements for Baylee Ann and Bambi. He had a feeling they wouldn't be around to dispute his recording of their account. The sooner he sat at his computer and banged those out, the better. He drove by Dixie's house without stopping.

CHAPTER—7

Doris finished entering the driver's license into the computer at the cash register for the box of Sudafed. With a quick signature for the database, a swipe of a credit card and a final signature, the sniffling driver afflicted with the bounty of spring was on his way. She sold a lot of Sudafed, especially during pollen season, and the pharmacy satellite had been a great move. And the old town pharmacist only came over once a month or so anymore to catch up on the pseudoephedrine paperwork.

She started cleaning the coffee pots behind the counter now that the lunch rush was coming to a close. Her feet ached and she could feel the tiredness in her shoulders. She wished they could afford to hire more help, but the mortgage of Dixie's little house was a struggle. As were the prices of Ed's medications. Push comes to shove, that's how she was lured into this mess in the first place.

As she turned to hang a glass coffee pot on the drying rack, she saw the Sheriff's SUV pull up to the front glass window. As he strode out the Durango's door, she gave herself a slight sigh of relief; no one makes haste to share bad news. But he didn't give a wave and smile through the window at her either. But then, that wouldn't be Chandler. She dried her hands on the dish towel, and readied herself at the counter.

"Good afternoon, Miss Doris," he greeted her in a flat tone.

"Sheriff. Any word on my girl?"

Sheriff Fouche stood erect, not compromising his posture to lean forward for privacy. Three stools down, Braxton Greene quietly rested his fork on the biscuits and gravy.

"Mr. Jager used his dog to follow a scent trail from the break-in to the curb. Buck got a license plate number from a witness and served a search warrant. Dixie wasn't there. I don't think her being gone has anything to do with all that.

Buck confessed to him and Dixie having some soul searching conversation before his shift. She may just need some space for a bit. I think she'll turn up really soon."

Doris nodded as Chandler's Corfam shoes angled toward the door, even as he kept his body square to her.

"Please keep me posted, Sheriff. Anything I can do to help your search?"

Keep you searching, thought Doris. Dixie never became emotional to the point of needing space. She would never call her daughter cold, she knew and loved her too well. But the idea of her willfully disappearing when her responsibility was to be on shift didn't sit well. She'd raised her much better than that. The family business had depended upon it.

"If you become aware of any additional information, or if she contacts you, please let us know, Miss Doris," and with that, walked back out the door.

She stared at the front window as the big SUV backed up, turned and exited toward the interstate. Doris knew he lived north somewhere from watching him come and go all these years, but of course had never been there.

But it was the reflection in the window she was really looking at. Dixie had grown up in here. So had she really, as a teenage bride. Ed and her were farm kids who watched his daddy's dairy struggle to be profitable after so much land was lost in eminent domain for the interstate. Ed pushed his father to change direction and she'd been swept off her feet with the vision of a traveler's oasis.

She had thought she was signing up to be a powerful business woman. Now she lamented being merely a gas station clerk and truck stop's waitress. But it was far from being all bad. Ed was smart and loving, even if he hadn't taken care of himself over all those years. There'd been too much sitting and too many pork rinds. But they had waited until they were established to have Dixie and she was pleased with the way she'd turned out.

Dixie was independent, and a beautiful young woman. Doris wished she'd be romanced by someone like an attorney or one of the up and coming city leaders, but at least her girl hadn't fallen in with the lot lizards. But that came with the price of giving her money they didn't really have. With Ed being sick they couldn't keep it up. And now there was trouble. She could feel it.

Her husband came in through the kitchen walking with a slight limp from his considerable girth. His hair was graying and thinning before its time, but he still smiled at her.

"How's my darling?" he said kissing her and reaching one arm around for a hug.

"Tired, Honey, and I need to stop by Dixie's. Can you hold down the fort for a while?"

"Sure thing, Baby," he said as he sat down on the stool by the register.

He wouldn't get off of it for the next several hours, letting the one waitress do all the walking.

Doris took her purse from underneath the register, and also walked through the kitchen. A set of stairs out back led to their apartment above the diner, but she made straight for their old Mercury Cougar instead.

Twenty years ago it had been quite the stylish little two-door, although the blue paint was now peeling in spots. Given its age, it didn't have very many miles. Ed couldn't easily get in and out of it anymore due to the low ride, and with running a diner groceries came to them. It took a couple turns of the key before roaring to life, but the seats were leather and the air-conditioning still worked. Less than five minutes later she was parking on the street in front of her daughter's house.

She decided to knock first, but didn't wait before inserting her key into the door. It had always been the dream of her and Ed to have their own house like this. Never did she think they'd still be in that same little apartment for all those years. When space got tight and business was slow, which had been most of the time, Dixie's room had been one of the motel rooms. But even that nest needed to be flown from eventually. Sometimes adult dreams were best realized through your children, she thought.

Patsy the cat meowed for attention, jumped down from the recliner and trotted up to rub and purr against her legs. It had been a few weeks since she had last visited, but everything seemed to be in order. There was nothing in the way of overturned furniture, or the content of drawers littered about. Doris sat on the small couch, more of a loveseat, and reflected a moment stroking Patsy in her lap.

She stared at the end table containing all manner of tiny glass figurines from carnivals going back to when Dixie was a little girl. It reminded her that even though her girl was all grown up, in many ways she was still just a girl. A hard stomp on the floor would knock the figurines over, but they stood proudly under a light coating of dust.

Dixie was a tall assertive woman, with just a bit of attitude from dating a sheriff's deputy and working in that office. If someone had tried to take her, it hadn't been here. That meant Dixie had gone willingly, or been taken by a strong and shrewd man on the street somewhere. Rebel was such a man. She chided herself for pretending to go through this deep analysis. Of course it was Rebel. That wasn't the question.

The question was, how badly did Dixie have to be hurt before she blew the whistle on everything. Before she dropped an atomic bomb that would envelope everyone. Would she send herself to prison, and Ed to poverty and terminal sickness if Dixie had been killed?

Yeah, she would. It was her child, the fulfillment of her hopes and dreams. If Dixie was lost, not even Ed would matter so much. She'd do it quick, before any resolve could fade. But she would make everyone pay with their freedom.

If Dixie had only been slapped around a little? She'd be raging mad, that's for sure. Hell, she was raging mad now even if mother worry suppressed that. But would she go full nuclear if that was the extent of it?

She was quick to say, "Hell Yes!"

But maybe not. She'd want to find a way to punish them, surely. Even if it took years to plot revenge. But if Dixie wasn't really hurt, her better nature would prevail with so much at stake. She didn't want to go to prison for this conspiracy, or condemn Ed with substandard care.

What if Dixie had been raped? That was a lot more than being slapped around a little, even if she was alive and physically would get better. But some recovered from it enough to get on with their lives. It was a common theme of daytime television. But, her blood boiled at the thought. She just might drop the bomb at that too and be damned. Her fist clenched and she struck the sofa cushion.

On the end table beside the sofa, the clattering figurines surprised her and Patsy let out a protest. Doris gulped a deep breath, and tried to soothe her blood pressure back down to normal. Then came the knock on the door, and her heart jumped into her throat again.

She stood and with a couple of strides looked through the spyhole. On the stoop was Kelton Jager and his dog. Patsy sulked in a corner licking a paw. Doris opened the door a crack, placing her foot at the bottom of the opening to preemptively block any animals that may be inclined to tangle, but the black masked dog sat at attention without giving the scent of the cat any mind.

"Mrs. Johnson, I apologize for disturbing you. I was just checking to see if Dixie had returned since I was passing by on my way back to the sheriff's office."

"How did you know this was Dixie's house?" her eyes narrowed in suspicion.

"I found this purse in her desk. The address was on her license."

She nodded as he gave it back to her. The young man wasn't the police, but seemed genuinely concerned enough to be trying.

"She doesn't carry it that often. Dixie eats out on dates or walks down to the diner. Maybe a couple of times a month she'll borrow the car to go shopping at South Hill."

"Does she have a cellphone, Mrs. Johnson?"

"Please, call me Doris. No. We'd be trying to call her if she did."

Kelton gave a soft shake of his head, "I was thinking more of the carrier pinpointing the phone's location. Even if she isn't there, it may provide a clue of what direction she headed."

Doris took a turn shaking her head in kind, "Signals are so intermittent here, especially if you aren't right on the interstate. And they are pretty expensive for us to justify without needing it for business."

"I understand, Ma'am. Just one last question," he said rocking slightly side to side on his feet. "I was wondering if I might have a better scent article in case there is an opportunity to track. It doesn't sound like she handled the purse a whole lot, and I haven't had a plastic bag to keep other scents from contaminating it."

Doris straightened to her full height, modest as it was.

"What exactly did you have in mind, young man?" she replied with a scowl.

"I was hoping for a sock from her dirty clothes basket and a zip lock sandwich bag to put it in."

She softened, "Please wait here a moment. I'll find something."

What he asked was easy and far from inappropriate, so she provided it and sent him on his way. Then she gently closed the door and started a silent prayer that her daughter could be delivered back to her without exposing the conspiracy in which she was entangled. The prayer died on her muttering lips. She hadn't been to church in decades, and only a handful of times after she was married. The "always open" nature of their business precluded that. Some enjoyed the luxury of religion, but she had to be much more practical.

That meant breaking the problem down into small pieces and using simple logic. She couldn't steal her daughter away from Rebel. She didn't have the power. Buck did, but sacrificing Dixie was something he was willing to do for the money. The only reason he didn't, was her threat to drag him down too. But perhaps there was another way.

Kelton could rescue her Dixie, and possibly not expose her wrong-doings. Perhaps the question was how to lead him to Rebel's and not let him see behind the curtain? She sat and pondered while stroking Patsy in her lap.

CHAPTER—8

Kelton and Azrael walked west from Dixie's house on the north side of Main Street toward the sheriff's office. Occasional cars were parked along the curbs, most tired and dated, and there were very few pedestrians in the midafternoon. After the recent rains, green swirls of cedar pollen lay in the gutter. A cool breeze fluttered his shirt collar and the sky was clear and bright.

He paused on the sidewalk where the blue truck had supposedly been and Azrael took an obedient sit. Overhead were the upstairs apartments of the shop keeps, windows staring down like empty eyes. There were no lights, no rustling curtains. With the realtor still out, the nearside shops were vacant. Three African-American men were in the barber shop across the street, two hunched over a table in the sitting area and one in an apron relaxed in the barber's chair.

Looking to the right of the barber shop he could see the hardware and feed stores across from the sheriff's building. To the left were a florist and a doughnut shop. Kelton came to the conclusion that Sheriff Fouche may not be right. If one had control of his victim, it wouldn't be hard to wait between the buildings until the road was clear. The barber was most likely the only chance for a witness after the morning commute was over, but they didn't look especially alert. He and Azrael looked both ways and jay-walked across the street.

As he approached the window he could see the two men were playing checkers. It was a folding two-dimensional battlefield of red and black squares next to a long cardboard box containing chess pieces and dice. Kelton assumed there were backgammon chevrons printed on the underside. A magazine rack near the waiting chairs contained several months of both Sports Illustrated and Playboy. Behind the big chair, a counter held small bottles of various lotions and creams of the trade, and a small dust covered TV with sagging rabbit ears. Above that a mirror, in which Kelton could see his own reflection not quite up to standards for being "in-garrison." He told his dog to sit, and the tarnished brass bell on the door jingled as he went inside.

"Good afternoon, Sir. What can I do for you?" the old barber asked as he stood up and raised the chair cloth like a bullfighter.

"I suppose I'm in the market to get my ears lowered," replied Kelton.

The retirees smiled up from the checker's game. The pieces weren't in their starting positions, but at a quick glance, it looked as if all were still present on the board.

"You've come to the only place, unless you're a metro-sexual who uses a woman's salon."

The barber's smile had a relaxed charm to it, despite the stained teeth and creased skin. Kelton took off his pack and settled into the padded chair. No one paid the huge automatic on his thigh any mind.

"You must be Sheriff Fouche's new deputy I saw this morning. I never thought the county would find the money to hire one."

"Well I wouldn't mind being paid a bit more than I am," feigned Kelton.

The retirees laughed with the barber.

"Shit. They tax the businesses. They tax the farmers. They pass out speeding tickets and soliciting citations to every trucker they can find," he said tucking Kelton's collar in and buttoning the chair cloth around his neck. "But they still don't have the green to fix that pothole out there. Getting to the point you need a four by four to drive on the streets of downtown."

"Ain't that the truth," said the red player. "All our money is going to that teen program over at the clinic."

"If it don't, you'd be buying food stamps for babies, Fool," replied the black player.

"King me, Bitch."

The slap of the one checker on another echoed over the hum of the clippers.

"That your dog outside?" asked the barber. It sounded like "dawg".

"My partner. I was hoping you could tell me more about that blue truck you gave the license plate number to Buck this morning."

"That'd be Deputy Garner to a humble working man like me," he shrugged. "Didn't give him no plate. Can't rightly see it from this angle in the shop and kind of far, no how. But it was a big truck. Ford, I think, with the extra wheels on the back. It had tool boxes and a fuel nozzle for topping off tractors in the bed."

Kelton nodded looking over Azrael sitting at attention in his brown harness vest to across the street. It wasn't side on, but reading the front plate would require moving left down the sidewalk past the building's west wall.

"This helping your case any?"

"Absolutely. Do you remember what time it drove off?"

"Can't say I rightly noticed. Must have been close to noon though. My clients were showing up."

Kelton considered, "Did you have a lot of people coming in and out today?"

"Naw. You the first walk-in I've had in a while. Picks up more come end of the school year. My regulars mostly call ahead for times around their lunch hour. Walk over from city hall and such."

Kelton considered getting a list of the appointments and going to interview those people on what they saw. But then, he wasn't the law and that would be exceeding his brief. Maybe he would suggest it to the sheriff later.

"Lots of people walking the sidewalk then?"

The barber shrugged, "All the café's and such are more up around the square. I usually walk down for a sandwich in the afternoon.

What you carrying around that big pack for? They not given you a car or something to keep it in?"

"Mostly dog equipment. They don't have me settled in yet." Kelton tried to divert attention away from him, "Do you know Dixie who works for the sheriff?"

"Can't say I've met her, but we do enjoy watching her walk across our sidewalk every morning. Gets me up to open early. Sometimes I'm too late though and those are like days with no sunshine. Other days she walks by at lunch and we are treated to additional viewings," he bragged and the men playing checkers shared in some snickering.

Turning him around in the chair so Kelton could see the mirror, the barber lamented, "But no extra sunshine today. How's that for you?"

"I feel ready for my official photograph. Thank you for getting me presentable."

Within a minute cash traded hands, including a handsome tip, and Kelton was back outside with his dog. In his head was the undisputed notion that Deputy Garner had lied for some reason. The tiny under furnished room at the truck stop held no appeal, so to avoid a long evening there he headed toward the town square. The manicured greenspace would be ideal for some more throws of the Kong.

Bambi's afternoon in the vault had passed slowly, rising occasionally from her seat against the wall to try and soothe Baylee Ann when the whimpering became worrisome. There was no window to the outside, but the coming evening gave the air a different feel. She didn't know if it was temperature, humidity, or maybe some rhythm of her body telling her that the quiet solace of the afternoon would soon be over. But regardless of the reason, a change was lurking like some phantom shadow. Her eyes kept drifting upward to the trap door, like she used to steal glances out the living room window at the sidewalk for her alcoholic father coming home.

"Any idea why he keeps you two?"

Bambi turned toward Dixie with some annoyance, "Why did he take you?"

"Ransom, maybe?" said Dixie with a half-smile.

"It's sure as hell not the reason he took us," dismissed Bambi.

Dixie was quiet for a few minutes and then replied, "If he's keeping the three of us in this pit, I feel like we must have something in common."

Baylee Ann coughed from the table and croaked, "Does that bother you? Thinking you have something in common with the likes of us?"

Bambi rushed over, knelt beneath Baylee Ann's downward face, and reached up to hug her. But it was all she could do because there were no tools to release the metal bracket that pinned her neck to the table.

Dixie considered a retort, but before she could compose the words a screeching noise could be heard above them. A minute later the hatch opened, and a ray of florescent light poured down, dwarfing the output of their single greasy bulb.

A hefty gruff voice called down to them, "Dinner, you bitches."

A paper sack landed with a hard thud, and the light went away again. The screech followed, as something metal and heavy was dragged back into place across the concrete. Dixie rose slowly, greatly favoring her ankle, so Bambi easily reached the bag first. She tore open the paper sides with no ceremony. The contents spilled all over the floor.

It looked as if someone had raided a vending machine. There were a few packs of the small orange crackers filled with peanut butter. A couple of snack cakes, feeling hard and stale through the wrapper, a plastic tube of peanuts and some rock-hard red Twizzlers finished the edibles. There were also three plastic bottles of water, only twelve ounces each, but cold enough to be sweaty in the southern humidity.

Dixie tore into a package of crackers while Bambi opened a water bottle and strode back over to Baylee Ann. She raised the bottle to her lips, but Baylee Ann couldn't tip her head back far enough to take a sip.

"Try from the side," advised Bambi to her friend and used her free hand to support Baylee Ann's cheek. Bambi watched the parched lips greedily suck at the bottle as she slowly poured, but much was lost onto the floor.

"You need a straw," said Dixie.

Bambi considered, looking around the debris on the floor. There wasn't much, and certainly nothing that even a girl like her wanted to put in her mouth. Then she saw the Twizzlers and her eyes widened.

"Give me those red licorice things!"

Dixie gave a quizzical look at first, but her face lit up before Bambi caught the tossed package. The girl ripped one from its wrapper, bit off both ends and spit them onto the ground. It had made her teeth hurt, but she was already putting the makeshift straw into the bottle and offering it to her friend. The water disappeared in a few determined slurps.

"Thank you," muttered Baylee Ann before letting her neck sag again.

Bambi knew her muscles must be aching from being pinned in that position for so many hours. She fed her all the crackers she would take, and even shared most of her bottle of water.

"Can you free me?" Baylee Ann implored.

Bambi's eyes fell in disappointment.

"Are they flathead screws? Can you use the edge of a dime or anything?" asked Baylee Ann, weak but well-motivated to problem solve.

Dixie took a staggering step to gently move her hair aside and bent over to look again.

"Cross-headed. And not very big. A dime would be way too thick, and they're mostly stripped anyway," Dixie turned to Bambi. "Can we just pry it off?"

Bambi looked around the vault. Once upon a time it had been one of a couple of mechanic's pits, where one could change the oil easily without having to hoist a vehicle. But the wall dividing the pits had been excavated away, making a small rectangular room. A ladder in the corner led to the hatch in a roof of old railroad ties supported by steel beams improvised from the frame of a large truck. A few metal posts, like one sees in a basement, supported the beams in lieu of the torn down wall divider. The concrete floor of the garage above was merely a veneer, but an effective one.

Nothing looked promising to use as a lever. There were some concrete chips, and small rusting pieces of metal like the occasional dropped washer or oil-pan bolt but nothing big. She opened the desk drawers and Dixie joined in, both being careful to avoid contacting Baylee Ann's exposed posterior. Some loose paper fragments and a couple of paper clips showed the desk had been cleared out before being placed in here. Other old screw holes in the desktop made clear its new purpose.

"There's nothing," lamented Bambi. She felt herself shutting down, trying to get small in the face of failure so it wouldn't notice and punish her. Her heart began to race, and she sat down to pull her knees into her chest and cover her eyes. Dixie shook her shoulder and looked into her red eyes.

"Stay with me, Bambi. If we all can't breakout, maybe you can and get us some help."

Bambi sniffled and took a breath. She tried to relax her heart. Breaking out and running away appealed to every fiber of her being.

"How?" she asked. The concrete walls imposed upon her brains as well as her body.

"He's shown he's going to feed us. Maybe not much or often, but if he did it once he's going to do it again.

And we get good warning when he does it. There's that tool box or supply cabinet or whatever it is he keeps over the trap door. When we hear that, we climb the ladder. Me first, with you right behind.

We'll gather up every single piece of whatever we can find. Pebbles, nuts and bolts, break-up the desk drawers if we have to. Even Baylee Ann's shoes. When he opens the hatch, we throw it at his face and I charge him. He'll grab me and tackle me to the ground.

That's when you pop out behind me and run for it. I'll hug him tight and not let go so you can get a good head start. If you get on the clear of the train tracks away from all the brush and vines, you'll be able to outrun him and plenty of backyards face the tracks. Someone will notice you and can call for help."

"Why don't you run for help?"

"With my ankle? I won't get far. And we can't free Baylee Ann so it has to be you."

"Won't he hurt you?"

"He might. But there's a reason he hasn't hurt me already. I don't know why he took me, but with the two of you already here he wasn't procuring additional entertainment."

Bambi nodded and sniffed again.

Baylee Ann turned her head sideways to look up at her and croaked, "Dixie's right, Bambi. Get out of here if you can and get help. They might not come for me, but they'll definitely come for her."

Bambi turned back to Dixie who offered a soft pleading smile.

"Okay," nodded Bambi.

A few breaths and tears later they were scouring the edges of the pit, picking up every small object they could find. The vault was barren, but poor housekeeping gave each of them a sizable throw. They sat on the desk clutching their handfuls, eyes locked upon the hatch. It was simply a matter of time before an opportunity.

CHAPTER—9

Deputy Buck Garner settled into his office for evening paperwork. He started a small coffee pot on his sideboard and turned on the old desktop computer to begin booting up. While he was waiting he picked up the phone and dialed the city's fire department control room which served as the county's emergency command center. They picked up on the first ring.

"St. Albans Emergency Center, this is Mr. Kissel," came the crisp voice.

"Evening Brett. It's Buck. Just checking in to see if anything was going on," he explained.

"Hello, Deputy. Old Mrs. Myrtle down Smallwood Street passed away. Her son stopped by in the afternoon to check on her and found her in bed. Dr. Fairborn is there now and says she passed in the night. Think she was ninety-three. Other than that, all is real quiet. Not even a cat stuck in a tree."

"She was a proper southern lady of the old guard," Buck said without any emotion in his voice. Personally, he could care less. The young were born, the old passed away. Even a small city had its people always turning over with the march of time. "I'm at the office catching up on paperwork. If anything comes up in the next couple of hours, you can reach me on the landline."

"Ten-four, Deputy. You have a nice night."

Buck set the receiver down to end the call and entered his password. The first order of business was finding a way to chase the Jager fellow and his dog out of town. Rebel's Dixie stunt had driven the sheriff to give the drifter a sense of purpose. That could cause him to stick around. The longer that went on, coupled with an anointment of special authority, the greater the chances of things getting even more snarled up than they were. Right now there was a pair of loose ends to get tied up so things didn't unravel.

First, Dixie's absence needed to be resolved. Rebel was financially desperate with the lost cash and taking Dixie was his leverage for keeping everyone he needed in the game despite the heat. Buck would talk to him again. The point had been made. The sooner Dixie was back in view, the quicker things would go back to normal and they could start making money again. Rebel would just have to suck up this short term loss and drive on. Dixie could be coached on answering questions, but may not hold up to the scrutiny of the mysterious stranger.

Second, there was the break-in issue. For all Kelton Jager knew, reasoned Buck, plumber Braxton Greene was the perpetrator and had been released on bail. That wouldn't hold up with Chandler, especially if Dog-Boy kept asking questions, but the old sheriff hadn't seemed too fazed by the trespass. If given a chance, he'd probably forget all about it. They were more about keeping the peace and fining trucker passersby to fund the county than playing detective.

To get rid of someone, Buck normally would put the fear of God into them. Everyone knew Sheriff Fouche was coasting toward retirement with no fire to fight over anything but his own legacy. That made Buck the face of the law and provided no recourse to those he leaned on. They could only run away.

But with the Kelton Jager case it was different because of the possible murder indictment working against him. If Kelton ran away, the long arm of the law threatened to chase him down and bring him back to face consequences for that. Buck needed to change the threat of indictment to actual indictment to send him on his way. Whether that way was out of town as a fugitive or off to prison really didn't concern Buck very much. Fortunately, there were a couple of witnesses he could control.

On the computer screen he opened a witness report form, and to the left of his keyboard, his notebook. He poured the now ready cup of coffee into a stained and chipped department mug and settled in, working hard to get the details right. He wrote how the rain caused the members of the Lowland Outlaws motorcycle club to stop under the shelter of the bridge. How the president wanted to privately address his riders in their formal club ceremony of inducting a new member after their initiation ride, and moved them all away from the women folk to do so by having them line up at the far side of the bridge. That this normally would have taken place at their clubhouse, but people were wet and tired and ready to break up and go home. They began bellowing their sacred and bawdy song, when the insecure hidden drifter felt threatened and senselessly gunned them down.

He printed three copies, placing one in Sheriff Fouche's in-box to be found in the morning. The others he would get signed by the girls when he went to visit Rebel. He didn't want to forge anything, and have Baylee Ann and Bambi show up later with different handwriting. That was probably remote, but he wasn't in the mood for any more chances.

The caffeine surged in his veins as he left the office and locked the metal doors with his key. If he were to reassure Rebel, actions would speak louder than words. Buck had to find a way to convey that he was still serious about the continuation of their enterprise. He cranked the key of the Chevy patrol car and headed toward Ed's.

Once he was through the flashing light at Thigpen, he pressed the accelerator. If a truck driver was alert, there was little he could do to avoid being seen. Before he could get to the cab, the girl slipped out the passenger side of the truck and raced toward the woods behind Ed's to disappear until their next visit. Being quick, mitigated this problem.

As he raced down Main Street with his lights off he did a quick survey of the lot and saw a big white International parked in the far corner. He made a hard turn into Ed's parking lot, and went right past the motel, diner, and pumps to pull up alongside. Buck jumped out without closing his door and sprinted to the driver's side. Grabbing the hand bar as he leapt up onto the running board, he used his other hand to tap on the window with his badge.

"Deputy sheriff, open up."

Inside the cab was dim, but the big parking lot lights allowed him to see inside well enough. The driver was behind the wheel, but his jeans and jockeys were down at his knees. It was a bench seat and she was splayed across it face down, although now getting up on her hands and knees with big eyes. Excess lipstick smeared across her plump cheeks. Buck didn't bother to look down to see how much lipstick was left behind there. Some things can't be unseen. The window came down as the driver's left arm made several circles.

"Hey, man, me and my new special friend were," he began groping for an explanation.

He was a dirty greasy blond, mid-thirties, with lots of stray facial hair.

"Shut up," ordered Buck in a flat, disappointed tone.

He turned on his flashlight and shined it on the girl for a better look. She was dark haired with crooked teeth. The pink spaghetti top was low enough but still failed to show cleavage, although her braless nipples budded enough to make an impression on the thin fabric.

"Did he pay you?" he asked firmly.

Her eyes dropped down with uncertainty over the best response. Buck turned toward the driver.

"Pay her," Buck ordered with a sneer.

"But I already paid her," the driver protested.

"Then pay her again," Buck demanded firmly.

The driver reached toward his knees to fish out his wallet from the twisted jeans. He had plenty of cash and handed the girl $20. She smiled a bit as her hand grasped the bill tightly.

"Okay. Exit the truck from your side and go wherever it is people like you go."

She looked a little surprised again, and then raced to comply. They usually were barely literate so tickets were meaningless, and there wasn't the manpower to bother holding them in a cell. Besides, he didn't want the girls afraid of him and be inhibited from doing business. He needed them for the scheme to keep working.

"Give me your driver's license," Buck demanded.

The driver opened the worn wallet again as the passenger side door slammed with the girl's exit. It was under a cracked plastic window sewn into the leather. He had to pry at it a bit to free the laminated card, then handed it over. It was a Georgia license.

"Wait here. And pull your pants up."

Buck climbed down and got back in his cruiser. He started an incident report with the usual litany of charges for being caught in public committing lewd acts with a far under-aged prostitute. However, he chose a local drive "save" rather than "submitting" into the official database. He placed the license into an envelope.

When he returned to the driver, the sweat was noticeably dripping down the unkempt sideburns. The musty body odor from days on the road made Buck wonder how the young girls did it.

"Well, Mr. Branson, you are in a heap of trouble aren't you? Solicitation of a minor, child endangerment, public lewdness, even sodomy if our prosecutor has a mind. The old geezer often does, too. Very conservative and Christian. Always re-elected for his long and notorious record of no leniency in such cases. What do you have to say for yourself?"

"Look man, the roads are long and lonely, you know and," he began shrugging and cocking his head to the side.

"They are long and lonely. I spend a lot of time in the patrol car, but I get to go home after each shift. It's harder for you, but at least I can relate some. Tell you what I'm going to do.

I'm going to keep your license. I've got an incident report started in the car. If I see this ugly rig fouling any pavement within Lowland County, I'm going to see Mrs. Doris for a big pot of coffee and slap on every charge I can think of and get it over to our commonwealth attorney. Our inmates don't take kindly to child molesters and you will be with them for a very long time.

But if you drive away, and stop polluting our air, then there's a chance that by the time I get up in the morning and start a new day I will forget about it as I find other things to do.

You got me?" Buck leaned in the window to finish with a cold stare.

The driver nodded, face twitching with nervousness and adrenaline.

"Then fire up this heap and get across my county line. I suggest you begin avoiding my section of I-85 and find some alternative routes."

Buck stood hands on his hips like a disapproving coach or parent as the big rig rumbled toward the interstate entrance ramps. Once its lights faded from view, he started walking toward the diner.

He'd had that same conversation many of times. He used to bring in the young girls, but it cost the county more in jail supervision than any legal fines that could be imposed. They were in this particular line of work because they had no money. And Chandler hated the bad press of "prosecuting the victims of sex trafficking" editorials in the county newspaper. The national conversation on whoring had shifted toward victims of sexual exploitation, and even old Fouche still paid enough attention to things to shift with the winds.

With the truckers, fines were best his boss had explained to him. The problem belonged to someone else so let their jurisdiction pay for jail, legal, and other fees associated with starting the pipeline to the state penitentiary. He'd been told to instead look at them as a revenue source for the county to tap. Well, thought Buck, if it's moral for the county to tap nonresidents for money, it was for him too.

He opened the door to the diner and gave a quick look around. A few drivers were tanking up their bodies and trucks for their night runs. Doris manned her counter with hard set eyes. Buck sat on the usual stool and placed the envelope on the counter without saying a word. She reached up, took it, and felt the hard plastic card inside. He thought she might refuse to take it on account of Dixie and thoughts of laying low.

Instead, she gave him a slow nod and walked over to the locked cabinet of pharmacy goods for a package of decongestants. Upon returning to the register she scanned the small cardboard box, then opened the envelope to do the same with the license. The query went to the state database tracking pseudoephedrine purchases, and a response came back authorizing the sale.

Buck knew no single person was allowed to purchase more than 9 grams per month under the Combat Methamphetamine Epidemic Act of 2005, a law designed to choke off a key ingredient in making "kitchen sink meth." Retailers, like the St. Albans' Pharmacy or its "satellite location" at Ed's truck stop, were required to keep detailed records of purchases along with a rigorous host of storage and security requirements. Nowadays the reality was with the instant check system, one couldn't commit the crime of over purchasing. Illicit drug manufacturers now needed armies of "smurfs" to try and obtain enough raw materials to stay in business.

Buck and Doris, well-motivated by financial insecurity, had developed a scheme of sorts to bypass that purchasing limit hurdle. Before long they had an entire stack of mostly out of state licenses to make purchases. Any auditor of Ed's would declare the business of providing allergy relief to travelers "amazingly good".

It was possible someone could be denied a purchase somewhere, and raise a fuss to cause an investigation. But most people didn't purchase very much, unless an allergy sufferer, to run into their limit. On top of that, the state databases weren't linked with each other. If this recently busted driver bought some cold pills back in Georgia, the rulers of the land of the peaches had no idea there'd been a purchase in Virginia to count against the limit. The reality was that with child sex charges hanging over their heads, the busted drivers merely reported their license lost to obtain a replacement in their home state and went on with life.

On occasion, the Virginia state database provided a report of people who consistently made purchases at or near the legal limit month after month. In local law enforcement circles this useful tool had been informally dubbed "the smurf report". Given that the report came to Buck, their little conspiracy had no fear from that. Instead, Buck identified names from their stack of licenses who had made the list, and rested them for a rotation. If someone made the list twice in a row, they disposed of the license.

If anyone were to come investigate the store's success, they would find everything in order. Sure they moved a lot of pharmaceutical product for a truck stop. But it was next to an interstate, and the rural surroundings provided lots of molds and pollens to torture allergy sufferers. The town pharmacist was meticulous in his supervision, yet totally ignorant of the scheme to be able to tip their hand. But no one had ever come knocking.

A decade or so ago Rebel had done six months for breaking his then girlfriend's nose, jaw and cheekbone. There he'd met a dealer from Church Hill in Richmond. The rural community made it easy for Rebel to cook and his contact in the big city readily moved the product. Together, they could both produce and distribute. Buck and Doris fed the machine its most important input.

The money was okay. A quarter gram hit of their meth sold for around $30 wholesale, and they could make a gram or more from just four boxes or so of cold pills and some other common ingredients. Buck wasn't sure what it went for in the big city, but Rebel was always able to quickly take every cold pill they could procure. And that was fine with Buck. He didn't want to be near the distribution and street sales. Too many people would know who he was that way. The wholesale side of things was just fine. It wasn't buy a mansion and a sports car kind of rich, but for a small town deputy and a truck stop clerk it really changed things. Especially over the long haul.

Doris handed him the box of cold pills. They'd just done it to test the license really quick, but no sense in putting the box back on the shelf. Buck slipped it into his pocket and drove home for the night hoping there wouldn't be any calls. Tomorrow, when Sheriff Fouche read his report, would likely be a lively day and he still needed to have a conversation with Rebel before hitting the sack.

CHAPTER—10

Kelton walked his dog west down Main Street just after the morning rush. He'd slept a little on the later side again, for him anyway, made easy by a motel bed rather than being under a poncho on the ground. Like before, he'd availed himself upon the diner for a huge American-style breakfast, and sat pondering Buck's motivation for lying about the blue pickup. He had still been at his table when Doris wandered in from the back and immediately approached.

Dixie still hadn't been seen or heard from, and understandably Mom remained worried. She told him it was probably a long shot, but there'd been a wild boy in town that once had an interest in her girl. His name was Rebel Tarwick and he ran a garage just south of town on Lowland Road. She said she'd mentioned it to Buck who'd scoffed.

He'd considered he wasn't a police officer with any special authority to trespass or interfere in an active investigation. However, since it had supposedly been made clear that this wasn't a lead the deputy considered worth pursuing, Kelton had decided that the interference opposition carried little weight.

Normally, he would have declined the request as someone else's business. Especially since Doris offered no firm evidence other than a mother's hunch and law enforcement was actively involved. But young idealism, in the mold of an officer and gentlemen, didn't like to pass on rescuing young ladies. It didn't endanger his dog, and it gave him something to do while the slow wheels of justice turned for his ticket to walk out of town.

His plan was to stop at the top of Rebel's driveway, let Azrael scent Dixie's sock in the plastic bag, and then approach to knock on the door. He could play "lost out of towner" and ask for directions if anyone was there, but the real aim was to see if his dog gave any indication Dixie had recently been there.

It was not just a long shot as Doris termed it, but also a long walk. He decided upon a route that avoided the residential areas to avoid trouble from other dogs who weren't as well trained as his. The fresh doughnuts of the St. Albans' bakery smelled good, but with a full tummy it wasn't hard to not stop in. Dixie's house remained dark and quiet. He gave a friendly wave at the barber's window and noted both sheriff's vehicles were at the office. A couple minutes later he and Azrael reached Lowland Road, and Kelton paused to look around.

His dog sat and whined softly looking north up the railroad tracks that stretched behind the city offices. Kelton decided the city office building looked like an old rail terminal. It had "architectural character" as one of his old professors would say. So did the church beyond it with its tall stained-glass windows. But it wasn't what caught Azrael's attention. It took a minute for him to hear the train himself and then he understood.

He slipped off his pack, unzipped a side pocket, and placed the "mutt-muffs" over Azrael's ears. It wasn't his dog's favorite thing, but after helicopters and gunfire during the war the dog was well conditioned to them. Kelton was remounting his pack as the big diesel locomotive came into view, black with a white rearing horse painted on the nose. The engineer extended a hand from the window and gave a friendly wave. Kelton gave a wave back. There were several power units on the front of the train, followed by an endless metal snake of boxcars and container carriers.

An ancient relation of his mother had driven locomotives long ago, and sent him a toy train set at one of the first Christmases he could remember. To the best of his recollection he never met the man, nor knew what became of the toy train. His mother had kept a neat and tidy house in those early years, being quick to participate in garage sales or use thrift store consignments for things not in active use. It seemed they moved every few months as she struggled with evictions or chased the next minimum wage job.

He'd been ten when they had finally settled down into the little house in Fayetteville, North Carolina, near Fort Bragg. She got a job at an herbicide factory, and sold the car due to the convenient bus stop. Her shifts were erratic but the retired cop veteran next door, despite being on disability, took a keen interest in him. At one point Kelton hoped the old cop and his mother might get married before he was old enough to appreciate the thirty-five-year age difference and his physical infirmaries.

Patrol Sergeant Hesp saw to it that Kelton had done his homework, and done it well. He'd made him give presentations on the lessons. Then the old sergeant quizzed him mercilessly not just to make sure the lesson had been thoroughly understood, but to help young Kelton learn to keep his mental balance. The reward had been shooting. Lots of shooting, which also meant lots of reloading using a press to turn empty brass casings back into live cartridges again. The boy he'd been thrived. The lonely old policeman thrived too, with renewed purpose in life.

Kelton had felt he was on his way. There was an appointment to the United States Military Academy at West Point. Old Sergeant Hesp passed his sophomore year, but a bachelor's degree in mechanical engineering and an officer's commission in the regular army soon followed. Then he was off to war and wasn't looking back, extending his tours and then getting waivers to further stretch his deployment.

Then, through the American Red Cross, he was notified his mom had died and he came home. An aggressive form of cancer, perhaps brought on from years of chemical exposures in the herbicide plant. She must have known, but never told him. He knew he might or might not come home from the war. It never occurred to him that home may not be there when he got back.

The army hadn't been there for him either. Despite four years in the warzone, volunteering for special duty and performing it well, his military career was completely off track. He had the wrong assignments for a developing engineering officer and the army was drawing down. A personnel officer, a friendly old major with graying hair, advised Kelton he had no future there, so he separated.

The train finally rumbled on, and Kelton took off Azrael's "mutt-muffs". They turned left on Lowland Road to start heading south. Within a block were the neatly kept old track houses of Coalson Street, with white asbestos siding and rusting tin roofs. A quarter mile later they were deep within the wild rural lands ornamented with scrub cedars, barbed wire, and giant purple pokeberry stalks.

On his right, the railroad bed had been built high enough that when walking on the road he couldn't really see much on the far side. There were old telephone poles with glass insulators, wires broken and tangled with kudzu vines. To the left, it alternated between pastures and woods with the occasional modest house much like over on Thigpen.

As was their custom they walked on the left shoulder to see on-coming traffic, and occasionally stepped into the briar clogged drainage ditch for cars reluctant to drift into the other lane to give them space. He used his iPhone briefly to check his location, and noted it was probably another half hour to Rebel's address. Putting the mobile device away, he saw the two sheriff's vehicles coming up fast behind them with blue lights flashing but no sirens.

He turned to watch them curiously, as Buck's Chevy Interceptor skewed sideways in the road and came to a stop. As the Sheriff's Dodge Durango pulled up close behind, Deputy Buck Garner opened his door, stepped out kneeling, and leveled his gun at him over the car's engine block. Kelton cocked his head to the side while Azrael sat panting. Sheriff Fouche exited his vehicle behind, but didn't feel the need to walk any other way than smartly erect.

Kelton called to them in greeting, "Good morning, gentlemen. Would you please not point that at me? And what can I help you with this morning?"

Buck called out, "Kelton Jager, you are under arrest for murder. Raise your hands high above your head!"

Chandler quickly corrected him, "Not arrested, detained. The county prosecutor has some questions. I need to take you back to the office."

Buck's sunglasses and raised pistol kept Kelton from reading his expression, but he leaned forward with his weight on his front foot and his shoulders were high and tense. His knees were bent, taking as much cover as possible while still being able to aim. Kelton briefly considered, fingers tingling, but heard the soft voice in his head reminding him that one can't outdraw a drawn gun. He raised his hands, but with bent elbows.

"How do you plan to detain my dog?"

Chandler's head cocked slightly to one side as he considered the question but Buck quickly yelled, "We'll turn him over to animal control."

Really it was their only choice, Kelton thought. They couldn't put the dog in the jail cell with him any more than they could leave him with his gun or any other weapon. But Azrael was a Military Working Dog, an "M.W.D." in K-9 parlance, and most likely far beyond the handling capabilities of the small town dogcatcher. They might put him down in the interests of public safety.

Sheriff Chandler Fouche was advancing, circling as wide as the drainage ditch allowed around the front of Buck's car so as not to interfere with Buck's line of fire. The old-timer had his left hand out for balance as he walked gingerly with firm flat foot placement so as not to scuff his shoes. His right hand was on the butt of his revolver.

Kelton knew Chandler was coming for his gun and considered. There was a good chance he could kill them both, despite Buck at the ready, and save his dog. He didn't believe Buck was very practiced, and firing a double action revolver wasn't easy. But becoming a fugitive may not be necessary to do that. Kelton was confident there was no true murder case against him. So the impending detainment was temporary, although possibly a year to trial if indicted.

Kelton made a soft kissing sound with his lips as Chandler got within fifteen feet, still stepping slowly and deliberately. Azrael looked up, bright eyes in the black masked face answering. He pointed his right index finger with a soft stabbing motion toward the near field, where Azrael's path would take him in front of Chandler so that Buck's line of sight would be blocked.

"Voraus," he commanded softly. Go forward and run out. Dogs have great ears. There was no need to aggressively shout. Kelton figured that was a good thing when someone was pointing a loaded gun your way.

Azrael launched himself in a deadbolt sprint in the direction Kelton had pointed. Chandler wobbled in surprise, but didn't lose his balance. In a single leap, the Belgian Malinois was over the drainage ditch and barbed wire hedge of cattle fencing. He found a low roll in the ground, and then poured on the speed. Buck's pistol banged after him, shot after shot, until clicking empty. A dog is a small target, moving low and erratically, and the range was long for a handgun. Buck wasn't a great shot either. Azrael probably didn't even know the gunfire was meant for him.

With the deputy's gun empty and the sheriff's still holstered, Kelton's fingers tingled again. A common firing range drill was the "El-Presidente," where the shooter started with his hands above his head and back to the targets. This would be easy in comparison, but it was not about the police. It was about his dog.

He extended his arm and finger to continue the voraus. He didn't want Azrael becoming protective, breaking the command, and returning. As Chandler approached, Kelton gave no resistance, and let the old sheriff take possession of the Glock 40 once again. He made no sudden moves that Azrael might interpret as the beginning of a struggle. Azrael liked putting teeth into flesh.

Chandler ordered in a conversational tone, "Please drop your hands and slip off your backpack, Sir."

Kelton did so, in slow steady compliance, before standing relaxed.

"Please place your hands behind you, Sir."

Kelton was a little surprised to be handcuffed by the old sheriff, the action interrupting his amused view of Buck fumbling with a speed loader for his empty revolver. The cold steel bit at his flesh, clearly indicating they weren't decoration for procedure's sake. In a few moments, Buck was reloaded and joined them with the now holstered gun. It took the deputy a few minutes to strip away Kelton's Leatherman tool, spare Glock magazines, and the like from his belt and pockets. At least they placed them in the top of the backpack for safe keeping, he thought.

Kelton stood quietly, waiting for Chandler to scold his deputy for the half dozen shots. But if there was going to be a tongue lashing over it, it wasn't going to happen here. Chandler directed Buck to pick up the backpack and they started marching toward the sheriff's SUV.

There was a possibility, thought Kelton, that the sheriff did such chastising in private and wanted the facade of a unified law enforcement front. But he'd been quick to loudly correct Buck about arrested vs. detained. And now the sheriff didn't even bother to use his voice to defend a dog which had helped him just the day before. Kelton, in the mental filing cabinet of the brain, lumped him in the bottom drawer with the jihadists.

Buck pushed him roughly into the back seat, but didn't get to bang his head against the car roof given the additional headroom of the Durango. The deputy also didn't bother with his seatbelt. Kelton wasn't sure if that was because of the short ride, or Buck feared him biting into his throat when he leaned over. The backseat door was closed, his pack thrown in the back with the spare tire and he and the sheriff were headed north. Kelton stared down at the surplus ammo can which was bolted to the floor with a padlock on it for a second to collect his thoughts and then looked out the windows for any sign of his dog.

Kelton took a look over his shoulder to see Buck return to his car and head south, and then looked to his right, east out over the pasture land again. Azrael was nowhere to be seen. The separation filled him with anxiety, and Kelton strained against the cuffs. He knew it would be fruitless in breaking free, but the exertion felt good to burn off the adrenaline and frustration. Before he came to terms with the state of affairs, they were pulling into the parking lot.

"Are you going to give me any trouble?" asked the old sheriff.

Kelton took a deep breath to relax. If he was going to give trouble, handcuffed in the back of a SUV was absolutely the worst time to do it. He'd made his choice when he gave up his gun and sent his dog away. Kelton stuck with that decision and shook his head. He also noted there wasn't a single hair on the upholstery he could see from his dog's ride just yesterday.

Minutes later he was led through the alley entrance to one of the holding cells and gently pushed inside. The door slid closed, and the sheriff locked it with a large key. There were no fancy electric locks in St. Albans. The other cells were still empty.

"Back up to the door," instructed Chandler and Kelton did so.

The sheriff reached between the bars and removed the handcuffs. Angry red circles, some already darkening into deep bruises, were plainly visible on his skin despite it being darkened from years in southwest Asia. And then the sheriff disappeared through the central hallway door, the same one he and Azrael had tracked through just yesterday, without another word.

All the water had evaporated from the stainless steel commode, although things worked appropriately as Kelton took advantage of being alone. The dusty furnishings were sparse as to be expected, with only a sink and a cot with a thin mattress. The cells were really just separate cages erected in a large bay with a concrete floor. No matter where one was, one could see absolutely everything.

He figured the prosecutor might come within minutes or hours, but not days. Else they would need to feed him and check on him regularly. They didn't have the staff for that. But they might be thinking it would be a good move to let him cool down awhile before starting their interview so he was more in a mood to talk. Lawyers didn't like to be kept waiting for someone to speak.

Kelton made himself comfortable on the cot and tried to contemplate returning to life in the absence of a special dog. It was distasteful, and he began to regret honoring the authority of law.

CHAPTER—11

Rebel Tarwick closed the manila folder, sat back in his desk chair, and rubbed his hand over his greasy beard. Despite his troubles, he'd slept soundly without suffering from heartburn, and even his morning coffee sat well with him for a change. It felt good to be calm again after all the rage, but his problems remained and he had to face the issues. He took a deep breath again, and wiped his palms on his denim clad thighs without letting go of the pencil he'd done his figuring with.

He owed a lot in property taxes, with compounding penalties and interest, and had for a long time. He'd never liked tractors that much, finding their crude simplicity boring, and neglected the cornerstone of his daddy's business. He'd always enjoyed working on racecars, or at least cars since there weren't too many racers who didn't have their own mechanic at their local dirt track. Every year he had to purchase more specialty equipment as automotive systems became more sophisticated, but St. Albans lacked the volume to recoup his investments. The Commonwealth of Virginia's letter was demanding immediate payment, or they were prepared to move forward with seizing his assets. The shop was the only asset he had.

The Environmental Protection Agency's letter was similar, but in addition to fines wanted excavation to start on soil contaminated with oil, heavy metals, and assorted solvents. His attorney had described it as a "remediation effort." That was all well and good, but contractors with big machines didn't work for free. Neither did lawyers, and the man had stopped returning his calls.

Rebel was tired of failing. He'd pretty much flunked school, only staying for shop classes before dropping out. His daddy had bled the business dry keeping his racing dreams alive, but when he got hurt Rebel had to take over and the business side of running the shop was not the same as replacing a head gasket. When the pressures got to him, he'd hit his girlfriend for insistent nagging, and she'd disappeared while he was in prison for it. Now, he couldn't seem to make it as a drug dealer. Digging out the pit for a secret place to cook the meth had been an expensive and dumb idea and now the latest profits from his largest batch ever had been stolen.

He shook his head at the stack of fake work orders for tractor maintenance activities, oil changes, tires that had gone flat over winter, sharpening of bush hog blades and the like, he'd use to launder the money. The only problem was no money to launder. He'd invested in security, nearly a half dozen rough and ready who'd paid with their lives, and the green had still walked.

He had to go for the money. It wasn't enough to solve his problems, but it bought him some time. Buck and Doris wanted to lay low, but he didn't have time for that. Moving on to the next batch just wouldn't work. They would have to smurf up the pills, which wasn't free, and then he would have to cook. Then there was delivery to Church Hill in Richmond whose customers would still be enjoying the current shipment. Prices wouldn't be back up for a while. They preferred crack cocaine there, but he couldn't supply that and lacked the contacts to find other meth markets. Add in laundering the money, and there was no way he'd be able to make a large enough tax payment in time to avoid being swarmed with armed agents.

His father, the useless crippled drunk, would say he needed to pray. Rebel slammed the table with his clenched fists as he heard that irritating voice inside his head. How he'd been made to get scrubbed up and go to the great stone church on the city square for Sunday school like it was a gateway to living in high society. Instead the old lady had brought him to the minister for punishment for taking an extra Graham cracker during snack time. His fist clenched hard around the pencil, shattering it like he had that minister's neck for doing that to him. He should have paid the Sunday school teacher a visit too, but she'd already died.

Rebel's erection reliving those events surprised him, and he thought of going down to the pit again, but then thought better of it. He'd attacked that fantasy with elation, fueled by the meth like a fiend the past couple of days. He didn't want to embarrass himself by being unable to complete, and he needed to come off the ice for the mental clarity to save his shop and the Gray Ghost. It wasn't near as much fun when he wasn't high, and Baylee Ann would be there when he was ready again.

The soft rumbling of rubber on gravel made him look out through the greasy shop window to see Buck's patrol car making its way down the drive. He wished the deputy would be more careful, but at least Rebel did work on the patrol vehicles from time to time. And they did need to talk. Rebel wasn't sure what to do with the Dixie girl and still manage to save face. It wasn't something he'd been able to think through beforehand. The money wasn't in the safe, and when she was walking down the alley he grabbed her in a mad fit.

Dixie was useless for ransom. Neither Buck or Doris had much money. That's why they were involved in his scheme. Doris would never tolerate her being used as payment to Shep for another group of bikers. He didn't need her as leverage over Doris and Buck. They were in much too deep to get out if he was still alive.

Was that why Buck was coming, he thought, to kill him? Of course not. Buck was a coward and bully. If that time ever came, it would be a bullet in the back. But not yet, because they still needed cash. He was coming to beg for his woman.

"What the fuck are you doing here?" Rebel snarled as Buck came in the door.

He didn't bother to stand up from where he slouched in the grease stained overalls. It didn't make the snarl particularly menacing.

"You took something that belongs to me," said Buck coldly, eyes hidden behind the sunglasses.

He stood in the doorway, backlit by the brightness of outside, with his arms folded across his chest.

"What have you got to trade?" countered Rebel.

Buck's head looked down and to the side as he considered. Rebel helped him out.

"Where is the money now? If Chandler didn't put it in his office safe, where would it be?"

Buck exhaled, and considered.

"His house. His car. Maybe he took it to the bank and put it in a safety deposit box."

"Do you think he has gone to the bank?"

Buck's lips contorted as he thought, and shoulders shrugged. Rebel rose, and leaned in near the side of Buck's face.

"Bank or house? We only get one more shot at this," said Rebel.

"It has to be house. He's an evidence box on the backseat floor of his Durango. It's just an old ammo can with a padlock on it. Banker hours are pretty narrow, and he's been busy with interviewing the dog guy, cleaning up after your break-in, and consoling Doris."

"Okay then. His house it is. May even help you win the next election. Legit sheriff's homes don't get raided."

"Don't overdo it. We don't want some sympathy backlash starting a manhunt. It has to make Fouche look shady."

Rebel nodded in agreement.

"Okay. You want your bitch back?"

Buck nodded.

"She's not stupid, you know. I haven't hurt her, but she'll figure out where she was and raise a fuss. If it weren't for Doris, I'd sell her to Shep and a biker gang riding way out west or something. You'll have to explain it to her."

"Doris won't like it."

"Doris will want her to be alive. Dixie's a cold bitch, but she won't want her mom and dad in the slammer, or lose their help with the rent."

"I'll tell her the details," agreed Buck.

"Not all the details. Just about her mother will be good enough. Don't tell her shit about me."

Again Buck nodded.

The garage was a typical layout of a two stall bay with a front office on the side whose large front window faced the road along with the door Buck had entered. A back office served as Rebel's living space. Another door from the front office opened into the bays, which Rebel led Buck through. The near bay was cleared for use, but the far one had degenerated into ad-hoc storage with surplus tools, parts, and other supplies choking the floor.

Rebel took him to the squat metal shelving unit with boxes of assorted motor oils and radiator fluids standing between the bays.

"Give me a hand with this, will you?"

Rebel started to push it, using his back against it and extending his legs. Buck joined in, the unit sliding and grinding upon oil soaked kitty litter on the shop floor. They had only moved it about a yard before fully exposing the trap door of plate steel.

Rebel knelt at it, while Buck stepped off to the side with hands on his hips. Rebel grasped the handle, began to pull, looking up toward Buck.

"I should get some food and water for the b-," he began, his words cut short as debris pelted the side of his face. He groaned, clutching at his right eye as it squinted shut in protest over sand and other grit. A blond woman sprung from the hole like a rabbit, and made for the open bay doors. Rebel reached for her with his off hand, but missed the tackle as his fingers didn't quite manage to close about her ankle. His belly hit the floor, the pork rinds in the chest pocket of his denim overalls crushed into powder.

"I got her," said Buck.

Rebel looked up to the see deputy dragging Bambi by her hair back toward the hatch. She screamed and twisted, pounding at him with her fists, but his grip was too strong and no one was within hearing of the remote garage. Another blond head poked up from the hole in the floor. He pushed himself up onto his knees, eyes wild and face flushed with raw red anger.

Buck raised Bambi by her hair just high enough to be able to throw her down on to the floor. Then he kicked her with his steel shank patrol boots. She curled up into the fetal position crying. Showing just above the hole in the floor, Dixie's eyes went wide and her jaw dropped.

Buck pulled the wooden nightstick from his utility belt, and tapped the open palm of his off hand as he towered over the girls. Their resolve died as quickly as their plan.

Rebel pushed himself to his feet and pointed an angry finger at Dixie.

"You! Go to him," he said with a thumb flick toward Buck.

Dixie made her way out the hole, limping a tad on the slightly swollen ankle. Rebel bent over to make a grab at Bambi's hair. Dixie turned on him in a quick whirl.

"Leave her alone!" she exclaimed as she slapped at him with her right arm.

Rebel easily caught her hand and pushed it backward. With the hurt ankle, Dixie lost her balance and tumbled to the floor. Buck reached down to help her up, and as she took his arm he threw her up over his shoulder. Her legs flailed, but he refused to let go or set her down, easily holding the nightstick in the other hand.

Then it was Bambi's turn, Rebel grabbing her by the hair and raising her, forcing her folded body to unwind. A couple of steps, and he was lowering her back into the pit. She grabbed the ladder rungs, and Rebel stepped at her hands to keep her moving downward. A quick slam of the steel plate and a slide of the latch and he had his biker girls secure. He would have to move the shelves back himself later. Buck had his hands full.

"Anything else, Rebel?"

Rebel thought about coordinating the raid on Chandler Fouche's home with Buck, but shook his head no. Dixie would hear, and despite Buck's best efforts she may give the secret away. The raid would come in the night just as soon as he could buy some new muscle. And you could only buy muscle with four things: money, drugs, guns, or pussy. A third of his only account walked out the door on the deputy's shoulder.

Buck sat Dixie upfront in the Chevy and took his time walking around to the driver's door. She didn't make a run for it. Her ankle wasn't that bad, but he didn't think she'd get too far on him. He sat down behind the steering wheel and turned toward her. She sat glaring out the passenger side window, arms crossed over her bosom.

He waited, but she was stubborn and didn't turn toward him.

"Most people I rescue are grateful."

She turned toward him incredulously.

"Why aren't you arresting him? Why aren't you rescuing the other women?" she asked with tears starting in her eyes.

"Because I have to draw the line somewhere, Dixie."

"What in the world does that mean?" her jaw dropping.

"Your mom is in business with Rebel to pay your dad's medical bills. I like you, and don't want to put your mom in prison and have your dad wind up in a home. The state will take his business to pay for his care, and you'd not be able to keep your home.

If I take those skanks from Rebel, things will unravel and he'll drag us all down. But I can't have him bothering classy southern ladies like you now, can I?" he smiled.

"What are you saying Mom is into?" asked Dixie sharply, but the intensity of the question faded before the end of the sentence.

She'd always felt on the rich side of poor. She'd always had nice clothes, food and money for movies and such. It made her feel wealthy amongst her friends growing up. But she also knew the other truth. Her bedroom had been a motel room. She couldn't afford her own car, even if she had needed one. She'd never been on an airplane. There weren't vacations down to Myrtle Beach in the spring other than the one time, the only other time she'd been out of the state than a school field trip to the North Carolina Zoological Park. In the world, despite all the money that passed through their hands, the Johnsons were very far from well to do.

"It doesn't matter," he said. "The less you know the better. And she doesn't do it because she's a bad person. She loves your dad and this is the only way she has to make ends meet and not lose their business. And if you make any fuss around town, I won't be able to keep covering it up for you."

Buck started the car. He would have liked to get the witness signatures, but this was much more important.

She nodded. A few minutes later they drove past the empty sheriff station parking lot, did a U-turn, and stopped in front of her house. He turned off the engine.

"Thanks for taking me home," she said getting out.

He got out after her. His door closing caused Dixie to look back at him over her shoulder as he followed, her tape-savaged eyebrows raised and mouth terse.

"I'm coming in, too."

Her eyes flickered with defiance briefly, but she turned around and put the keys in the door. He pushed through the doorway behind her. Patsy meowed, and started rubbing her legs as Buck threw the deadbolt. As she reached down to stroke her, she felt Buck's strong arms encircle her waist from behind and his hips start grinding her bottom. Dixie tried taking a step forward to break the encirclement, but he stayed with her taking a heavy step forward. The glass figurines spilled off the end table.

"Not now. I'm gross from being in that pit," she protested.

He used his nose to move aside her blond locks, kissing and biting at the back of her neck. Dixie grabbed at his hands, trying to break his embrace, but his grip was too strong. Buck picked her up, his mouth never leaving her neck and carried her forward through the door of the small bathroom.

She squirmed and twisted, and the shower curtain rod fell. He kicked it aside as he put down her feet in the pale green tub. As Dixie turned her head, his kisses left her neck and blazed across her cheek toward her lips. Buck's grip loosened as one hand reached to turn on the water.

"God it's cold!" she screeched.

He found her mouth and she opened it, kissing him back. His utility belt's steel buckle clunked loudly on porcelain, as it landed between the tub and toilet. Buck lifted her wet skirt and gripped the thin cotton panties. She grabbed at his wrists, but he tore the fabric away and spun her, pressing her chest to the lime spotted tiles. He stepped into the tub, standing behind her.

Patsy sat screeching in the bathroom's open door, twitching her tail, as the wall was battered and water splashed across the walls and floor.

CHAPTER—12

Kelton kneeled on the brushed concrete floor to do another set of pushups, trying to keep some level of rage up. The long hours in confinement, with no food and marginal water, were mellowing him and he resented it. When his arms trembled, he sat on the cot with his head in his hands. He'd done nothing wrong. He and Azrael had tried to help them. They had locked him up. Worst of all, they had shot at his dog, and he didn't know where Azrael was or his status.

The light through the high bay windows, much too high for him to see out of even standing on the cot, was steadily growing in intensity. It must be getting late in the afternoon he thought. There wasn't a visible clock and they'd taken his phone. His stomach grumbled in emptiness, even if he knew he'd eaten plenty of calories at breakfast. The glass and steel door to the office hallway was dark with shadow.

He slapped one of the steel bars in frustration, listening to the ring until it died. He repeated it again and again. With intense auditory focus he heard a truck parking outside. It was in the parking lot, and not the alley. It might be the sheriff's Durango, but it sounded bigger and deeper. It wasn't a diesel, but there was no mistaking the big engine. When it shut off, he heard the slam of the door and then nothing.

Kelton's ears strained, hearing the soft buzzing ringing of nothingness. With a fingernail he tapped the bar yet again, to help his ears calibrate to hearing something real instead of imagining something. Yes, he was sure he was hearing it. The distant footfalls echoed on the linoleum tiles, announcing the advance. They were booted feet, in a confident steady cadence with a heavy but powerful stride. And they were growing louder. There was a flicker of movement in the glass door, and a pausing of steps just long enough to work the door mechanism into the cell bay.

The man stopped as he entered and briefly surveyed the entire bay as if to ensure everything was as he'd been told to expect. He was tall and white, skin with a bronze healthy glow that bespoke an active outdoor lifestyle despite approaching sixty. His hair was silver, but very full, and trimmed short with long sideburns. Draping off his powerful shoulders was a tweed sport coat over a forest green shirt with an open button-down collar. He wore slacks of French khaki, neatly folded to tuck into knee-high Irish boots. With his right hand he pushed an office chair on its casters. He carried a brown buffalo hide satchel draped over one shoulder.

Kelton said nothing, merely standing with arms gripping the bars like an extra in a prison movie. He watched as the gentleman positioned the chair in the aisle across from him, put down the satchel and removed his sport coat to drape over its back. Removing the coat revealed a 1911 pistol on his right hip, the hammer back, in an "inside the waistband" type holster. On the left hip was a spare magazine and a small tactical flashlight in a leather carrier. He sat, feet shoulder width apart, and placed his hands on his knees leaning forward slightly.

"Captain Jager, I presume. I am James Redigan, the Commonwealth's Attorney of Lowland County. Please, have a seat," he said with a small hand gesture and a commanding voice, but with a friendly undertone.

Kelton remained standing for a moment regarding him, but the prosecutor patiently gazed upon him with bright eyes. He let go of the bars, and sat upon the head of the cot facing him.

"I am told you have been detained for my questioning, but have not been placed under arrest. I'm sorry the detainment has been inconvenient. The sheriff did not inform me beforehand he was taking this step, and I needed to work through some schedule challenges before coming to see you. Even in a small town, that tends to be the burden of holding office."

Kelton shrugged to acknowledge the apology. It seemed reasonable and he didn't want to delay the situation any longer than necessary. He wanted out as soon as possible to go find his dog.

"I've of course read the draft reports from the on-scene personnel associated with the events of the other night to include Coroner, Sheriff, Deputy and various technicians. We may not have full departments in little St. Albans, but since things like this are so rare we can bang things out in short order. I insist upon it due to the sixth amendment. I consider my oath to support and defend the constitution one that did not expire with my military service and I'm sure you feel the same way."

Kelton nodded again. A speedy resolution was fine by him and he'd rather deal with a veteran.

"I understand you told the sheriff it was self-defense and the disparity of force, five to one, was the driver of your decision to resort to your firearm?"

"Yes, Sir," answered Kelton without nodding.

"Why did you discount non-lethal options?" asked the prosecutor with a passive smile and steady eyes.

Kelton's eyebrows knitted up as he replied, "Sir, I do not understand your question."

"You had a working dog at your disposal. They can be very good at deterring mob advances."

Kelton's lips parted and his eyes looked down as he considered.

"I suppose that was an option," Kelton stated slowly, "but it carried some risk for my dog."

"Are you telling the Commonwealth of Virginia," he said leaning in "that five of its citizens are dead because you didn't want to put your dog at risk?"

"Well, I guess I..."

"You do know that the law places human life, five such lives, above that of mere property, like a dog?" the prosecutor half rose from his seat, his voice rising in volume as he did so.

"I," said Kelton answering in kind, "don't place their lives above my dog's."

The prosecutor smiled, and then sat back. Kelton remained a few more seconds before settling back on the cot.

"Neither do I. The spectrums of the worst to best dogs and worst to best humans, overlap. Especially those five. Worse than the worst dog. Good riddance," he said and upon seeing Kelton's shoulders soften suddenly lunged forward again. "But kid, you need to understand something. I know you are smart. I know you are well-versed in the law. But you'll still wind up in prison if you don't heed what I'm telling you. Don't talk, and get a defense attorney."

"Is there someone you'd recommend here in town? Or give me a list so I pick them instead of you."

James Redigan sighed, "No, I really can't. We don't have enough crime for a local defense attorney. They'd starve down here. Other than me, there's just a couple of real estate guys specializing in agriculture. I even serve as the county attorney when those duties don't conflict with my primary office."

"How long have you been the Commonwealth's Attorney?" asked Kelton.

"Nearly twenty years. I met Lauryn on a Friday night at the officer's club while I was stationed at Langley. I'd just come from Sheppard Air Force Base down in Texas where I prosecuted desertions. She'd been to college and was administering the base elementary school. We married when I received orders for the pentagon. After following me around to a half dozen other bases, she wanted to settle back home in St. Albans when I retired from being Colonel James Redigan, Judge Advocate General's Office, United States Air Force.

No one local could compete with my resume, and no one would want to come here to start a career.

Other than our preacher who went missing several years ago, odd duck that he was, nothing ever really happens here. I don't need indictment or conviction rates to win elections. The next town you shoot up might have that working against you.

In truth, I think our little county would do well to fold. There isn't the tax base to support the services the citizens need. Taxes on the landowners are draconian. I'd be happy to see that happen and fully retire.

Now tell me something," he asked as Kelton nodded in response, "What the hell was a captain doing as a K-9 handler? Weren't you supposed to be leading a company or serving on staff?"

Kelton's head bobbed side to side. It was a good question and he saw no harm in sharing. He needed a good relationship with this guy and didn't want to antagonize.

"The short answer is the army," said Kelton.

James smiled and Kelton continued, "I was branched engineering on account of my degree and the need in Iraq, just like every other engineering graduate of my class. But by the time we were trained and deployed in the pipeline, the engineering demands were stabilizing and the units were saturated with inexperienced lieutenants and not much to do.

Then, the senior NCO who ran the kennels was killed in an auto accident. They asked for a volunteer to lead it for a couple of months, pending an "out of cycle" replacement and I raised my hand. The replacement turned out to be hard to come by as they were ramping up stateside training programs to answer the cry for more multi-purpose K-9's. Then, when the first guy actually showed, he had to go home two weeks later due to a bleeding ulcer. By then I had traction with the local infantry brigade who loved us for finding weapon caches and improvised explosive devices, and nobody was missing me over at the engineering battalion.

A year later, when my deployment should have been ending, the engineering battalion's leadership had not only turned fully over, the unit had moved from Baghdad's Green Zone to up around Erbil somewhere. When my orders came to them, they had no idea who I was or my status. That was fine with me, and I think the local personnel NCO's put up a smokescreen for me saying they had no idea who I was when someone called brigade, threw out letters, filed extensions on my behalf, etc. The army still might not have found me if my mom hadn't died.

Anyway, the guy killed in the car crash had used back channels to get a breeding pair in the country after all the frustrations with getting replacement dogs. The first litter was six weeks old when I took over. I had a lot of spare time, and was surrounded by a lot of guys who spoke fluent dog, including a well-seasoned civilian contractor from Israel. Azrael was one of those dogs, and didn't exist on army property inventories. That's how I got to take him home.

Fun as those years were, it didn't set me up for an officer's career. Those commanders over there kept me where I helped them the most during their one-year tour. When the real army found me, I was way off the career track and they encouraged me to separate."

"Even with two silver stars for valor?"

Kelton looked surprised.

"A copy of your DD214 was in the file, but not the citations," he explained with a gesturing open palm. "Tell me."

Easy enough for one of the technicians to take a digital photograph of all his processions.

"I went out on patrol once a week to stay in touch with what my guys were doing on the front lines. The first couple of years, I would pair up with someone, rotating through the entire platoon. Later, when demand for us was so high with everyone knowing what we could do, I'd go alone to stretch our resources.

On one of those, the platoon I was embedded with started taking heavy fire to the front. We were in low rolling ground, between a lot of small stone houses, with these low walls crisscrossing everywhere. It was good cover against the incoming rounds, but dead space was everywhere."

"What's dead space? Remember, you're talking to an air force lawyer."

"Ground that can't be covered with direct fire, from like your rifle. That you can't see into. It's a way the enemy can more safely approach your position. Which is what happened.

The platoon leader had everyone on line facing front, not realizing his brother platoons on each flank were a little far off to secure his. Some bad guys got between the units without us seeing, and popped up to our side and rear with light machine-guns and a rocket launcher.

I couldn't see to the front and had only brought a pistol. It made things a lot easier working the dog. So I was just lying on my back looking to the rear when I caught a brief glimpse of a head scarf in a gap in one of the walls. When they popped up over the top a second later, I was ready for them. It took them by surprise. I killed all four before they could get off a shot. They credited me with saving most of the platoon."

"And the second?"

"An ambush initiated by an IED on some marines. We were nearby. I saw a wounded dog in the kill zone so I crawled out there to get him while everyone else was busy firing. He passed soon after I got to him, but it positioned me to make my way over to check out a burning Humvee on its side. There was a wounded man inside, and I dragged him to safety while everyone gave cover fire. A corpsman and another guy met me halfway to safety at which time Azrael and I turned around to try and find other survivors. We didn't, but I was sure proud of my young pup under that pressure, bullets flying all around, and keeping his nose to the ground.

The medals definitely would be a help with a military career, but there are a lot of brave men and women serving who have earned medals, too. And they served in positions that have prepared them for staff work or company command. I did not."

"Justice is supposed to be blind, but please pardon me for wanting to peek under the blindfold a little bit and know who you are. Seems only fair since I knew who the others were. Not my fault they don't measure up.

The only other thing I have to discuss with you is a witness statement taken by Deputy Garner which says you were the aggressor under the bridge, ambushing them from the darkness because you were so afraid and all alone. What say you to that?"

Kelton scoffed, "I'm a combat veteran. I had a weapon, plenty of ammunition, and am skilled in its use. And I wasn't alone. Azrael was with me. If they didn't know I was there, I would have just sat quietly until they left so I could keep on walking. It's nonsense. It's a lie."

"Bullshit is the term I would use. The statement is also unsigned. Even a second year law student, with a little collaboration from you, would eviscerate it in court. And it's the only piece of evidence contrary to a very strong self-defense case.

I see no reason to detain you further, or confine you to town.

Come on, I'll give you a ride to animal control so we can get your dog," he said as he rose and reached for his sport coat.

Kelton stood too, "My dog is missing. I told him to make a run for it, and Deputy Garner emptied his sidearm at him. But if my gear is nearby, I have GPS on him."

James' eyes narrowed at the explanation, but he confined himself to actions instead of words. He left through the bay doors, but returned within moments with the cell keys. They left them in the lock, and the chair in the cell bay. Chandler had placed Kelton's pack in the hallway just outside his office, and James waited patiently as Kelton opened the top and began hurriedly donning his gear. He checked the pistol, and found it was still loaded.

"I can't believe your sheriff left an unattended loaded gun laying in the hall."

"The front doors were locked when I came over and I'm sure he expected me sooner," James shrugged, "but I agree with you that it was poorly done."

With phone in hand and pack slung over one shoulder, Kelton hurried toward the front doors. James followed, and used his keychain remote to unlock the doors and start the engine of his vehicle. Kelton saw it was a big silver Dodge Ram 4x4 with a V10 engine. He threw the pack in the bed, and jumped in the passenger side. James was already putting it in gear.

"Which way?" he asked.

"Head south out toward Lowland Road while it loads up. That's where I lost contact. It's being a little slow."

"We don't have the best satellite coverage out here," James explained as he took a right out of the parking lot and then a left at the stop sign by the railroad tracks.

Kelton didn't acknowledge him, eyes fixated on the tiny screen. He began working his fingers to zoom in and out, trying to have enough perspective to know where Azrael was but detailed enough to navigate. It was a hard balance on the tiny screen.

"We're way to the west of him."

Tires squealed and Kelton banged his head on the door as James whipped the big truck left onto Coalson Street. The tiny yards were mostly quiet, except for some young boys throwing a baseball.

"Looks as if he's this side of the interstate."

"Coalson dead ends into Thigpen and we'll need to pick left or right," informed James.

"Left. We're just a little south of him, but mainly west," said Kelton, not looking up from the small screen for even a blink.

James took the next turn more modestly, running the stop sign. Within a moment they were at Main's flashing light, where it intersected at Thigpen.

"Go east. Right," directed Kelton.

James was quick to comply, the giant V-10 engine roaring as he mashed the accelerator. Kelton began scanning the scraggly bushes and brush maple trees of the vacant strip just west of the truck stop.

"Okay, he's just a little south," said Kelton looking back down at the screen. They were just north of the truck stop's parking lot.

A faded blue sedan with peeling roof leaving the diner started to coast across their path. James angrily hung on the horn, the long blast lasting several seconds. The driver extended his hand from the window with raised middle finger. James gave him a second horn blast as he raced on by. The car turned and started to follow them behind the parked rigs.

"East west is good. Head south."

Fifty feet later they were out of asphalt, but James didn't slow down. A quick pull at the floor lever and the four-wheel drive indicator glowed on the dash. The rough ground bounced their heads to the ceiling as they left the parking lot for greenspace. Tires ripped into the grass and they barreled toward the wood line. Only when within a few yards did James apply the brakes. Both men hit seatbelt releases and door handles as the rock back of the truck's suspension shook them.

"Azrael!" called Kelton.

An explosion of leaves and branches followed by paw pounding joy, greeted them. Kelton dropped to the ground, patting at his dog while fangs tickled his wrists. Azrael rolled and ran circles, letting out a series of short high-pitched barks. Behind them, at the edge of the parking lot, a young man in a wife beater and backward ball cap got back in his car and drove away.

"You drive like a wild man," admired Kelton.

"I want all my veterans home safe regardless of their branch of service, or species," proclaimed James.

Azrael sat proudly in his drab-brown vest, panting after his excitement while a kneeling Kelton rubbed his ears.

"You two are free to continue your pursuits of life, liberty and happiness. Let's get your gear out of my truck, and I'm going back to the office."

"Kind of late for that isn't it?"

"I want to get a jump start on my filing against Deputy Garner. Reckless discharge of a firearm and cruelty to animals," shrugged James. "He should have called the dogcatcher."

Kelton donned his pack and the attorney handed him his card.

"In case you get into further trouble, young man," he explained. "You are a fellow oath taker and will be standing up for what is right. I will do what I can to help you, provided you don't lie, cheat, or steal."

Kelton shook the old colonel's hand. He'd actually enter the information into his phone before throwing the card away. Then he'd get dinner one more time at the diner, a good night's sleep, and would be walking down the road come morning toward nowhere in particular.

CHAPTER—13

Chandler pulled into his old saltbox on the grassy knoll on Caisson Road. The house was two stories facing the road with five upstairs windows over four below, the middle spot taken by the front door which nobody ever used. The white asbestos shingle siding needed a pressure-washing to chase the pollen and mildew away, but so did all houses here this time of year. The crepe-myrtle trees were well pruned and blooming their pinks and reds. No debris lingered under the magnolia. He had lots of pride and was pleased with how his home looked.

Image was everything for a highly visible public figure like himself, especially for a negro sheriff in a small rural southern town. He embraced using the term "negro". It made other people uncomfortable and off-balanced like they had done something wrong, while he stood before them firmly grounded and impeccable. Relations on occasion over the years would try to tell him he should say "black" or later as the decades went by "African-American". He'd just smile softly and tell them that the term might describe them, but he was seventy and didn't need to change his ways. He was the law of the county, and that credential sounded much more impressive given the proper historical perspective of the achievement. Using a term other than negro seemed to undercut it.

As such, he always gave his property a real critical eye. He paused as he exited the Dodge Durango, noting his wife's old Buick was in the carport on the side, and made his list. The gravel drive could use a grading after the spring rains he decided. The usual pothole had formed in the middle near the bottom. The white picket fence running along the drive and road would need a coat of paint when the weather became warm and dry. The house's metal roof, which had been painted silver a couple of years ago, showed no signs of peeling or rust breaking through. Mortar on the weathered brick chimney looked like it had weathered another winter, although he wanted to get up there and be sure. All in all, it was simply maintenance he could mostly pass on to his grandsons. He wasn't behind on anything. Chandler didn't want to leave for fishing with anything hanging over him.

He looked up and down Caisson Road at the small ranchers and cottages, the lots sold off over the years to fund the farms through the hard times. It was quiet, the houses much too far apart to be considered a neighborhood. If you needed to borrow a cup of sugar from a neighbor, you were driving. During the civil war, when the railroad couldn't run, the lonely country lane was rutted with wagon traffic and earned its name. After the war, the movement of goods returned to the restored railroad and later the interstate, making it once again a quiet county backwater without enough traffic for any type of business to make it. Chandler thought it was the perfect retreat.

He walked on the paver stones around back and saw his wife still had clothes out on the line. There was the small weathered wooden barn which was his workshop and housed the Cub-Cadet tractor with its belly mower, and a woodpile under the overhang for the old stove when the power went out. His picket fence ended against a cattle farm's barbwire, with rolling green pasture and dogwood trees. There didn't seem to be any cows about this evening.

He opened the screened door on the porch. The large double doors into the living room were open, making one large gathering place.

"Evelyn?" he called before grunting to himself at the smell of boiling collard greens.

"In the kitchen," she called.

Little feet, carrying braided pigtails tied in pink ribbon, raced out from behind the pantry.

"Grandpa!" she called excitedly.

He knelt down so he could see her face.

"Which one are you?" he asked skeptically.

She giggled, "I'm Latoyia."

He was taken aback, putting his hands on his hips while still kneeling.

"What kind of name is that?"

"My name, Silly!" she proudly proclaimed.

Evelyn called from the entry way to the kitchen, wearing a pale blue house dress and a faded navy and white checkered apron, "Chandler, you know better than to issue judgement on the little ones for the sins of their parents."

He stood, and Latoyia began running around and talking to a small plastic doll she was holding.

"She's Juliette's daughter."

Chandler's eyes narrowed over a blank face.

"My third sister, Delia's, stepchild from her second marriage, Catarina. Juliette's her daughter. She's visiting while Juliette takes her state cosmetology exam. Gives me company while you boys are out in the southern wild."

Evelyn sighed as he shook his head to clear it.

"Did you go to the bank like I asked you?"

He nodded.

"Also, Deputy Garner left a message on the answering machine just as you came up the drive. He said that Dixie was back and there would be no concerns. Office romance drama?"

He nodded again. That had been a worrisome headache.

"Go change. Everyone will be here soon."

Chandler climbed the stairs to their bedroom which was over the kitchen on the driveway side of the house. Its open screened windows looked over the road in front and the roof of the living room and porch outback. Furnishings were simple. Evelyn wouldn't abide a television set in there. She barely put up with the gun cabinet, holding a lonely over-under shotgun, but with the small kids frequently in the house had relented to its residence in the bedroom. What she hadn't relented on over the years was giving that shotgun some company, but she took good care of the one. Every week it moved positions in the cabinet and there was never any dust. She made him refresh her how to use it every few months.

He removed the bank envelope from his pocket and placed it on her vanity, as always confused at the endless bottles of lotions, oils, perfumes and such. An array of wigs hung to the left of the mirror. Small shelves on the right contained assorted acrylic nail kits and polishes. While he appreciated her effort over the years in looking the perfect part as the sheriff's wife, he wondered if she'd ever gracefully accept her advancing years. She was sixty now. It was beginning to border on undignified.

Chandler sat down on the bed, took off his shoes, and wiggled his aching feet. He meant to get up and give them a polish as was his custom, but he just felt like sitting. A moment later he lay back, looking at the Jesus portrait above their bed and wondered where he stood in the eyes of the Lord. It had been a really hard couple of days.

He didn't want to be seen as weak, but in retrospect he wondered if he should have called in more help from the state police than the contracted lab technicians. No one expected him to be equipped to handle a shooting with five dead. But it would have been another piece of ammunition that the opposition would use in the newspaper about it being time to fold and join a neighboring county. When that happened, he would never work again.

Something was afoot with Buck. He wanted to fire him, for no other reason than he didn't trust him anymore, but that wouldn't look good. Like he was losing control of his department. But lots of things weren't adding up right. The Lowland Outlaw bikers had been a scourge upon the county for years. Mr. Jager's pedigree was impeccable. Buck's witness statements didn't quite fit, and he must know that as well. The break-in upon his safe wasn't a coincidence. There had to be someone else playing this game, that didn't die under that bridge. Until that was figured out, Chandler felt it prudent not to commit to any course of action.

And Dixie didn't sit right with him either. She was a cool one. It was hard for him to believe that she'd been so riled up that she'd abandoned her post without a word. Buck hadn't acted like he was particularly worried, like he knew that Dixie and the break-in weren't connected at all. Maybe Buck had been embarrassed by something and was trying to cover it up. He'd pull them both into his office Monday morning for a counseling. Maybe dock them some pay. He wasn't going to have this type of crap going on in his department.

It was probably best that the stranger was in the jail for safekeeping. Hopefully animal control would find that dog and euthanize it before anyone was hurt and it blew back on him. Still, the question of why Buck had taken a dislike to the man vexed him. Did Buck feel inadequate? He was too big-headed for that. But making that arrogant upstart Jim Redigan do his job and be the one to stick his neck out was probably the right call.

The low throaty grumbling of an aged pickup truck turning into the drive came through the front windows and he hurriedly changed into jeans and donned a long sleeved work shirt with lots of pockets. Evelyn had packed the small bag for him already, and he slung the strap over his shoulder without a glimpse inside. Evelyn knew what he needed.

He slipped his service revolver from his duty belt into a side zipper pocket. The big six-shooter barely fit, but he'd never trade down for convenience. More times than not it wasn't about shooting, it was about intimidation. Chandler never even considered leaving it behind. He'd carried a weapon his entire adult life, even at church, and couldn't stomach being without one.

Chandler then sighed, as he realized he left the charger for his cellphone at the office. With the radio he didn't take a lot of calls, but he never wanted it to go dead on duty either.

He never used it at home, and usually the battery got him through the night to his next shift where he could plug it in again. With the charge down to twenty percent he turned it off to save what was left in case he needed it. He wasn't going to bring a police radio on his day off.

He began to make his way downstairs, but then hesitated and slipped into the attached bathroom to make water as voices rose from below. Holding things wasn't as easy as it once was. By the time he trotted back down the stairs he could hear the truck rumbling away and found four boys, ranging from ten to twelve, around his kitchen table.

"Hey Grandpa!"

"Hello, my boys. As soon as we eat, we'll get going."

Evelyn had made fried chicken to go with the collard greens, and the boys ate like growing boys who never quite get enough. There was small talk about school, how Easter Break was going and tangled tales of family gossip which his wife tried to make sense for him. His wife let him know their son had called from Colorado on his latest run driving cross-country trains for the Union Pacific. Thirty minutes later, the boys piled into the Buick while Chandler put bags and fishing poles into the trunk. Evelyn watched while holding Latoyia's hand. It was beginning to get dark.

"While you were still upstairs, Jerome asked if you could call the sheriff in Halifax. Seems his son got himself into a little trouble last Saturday night," informed his wife.

Chandler froze, "And what did you tell him?"

Her head moved backward as she answered, "Not to bring us crap like that. You do the crime; you do the time." Theirs was a big family and such requests were common and always offended him.

He nodded approval, and began to turn toward the car.

"When you going to retire and buy that sailboat? You been talking about it for years."

"I know, Evelyn. It's just that," he struggled for words "down there on the river I'm nothing but another negro with a cane pole and straw hat. Here,"

"I'm the sheriff," she finished for him nodding.

Chandler flew to the driver's door before she could lay a lecture on him about aging gracefully. The boys sat quiet as he got in and started the engine, cowed by the heavy-handed discipline of impatient and often reluctant parents. He watched as Evelyn and Latoyia waved in the rearview mirror as he creeped down the driveway and on to the road.

"What's the biggest fish you boys ever caught?"

He looked in the rearview as the youngest raised a pair of hands separated by about six inches.

"We'll get catfish bigger than that. We will catch catfish bigger than you!"

They looked at each other skeptically, not used to being in the conversation while riding in a car. They began to warm up to the idea.

The second oldest raised his hand.

"Ain't that like a really big fish?"

Chandler bit his tongue about proper words and nodded his head instead, "We will catch some really big fish."

But his mind was drifting to catching another type of fish. He stayed in the conversation long enough to get them talking and then he eased more into his own thoughts as they engaged with each other. By the time he was driving south on I-85 and passing the lights of the St. Albans' exit, he'd decided not to take it all the way to River Road.

He weighed the risk with the boys in the car, but ultimately it came down to this being his only chance to do a drive by in a civilian vehicle. Chandler changed lanes, interjected a "huh" into a spirited super-hero powers discussion, and looked ahead for the exit sign. Azalea Estates Lane was the only off-ramp between St. Albans and River Road, and some seven miles south of Ed's Truck Stop.

It was originally zoned to be a middleclass housing development for those that lacked the means for a place directly on the river. But the river parcels proved too out-of-the-way from any large cities to truly blossom into wealthy estates. The demand just hadn't been there. Which meant the overflow development of Azalea Estates hadn't developed at all. Or at least not in the way the cutesy road name implied county planners and real estate investors had hoped for once upon a time.

What it had become was the hub of the Lowland Outlaws. There was an old dairy barn, owned by a guy named Shep Primrose, adjacent to a service station specializing in two-wheelers. Shep hadn't been terribly abused in the transaction according to county tax records, but old farmer Casey had been concerned about construction noises throwing off the milking of his cows and had sold out. The structure had been well maintained and sound. Slowly it was converted into a clubhouse. Now, it had become more of an underground biker bar and grill known as the "Outlaw Saloon". It had direct interstate access, was remote from the homes of gentlefolk, and connected to a good many country roads. With no complaints from locals and only him and Buck to patrol the county, they were left alone.

Whether they were a motorcycle club, gang or loose affiliation was really just a matter of semantics. What wasn't a matter of word games was analyzing the real trouble within the county. Not the "your dog relieved himself in my yard keep the peace" type of trouble which dominated the calls they received, but the "real crime" type of trouble. It was either transient, like the truckers looking for young prostitutes, or it was local trouble. And when it was local trouble, it usually traced itself somehow back here. He started down the ramp and could see the barn's security light glowing on a utility pole.

"Grandpa, I think you got off at the wrong exit."

"I think you are right, young man. Grandpa's just excited to go fishing with his boys and turned too early. We can get there going this way, too."

"A shortcut?" asked the smallest.

"It won't be any shorter but we'll be there soon."

On the south side of the road, the service station of grimy white cinderblocks was dark with its two garage doors shut tight. To its east side and snaking around the back, was a mound of tires. Mainly motorcycle tires, with a few truck mudders showing in the Buick's high beams as he turned right at the stop sign partially obscured by scraggly bushes. However, the gas pumps glowed on a lonely island ready to accept plastic money. There wasn't any overhead cover for filling up in the rain. He dimmed his lights.

A little further down on the right, the north side of the road, the saloon was having a good night. A protruding beam, that once helped alfalfa bales into the hayloft, now supported a faded sign in red letters "The Outlaw Saloon". His grandsons strained their necks, eyes wide, taking in the chrome and black leather of choppers and trikes in the gravel parking lot. An engine revved, and then idled. Music blared from speakers hanging under the rusty tin roof of the covered porch built around the barn doors. Cigarettes glowed orange in the small groups of shadowy figures. He guessed there may have been some three dozen people present, inside and out. A lit marquee sign trailer by the road, leaning with a flat tire, promoted local guitarist Braxton Greene.

Chandler's mouth opened slightly as he read the name to himself again, continuing west down the road. No on-coming headlights shone in the darkness so he hit his high beams again and sped for a few minutes to gain some distance. His worst fear was to see a cloud of single headlamps, like fireflies in his rearview mirror, giving chase while he had the boys in the car. But it was all darkness and he gradually slowed until finally reaching Thigpen Road. He turned left at the four way stop and soon hit River Road along the Roanoke River.

He breathed a sigh again, as the rearview stayed clear. His young companions, with very full bellies and the country darkness far from the lights of the interstate, had drifted to sleep. Chandler slowed down, not wanting to arrive at the cabin too early and have his thoughts interrupted getting his charges settled in. No lawman believed in coincidences, and he'd been a lawman for nearly fifty years. Braxton Greene was who Buck claimed owned the truck seen by Lutheran Butler across from his barbershop. The shootout, the break-in to his office, and the strange kid in his jail had his mind working overtime. For the first time in years, he had a real case. Nothing like sitting with a fishing pole to consider his next moves.

CHAPTER—14

Dixie sat in the small rocking chair by her bed and exhaled again, hung her head and rubbed her eyes. The white painted wood creaked softly in-time to the thudding of the runners. Buck hadn't stayed real long. Caught up in the steamy moment, he'd finished within a half dozen thrusts. As he'd gathered his wet clothes and discarded equipment, she'd wanted him to stay. She'd felt safe with him. He'd rescued her, instead of letting her wind up like the other two women.

But as he'd tried to pull himself back together enough to make the dash from her front door to his patrol car, she'd lingered in the shower. The pit had been nasty. Buck taking her when she was mentally off-balanced, just rescued and reeling from tales of her mom's malfeasance, felt nasty. The way he'd taken her, and then started to dress so he could immediately leave felt nasty. His sticky seed running down her thighs instead of captured in a condom felt nasty. There had just not seemed enough shampoo or water to wash it all away.

She'd again considered calling to him, searching for something more, but instinctively knew there was nothing more to be had. Dixie hadn't wanted him to be seen leaving her place in such a disheveled state, but it was better disheveled in the evening than immaculate first thing in the morning. Even after the hot water gave out, she had stayed silently under the showerhead, nipples erect in the chill. She heard him hanging up the phone in the kitchen and his footsteps toward the front entryway. The fogged bathroom mirror was angled right to give her a brief glimpse of him reaching for the doorknob.

"Go see your mom," he had said over his shoulder. "She's worried about you."

And then he had gone, leaving her cold and dripping wet, with a mess on her hands.

All her towels, bath and hand, had been soaked. Even the fuzzy commode cover had needed to be wrung out, the cheap dark green dye staining her hands. Dixie had cracked the tiny window, spinning the handle until it would go no further and fretted about things drying out properly. The heat and humidity of the south already punished her with blackened tile grout and rusty fixtures. She'd hung the shower rod, the mildewed curtain still dripping. It took her half an hour on her hands and knees, soaking up the water with a bath towel and wringing it out in the tub, before there was nothing left to do but let evaporation take its course.

Dixie had used the few dish towels in the kitchen to dry herself off and started a load of laundry before sitting. It was a girl's chair, sanded down and repainted by her grandfather as a birthday gift long ago. Although a little low, she'd stayed small and it was a good place to put on her shoes in the morning or drape clothes she'd wear again. And its finish resisted the water better than the living room upholstery. Patsy sulked somewhere under the bed, refusing to come out, rather than jumping into Dixie's lap as usual.

"Okay. Mom. I must go see Mom," she told herself out loud.

She opted for a favorite pair of capris jeans, so tight that commando was a necessity. With black heels, it made her feel like a rock star. The walk to the truck stop be damned, after a couple of ibuprofen her ankle was feeling much better. Pushup-bra and black V-neck T-shirt with a heart of silver rhinestones on the front fit her mood. The jeans were too tight to tuck the shirt in. No belt. Dixie dried her hair and put up her blond locks with a dark red ribbon, leaving things edgy and frilly. Metallic red lipstick and thick eye makeup to cover her duct tape wounds. Nights could be cool. She donned a thin black leather jacket, with accent zippers on the pockets.

Come rock me, she thought looking in the mirror. Dixie craved men's attention, feeling terribly unfulfilled from Buck who wasn't to be denied. The power of turning them down energized her. That's what uplifted her, made her feel in control. It's what fueled her self-esteem.

She didn't bother to stand-up the scattered figurines on the end table. She could finish tidying up tomorrow. A scoop of dry food and fresh water in Patsy's dishes and she was out the door. Upon the sidewalk in the darkness, she could see the flashing yellow light and the orange glow beyond of her daddy's business.

Dixie walked near the curb, glancing warily into the black mouths of the alleyways between the buildings as she strode along her way. She took a deep breath trying to calm herself a little. She didn't used to be as jumpy. The sidewalk ended at Thigpen, so she crossed to the other side of the street, and continued on the well-worn trail of dirt, cigarette butts and pop-tops. Her dad's land here was undeveloped, now a tangle of briars and scrub trees.

They'd talked as a family about selling it as a commercial lot, but the legal and surveyor fees with the county would be an expensive hassle and it might develop into competition for her parent's business. Once, while in 4-H club, she had wanted to fence it and get a trip of goats. Instead, it remained as a place to expand the parking lot although that seemed increasingly unneeded and unnecessary as the years went by. There were a healthy number of parked semis for a weekday evening, and they could still arrange themselves with plenty of separation.

Her dad always condemned the girls, as parasites taking money away that otherwise might be spent on diner meals or convenience items. But as she grew more savvy in recent years, she began to appreciate that it might be the other way around. Bigger and better facilities weren't much further away. Truckers stopped here to spend money because of the girls.

As she reached the corner of the parking lot, she leapt the drainage ditch beside the road. Three more steps, and she was on the cracked asphalt with faded striping, and last year's dried up grass poking up between rampant cracks. A driver at the back of the lot rolled down his window and waved for her to come over, but she just kept on walking.

"Can't afford me, Baby," she muttered under her breath and then swayed her hips. "I own the place."

A number of cars were at the diner, but none she recognized as locals. They mostly came for weekend breakfast or late after the bars had closed. Else they would take in a café or restaurant in town. Dixie paused outside the foggy door, took a breath, and went inside.

The rush was over, the waitress mainly concerned with keeping glasses full and running tickets and payment back and forth to the register. They pushed dessert, but seldom had takers. Her mom swiped a card at the register, and placed the printed receipt on a tray. Doris looked up, saw her, and began to tear up.

"Rachel, can you handle things for a minute?" she called out, voice nearly cracking.

"Sure thing, Miss Doris," Rachel replied while pouring a cup of coffee without looking. She didn't spill a drop and scooped up the cash in a tray with her other hand.

Her mom turned from the register and walked back toward the kitchen. Dixie followed until they exited the back, and Doris sat down on the steps leading up to her parents' apartment. One of the dishwashers in a greasy apron was having a cigarette, but quickly put it out and went back inside. Tears began to flow down her mother's cheeks.

"Mom, I'm fine. Nobody hurt me."

"I'm so thankful, Dixie. But I hate you seeing your father and me like this."

"I know, Mom. But I'm a big girl now. I know you and Dad love me," said Dixie leaning down toward her mom and stroking the side of her face with the back of her hand. "Things will be okay."

"Then you should know. Things might not be okay. Rebel is desperate, and Buck isn't smart enough to control him. If it blows up, I'll be dragged down with them."

"Can you get out?"

"It's much too late for that, my dear. But you might be able to get out."

"Me get out? Why? How?"

"If this thing unravels, Buck is going to prison for a long time. Chandler's little department will be done and you'll lose your job."

"Then I'll just come back and work for you," she said dismissively with her hand.

"We won't be open. Your dad's medical bills are drowning us. There are environmental and VDOT upgrades we are supposed to make. The place is falling apart. It's old and wasn't well built to begin with. The only thing to fix it is a bulldozer," her mother declared with eyes now dry.

"Okay, but I can't just walk down the road by myself and have it lead anywhere good."

"Not by yourself. You haven't met him, but in room three is a young man named Kelton Jager and he is leaving tomorrow morning. I sent him to rescue you, although I know now that Buck interfered with that. But he went. He tried. He has a good heart and a brighter future than anything that will ever be had here."

Dixie smiled, and caressed the back of her jeans with her palms. Timing was good. She looked the part.

Extending a hand to her mom she helped her up, and they both walked back through the kitchen into the diner. Dixie made for the front door, but not before hearing one of the regular truckers.

"Doris, what's yours and Ed's secret for staying together so long?"

Her mom's response came quick as a whip, before the door closed behind her.

"Thirty years of marriage and I've never once had to lower a toilet seat."

Rough laughter howled along the barstools.

Dixie licked the corners of her mouth, wishing she was able to freshen her makeup. It was too far to walk home and back again for a quick application of lipstick. Instead she slowly meandered down the chipped sidewalk in front of the motel doors facing the road, picking her words. She didn't hesitate at the moment, tapping gently at the door as soon as she arrived and smiled.

A quick darkening of the spyhole, and the door opened. She was so startled by the black muzzle below, she didn't look at him at first.

"Ma'am, may I help you?"

He was a handsome man, although plainly dressed in his brown shirt and pants like some farm laborer. But he smelled clean, hair still dripping and his face freshly shaved. She reckoned he was about her age, but his eyes seemed older.

"I'm Dixie. Doris is my mom. She said you tried to help me out. Can I come in?" she said cocking her head to one side with a smile.

"Uh, okay," said Kelton blinking. "I guess."

He stepped aside to open the door as wide as it would go, giving her a clear path around Azrael who hadn't been gracious enough to back away.

She kept her eyes on the dog as she came through the entrance, "Does he bite?"

"Oh, yes. He loves to bite people," he replied instantly, like a reflex. It was a favorite line in the K-9 world.

She could tell he'd used that line before, but as Dixie looked at the dog she realized it was only partly a joke and shivered slightly. She regathered herself as he closed the door, and then sat on the bed. There was only one chair in the room so it wasn't particularly forward. As he turned back around and saw her there, he stopped dead in his tracks. Azrael came up to his side, and sat down at attention without command.

She lay back on the bed, using her elbows to work her head back to the pillow and the battered wall. The dog looked back and forth from her to him, and then again. Kelton stood there, his mouth slightly open. Dixie bent her knees, and then let them fall apart until the tight denim resisted, framing her view of him with the V formed by her pulled up legs. The side of his neck quivered and his hand went to massage the base of his throat.

"Do you bite, Kelton?" and then in a softer voice, "I sure don't."

He walked around the end of the bed, to sit on the left side where there was more room. Kelton used a hand for support, elbow locked like a pillar, to keep himself upright with lots of daylight between them. His breathing was shallow, the chest working up and down in a quiet panting. Even in the poor light of the room, she could see the glimmer along his hairline.

"I'm really grateful you tried to rescue me from Rebel's pit. It was hell down there."

"He had you in a pit?" Kelton asked suspiciously.

"It was under a big shelving unit in the middle of the garage. There was this metal trapdoor and a ladder."

"What did he want with you? Did he hurt you?"

"No, he didn't hurt me. He was sure hard on the other women, but he knew I was too good for him," she said smiling. She pulled back the unzipped leather jacket to show her cleavage.

"What other women?"

"But I was still glad to get out of there. It was dark and dirty, and I felt so scared. I'm so glad you came for me."

Kelton repeated, "What other women?"

"Huh?" she said with pursed lips.

"The other women that were being held in the pit with you. Are they still being held there?"

Dixie pulled her legs together and up underneath herself as she sat up on her side of the bed with eyes narrowing in confusion.

"I don't know. Maybe. But you're here with me now."

Kelton sprung from the bed into the chair, and knelt forward to grab his boots. Azrael stood and began to wag his tail excitedly.

"How many other women?" he asked gathering some stray equipment into his pack.

Dixie folded her arms across her chest, "Two. Just a couple of local skanks. Nobody important."

Kelton stood and then donned his backpack.

"Where you going?" she said bewildered.

He took a quick, but thorough, look around the room carefully eyeing the nightstand and the electrical outlets. A couple of strides and he checked the sink, finding nothing.

"Come on!" she implored.

He knelt by Azrael, checking the vest, it's attached light, and the collar before rubbing him on the shoulders and standing.

"Please don't go," she pleaded.

"It was nice meeting you," he replied firmly and then raced through the door with his dog.

She collapsed backward on the pillow, with one leg hanging off the side of the bed. She exhaled, and half-heartedly slapped at the mattress a few times while stomping the opposite foot. Dixie turned to look at the clock on the nightstand and saw he'd left the room key. Then she curled up and began to cry.

CHAPTER—15

Inside the Outlaw Saloon, Shep Primrose sat at the scarred wooden desk in the middle of his oblong mezzanine hayloft office, comparing inventory reports to sales receipts. He faced a window, where the old hayloft doors used to be, that looked out over the covered porch into the parking lot. The rectangular sign hanging from the beam above split the view. Behind him and opposite that window was a balcony of sorts where the floor of the old hayloft had been cut away. This allowed him to survey the bar below or relax in a chair to enjoy the small stage without mixing with the clientele. The open shutters were full length to be able to block out the noise or meet people to discuss nefarious plans without being overhead. Some discussions were heated. One short-side opened to a spiral staircase going down, or if one wanted to among the rafters and beams. The other led to a small private bathroom, with just a commode and a sink that tied into the old dairy-waste septic tank.

His bed was in the corner. An old G.I. footlocker that he'd won in a card game during his brief stint in the air force sat at its end. The only other furniture was a couple of chairs for visitors and a venerable filing cabinet. A couple of torn and sun faded Baja 1000 posters, the off road Mexican desert motor race, decorated the walls. An old pilot's survival knife stood vertically near the stack of receipts, its point embedded in the wood. He stabbed the desktop when frustrated. The desk bore many knife wounds.

It smelled in there, even to him. Washing clothes and bedding was a trip to a laundromat in town, and not an easy thing to do on a motorbike. It also looked stupid to be riding a chopper with a plastic basket bungeed on the back. Once every couple of months sufficed if he remembered. His type of women weren't around long enough to tend to such things for him. Deodorant cost too much money. And the stink wafting upward from the saloon floor, stale beer and biker funk, never went away no matter how hard the staff cleaned. And they didn't really clean all that hard. The local health department never bothered to come visit them. Their expanding clientele didn't seem overly sensitive to the issue.

Shep wasn't an educated business person or a forensic accountant, but he wasn't stupid. Not stupid-stupid anyway. He compared the items rung up on the cash register to the money in the till every night. Some hard words and the slamming of a billy-club on the bar top, while the bouncers barred the wait staff from leaving through the doors, usually made sure those two things were pretty close together. Or ended up pretty close together on the occasional night when the first count seemed off for unexplained reasons.

But the inventory check was never coming together right. Word would come they were out of something, like bacon, and he would arrange for more. But when he looked back at how many pounds he had ordered, and how many items containing bacon were sold, it was coming up to a ½ pound per order. That was one hell of a BLT. Or a cheeseburger with more pork than beef. And it wasn't just bacon, but everything. Even beer and booze. And he couldn't control it like the register cash. Performing inventory and counting everything took way too long to do regularly.

He'd never run a bar and grill before, and could tell he was missing something. Losses were getting to the point he was considering looking for someone with experience to be the manager. Once he learned a bit more and put some new practices in place, he reckoned he could always fire them. Or not if it freed up his time for other pursuits. Putting up a help wanted sign in the door though was probably not going to bring him the type of help he was looking for. Of course that wouldn't help if the problem was really his boys helping themselves a bit too often. He'd have to think some more on how best to address the issue.

He turned off the desk lamp, stood and wandered out to the balcony. Spotlights with colored lenses were mounted on the rough dusty beams, illuminating the tiny stage and making him very difficult to see for the crowd below. Shep moved slowly nonetheless, not wanting to make a big motion that might attract attention. He studied the happenings, and pondered again how to improve. Too bad there wasn't a local community college where he could take a class.

Braxton Greene gave a passable imitation of Neil Young on the tiny stage, but none of the black leather and blue denim patrons seemed to pay his act much mind. At least he only played for tips. That didn't bode well for him. Bikers had pretty tight wallets most of the time. A couple of weathered and tired waitresses, moving hurriedly through the tightly packed tables, ran trays of hot sandwiches with fries from the kitchen behind the stage to the middle of the floor.

It had been a good move to get rid of the pool table in the center floor a few years ago. After riding all day people wanted to eat as well as drink and there were a lot less in the way of furniture breaking fights. The change encouraged the local idlers elsewhere and brought a new kind of clientele, the mainstream bikers. The type of rider not just looking to go on an interstate trip, but to embrace the whole biker cultural experience. It gave them something to connect to. At a typical gas station or road house, they were the odd ones without a car or truck. Here, they were part of an open road community. The saloon's reputation was growing in a positive way and, especially during summer, some larger riding clubs up and down the east coast doing multiday rides planned their itineraries to stop here. Legitimate business was growing, and that was a good thing.

The increasing crowds brought good cover for his boys, the Lowland Outlaws. He wasn't really in the drug business per se, but rather in the transportation business. The drug manufacturers in Mexico needed to move their products north to the big cities like Baltimore. And the money needed to find its way from the dealers back to the manufacturers. Everyone along the chain, including Shep, got a cut.

When crossing the border there was a school of thought, that to minimize exposure to risk of discovery, a single large shipment with key confidantes, be it drugs or cash, was the best way to go. But once through the border, it was far better to keep all the eggs out of a single basket. Breaking it down into parcels made distribution much easier too. It made for more tracking, but computers and tracking tags made that easy. At least for people other than Shep.

His gang was part of a network usually connecting up north around the District of Columbia, and ranging south to the outskirts of Atlanta. Their packages were small and light, perfect for the saddlebags of a bike, and moved with a low profile. The large number of small packages made it impossible for the DEA to try and interdict them all. In the event of a nosy police car, riders could block while the package sped away. Using a group instead of a couple of guys made "self-deals" and "skimming" less of a problem as too many were in on it, and all types of cheap GPS trackers and anti-tampering seals available these days helped with that too. Security wasn't a problem either, as no one wanted to mess with a half dozen biker dudes by themselves and things were always rolling on before whoever it was could get their own group together. It worked well. Some of the guys in the group he didn't even have to pay. They just rode along in ignorance for the sense of belonging, enjoying their "I'm a tough biker" fantasy with no idea of the cargo the group was carrying.

On the drug side, it was usually heroin and cocaine, but Shep cared little about what was in the packages. He was a mover, not a user or a pusher. Sometimes the boys did a little human trafficking on the side, passing the girl off riding behind as just another biker bitch. This didn't concern him either unless they disrespected him by denying free service when they came through. That was a different type of profit that wouldn't need a legitimate business to launder.

Braxton Greene finished the set with his rendition of "Down by the River". No one clapped, but the briefly quiet speakers allowed Shep to hear the big diesel in the parking lot behind him. He turned and strode to look out the parking lot window. He immediately recognized Rebel's truck and his eyes narrowed. It hadn't been Rebel's fault, but Jessie and his boys had been one of his top crews.

They would be hard to replace. It was a dubious business that would quickly fall apart if people didn't follow through with what they were supposed to. Foot soldiers were easy to recruit, but lieutenants were harder to come by. Trust and respect couldn't be developed overnight with the up and comers. Jessie had been tough and reliable, and Shep had been considering promoting Grover to his own crew. Right now the roster felt thin facing growing demand.

Both doors of the truck opened, and Shep looked down fondly at the little blond. His eyes softened and a slight smile tugged at the corners of his mouth. He turned around again to close the balcony shutters. Braxton was done for the night, and he didn't want to risk the upcoming conversation being overheard. He settled into his desk chair and waited, feeling a stirring.

He waited quite a few minutes. It took Rebel a while to navigate the layers of bouncers, henchmen really, between his abode and the general public. Having the girl in tow sped the process a little as he wasn't to be outright refused, but they would want to gawk at her or have a feel so it went far from quickly. Eventually came the soft tap on the door.

"Enter," he grunted.

Rebel opened the door and pushed the blond girl before him. The desk faced the parking lot window so they moved around to their left to stand before it and Shep, standing by the two chairs.

Shep looked her up and down slowly, lingering briefly on her face. The tight faded jeans were cute as was the black Harley tank top. Both were clean and fresh looking, but the girl's hair was frazzled and grimy and her skin bore an oily sheen. He noted the tattoo of a fawn on her forearm and recognition came to him. It was like she was wearing a name tag.

"Bambi," he said "you're back again. Sit down, please. Both of you."

It wasn't a matter of being polite, although Shep wasn't particularly looking to be inhospitable at the moment. He was always up to listen to a good deal or proposal. But even though his men would have searched him a couple of times for any gun or knife, sitting while the others stood made you vulnerable. They could rush and tackle you or make a kick at your head and it would be really hard to block it or spring out of the way sitting back in a chair. He always wanted to get them settled on to their asses as quickly as possible. Shep had no need for "you stand while I sit" power plays. His power was undisputed. That was evident as they sat and remained quiet, waiting for him to bid them speak. Shep kept them waiting a little bit to highlight that dynamic of their relationship and let its meaning sink in.

"Okay, Rebel. What the fuck now?"

"Need some more boys. Fouche has my money at his house and gone off fishing. Ain't gettin nother shot like this."

"How do you know?" asked Shep skeptically. He shifted in his chair as his underwear put the bind on his slowly expanding member.

"Buck told me. Man been running hard all week. Had to deal with the dog guy and the missing chick. Hasn't had time to hide my money away."

"How many boys? What's the plan?"

"Only two. Don't want to hurt nobody this time. Just want to keep her down and crying while I search around. Could take a while. And that Evelyn woman is sure mean. Wanna go t'night before the sheriff comes back."

Shep paused before replying to think it over. It sounded reasonable, but he had two concerns. One, Fouche was law enforcement and the law could be pretty forceful with taking care of their own. Second, the Department of Justice was very aggressive concerning possible civil rights issues. If anything went too far, it could all blow back on to him, even if race had absolutely nothing to do with it.

"That could still bring down a ton of shit that we don't need for your little bag of cash."

Rebel's head and right shoulder made a small shrug to the side.

"With the cash he's looking at corruption charges. Don't hurt no one badly or break shit up much, I suspect he'll stay real quiet. Need two special dudes who won't get bored and want to dip their wicks or tag the whole house."

"So you want to go out on your little raid with men who have been well satisfied?" sneered Shep.

"That's why I brought the payment," said Rebel spreading face up palms.

Bambi shrunk down into her chair and Shep felt his member harden at her meekness. There was a knock at the door.

Shep called annoyed, "Enter!"

The door opened quickly followed by confident steps which rapidly faltered when Braxton Greene realized that Shep wasn't alone.

"I'm sorry to interrupt. I just wanted to bring you your half of the tips," he explained.

Braxton held out his hand, with the handful of bills and loose change. Shep looked down at it, trying to come up with a figure. Probably around a pathetic thirty bucks.

"Fifty-fifty split was what our deal was, right?" Braxton tried to clarify, stuttering slightly with uncertainty.

"I saw Neil Young play once. Way back in California when he played guitar for Buffalo-Springfield. My parents took me. I don't think I was even ten years old," Shep grew quieter as he reminisced and then in a bold assertive tone, "My half is the paper half."

Braxton handed over the bills without making eye contact and backpedaled to the door, "Sorry to have interrupted. I appreciate getting to play."

"Don't be late tomorrow night, Braxton," replied Shep and turned back toward Rebel and Bambi.

"Alright, I will take her here and now," decreed Shep. "Then we'll show her to the boys. They'll hold off on an old nigger grandma when they got a smoking hot blond to come back to. That way you can go and do the job tonight. Else you might not get away until morning when it will be too late. I'll keep her here while you all are away. May even play again if you take long enough. When the boys finish, you take her back. Deal?"

Rebel rose from his chair and nodded, "I'm down with that."

"Where you going then?" asked Shep confused.

Rebel gestured over his shoulder with a thumb.

"Downstairs to meet the boys, I guess."

"We'll go pick out a pair after I'm through. Sit down," ordered Shep.

He turned toward Bambi and leered. There were many ways to wield power. This one just happened to be his favorite.

CHAPTER—16

Azrael and Kelton hustled south on Lowland Road, making pretty good time for boots and a rucksack. They kept a steady rhythmic pace without interruption, covering most of the four and half miles in just over forty-five minutes. There was no traffic at this late hour, no reason to duck off the road into the brush and lose time hiding from sight. The clouds were broken and the fuller than not moon provided plenty of illumination on the dark rural road.

Kelton had briefly considered taking a left on Thigpen Road to cut over on Coalson Street instead of going down Main. He recalled the iPhone map application saying it was five minutes faster when he had planned the trip for Doris the first time. But it was a residential street and that could mean problems from other dogs. Even with the late hour, versus the early morning timing of last time, the risk didn't seem to justify the gain.

He moved at the "Ranger Quick Step", a technique from academy days for long road marches during field exercises. Running with equipment was particularly strenuous, especially over rough terrain. By walking quickly for fifty steps and then doing a slow lumbering jog for fifty steps, one covered much more ground than by walking alone. The intermittent nature of the run steps allowed the pace to be kept up over longer distances, and counting the walk steps coaxed people back to the run when they would otherwise be inclined to continue walking.

But despite the urgency he felt at getting to Rebel's garage, Kelton knew he needed to restrain himself. It wasn't a race, with the goal of getting there the fastest only to collapse over the finish line with all energy reserves exhausted; it was to get there quickly in a state of being able to mount a rescue. That might mean being able to fight. So, as they passed the place on the road where Chandler and Buck had apprehended them, he slowed to a walk. Whatever had happened in that pit had happened by now. He couldn't save these two women from that. But he could save them from the pit overall, and the best chances of that were him arriving on scene with breath and brains at the ready.

He actually smelled the grease, oil and exhaust fume soot before fully seeing the mailbox with the address. It was a big mailbox that handled a volume of correspondence larger than most households, with the dings and knocks of rural living. Immediately, he led Azrael into the shrubby cedar trees for cover and listened a spell. Azrael listed too, and scented with nose stretching into the air, but gave no indications that anything was amiss. In truth, it was hard to listen. The frogs singing along the soggy soil of the drainage ditches were almost deafening.

Kelton removed his pack, and placed it at the base of one of the larger trees. He wished he had a chem-light to put on the pack, but he wasn't as well equipped with expendables as he'd been in the warzone. A chem-light was a plastic tube containing two different solutions separated by a membrane. Bending the tube and giving it a gentle shake broke the membrane and mixed the chemicals, resulting in light that he could use to mark where his pack was and be sure of finding it again in a hurry. Azrael's nose would work just as well.

Kelton put on his yellow lens shooting goggles and bionic ears, and then did the same for Azrael with his doggles and mutt-muffs. Azrael would need to use his nose to spot trouble. Kelton didn't want to hurt his ears with a gunshot. He clipped Azrael's short leash to the ring on the back of his harness and drew his pistol. The tritium night sight glowed as it should and he validated a round was in the chamber. They crept forward slowly until they could see the north side of the garage. He kneeled on the pine needles just inside the thicket, perhaps twenty feet from the wall. Azrael downed himself alongside.

There was no window on this "short side" of the rectangular building, and not much to see but an old rusty fuel tank labeled "No. 2 Diesel" supported six feet off the ground on four narrow legs. For refueling tractors, he guessed. He scanned and listened, adjusting the knobs on the electronic hearing protection, but detecting no sign of activity other than singing frogs and the buzz of a mercury-vapor security lamp on the front of the building. He couldn't see the fixture, but its blue-white halo glowed over the roof. Kelton returned the pistol to holster, and unbuttoned his right breast pocket for a small pair of binoculars. Off to the left, beyond the building, he could see the outlines of scrap cars in some type of junkyard. Behind the building to the right, vegetation had grown up through a garden of old tires at the base of the railroad bed. He decided to shift to his left for a better view.

They fell back into the thicket again until they couldn't see the garage wall, and then shifted using the security light visible through the trees to keep their bearings. This time Kelton approached the edge of the wood line crawling on his belly, Azrael again right beside him. Again he scanned with the binoculars, now being able to see the front of the building with its pair of garage entrances and an office off to the far side, well-lit by the security light over its door. He could also see the gravel drive and a little around the far corner, not seeing any parked vehicle that appeared to be in-service.

"Okay, Azrael. Let's go and see if anyone is home," he whispered. He put away the binoculars and again drew his sidearm.

They fell back into the woods once more, half circled back to the original location, and then dashed to the wall to kneel in the moon shadow of the diesel fuel tank. He waited here listening again, knowing that his approach from the woods would be the most likely time to have been seen. Nothing.

He decided to check the back first, as it was the only side he hadn't yet an inkling. He kneeled at the corner, firmly placing his left knee and right foot in position, before leaning out to take a peak over the barrel of his ready gun. This exposed only his right eye and shoulder, while the rest of his body, and his dog, were protected by the building's concrete. It was blackness, full in the shadows of the trees and building itself. Overhead a powerline showed as a dark line against the sparkling heavens peeking between clouds. He picked a spot, a door about a third of the way down the wall whose frame was silhouetted by the distant sky over the junkyard and dashed for it. It was a steel door, of heavy commercial manufacture designed to take hard knocks in a shop environment. He tried the knob, but it didn't move.

He took a step further down the wall, paused, and then took a step back. Transferring the end of the leash to his gun hand, he then used the end of his sleeve to give the doorknob a superficial wipe. Kelton noted he needed to add a lot of forensic technique research to his internet reading. Or maybe his Audible App for reading books while they walked. This was different from what he did in the military. He considered putting on his gloves, but they were heavy and stiff.

They advanced rapidly toward the far corner, finding another locked backdoor just before getting there. It was a narrower door, not designed for carrying equipment or car parts through. More a personnel back entrance. To the right of it was a clothes line, a pair of posts with wide arms, winding back and forth a half dozen times. He reached out and felt with his hands, not wanting to turn on a light. There were several pair of heavy duty wool work socks pinned up. Behind it, several garbage bags were piled up in a heap. They didn't readily smell like old food, but the weather had been mild.

On the far building short side was a gravel parking area, and the security light allowed him to see impressions in the rain softened ground and gravel from a dual rear axle truck. The junkyard beyond was quiet and unmoving, but shadows danced as swaying tree branches caught the ample moonlight. His suspicion of nobody being home was growing. They approached the corner to the front and paused for one last look and listen before stepping out into the light. Still nothing.

The front office window was plate glass, perhaps three by six feet. The security light overhead made it reflective, so he paused at the edge to place his left eye close to the glass. His floppy hat brim allowed him to see inside for a quick glance, and he noted nothing but office furniture. The wooden office door, with small panes of glass and many generations of paint, was to the right of the window. He tightly gripped the shiny brass knob and tried to turn it. It was locked tight, and he wiped it like the other. There was also a deadbolt, and both brass faces sported telltale scratches among the tarnish of being operable and in use.

The two of them slowly walked down to the garage bay doors with the heavy metal panels and tinted windows. Inside was quite dark, and even with the moon over his shoulder he couldn't see much. The security light down by the office just made glare off the glass. He holstered and dropped the leash, cupping his hands around his eyes. There seemed to be some stuff between the two bays as Dixie had said, but he couldn't say for sure what it was. Azrael continued to stretch out scenting with his muzzle, but gave no indication of anyone about. He walked slowly down to the other bay, Azrael following dragging the leash, but the view in its window brought no new information.

He felt vulnerable under the light and continued back to the woods, rather than ponder his next move in the open. Was Dixie playing him? He'd never been hit on like that before. But was it an act? Of course it was an act. A homeless wanderer living out of backpack is hardly the typical desire for young pretty blonds. And wouldn't Buck have freed the other women at the same time as Dixie rather than leave them with Rebel?

Did Buck send Dixie to his room? Was Buck trying to set him up for breaking and entering? Surely Buck realized that his Braxton Greene story didn't hold water and that was why he'd leaned on him with the shooting witnesses. Maybe Buck didn't realize he was planning to just leave town and not come back? If it was a ploy against him and his dog, why did Buck feel the need? Kelton considered it irresistibly curious.

The doors were all locked tight, and Kelton suspected there wasn't any additional security given that someone lived here as evidenced by the laundry. This junkyard didn't even have a dog. He holstered his gun, and used his flashlight to find a stout piece of wood. In the copse of trees, it wasn't hard. Then he marched back to the building, his grip about the club strong with resolve. Azrael again followed at the heel, dragging his leash behind.

He smashed the rectangular office window, with a wild blow. The shattering silenced the frogs and sprayed glass in all directions to including some back upon them. Thank goodness for eye protection. Next he turned to the frame, clearing away the shards with a back and forth sideways motion. The frogs resumed their chorus. Kelton didn't pause in his quick work, being thorough but not wanting to dally. He tossed the branch aside, Azrael's eyes following it with some hope.

"We'll play soon," he promised. "Platz."

Azrael lay down flat on the ground.

Then he put on his rappelling gloves and climbed through the window, being careful of his right index finger where the leather tip had been cut away for better trigger control. He used the flashlight on his phone, the tactical flashlight was much too bright for indoors, while he was still straddling the windowsill. He kicked away a rickety magazine rack for a good landing spot and swung over inside. Stray glass crunched under the thick soles of Kelton's boots. His electronic earmuffs heard nothing but the frogs in the distance and Azrael's panting.

The door to the garage bays was both obvious, and unlocked. He went as quickly as he dared in a strange shop building using a flashlight. He didn't move tactically, checking corners as he went. Kelton opted for speed, wanting to be on his way quickly in case it was bait.

There was quite a bit of stuff between the two bays, but even with the small light the scuff marks in the dust on the floor indicated which had been frequently dragged aside. Rebel apparently wasn't much into housekeeping. Kelton muscled it aside easily enough, found and opened the hatch.

He shone the light downward and called in a normal tone, "Is anyone down there?"

Kelton heard a cough and then a croaking, "Please help me!"

He sprang down the ladder where Baylee Ann was trapped, still sprawled across the desktop. He examined the screws and bracket, and bounded back up to search the garage for tools. She cried out again imploring him not to leave her, but he was back to her side in under a minute. Moments later she was freed, crying and trying to dress in torn clothes with aching and cramping muscles. He removed his earmuffs and pulled up the dialer on his phone.

"911, what is your emergency?"

"Ambulance needed, 643 Lowland Road. Injuries are non-life threatening, but require medical attention."

A flurry of other questions came, but he put the phone in his left breast pocket.

"Can you climb out?" he asked.

She gave a nod that she would try. He stood beneath, pushing gently under her feet as she made her way up the ladder and crawled upon her belly on to the garage floor.

"Is there anyone else here?"

She shook her head side to side, making a grasping motion at her throat as she mouthed "no."

"Let's get out of here," he said grabbing her wrist and leading her back to the office. Glass cracked under their feet, but she had biker boots. He opened the front door so she wouldn't have to climb over the window. Azrael lifted his head where he stood sentry.

"Come on, up to the road," and then toward his dog, "Hier!"

The three of them made it up the gravel driveway, and Kelton removed doggles and muffs. Looking north, the sky was black, without the telltale flashing lights of approaching emergency vehicles.

"Just sit here by the mailbox. Help will be here soon. Do you want some water?"

She nodded.

"I'll be right back. Just got to go get my pack. Azrael, find it!"

He was back within a couple of minutes and helped her work the CamelBak. She was clearly dehydrated, overdrank and doubled-over coughing. Kelton tried patting her back in a steady rhythm, so she could synchronize her clearing efforts, but she flinched away. Baylee Ann closed her eyes and sat back against the mailbox post. He let her rest and scanned up the road again.

"I see red flashing lights. That must be the St. Albans' squad," he turned toward her to see that she had heard.

She opened her eyes, but stayed curled up on the ground with her chin on her knees and arms about her shins.

"I probably don't need help and they won't want to waste their time on me anyway. And I don't have no money no how."

"I'm going to provide the help you need," he promised.

Kelton removed his flashlight from its belt carrier and gave a few flashes across the pavement as they approached, being careful not to aim it directly at the windshield and blind the driver. The ambulance pulled up alongside them and the backdoors opened. A man and a woman, adorned in one-piece jumpsuits with rescue patches on their shoulders, wheeled over a gurney and collapsed it to the road's surface. An older man with similar uniform and an orange windbreaker opened the passenger-side door and sized up both Baylee Ann and Kelton.

"Does she have insurance? It's an expensive ride if injuries aren't critical."

"I'll pay. I'll pay for the IV fluids, too," declared Kelton forcefully. Azrael walked to his side in heel position.

The man looked at Baylee Ann, and then back like he was going to argue. But he shrugged instead.

"It's your money. You can ride in the back with her. Can't say your dog is dirtier than her. I'll let Doctor Fairborn know you are coming. He's working the emergency clinic this evening."

In short order they were loaded, the driver pulled into Rebel's drive to turn around, and they quickly covered the three and a half miles to the St. Albans Clinic.

CHAPTER—17

Kelton waited on the front steps of St. Albans Clinic facing Smallwood Street. It was next door to the town's fire department on the north side of the park opposite the sheriff's office to the south. The squat cinderblock building was painted white, everything it was supposed to be but nothing more. He'd seen signs through its glass doors for an x-ray machine and a small lab for routine blood and urine work. The whole structure was on one floor for better access to the old and obese, and to save the costs of elevators.

The firehouse to his left appeared quiet, the rescue crew back in their ready lounge he supposed. He hadn't been invited over. There was a small bay for the ambulance and a couple of other large ones he presumed for the "hook and ladder" trucks. It was in the brown brick of the rest of the town, but there was an array of antennas on the roof giving it a modern feel. He almost expected a sign out front bragging "Number of Cats Rescued from Trees this Month" given the small quiet town, but that was unfair. Unlike other areas around government buildings, the surrounding green space was impeccable and the walls devoid of pollen stains. The yellow curb paint was fresh and unblemished. Clearly, the men here had a special type of pride.

Azrael lay relaxed on a stone stair by his side and panted, watchful for anything of interest. Kelton had fed him and the meal, combined with lots of outdoor time, had mellowed the energetic dog. He'd also found a water spigot on the side of the building and filled the bowl for a clean fresh drink. With Azrael feeling a little docile, Kelton had also gone through the pads of his feet looking for any broken glass or gravel that he might have picked up but things were fine.

When the ambulance had arrived, the two of them were promptly banished to outside because they were inseparable and one of the wrong species. However, the receptionist had waddled out to him the billing paperwork on a clipboard. For things like medical history, HIPAA medical privacy compliance and such Baylee Ann had been on her own. Kelton hoped she'd been able to navigate that okay in her current state and suspected she was suffering from shock as well as dehydration and low blood sugar. The office visit was $200 alone, not including the ride or any additional supplies or services that would be required. He'd seen the dried blood in the pit and knew there'd be more. But he had the funds and it seemed like the right thing to do, so he made his credit card available for payment. The reward had been several pages of hospital and financial legalese.

Kelton spread the pages on the steps one at a time, and took a picture of each side with his phone's camera. The next time he was on a wireless network, which was getting very common at most retailers or café's, it would load to the cloud, the big data warehouse in the sky. Then he folded the papers into his pocket for when he could use them to start a campfire.

The night air began to get a little cool, and he opened his pack for his old army sweater. He pulled it over the top of his shirt. Then the brushed concrete steps began to get really hard and he balled up his jacket for a seat cushion. His eyes began to get heavy, and he rubbed them and blinked.

He studied some of the old homes across the street, but couldn't see much given the trees and the darkness of the hour except that they seemed to be two floors with an attic and sweeping covered front porches. The nearby sidewalk along Smallwood Street was vacant as would be expected after midnight on Thursday in a small town. Some trees along it had grown large enough to heave it's concrete.

Kelton considered if he should call Colonel Redigan, but decided not. He didn't need legal advice. The sheriff would be a more appropriate choice, but Fouche wasn't too high on his list right now. He shook his head to scatter those thoughts away.

"Come here, Azrael."

He removed his dog's vest and began taking a shedding comb to the coat. The Belgian Malinois is a breed of constant shedding, heaviest with the change of seasons. Azrael sat proudly with tongue hanging as the tiny teeth of the brush carried away the hair in small tuffs. He cleaned the comb with his fingers, tossing the hair into the bushes beside the stairs. Some blew back on the night breeze to his face, making him try and spit it away after landing in his mouth. A half hour later, he gave up and dressed his dog back in his vest.

Finally, a noise inside made Azrael look up so Kelton turned to glance over his shoulder. Doctor Fairborn was behind the counter talking with Baylee Ann and the pudgy receptionist with her clipboard came out to him once again.

"Just wanted you to sign the receipt for the final charges," she smiled.

Kelton looked at the figure on the clipboard.

"That's a lot less than I was expecting," he stated in a questioning tone.

"Doctor Fairborn gave you fifty percent off since you don't have insurance. She's all ready to go. There's some prescriptions you can fill at the pharmacy in the morning on the west side of the square. It's on this side of the church that's next to city hall. It's by the coffee shop," she said gesturing. "Doctor Fairborn gave her a few pills to last until then. He'll also send the rape kit on to the lab for DNA testing so she should expect to be contacted by the State Police. Have a nice night."

"Thanks," he said handing her back the clipboard with the signed receipt.

He wondered how rape kit and nice night could be in subsequent sentences.

Another quick photograph, and yet another piece of paper was in his pocket. He didn't harbor any hopes of reimbursement. It was more to defend himself against future accusations of nonpayment. And the army had been big on paperwork. As an ambitious young officer among many likeminded, with no real responsibilities, they had all tried to distinguish themselves with excess administrative prowess.

At last they finished talking inside, nodded heads at each other, and Baylee Ann came walking stiffly toward the front door in gray sweatpants and matching hoody. The torn jeans, the denim slit from cuff to waist on both sides probably while she was bolted to the desktop, was gone to an evidence bag. He stood as she approached, as a gentleman would at a formal dinner table, and Azrael rose also to sit at his side. She paused, a few steps before the door, and stared at him through the glass. Kelton guessed she was his own age, or maybe a year older, but life hadn't been particularly kind. And that was from the perspective of someone who had been to war.

Her brown eyes were clear and bright, although the skin around them looked inflamed from rubbing. They looked him up and down, lingered on his gun, shifted sideways to his dog, and then returned to his face. She exhaled, and then tried to force a small smile. Baylee Ann then crossed her arms, hands grasping opposite elbows like she was giving herself a hug and resumed walking toward the door.

With a single big step, Kelton beat her to it and pulled it open while standing at attention like in an honor guard ceremony. She took a half step back in surprise, and then shuffled through the entrance brushing away moths and other small insects anxious to get at the lights inside.

"Ma'am, how are you feeling? Are you able to walk?"

"Not much, but I think I'll be better after I get some food. They only gave me some nabs from the vending machine. The stitches don't really hurt any worse when I move around. When I got to shit it will be another story. So you're only going to get straight," she declared.

There was a long silence while Kelton tried to decode what she had meant, and Baylee Ann figured out he wasn't anticipating. Then she shrugged.

"I'm so tired. I've no money and nothings open anyway. And I'm cold. And I don't know where Bambi is," she began to cry, hands letting go of her elbows and coming up to her eyes.

He slowly extended his arm to wrap them about her, trying awkwardly to avoid contacting her other than his hands on her back. Baylee Ann was a buxom girl. Even the heavy and baggy sweatshirt hoody couldn't hide it.

But she had no inhibitions and collapsed into him. Her large breasts, unbounded as all her own clothes were now gone, were easily felt through the fabric. Baylee Ann's hips were substantial as well, the net result of unhealthy diet and little exercise constrained only by considerable smoking. He held her, but didn't have to long.

"I'm okay," she sniffed. "Thank you. Ain't you a weirdo."

"Come on, let's find a park bench and get you off your feet for a bit. Things won't open for a few hours and I don't think you can make it to Ed's."

"The cops will ticket us for vagrancy if they catch us sleeping in the park," she warned.

"You have absolutely nothing to fear tonight. Not even cops," he declared as he took off his pack and sat down on the edge of a bench with his right thigh against the armrest. He knew she would be sitting down next to him and didn't want his gun side wedged between them. The bench was flanked by a pair of stone planters littered with cigarette butts.

She nodded, remembering Jessie's crew, and sat down next to him. Azrael, who heeled, sat and performed other commands based upon Kelton's left side must have felt she was in his spot. The dog climbed up on the other edge of the bench, and sprawled across Baylee Ann's lap to be able to get his head on his master's thigh.

"Never had no dog before."

"He just wants to keep you warm. And you don't. He has you."

He pulled out the poncho from the pack at his feet and draped it over the three of them as a blanket, putting the center hooded hole over Azrael's head. He then offered her a protein bar.

Baylee Ann tore the wrapper and then sniffed at it uncertainly. Azrael eyed her suspiciously, but didn't dare move for fear of being banished to the ground below.

"What is it? It smells kind of nasty," she protested.

"It's an energy bar, and yes they are sometimes a little greasy from all the calories they try and pack in."

She bit into it, chewed and shrugged at him before taking another bite. A few more chews and it was an empty wrapper. She crumpled it and coughed. Kelton handed her the CamelBak hose for a drink of water and took the wrapper from her before she could litter.

Shortly after she fell asleep. She had a bit of a rasping snore, but nothing really loud. Kelton dozed himself some, in and out, but each time his eyes searched around all was still and quiet.

Toward dawn, just a couple of hours later, he thought he saw a figure watching them. While it was getting light in the east, the park was still really dark and the town just as quiet as before. His right arm went to the butt of his gun, but Azrael and Baylee Ann still slept fast. He stared back, trying to make up his mind if there was a threat. A few more minutes and rays of sunshine he realized he was looking at a bronze civil war soldier by a marble slab in the middle of the square. He let go of his gun and rubbed his eyes.

Baylee Ann stirred, and then awakened but made no move to get up. Seventy-five pounds of dog may have influenced that.

"Why did this Rebel guy let Dixie go, but hold you and Bambi?"

"You mean, why'd he want us skanks instead of prissy stuck-up?"

"Something like that," Kelton confirmed.

"Dixie is Buck's girl. Rebel throws his weight around, but even he won't tangle with the law. She was going to be more trouble than she was worth."

"Any idea of where Rebel is now, or where your friend Bambi might be?"

"I don't know for sure where they are and what he was going to do. But Rebel most likely took Bambi to sell her at Shep's place."

"Then that's where I need to go next," declared Kelton.

"No it's not. Those are some real rough dudes. Rebel is nothing compared to Shep. And there's a bunch of 'em. They don't take to outsiders poking around in their shit very well. Some of them might even be killers."

"Maybe, maybe not," said Kelton with cold steady eyes, "but I am a killer. And I'm going to find your friend Bambi. And I don't really care how many thugs get buried in the process."

She shivered and then made to get up. Azrael hopped down dragging the poncho and looking like a lion with an oversized camo mane. As Kelton helped him out of it, he heard peeing and a soft fart. Baylee Ann had squatted behind one of the planters.

"Would you like a tissue?" asked Kelton keeping his eyes averted.

"Naw, I'll just give my ass a shake."

Kelton stood, considered and found a tree himself. It could be a few hours before things opened and soon people would start moving about.

"Think you can move about?"

"If we take it slow. I really stiffened up on the bench. Where are we headed?"

"The pharmacy opens pretty early so we can get your pills. Then, I think we head to Ed's. Even at a slow pace we'll get there long before anything here opens. Get you some real food, and a room for a real rest. Then we can plot our next move to find Bambi. Sound like a good plan?"

"You're the man. I just follow."

Right, thought Kelton. They started toward the west side of the square where the church steeple was visible above the scattered park trees.

CHAPTER—18

While Kelton waited on the clinic steps in the small hours of the night, Rebel rolled in his truck on I-85 North. He watched the headlights of the pair of hogs that were following him, making sure their riders hadn't gotten cold feet and backed off. Bambi, anyway you wanted her without a time limit, was proving to be sufficient motivation. She'd started crying as Shep took her a second time in the middle of the planning meeting, and these two had leered. Rebel took the Virginia 903 exit well north of St. Albans and turned left at the top of the ramp, to pass over the interstate heading away from the scene where Jessie and his gang had fallen.

At the corner of Chandler's road was a dilapidated country store, the old sign no longer legible. The antique gas pumps had been removed from the crumbling island, and the plywood window coverings had long since rotted away to let the weather inside. Kudzu vines were doing a credible job of reclaiming the lot for Mother Nature. It smelled of rat feces.

But they weren't there to fill up or grab a six pack like customers of long ago. It had a small gravel parking area and was unlit. Behind the decaying building was room to stash the motorcycles. And it was in walking distance of Chandler's house, if a bit of a long walk for guys who drank too much, smoked too much and sat on their bikes all day. It was a wonder he hadn't had to throw in several pills of Viagra for these guys to seal the deal.

The thugs, Ripper and Burt, had wanted to ride all the way to the house. If things went badly, they had their own way of bugging out if it became every man for himself. Rebel wanted to approach more quietly, as quietly as a truck could, without the roaring of the hogs shaking the neighbors for a half mile around. A single truck at night wasn't that unusual in the country. Three vehicles, of any type and especially at that hour, was a parade reserved for special holidays. The discussion had been lively, until Shep dictated using a staging point. It also kept the motorcycles away from the raid, which could potentially lead an investigator asking questions to his establishment if a witness noticed a "two-wheeler".

Despite the empty seat upfront, both Ripper and Burt opted to pile in the back of the crew cab whose last passenger had been Dixie. Ripper carried a machete, Burt a sledge hammer and a pair of bolt cutters. Rebel cracked the window a little. The guys really stank, like they had passed out on the bathroom floor and others had taken turns pissing on them the rest of the night. It probably explained Bambi's appeal. There was no other way besides a violent forceful rape that they would be getting any. Hookers in Tijuana were not only too far away, they also had some minute sense of standards concerning their clients.

No cars passed as they pulled out and made a right onto Caisson Road. Rebel killed his headlights and drove slowly to keep down noisy engine revolutions. He toggled the switch by the rearview mirror to keep interior lights from coming on when the doors opened. As they approached within a hundred yards of the drive he killed the ignition and let the truck roll to a stop without hitting the brakes.

"Y'all don't close the doors when we get out," explained Rebel in a soft tone. "Makes too much noise."

They piled out, Rebel taking his crowbar from underneath the seat. The house on the hill was dark, but the moon was bright. Frogs sang from the pastures behind where there was a cattle watering pond. The trio made their way up the driveway, Rebel tapping the green phone pedestal with his palm as they passed. The scraping of gravel with their boots was hardly audible. Chandler's driveway was pretty well graded which made for easy going. The Durango, with its blue light bar on the roof, sat in plain view on the side of the house under the carport. The carport was simply a metal overhead cover to keep off sun and rain, without any sides or back.

Rebel whispered toward Burt, "Get her phone."

Burt, with Ripper following, headed toward the side of the house and quickly found the gray box. It had a small lock on it, but the bolt cutters made short work of that. They opened the cover with such force, the plastic hinges broke. Inside were the tiny low voltage phone wires. A couple of savage thrusts from the machete point did for them. There would be no dial tone inside.

While the boys were doing that first essential thing, Rebel made a line to the driver's side rear door. He pulled out a penlight from his shirt pocket and touched it to the window before turning it on. Buck was right about the old ammo can with padlock. The question was, the $40,000 question to be exact, was the money in the box? He reached into his overalls' pockets for his work gloves and pulled them on. He took a look over his shoulder and rolled his eyes. Ripper was preparing to urinate on the flowerbed.

"What the hell he doing?" scolded Rebel.

Burt shrugged, "Ripper gets nervous."

Rebel shook his head and tried to lift the door handle to see if it was locked.

The frog voices were silenced by the drowning torrent of honking, as the anti-theft mechanism activated.

"Bitch!" shouted Ripper to be heard over the noise.

Rebel savagely jammed the crowbar into the seam between the door and frame near the locking mechanism and pried, tearing the thin sheet metal. A light came on upstairs in the house as Rebel speared again, making the opening wide enough to use the curved end of the crowbar for better leverage. The side-impact airbag went off, filling the interior with a giant white balloon. The pulsing honking continued its barking.

Burt warned, "Hurry up, Rebel."

"Bring the bolt cutters, dammit!" Rebel said as he ripped at the bag with the crowbar to hasten its deflation.

"Here," offered Burt as he traded it for the crowbar. He grasped both it and the sledge hammer tightly, not wanting to leave either tool behind. He hadn't thought to leave on his biker gloves.

"Back porchlights just came on!" shouted Ripper to be heard.

Burt walked around to the front of the SUV while Rebel wrestled with the airbag, trying to get the bolt cutters on the ammo can's padlock. The biker stabbed the crowbar's straight end several times into the grill, and on the third thrust the honking mercifully went silent. Barking dogs called out from all directions.

"Got it!" shouted Rebel in triumph as the tool's jaws finally met, even though the horn's demise made raising his voice unnecessary. The lock fell to the floor of the SUV with a clatter.

Something grabbed at his cheek and shoulder, tearing at his flesh as he felt glass pelt his face. The shotgun's report followed as he fell over backward on to the gravel. He lay there stunned, as he heard a second blast that seemed far away.

Ripper cried out, "Bitch! She got me!"

Ripper came running over to the Dodge, passed Rebel and kneeled by the radiator with Burt to take cover.

"You messin with the wrong black woman!" proclaimed Evelyn as she broke open the shotgun. The empty cases popped out and she smoothly took two from her front pocket and replaced them with a single motion.

Rebel came to his senses again as she slammed the action closed. He pushed himself to a crouch and made a diving leap onto the back seat as more glass shattered in the blast. He lay there sprawled across it as his arm fished around on the floor for the lid of the ammo can. He found it and yanked at the clasp.

The next blast was a little higher, and rattled the sheet metal of the ceiling in addition to bits of the tailgate windshield. Stuffed into the metal box, was the clear bag of heavy duty plastic, perhaps six mils thick, with bundles of cash. He pulled at it, the metal sides forming a suction that didn't want to let go, but Rebel wanted it bad. The angle denied him leverage, but he strained until it yielded.

More pellets flew as the shotgun again roared, and he felt the searing burning across his backside. He reached for the passenger side door, prayed the backdoor safeties were deactivated and got lucky. It opened, to give him a view of Burt and Ripper running down the driveway with short choppy strides. Rebel scrambled out the door after them, falling to the gravel and chipping a tooth. He almost let go of the bag. Almost.

"Fuck!" he complained.

As he struggled to his feet, he felt the searing burning sensation of the laceration on his butt cheek. Another shotgun blast and he cringed, frozen in place, waiting for the pain of ripped flesh and gushing blood to register. He watched Burt fall down instead some fifty feet in front of him. His nerves unlocked and he plunged forward down the driveway after the two bikers. Ripper raced ahead, either unaware or unconcerned that Burt had fallen.

Rebel reached him and paused long enough to hook his free hand under his shoulder and help him to his feet. Ahead of them, and nearly to the road, Ripper stepped in a slight depression and his ankle rolled over. The big man fell hard, the impact of his fat gut on the ground pushing stomach acid into his throat and nose. Burt and Rebel staggered past and turned at the road toward the dark empty truck.

"You want some more of this, you just come on back now!" Evelyn screeched from the top of the hill.

Two more shots sounded in quick succession, fired up into the air. Rebel reached the driver's door, threw the cash bundle inside, but stood bent over while holding the arm rest. A moment later, he vomited onto the road.

Burt hoisted himself into the back making use of the running board, also on the driver's side, and yelled encouragement, "Come on man, we got to go!"

Rebel reached in to grab the steering wheel, using his arms as much as his legs to mount the truck. He turned the key, not waiting for the glow plugs. The engine was still plenty warm and roared to life. With his other hand he put his seatbelt on, by racecar driver reflex. He closed his door and put it into gear at the same time, mashing the accelerator as soon as he had a free hand for the wheel. The sudden acceleration closed the passenger side rear door. Up ahead he could see the silhouette of Ripper hobbling down the end of the driveway waving his arms at them.

Rebel stopped at the mouth of the drive. It wasn't out of great love for Ripper, but no one left behind meant no one the cops could turn with a deal to implicate them all. Ripper ran around the front of the truck as if to bar them from leaving, using his right hand on the hood to take weight off the ankle. It was torturously slow for him to reach the back door and pull on the handle. The door didn't open. The locks had automatically triggered when Rebel had put it in drive.

The shotgun fired again, just as Rebel hit the lock release, and pellets rattled on the truck's side like hail on a tin roof. Ripper had already moved away from the door though, going for the bed of the truck instead. Even without a hurt ankle and a shotgun wound, it would be doubtful his athletic prowess would permit him to climb the side of the bed. He was having to go all the way to the rear bumper.

Rebel took his foot off the brake, as Ripper yelled "Don't leave me, Bitch!" but all he was doing was trying to get the rear of the truck up to Ripper. He overdid it slightly. Another boom of thunder, this time a slug that shattered plastic upfront near the grill. Then the truck rocked on its shocks as Ripper made it over the tailgate and collapsed into the bed.

Burt screamed, "We got him! Go, go, go!"

Rebel mashed the gas again. The big turbo diesel roared, and carried them forward.

"No way man, that was close!" Burt celebrated looking back at the house on the hill.

Rebel turned on his headlights to see ahead, leaning forward to peer through the windshield. Only the passenger side lights came on, and using high beams didn't help much. He wiped at his face, feeling grit and fragments wet with sweat and blood.

"Got to go get the bikes, Man!" demanded Burt.

"You want to pass her house again? Bitch probably at the end of the drive just waiting with that shotgun. We'll be like fish in a barrel!"

"Got to get the bikes, Man!" yelled Burt again.

"We'll double back. Stop bitching," snapped Rebel.

The road came to a dead-end up ahead, with turns to the left and right. He ran the stop, slowing just a whisker shy of rolling it, and flooring it to pull through the turn. Unlike his passengers thrown about by the centrifugal forces, the tight seatbelt held him to the truck's controls so he could work his magic. The boy could always drive.

Ripper rolled in the back, being mashed by various tools and howled "Take it fucking easy!"

Rebel ignored him, and whipped around another turn and then another in a panicked flight through unfamiliar backroads to get away as far as he could as fast as he could. He had his money. There were no witnesses who knew them. The bikes weren't his concern, but they were safe. The boys may have to ride like bitches to go pick them up later, but they weren't really out anything. All was well.

Until it was not. He didn't know these roads, didn't see the faded orange warning sign in his panicky flight and limited headlights. Rebel merely barreled ahead down the slight grade, speed far over the legal limit, the way ahead dark with the trees making a thick canopy over the winding lane. The black and yellow barricade crossed all lanes, but he saw it much too late. He slammed on the brakes in panic, but the loose gravel gave them no chance. The truck splintered the wooden warning in all directions, larger chunks trampled under skidding tires.

It was a small bridge, under replacement, just enough to get over a narrow creek. It had been a slight wooden structure that had slowly weakened over decades of service. Now cleared away for a large steel culvert design not yet in place, there existed a twelve-foot gap and four-foot drop to meeting the road on the other side. The law of gravity made it not even close.

The nose of the big Ford began falling as the front wheels went over the edge. There wasn't a ramp to launch them up into the air in some "Dukes of Hazard" rerun. Their high speed, despite the hard braking, carried them across the gap for the bumper to impact the muddy face of the far side. The frame crumpled with the impact, Ripper thrown from the bed over the cab with an assortment of tools. Burt, not wearing his seatbelt, was slammed into the back of the front seat. Rebel met a violent white explosion as the airbag punched his face, but the seatbelt held his hips in place so he didn't take the edge of the steering wheel deep into the gut.

A moment after the shattering impact all was unnaturally quiet, the truck wedged into the depression with tailgate up in the air. The big diesel died in the impact, spinning wheels rotating freely until coming to a rest. No shred of consciousness betrayed any human existence to the birds and frogs who resumed their natural routines of a few minutes before.

CHAPTER—19

Buck stirred in the small bed where in his dream he'd been reliving his most recent encounter with Dixie in her shower. His body was warm under the blanket and content with the rest, but the dream had left him unsatisfied as his erection continued to strain against his Jockeys. He tried to drift back to sleep before even opening his eyes, hoping the fantasy could resume where he'd left off. The sexual frustration dragged him to consciousness instead. The red digits of the clock said it was five in the morning.

Pulling his knees up to his chest underneath the blankets, he slipped his thumbs into the waistband and pulled down the white underwear to his ankles. Buck stroked his flagging member gently under the head, arousing himself back to full firmness. Then he grasped the whole shaft, moving quickly as he remembered pushing her up against the tiles. He pretended, as he relived it, that he'd entered her backdoor like in the movies.

A couple minutes later he could feel the surge was coming, but his arm muscles were beginning to burn. Would he get there? Could he get there? Sweat rolled from his temples as his hand stroked harder and faster. Almost. A big breath. Almost. Faster. Nearly there.

The phone rang and Buck slammed the bed top in frustration. He snatched it from the nightstand and put it to his ear.

"What?" he greeted with all the disdain he could muster.

"Deputy Garner, this is Evelyn Fouche. I'm sorry to call you so early, but a pack of vandals broke into Chandler's car a little while ago here at the house."

Color drained from his face as sat up on the edge of the bed.

"Forgive me, Mrs. Fouche. I didn't look at the caller I.D."

"It wouldn't have helped you. The phone at the house is dead for some reason so I walked down to the neighbors."

"Are you safe? Did you call 911?"

"Should I? I thought I would just bypass the middleman."

"You did well, Mrs. Fouche. I'm on my way and will be there as soon as I can."

"Thank you, Deputy. I will walk back and meet you there."

She hung up before he could, and he held the phone briefly with forearm throbbing. He looked down and tried to decide if things were still aroused enough to resume, but thoughts of how Rebel's raid went, did they have the money, and then the phone's "off the hook signal" pushed the Dixie fantasy away. Buck hung up and went into the hallway bathroom, the only bathroom, to splash water on his face. He quickly donned yesterday's uniform that was draped over a chair. He would look disheveled, but that would be forgiven. Failure to be prompt would not. This could drag Sheriff Fouche down and line him up for the job, but one sentence in the newspaper about "the deputy took over an hour to arrive" would not play well in any special election.

Buck lived in a little two-bedroom farm laborer house four miles to the east of I-85. Essentially it was on Main Street, but the name changed to Virginia Route 605 past Ed's. It was an eighth of an acre backed up to large fields, with neighbors in similar digs who drove combines and other farm equipment depending on the time of year. But it met his needs and his neighbors rose too early and were always too tired from their labors to ever stay up late and be rowdy enough to bother him.

Walking through the common room, he unplugged his cellphone from the charger and saw he had missed a call. He'd sat out on the porch with a beer last night for a while, listening to the baseball game on the radio like he used to with his dad when he was a kid. He must have missed it then. Buck checked the call log, and didn't recognize the number. Rather than play it now, he made his way out to the patrol car. There was a Twinkie in the glovebox he could scarf down on the drive over.

The sheriff used to have the entire department over for a grill out every summer, but the steady decline in funding drove the departure of the other deputies. And as the department had finally shrunk to just the two of them, Chandler had stopped hosting get-togethers. Which is to say Buck had been over to the sheriff's a few times over the years, and even though it had been a while and it was still dark, had no problems quickly getting over to Caisson Road.

As he was approaching the drive, the silvery reflections of assorted plastic fragments twinkled on the dark asphalt. He stopped, leaving the blue lights on, and then went back to the trunk for the portable barricade. It was essentially a white sawhorse of tube steel with blue reflectors and a sign on the side "Lowland County Sheriff". It also had a couple of blue flashing LED lights, and besides his patrol car was the piece of equipment he used the most. He carried it around to the other side of the driveway to the middle of the road, unfolded the legs, and turned it on.

The last thing he wanted was someone driving through the crime scene because he failed to properly secure it. And he wanted Rebel not to be implicated, which would bring heat back on him. That could be the tricky part, that balance. A job well done, by the book, but no result or arrest. The immediate prize was praise for him, and with enough mud on Chandler to spark a no confidence vote. Or recall election. Buck wasn't sure how all that worked exactly. He was kind of hoping the county's Board of Supervisors would take over from there and he could simply ride the wave of subsequent events. And then they would hopefully forget about the perpetrators and leave him be as Sheriff Garner. As long as the county lasted, anyway.

Mrs. Fouche waved with a flashlight from the top of the drive and began walking down the picket fence along the driveway. He walked to greet her, also staying on the grass to the side for no other reason than she was. The heavy dew made his socks wet. His boots were "uniform boots" and not field boots. As she came closer, he saw the twelve gauge broken open on her right shoulder like she'd been out chasing Ruff Grouse though the season was over last month.

A little girl in her night clothes was with her, dead on her feet and dragging a stuffed bear. Evelyn wore a simple country dress, with rubber crocks, and a long unzipped sweater. The sweater's pockets bulged and the weight stretched the garment's fabric downward.

Buck guessed extra shells. As they neared, she turned off the flashlight, put it in the dress's bib pocket, and took the girl's free hand. The little one leaned her head against Evelyn's leg, like she might fall back asleep standing up.

"Is everyone okay? I just wanted to get that out of the way first. Everything else can wait."

"We all fine. Aren't we, Girl?" Evelyn gave a gentle shake of her arm and the child nodded.

"Any luck getting hold of the sheriff?"

"You know when Chandler is off duty, he is off duty. There's no phone down at the cabin. I was going to call one of the cousins to go tell him, but he'll be back late night. If I fetch him now those boys won't get to fish."

"You said they tried to vandalize his truck?"

"Look at it up there by the house. It's all tore up. Sure, it has some shotgun pellets in it. I had to protect little Latoyia, here. But you look at the back door and the radiator. You'll see," she said while nodding her head for emphasis.

He strode to the top of the drive, outpacing her dragging the small child behind her. Buck turned on his light, and did a full circle twice around like his boss had taught him. Always good to have a "big picture" perspective before diving into the details, he'd said. The second time around he saw the phone box.

It was partly hidden in the shadow of the chimney and a nearby bush, bent over and hanging from the conduit stub that rose out of the ground. Only a piece of sheathing, that bound all the wires together that wasn't trimmed during installation, kept the box from falling to the ground by catching in the entry hole of the panel's bottom. No wonder she had to walk down to the neighbors. Buck had thought Rebel would just use some of his mechanical expertise to slip in and out in the middle of the night. This might be better. He couldn't wait to look over the Durango.

Evelyn had certainly done a number on it. Small plastic crumbles of the windows were sprayed everywhere. Buck thought she must have hastily broke open cardboard ammunition boxes in the dark to stuff handfuls of loose shells into her pockets without regard to their type. Some shells had been surplus from the department's "nine-ball machine," the cop nickname for the 12-gauge pump shotgun with buckshot. In size "double-ought," the twelve gauge held nine pellets. However, unlike hunters that used soft lead, these were steel and tore through the sheet metal doors and chair cushions of the passenger compartment until stopped by the engine block. Other shells had been bird shot, leaving everything peppered with tiny pockmarks. But regardless, the car was clearly a write-off.

He noted the mangled door which had yielded under brute force, and the telltale red droplets across the back seat. Chandler's evidence box was both open and empty. Around front someone had stabbed at the radiator, but Buck didn't know why. Worried about pursuit, he guessed. Buck considered his next move.

The way he thought it would have gone, would have been more akin to the office break-in. Such as using a "Slim-Jim" to stealthily unlock the door. Sure the box on the floor would be sprung, and there might on an outside chance some minor vehicle damage like a broken window that could be quietly repaired. Nothing that would have raised huge questions or an investigation. Then Buck could have threatened Chandler by exposing that key evidence was lost because he hadn't followed proper procedure, imply that he might be perceived by others as dirty, and offer to let him resign and retire instead. Maybe even get him to endorse his bid for the office.

But there was no hiding this complete demolishment. Such things didn't happen here. Buck had never seen it during his tenure, anyway. Some cop-shop jurisdictions, like New York or Chicago, might lose a cruiser every couple of weeks. They would have processes and procedures for that type of thing. Here, everyone in the county would be circling the wagons to discuss it, trying to figure out what to do. The board might even hold an emergency meeting over it. Buck couldn't keep it quiet, even if he wanted to.

That might be better, anyway. He wouldn't have to confront Chandler and try and blackmail him. It was a conversation he knew he'd have to have to realize his plan that way, but also one where he wondered if he could go through with it. This way, the problem was Rebel getting caught, and then implicating him. Rebel had been to prison. His DNA was on file. There was no way they weren't going to find that DNA in Chandler's back seat. Buck had to find Rebel, and kill him, before the State Police lent a hand and brought a manhunt. The weekend, and his boss being away, might work in his favor. He was being blessed with a head start.

He turned around to Evelyn.

"How long ago now?"

She looked at her watch, "Probably close to ninety minutes by now. They long gone."

"What was he driving?" Buck asked, going through the motions while giving his mind time to work.

"There were three of them," she said, "in a big blue crew cab truck. They drove away to the north, the last man barely jumping in the back before they sped away."

He asked her a few more straightforward questions, trying to decide how best to handle things and not let on that he knew more than he should. Lights were beginning to come on in the little houses up and down the street, and the east sky was growing a lighter shade along the horizon.

"I'm going to call the lab technicians to collect evidence when their shift starts. Trying to rush them out here in the dark will just make it likely that something important gets trampled. Better to give them the extra hour, and get it done right when everyone can see.

Why don't you go inside and get some rest? I'm sure this has been an upsetting night."

"I'm up by now anyway, but this one could stand to lay back down. Would you like some coffee, Deputy Garner?"

The air was chill and he hadn't gotten to eat anything in his rush out the door.

"Mrs. Fouche, I would be much obliged," he replied. "But I do need to return to my cruiser and call in some help. I'll be back up in a few minutes."

In truth, he was down there for nearly fifteen minutes. He called for the state crime scene technicians, since Lowland County didn't have their own. Then he got out the map and took a look at the roads. They mainly ran north-south, with short "cut-overs" defining long narrow rectangles around agricultural or forestry plots. Rebel would have had lots of options with which way to go. But what Buck wasn't sure about was where would he go?

Evelyn had said there were three of them, but he assumed it was Rebel who was wounded in the back seat because of the evidence can. He wouldn't trust touching the money to anyone else. A quick hop over a cattle fence and a short sprint into the darkness and they would be gone with fifty "g's". Was he hurt badly enough that he would go to a medical facility? Rebel was one mean son of a bitch. If it was really bad though, thought he was going to die, he'd go to the closest: St. Albans Clinic. If it wasn't life threatening, he'd not go anywhere at all. He'd tough it out.

Evelyn hadn't gotten a plate number, and Rebel may have taken precautions such as obscuring it with red clay mud. Which meant Rebel might be hopeful that no one had identified him and he'd simply hole back up in his garage and lick his wounds.

There was a third possibility, that of a fresh start. Rebel had two girls in his pit to trade to Shep for help. Shep might have connections to get him a fake driver's license and such. Sell the truck, buy a bike, and go down the road a piece with the satchel of cash. Buck wouldn't put it past the snake to run out on him and Doris. The only family he had was the crippled drunk that urinated on statues in the square. The garage was nostalgia, and its day was over. This might cause him to clear out.

Buck thought he might let him go, with the money, if he was truly going. Doris would be out of luck, but that wasn't his problem as long as she kept quiet. He bet she would for Dixie's sake. It meant Baylee Ann and Bambi getting back into circulation, and that could be dangerous if questioned about his false witness report. The faster they dropped charges against Dog-Boy starving in his cell and escorted him to the county line, the better. And it also meant that Rebel would have needed to have thought things through.

And that, thought Buck, was the single most compelling reason to begin searching for Rebel locally and immediately. He'd get started just as soon as the technicians arrived. Feeding Kelton Jager in his cell could wait, or he'd call Dixie later and order her to do it.

CHAPTER—20

Kelton, Azrael and Baylee Ann stood in front of the little pharmacy, five minutes before it opened at seven, on the west side of Lowland Road. It was a two story brick structure, with windows covered by thick curtains upstairs. The front window had a variety of advertisements for snacks and school supplies, as well as medicines. Easter and St. Patrick's Day decorations were on sale.

Down the street the county offices were mostly dark except for one window on the second floor. The nearby coffee shop showed shadows of activity within, but its lights also remained off. Kelton briefly walked along the building's sides looking for a water spigot, but didn't see one. He squeezed some water into Azrael's bowl from his CamelBak instead.

A soft jingling of bells made him look up to a tired old man in a dingy white lab coat. He reversed the closed sign and smiled as he held the door open.

"Sitz," Kelton commanded and followed Baylee Ann inside.

They walked in leisurely, to give the old man time to beat them to the back counter. His steps were slow and painful, and his back was rounded. He curved to the side to get behind the counter, and stood smiling with the shelves of various pill bottles behind him. Baylee Ann handed him the prescriptions, and he held them fanned in one hand while the other adjusted his glasses. Then he nodded and began walking from shelf to shelf.

"We appreciate you being up early for us," said Kelton.

"It doesn't make good business sense, I must confess. But when you need something, you need it," he said as he took down a large white bottle from a top shelf with a red lid. "And with Lily gone, I suppose I'm just marking time trying to do my civic duty."

The old pharmacist shuffled around to the next shelf.

"Things are slow then?" asked Kelton, trying to keep up a friendly air to overcome his homeless look.

"Any faster and me and my diabetes wouldn't be able to handle it. But our satellite location sells enough allergy pills that I can pay the taxes."

Kelton kneeled down by some health products and grabbed a handful of protein bars, "Yeah, where's that?"

"The truck stop. Doris sells quite a bit to the truckers. I guess those boys get a lot of pollen driving through those farm fields and trees sixteen hours a day," he said as he returned from his workbench with a trio of the translucent orange bottles with white tops. "Do you have any insurance?"

"No," Baylee Ann admitted.

Kelton intervened, "I'm her insurance today. I'll take these, too," he said piling the protein bars on the counter. He would eat them first, as their expiration dates were closer than the ones in his backpack.

A few minutes and a $150 of plastic money later, they were back on the sidewalk and heading toward Main Street. They split one of the protein bars, as among the antibiotic, stool-softener and anti-inflammatory pill bottles, a couple were labeled to take with food. Kelton struggled to walk slowly enough for her to keep up, zig-zagging and driving his poor dog who was trying to heel to distraction. They reached the feed store and began to make their way down Main Street to Ed's.

"Kelton," she smiled sheepishly.

He turned toward her.

"Will you please buy me some jeans? These sweat pants don't really fit, and they rub and get too hot when we are walking."

Instinctively he felt denial rising up inside him, but rapidly reconsidered. A pair of jeans from a farm store couldn't cost much, especially compared to medical bills, and would go a long way toward helping her feel back to normal. And, it was going to be a warm day for spring. The heavy sweat pants had been great overnight, but if they were going to do any amount of walking she'd quickly be miserable. A T-shirt would be a nice add, too, he thought. It wouldn't be long before she'd want to shed the hoodie.

"Okay," he relented, "and try and find a shirt, too."

With it being a feed store, all three went inside. It was a brick warehouse, dating back to the town's founding days with solid wood beams and large square-headed iron nails. All the electrical wiring, be it for outlets or lights, ran in surface mounted conduits whose galvanized coating was tarnished with years of dirt and hay dust. Most of the store was pallets on the concrete slab floor with fifty pound sacks in a variety of brands and purposes. But there were a few odds and ends, like nuts and bolts or tractor pins, on some shelving near the cash register. And that included jeans and boots.

She found her size, while the old man watched from his stool. Younger backs, breaking down a just delivered pallet, didn't pay any mind at all to them.

"Nice dog," he complimented. "Can I sell you a biscuit?"

Baylee Ann held up the denim to her hips, trying to make up her mind about the cut and fit. She did the same with a pink camouflage T-shirt with "Browning" on the front. Then she carried them to the restroom.

"I'll buy if he'll eat yours."

The old timer grabbed one from an open box at the register with a cardboard and marker sign of $1.50 each. They were large biscuits, about the size of a man's palm and thumb, and came in three colors that must have denoted flavors. He tossed a reddish one, landing to crack on the concrete between Azrael's front feet. Azrael looked up at Kelton.

Kelton nodded, "Go ahead."

Azrael lowered his nose to the biscuit, lingered a few seconds and then looked up at Kelton with wide uncertain eyes. They seemed to be searching for understanding of what he had done wrong.

Kelton smiled with a shrug, "Sorry, no sale there."

"Can't sell them to anyone in town either. When I was young, our mutts weren't so particular."

"I've held him to a high standard," Kelton explained. "I guess he does the same to me."

Baylee Ann wore the jeans and T-shirt out of the powder room, the sweatpants nowhere to be seen. The hoodie was tied about her waist by the sleeves. Kelton started to say something about saving the other, but then just bit his tongue and paid instead. A few more pleasantries and they were back on Main Street and heading east.

Baylee Ann moved a bit better in the jeans, and their pace correspondingly increased. Kelton noted Colonel Redigan's truck in the city lot, easy to spot as it dwarfed the various smaller cars. Mr. Butler and his barbershop weren't yet open, nor was the florist. The doughnut shop filled the morning air with pleasant aromas, but they didn't stop in given their destination. Then, came Dixie's house.

If she knew it was Dixie's home across the street, Baylee Ann didn't let on. Kelton composed a few questions but then left them unasked. He'd gone to Rebel's garage and found her there because of Dixie, even though that had been more of a slip of the tongue than a pleading for a rescue. Dixie had been let go, but the other two had been kept. Even though the law had been there. Why was that? Kelton pondered.

"I'm sorry to be a burden," she said.

Kelton came back to the present.

"You're fine. We've nowhere to be," he shrugged.

"You mean you and your dog?" she asked. "People have dogs. With you it's like you're a pair of people or something."

"I guess that's right. Kind of like you and your friend Bambi, I guess. How long have you known each other?"

"Kindergarten, probably. Although I think it was second grade before we became inseparable. That's not real unusual here, it's just that then you get married and things kind of change. But no guys ever wanted to marry Bambi and me so we just kept hanging with each other."

"We'll help you find her. Just need to spend a day resting you up."

They crossed over Thigpen Road and its yellow flashing light. Ed's parking lot in the distance was nearly deserted.

"Bambi and I used to hang out and smoke cigarettes she'd stolen from her dad before he ran off. In that field, right there. There were other girls there, too. Then we got old enough that the truckers started to notice us. A few years after that, they didn't notice us at all.

Then one day some bikers stopped in. They didn't have the gas to get down to the Outlaw Saloon, so stopped in here. Nothing was happening and we weren't making money no more so we hopped on. Been hanging on the back ever since."

"I'm sorry about any pain I caused you underneath that bridge. I really had no choice, you know."

"Yeah, I know. It was just shock for me. Rebel needed someone to take his drugs to Richmond, and bring the money back. Jessie's crew was part of the Lowland Outlaws, and did that type of work. When Grover and Shawn wanted some girls for the trip instead of just cash, Rebel bought us from Rattler and then loaned us out for the ride. I don't think Buck knows all that and didn't want to get too involved. So when it was all over, he just took us back to Rebel."

Kelton held open the diner door for her, and saw Rachel was working alone. He hustled her to a booth as quick as he could so Azrael could get underneath before anyone took notice.

"I'm going to go to the girl's room. Please get me a pop tart," and she strode toward the back. Kelton guessed the pills were doing what they were supposed to do.

Rachel came over after filling a coffee cup three tables down.

"Still in town?" she asked sweetly. "Is St. Albans growing on you?"

"A new friend needed a little help," he explained. "Is Doris resting?"

"She went up to South Hill to do some shopping. It's not unusual. Let's her get away a little before the weekend rush. Goes early so she can be back when the lunch rush starts. You want the breakfast platter again?"

"Please. Make it two. And something fruity sweet. Maybe waffles?"

"I can do pancakes," she offered.

"Sounds good," he nodded. "And we'd like a room too. We've been out all night."

"I'll grab a key too," she said with an exaggerated flirty wink that he found embarrassing.

Baylee Ann took her time and Rachel was bringing out food before she returned. Kelton watched her closely, and could see that she wasn't feeling very well. He observed her staring at the food, trying to resist because of knowing what would follow, but the famine of several days won out. It was a large meal, one that the likes of her was never going to clean the plate, but in the end she gave a good accounting of herself and it perked her up.

Rachel brought a room key with the check, and Kelton sent it back with his credit card.

"You just live from motel to motel?"

Kelton shook his head, "Usually I'm out on the ground somewhere like us in the park last night. Rooms are expensive and I have no income. But I think you need it and probably want to get cleaned up better than a clinic sponge-bath."

She shrugged and said, "Okay," with bright eyes.

Kelton left Rachel a nice tip when the ticket returned and they walked down to the motel room on the far end. It was pretty much the same as the others, except a framed watercolor print of a flowering gazebo survived in this one. Baylee Ann untied the arms of the hoodie as he was closing the door and then lifted off the T-shirt with her back to him just as he turned around. She had no bra and her skin showed an orange hue in places where the iodine hadn't been wiped away. The low-cut jeans fit her curves rather well, and showed a strip of a barbed wire tattoo just above her backside. She looked at him over her shoulder.

"Changing your mind?" she asked.

His face went red momentarily and Azrael came up and sat in the heel position at his left side. She giggled at him as he tried to compose his thoughts.

"That, ah, wasn't what I had," he stammered, "in mind."

"Suit yourself. You're the man," she shrugged as she let her jeans fall down. She wasn't wearing any underwear either. The rape kit at the clinic had claimed that for evidence, too, he presumed. She strode into the tiny bathroom, and closed the door slightly. A moment later he heard the running water and imagined how refreshing its warmth would feel after a night on a park bench, but he didn't go in.

He took off the pack, and then kneeled to remove the harness vest from Azrael. Since the sink was occupied he filled the bowl with water again from the CamelBak. It was nearly empty, but he'd refill soon. Then he sat and pulled off his boots and socks to wiggle free his toes, rolling back the cuffs of his pants so they wouldn't drag. The warm running water continued to beckon. His shirt felt restrictive, and he pulled it off. His T-shirt soon followed, and he felt perspiration evaporate. The warm moist bathroom air condensed to a wisp of cloud as it escaped into the cooler room in which he sat.

He sighed and muttered to himself, "Lightning won't strike you dead." He dropped the remainder of his clothes and went in.

She greeted him with, "Get the shampoo bottle on the counter by the sink."

A large tattoo of an eagle with spreading wings covering her breasts looked a little distorted as she was beginning to sag. To him it was far from sexy, more akin to graffiti on a great work of art. Black hair peeked from under her arms and her stomach bulged from lots of fatty foods and little exercise. She'd lived a hard life, and even being young was struggling to keep those consequences at bay. Nonetheless, there was a confidence to her that was attractive.

He stepped over the tub wall and got wet. They lathered and they rinsed. Her stroking hands were stimulating, but inhibition kept him in check. After drying off they simply climbed into bed, and cuddled up into a spoon. It was both comforting, and awkward. Pleasant, yet incomplete. She was young, and female, and in his bed. It was nice, but his body didn't respond to her presence. While she wasn't what he wanted, he felt perfectly okay to share the mutual pleasant glow of being clean and warm. Sleep came easy to them.

CHAPTER—21

Shep stirred in his office at the Outlaw Saloon as a ray of light through the east facing window that looked over the parking lot found his face. His head throbbed like always this time of morning, complete with aching joints and a stiff back. Bambi still lay next to him, one breast exposed from under the sheet. Her breaths rumbled as her chest rose and fell, and he let her be as he stumbled over to the bathroom. Shep rubbed at his temples a few minutes, bent over the sink. Like most mornings he took a couple of aspirin and drank from cupped hands. He dressed in yesterday's clothes, which were the same ones as the day before a few more times than even he wished to admit.

He opened the shutters to his inside perch and looked down over the restaurant floor. All was quiet and the lights were off. It was peaceful, but he could smell the stale beer odor that even Pine-Sol never quite stripped away. Sunlight through the front doors below were making long shadows and he could see just a glimpse of a figure here and there curled up asleep. After it closed for business in the small hours of the morning, his concrete saloon floor was like a castle's great hall. Assorted henchmen, "Men at Bikes" with no place to go unless on a run, crashed here. And he was the king.

"Anyone seen Burt and Ripper?" he yelled out. He didn't expect them to answer his question. They needed to be awake for that.

There were a few moans as people slowly stirred from his shattering of their tranquility. But it was earlier than they were usually roused, and Shep was patient with them. He reached to his desk for the knife, and used its pommel to pound the railing. It reverberated all over, being an open room with a hard floor.

"Wake up, useless shits. Who has seen Burt and Ripper? Has anyone seen Rebel?"

Shep banged the railing some more. The rattle was insistent, but he wasn't angry. This was normal for his gang. Most had only been asleep for a couple of hours and were drunk and exhausted before they turned in. He'd save the rage for a time it would matter. Right now he was concerned. It was supposed to be just a couple of hours, drive out to the sheriff's, recover some property and come back. Burt and Ripper would have wanted their turn. It would have provided them a sense of urgency. But they hadn't come. Bambi was still with him when he woke. And that told him something was wrong.

He switched the knife to his other hand when one arm became tired from banging. Moans became more like groans and there was movement. Covering their ears wasn't making it stop, so they did the only thing that would. They slinked off of booths under the old stall windows and out from under tables in the middle of the floor. Slowly they shuffled into an assembly below the balcony, looking up with tired greasy faces. Their eyes were bloodshot and even up here he could smell the bad breath and the body odor.

"Has anyone seen Burt and Ripper since they left?" he asked a third time, in a more normal tone of voice.

Shep stopped the banging now that all were paying attention. He wanted information, not to torture them.

They turned and looked at each other, as if checking for their missing comrades, and then faced outward to check all the booths and tables. A couple of guys wandered to the kitchen doorway to the left of the tiny stage and peeked behind, only to look up at him and shake their heads.

"Randy, check outside for their bikes or Rebel's truck. Mauler, look in the cans. If you got to barf, do it while you're in there."

The two shuffled off while the others began to become more alert. They sensed their patron was concerned, and began to rally their focus. Randy came back first, raised an arm to make sure Shep had seen him, and shook his head. Mauler stumbled back into view with vomit on his shirt a second later, and wiped his mouth with the back of his hand before shrugging his shoulders.

"Crew leaders, get up here. The rest of you get yourselves ready to ride," he ordered as he turned back to his desk.

In the lower left drawer, he retrieved a county map under a pile of cellphones decorated in colored electrical tape and unfolded it upon the desk. Their knocks came a few seconds later and he bid them enter with a grunt. They quickly gathered around, and pulled on their riding gloves as they looked on.

"Here we are, and here is Sheriff's Fouche's house on Caisson Road," he stabbed with his dirty broken fingernail while the four of them nodded. All of them knew the area really well. They'd grown up here, riding with no place to go.

He gave their riding purpose. They were the closest he had to lieutenants, although none of them could take over the business. But they could keep their half dozen crew members in line and that kept the business rolling, moving cash and drugs across the nation's interstates. Shep supposed that made them more like sergeants than lieutenants, but he'd deserted during vehicular mechanic school just after basic so didn't have a long career to go on.

"Rattler, check this derelict country store for Burt's and Ripper's bikes. They had planned to stash them there before going on their raid. Then," he said tracing the roads with his finger, "ride these roads to the north to find our guys. We need to find them before Bucky the Pig."

They all sniggered at his pet name for Deputy Garner, but Shep didn't really hear as he paused to evaluate his hasty thinking. If the bikes were there, that meant they would have fled north or got nabbed at the scene. If there were no bikes, and they hadn't come back here, well, so be it. They made their choice and he'd enjoy their turn with Bambi. He glanced over at her and saw she'd shifted on to her side, blanket draping off her narrow hips and showing her bare back and long gold hair. Since they weren't here, the bikes would be there.

"Rattler, if you find the bikes stashed there, sit on them. Take a cover off one of yours like there's been some mechanical trouble. I'll send Beau with a trailer, and a tarp, for them when he opens his garage across the street. But that could be a couple of hours before he gets in. Everyone set for burners?"

They nodded their heads. Burners were disposable cellphones. Since they weren't registered to any particular person's banking information they were ideal for making calls without leaving a record that connected anyone. All types of places carried them these days, and Shep kept a file cabinet full in case the heat was on and he needed to do a mass reissue.

"Okay, find our boys then. Send a text if you learn anything or when its ten o'clock so I know you're okay."

Less than five minutes later he heard the engines starting, and watched the boys riding off in their respective crews while standing at his office window. Rattler's was the smallest; Burt and Ripper belonged to him. When the last rider faded from sight, the overpass kept him from seeing the north bound on-ramp so it didn't take long, he sat at his desk. He arranged the four burners in a line, one for each crew, stared at the map and waited. While he was arranging phones, he made sure a fifth one, with red electrical tape around it, had a full charge. Sure, he could have used just one phone to talk to each crew but this way made it harder to connect the activity. Burners were cheap compared to the cost of prison; prison cost you everything.

Bambi wandered into the washroom when she awoke, and he heard the sink running for quite some time. When she emerged, her dripping skin glowed from the scrubbing of the washcloth. He didn't have a towel for her to use. If he had, it probably would have been dirty enough to defeat her purpose. But regardless, she looked good standing there naked in the door. He wished his body would readily respond again so soon, but he was no longer a young man and last night's satisfaction had left nothing to be desired.

Shep watched her dress, rather than staring further at the unyielding map, into the only clothes she had. Then she came over and sat in one of the facing desk chairs. She sat up straight, arms in her lap like a lady. He leaned back and slouched, then let out a soft belch. His stomach felt acidic and irritated.

"Rebel has my friend Baylee Ann chained up down in a pit," she said.

He wasn't particularly taken aback. He'd seen and heard a lot of things in the underbelly microcosm of society in which he lived. But what intrigued him, was why she thought he would care. Shep nodded to encourage her to continue.

"If Rebel is taken, then whoever frees her will own her," she said looking at his eyes and choosing her words. "Just thought you might want to know of an opportunity depending upon how this goes."

"I'd rather have my men back. We're a little short after Jessie."

"She'll give you a way to pay new men. And me. All you got to do is go over to Rebel's garage."

He shrugged. He had plenty of money to pay men, but money didn't buy loyalty. And once given, it was theirs and that made them less hungry for more for a while. Especially in the amounts he had to pay them if using money alone. But sex, anything goes sex with no danger of being caught soliciting, was a powerful incentive that kept them coming back because they couldn't take it with them. And after a day or two, mother nature told them they needed more. That required a steady supply of fresh women, fresh to his boys anyway, to be able to pull off. He knew Baylee Ann. He'd had Baylee Ann. She wasn't bad, but perhaps she and Bambi were both too well known around these parts to be worth much anymore. But that didn't mean he couldn't trade them for two similar girls from the next organization in the chain, or the next pack that rode through carrying their own recreation. Definitely worth considering depending upon how things worked out. But for now, he concentrated on the most important, effective way to build loyalty of all. Proving to everyone, that no matter how low you were in the gang, everyone would go out looking for you if you didn't come back. That was the real reason for the whole operation.

He gave her a soft smile, "Do you want something to eat?"

Bambi nodded quickly.

"Candi will be in soon downstairs. She's a squat redheaded lady, about fifty, who applies her makeup with a trowel. Tell her I sent you and she'll make you some breakfast. Then come back to me up here. Okay?"

Bambi nodded, and headed out the door to the spiraling stairs.

The first phone beeped a quarter hour later with a text, "Found the sleds."

Rattler being cute. The bikes were there. Why weren't their riders? He texted back for them to sit, and called Beau across the street. They were lucky Beau was in at his garage early. Shep explained what he wanted and sent him on his way.

Then he put his face into his hands and rubbed. Okay, if there's no Rebel, Shep decided, he would go get Baylee Ann. Would be a waste for her to die there. Keeping his face in his hands, he put his elbows on the table. Then he caught himself nodding off, but decided not to fight it. There was nothing to do but wait.

The next series of texts concerned State Police vehicles with "Crime Scene" lettered on the front fenders. They seemed to be showing up in a steady stream. Rattler had noted three. There was no telling if others had shown before his men had arrived. There were no texts of "Oink!" which indicated Deputy Garner or the Sheriff. He liked keeping tabs on them as a matter of course. Rattler also mentioned an orange barricade erected at the end of Caisson Road that read "Closed to Through Traffic." It seemed things hadn't gone as a quiet little theft after all. A major investigation was mounting.

Next was word that Beau and the trailer had arrived. He'd asked Beau to use the tarp so they wouldn't be seen removing two bikes. Two bikes breaking down at the same time would look suspicious. And loitering close to a crime scene was a really lousy place to look suspicious. Shep breathed a sigh of relief with the text that Beau had departed without incident.

And then it was quiet again. The shutters were open, and he heard Candi come in. Bambi accosted her right away. The poor thing was clearly starving. Shep rose and stood on the balcony. Candi heard his footsteps, and looked up. He gave her a thumbs up, a nod, and a wink to add his legitimacy to Bambi's request. Then he turned back to the business at hand.

The smell of the eggs and bacon wafted up to his office and he rose again from the desk.

Shep yelled down, "Candi! Make me some of that, please."

"You want this one, Shep?"

"No, that's Bambi's. I'll wait. And please bring it up."

Normally he would have said "send it up", but there was no one to do that at this early hour. The grill was already hot and he had his breakfast in less than ten minutes. It did make him feel better. He expected Bambi to have returned by now, but with a turn of his head he could hear her and Candi yapping. Shep stood to yell at them to shut up and for her to get up here, but then saw Bambi working a mop while Candi moved tables. He closed his shutters instead.

Finally, a text came from team three.

"Have Rebel. Brothers lost. Returning."

"God dammit," he muttered to himself. Two more of his gang dead. A chunk of wood flew from the desk as he stabbed the knife hard.

One at a time, he picked up the other three phones and texted "Return". They acknowledged in short order.

Shep leaned back in his chair and closed his eyes, thinking about Rebel and how the interview would go. He didn't have much time to figure it out, and the quiet wouldn't last long. After a few minutes' contemplation he opened the desk's central drawer, removed a nickel plated .38 revolver, and placed it in the center.

CHAPTER—22

Buck skidded to a stop in front of St. Albans Clinic, with his blue lights flashing. It had taken a while to get the crime scene technicians on site at Sheriff Fouche's and he wanted to make up for lost time. There was a period in which he had hoped to arrive in time to talk with the night folks, but as it was he didn't even come close.

He slammed the door without shutting down his car, and ran up the few steps with a lumbering stride to the glass entrance doors, his utility belt accouterments bouncing against his sides. The receptionist looked to be a pleasant brunette lady in her thirties, but Buck didn't recall meeting her before. It was a lousy paying job with awkward hours that dealt with the general public. Turnover was high. She smiled at his hasty approach though, but then the smile faded as she looked his wrinkled uniform up and down. He brushed yellow crumbs away from the tops of his shirt pockets.

"Good morning, I'm Deputy Garner of the Lowland County Sheriff's Department. Can I see your admissions log, please?"

"Are you looking for someone in particular?" she asked as she reached for a white three ring binder on her work surface to the left of the computer.

"It's an ongoing investigation, Ma'am. Thank you for your support," he said, it sounding a little condescending although he didn't mean it to.

She opened the binder on the counter in front of him.

"Each page is an eight-hour shift. The top sheet is from 8:00 AM to 4:00 PM, the previous from midnight until 8:00 AM. Anything from before midnight last night has been transcribed into the computer and the paper log sheet shredded."

He was familiar with the log sheets from years in the department. It was simply a series of columns: name, address, phone, etc. with one entry per row. Buck quickly turned the page for the night admissions, looking for Rebel Tarwick or a name that just sounded like an alias for whatever reason. There were less than a dozen entries; it was a small county. Baylee Ann Langford made his job drop.

"What was Miss Langford seen for?" he demanded.

"I'm sorry, Sir, but that information is private and between the patient and their doctor. In truth, I don't even have that data available to me. Would you like me to call my supervisor?"

"No," he said quickly. "Thank you, but that won't be necessary. I have what I need. Have a nice day."

He beat a hasty retreat back to his car, his head reeling. Was Rebel trying to screw him over by releasing her? Hoping she would bring to light that his witness statements were fake? That could easily happen if she wound up at the office and Sheriff Fouche started asking her questions. Buck leaned forward with his forehead against the steering wheel and pondered for a moment.

Did Rebel even know about his witness report? And if Rebel released her, how did she get here? Did he drop her off? He'd be able to do it, at that time of night during the week, without anyone noticing. But Rebel couldn't be two places at once either. And Buck had seen the result of Rebel's visit to Sheriff Fouche's with his own eyes. It didn't make any sense.

He sat back when a flicker caught the corner of his left eye. Red lights began flashing over the rescue door at the Fire Department, and a second later it began to rise. A warning siren blasted several times to warn cars on Smallwood Street. The St. Albans' medics were gearing up for a run.

His radio crackled "Lowland Deputy 1, this is St. Albans Control. You out there, Buddy?"

He recognized Kissel's drawl right away.

"Hello, Bret. Read you loud and clear," he said thinking the radio was only having to go a hundred feet. All you got to do is look out the window.

"Hey, Buck. There's a crashed truck on Virginia Route 422, about six miles north of the Sheriff's house. Two men at the scene, best guess is they will be DOA. I ran the plate for you, and it's a Rebel Tarwick. Seems that," Bret's voice went on over the radio's speakers while Buck floored it before putting his car in gear, "a lady taking her horse for a morning ride came across it where some small bridge was being repaired."

Arid smoke and black streaks of rubber came off the tires as he made a U-turn at such speed he jumped the far curve before getting turned around. In his rearview he just saw the ambulance creeping forward from its bay as the driver checked the road before pulling out. Buck wanted to beat him to the scene. Wanted to beat him by quarter of an hour if he could, but in truth a few minutes was probably the best he could hope for. He hit the siren toggle switch to join with the already activated lights, and got the hand back on the wheel for a white knuckled weave through a series of potholes. Rather than turn south and east toward the interstate he opted for the direct line north up Thigpen Road, the car's rear end swinging wide while tires spun looking for purchase.

"Did you copy, Buck?"

He glanced at his rearview every couple of seconds, Buck dared for not more than a blink at a time, but lost sight of the intersection before he saw which route the ambulance chose.

"Buck?" Brett Kissel's voice queried over the radio again.

"Yeah, I'm en route," replied Buck while on a long straightaway where he felt he could risk a hand off the wheel for a couple of seconds. Then he really dropped the hammer, trying to gain time in the straightaways before windy rural roads forced him to back off.

The orange warning sign let him know he was getting close, and he slowed down. Of course Buck had the advantage of daylight and knew about the construction, but he was no fool. He sure as hell didn't want to wreck the way that Rebel had, and Rebel had been a much better driver.

A lady up ahead with a cellphone in her hand waived and he killed the siren. She wore tall boots and tan britches with a tweed coat. It was a cute outfit, but as he got closer he could see on it the wear and tear, frays and stains, that came from working with horses every day. Her auburn curls were matted like she had just removed a hat. Then he recognized her and his heart sank. Mrs. Lauryn Redigan, wife of Lowland County's Commonwealth Attorney. Her horse was tied to a tree with the reins a few long strides off the road, the strap of her helmet snapped around the breast plate. He stood relaxed, with drooping ears and an alert but soft eye.

Buck knew the ambulance was close behind so he wasted no time in jumping out.

"There's a man in the truck's cab, laying on the back seat, and another in the road about ten feet in front of the truck. I looked inside to see if they were breathing, and they looked like they had been dead for a while. Other than that, I didn't move or touch anything."

She stood there in the middle of the road while he glanced ahead to the raised rear-end of the truck. He had a better view of the suspension underneath than the back window of the cab, with its hood down off the edge.

"You did real good, Mrs. Redigan. The ambulance is right behind me and may be coming with their siren. You may want to get your horse out of here before they arrive. I'll call later for an appointment so I can get your statement."

"Shouldn't you be securing the scene, by putting up warnings for other drivers?"

"Please let me do my job, Ma'am," he said with a stiff smile.

He stood there for a second, and she took a couple of steps back toward her horse but continued to gawk.

His belt radio cackled, "Buck, I just heard from rescue. They are five minutes out. Where are you?"

Dammit! Leave, Lady! Please! No time.

He strode toward the truck's rear end while keying the radio mike on his shoulder, "Just arrived on scene. Give me a few minutes to assess and secure. Out."

He glanced over his shoulder but she just patiently stood there next to her horse, cradling the phone. Buck climbed up into the back of the truck and peered through the rear window. He could see the deflated airbags upfront, and the twisted figure in the back. It was a big man in jeans and a dark leather jacket, neck bent against the seatback. He hadn't been wearing a seatbelt. It also wasn't Rebel. The driver's airbag had blood on it, at the middle top. Probably from a broken nose.

Bucked straddled the edge of the bed on the driver's side facing forward, slowly lowering his left leg seeking the running board. He found it, although he shuffled his feet slowly along it as his boots didn't have the best soles for walking on hard plastic, especially at such a steep incline; he kept one hand firmly on the bed's sidewall. The side of the truck was dinged up and down with birdshot pellets. Gingerly, he pulled the driver's side door latch with his left hand, and gravity pulled it open. With a deep breath he let go of the bed's side wall while holding the door post, and slowly shuffled down the running board. A second later he could grab the steering wheel and pull himself inside. Inside stunk like a summer outhouse, and the guy had that waxy look of being dead.

Buck reach toward the man's carotid for a pulse since he felt Misses Redigan's eyes burrowing into his back, but his attention was on his other hand feeling under and around the seat. The truck was diesel, with minimal risk for a fire, but he reached up and turned off the ignition anyway. The firemen could give the environmental office a call if they wanted to concerning any radiator fluid and oil that might be polluting into the stream. Ostensibly, he had a crime to solve.

The windshield was cracked, but all things considered, intact. Through it he could see the figure in the roadway on the far side, along with an assortment of equipment like jack stands, chains, tire iron, bottle jacks and the like. It was possible he was hit by the truck, but Buck thought being thrown from the bed was more likely. And he didn't care. However, Lauryn was still standing there watching him and he had to put on a good show while he tried to find the cash.

Buck looked down at the creek through the driver's door and tried to find a dry place to land and easily get across. The short answer was, there wasn't one. Not that dropping down from the truck into a couple of feet of muddy water was an insurmountable obstacle, glad as he was to be wearing yesterday's uniform. Getting over the three feet of exposed concrete retaining wall while standing in two feet of muddy water however was going to be the real bugger. Instead he opted to wade upstream, for no other reason than that direction was on the driver's side, slopping water while he clambered up the muddy bank and the briars.

A couple of steps up the side, he paused. Tips of the tall yellow grass in places were red. Blood red. Whether from a gunshot wound or the accident he had no idea, but it was a good bet it was Rebel's. Buck had been looking for an easy place to climb out and cross just like he had. This was the trail. He was no outdoorsman, but even he could see the mashed grass where Rebel must have rested on his stomach after getting out of the water. Then the broken grass curved up to the right toward the road. He heard the sirens approaching, and then cut off as Rescue slowed their approach.

Buck clambered up to the asphalt, looking keenly for additional sign. The first blood drop he saw was on the yellow painted centerline, but its size and shape helped him to pick out others on the blacktop. Rebel had gone up the road, not bothering to check his compatriot. Made sense. Rebel was injured and the guy was out cold. No way he was going to carry him, even if he wanted to. And Buck knew that Rebel didn't.

He took a quick look. It was another big man, huge around the belly and lying face down. This one also wore a dark leather jacket, with the patch of the Lowland Outlaws sewn on the back. There were multiple penetrations. Clearly, Misses Fouche had dusted him once with her shotgun as he'd fled down the driveway. Flashing lights made Buck turn around, and he saw the ambulance arrive on scene. He raised a hand as their doors opened to grab their attention.

"One in the truck, one over here on the road. I've a blood trail I'm following for a suspect in the sheriff's home invasion. Get crime scene out here. They should still be just down the road."

"You got it, Buck. Go get him!" wished the driver as the medics ran forth carrying plastic boxes to the wrecked truck.

One of them cursed, as he came to terms with crossing the stream. Buck hoped Mrs. Redigan had noted his display of leadership.

Following the trail was hard, and soon he lost it. There just wasn't enough blood and Rebel could have turned off the pavement anywhere. Buck hated himself for wishing he had a stupid dog. Maybe they could get one as surplus equipment on a government grant as the war in southwest Asia wound down. They could keep it in one of the cells; they never held many people at a time. Dixie could clean up its poop and stuff. Chandler may actually like that after two incidents and it couldn't be that hard. Even that Jager prick could do it.

Okay, cowboy just think a second he thought to himself. Rebel is hurt, but he is mobile. Which means he will go and hole up somewhere or maybe go to the clinic. Perhaps not the clinic. He might have risked it before a response had been mounted, hoping to slip away once treated. But too much time had gone by and Rebel would know they'd be on the lookout for him. Rebel would go to ground.

He might go back to his garage. That had been Buck's thinking earlier. But now that the truck was found, even that idiot would know that the posse would soon be pounding on his door. There was nothing left there anyway; the property would soon be seized for back taxes and environmental violations. That must be why he'd let Baylee Ann, and probably Bambi, go. Rebel wasn't planning to go back there. He had his money, but now needed some help. Where would he get it? Injured, and on foot?

Buck walked back toward the bridge and watched as a trio of medical technicians lifted the body into a bag, and Buck saw the patch again. Rebel would go see Shep, and so would he. But first, he had to feed that stupid prisoner. On second thought, he'd call Dixie and have her do it. He pulled out the cellphone to dial the office, and saw he still had a voice mail.

Buck hated voicemail. A text message you could scan quickly on the move and know whether it was important. Voice mail you had to stop everything you were doing, dial, enter a password, and then listen. If you missed any part of it, you wound up doing it all over again. He almost dropped the phone when he heard Dixie's teary voice.

"Hey, Buck. It's me. I'm over here at Mama's and its close to midnight. That Kelton Jager guy and his dog left here about half an hour ago. He said he was going to Rebel's to get Baylee Ann and Bambi. I thought you might want to know."

Buck's face turned red as he choked the phone to where he thought it's shell or his fingers would break. Not only was Dog-Boy on the loose again. And that meant Mr. Redigan had set him free despite the witness reports. It also meant Dixie had told him something. That was the only way Kelton Jager would have any clue about those two geriatric lot lizards.

His to-do list had grown from killing Rebel and stealing the money to teaching that little bitch a lesson she would never forget since last time didn't seem to have made much of an impression. And he'd have to find some way to deal with Dog-Boy if he was sticking around. Buck hoped that Shep might do that for him, if someone without an Outlaw patch was playing with the biker girls.

He turned toward the arriving crime scene technicians and forgot all about Lauryn Redigan, "Hurry the fuck up! We got things to do."

CHAPTER—23

Azrael lay in the center of the motel room's floor, so he could see the figures on the bed. Or their bare feet dangling off the end, anyway. They weren't moving other than breathing, and at a time of day when he and Kelton were normally walking the roads. This wasn't concerning to him, but rather a curiosity given that it was unusual. Life's rhythm was a little different today, and one might think it would make him speculate on how the rest of the day would be different. But truth was, Azrael was more of a live in the moment kind of dog. Now was a time for rest, so he rested.

It was also a time to be alert and he was ever vigilant. There were many noises outside, as was typical when bright sunlight snuck around the corners of the curtains. Some were people, others were vehicles. His ears stood tall and erect, and he occasionally cocked his head to fine tune the direction and distance. Approaching steps caught his attention, and he rose with a stretch. A second later he admitted a soft cautionary growl.

Kelton awoke instantaneously to Azrael's warning and immediately drew his gun from his pants beside the bed. Baylee Ann barely stirred, and succumbed back to deep sleep before ever awakening. A moment later came a pounding upon the door. Azrael barked in response. A single deep loud bark.

"Mr. Jager are you in there?" came the voice of Doris in a strict schoolteacher type tone.

"Yes, Ma'am. Give me a minute to dress."

He shook Baylee Ann and she opened her eyes with a groan.

"Come on, wake up. Throw something one."

She rolled back over and ignored him, and he pulled on his pants. Azrael barked again, dancing in front of the door with his tail up.

"Mr. Jager," she pounded on the door again, "I'm not fooling."

He looked through the spyhole and saw it was only Doris. Kelton grasped the knob and turned, letting the door open to the safety chain. He didn't fear Doris, physically anyway, but putting his leg in the gap made it easier for him to control Azrael. Or at least keep his furry buddy from unduly affecting the conversation.

"Good afternoon, Miss Doris. What can I do for you?"

"We don't allow dogs on these premises. You must immediately vacate. Now, young man."

"You let us stay before. What's different," she cut him off before he could finish the sentence with the "now?".

"Before I had to, at the request of the sheriff. Now that your case is resolved, you aren't here at their hospitality."

"I've paid my own way," he protested.

"Dogs and whores are not allowed in my establishment. You have fifteen minutes to vacate or I'm calling the sheriff's office. I'm also keeping your room fee to clean up after all your filthy dog hair."

She turned on her pumps, grinding sandy concrete dust underneath, and strode quickly down the sidewalk toward the diner. Kelton let her go without calling after. It seemed his welcome here had been rescinded. He closed the door and returned to the bed to give Baylee Ann another gentle nudge.

She rolled on to her back with a heavy flop, her shaking breasts making the tattooed eagle wings appear like they were flapping. He had trouble keeping his eyes away.

"Do you want to lick them?" she teased grasping them, and giving a slight squeeze with each hand.

He turned a little red as he glanced away. In truth, he didn't. The ink work just made him think about how many others had been there. He wasn't naive about it; he just didn't find it appealing to have that fact thrown in his face.

"No time. We got to pack up and go. Something's wrong."

"You got a dog, that's what's wrong."

"Where he goes, I go. Never again," he said as he checked the Glock. All was as it should. He stroked Azrael's head as she got up.

"I've rested enough. I had to rest. But I want to find Bambi."

Kelton cocked his head to the side, "The watering hole where you say this Shep guy is. It's nearly ten miles. Are you sure you're up for that?"

"I'm going to find my friend. When I put my mind to it, I can do anything."

Her feet were reasonably steady as she rose. It didn't take long for them to dress and gather their things, for they didn't have much. Baylee Ann took the roll of toilet paper with a smile and a shrug. Kelton rinsed and filled the CamelBak. The day was likely to seem warm with lots of walking, and she would be more demand upon the supply.

They walked down the little sidewalk in front of the motel doors, weaved through the small automotive service island, and rounded the corner of the travel mart and diner. The soft buzz of the interstate hummed in the background, and a cool spring breeze rustled Baylee Ann's hair. The sun was bright, and Kelton put on his shades.

Through the window of the diner they saw Doris strolling with her coffee pot while Ed sat at the register. Dixie held a pad in her hands while standing at a table with a weary family. Baylee Ann waived to get the attention of Doris, who paused just long enough to let them know she had seen them. Baylee Ann then raised her middle finger as they walked past to the grassy field next to the big truck diesel pumps.

Baylee Ann didn't have waterproof boots, but with the morning dew long gone Kelton thought they would try and cut a few corners. Rather than walk down Main Street to the flashing light at Thigpen Road, they cut through the grass and woods on the truck stop's south side. Moving as the crow flies would save many miles, and Kelton reckoned Baylee Ann didn't have as many miles in herself as the tough facade she put on. Kelton knew what walking that distance felt like, and he was athletic and in-shape. Baylee Ann was recovering from the pit ordeal, and obviously had a long history of making less than marginal health choices.

It was the same woods where Azrael had hidden when Kelton and James found him. It was also the woods in which the lizard girls hid while awaiting wanting drivers. The used condoms strewn about were merely disgusting. Even the potential diseases they may have carried were harmless if they weren't handled, as if anyone would want to. Those germs had also been at the mercy of full sunlight for extended periods. The used syringes were what concerned Kelton. His boots were designed with a heavy mountaineering tread providing significant protection, but Azrael's feet were just pads. Tough pads, used to daily work, but just pads all the same.

Baylee Ann laughed curiously as Kelton kneeled and retrieved the four small dog boots from the bottom of his pack. They were a commercial product, common with hunters in the American southwest amongst cactus spines and sharp rocks. The K-9 handlers had used them in Iraq when the terrain was rugged or the locals had been messy with lots of broken glass. Azrael went obediently onto his back for fastening the Velcro, but his first steps came with a mid-air foot shake in his stride. They weren't his favorite thing.

But he didn't need to wear them long. A few hundred yards through woods and a pasture, and the drug paraphilia faded into standard rural street trash. Another quarter mile, even the mundane trash became a nonissue. Kelton paused again to remove Azrael's booties, while Baylee Ann stood sweating with hands on her hips.

"You need some water?" he asked her.

She nodded, not wanting to stop her breathing to make words. Kelton extended the CamelBak's mouth hose to her. Baylee Ann panted to make up for the breathing lost as she swallowed.

"Going to make it? It's for Bambi," he encouraged.

She nodded her head and trudged on.

"Tell me something to keep my mind off it. Tell me about your girls," she said. "Something juicy."

"I can't say I have juicy women stories. Mom kept a pretty tight rein on me, not wanting her mistakes to be repeated. There were a few girls at the academy that shared with me their favors. But there was also a lot of competition and they moved on pretty quick. At least I had a turn, is how I've come to think of it. After graduation they sent us to all these trainings measured in weeks at different bases. Then it was off to the warzone. Other than a hotel party I stumbled across in Bagdad, where I met a British flight attendant named Julie for a wonderful thirty hours, there just hasn't been time."

His story carried them another half mile and their route across the cattle pastures and hayfields converged with Thigpen Road. Kelton helped her over the barbed wire fence and the drainage ditch. Her cheeks were red, and perspiration soaked her shirt. They paused for another drink, and he threw the Kong toy for Azrael a few times who was frustrated with the slow pace.

Walking the roadside made for easier going. Only a couple of cars passed them in the next forty-five minutes, and neither slowed down to offer them a ride. Kelton felt they would have stopped if they were standing beside a disabled vehicle, as a courtesy to a fellow motorist, but people simply out for a walk were a different proposition.

"I need to rest again. I'm sorry," she said, leaning forward with hands on her thighs.

"It's okay. Lay down here on the shoulder and you can put your feet up on my pack."

"Wouldn't it be better to lay in the grass?" she asked.

"Only if you like ticks," he grinned.

Her eyes went wide, "Yuck. I hate those blood suckers."

"I think that is something all three of us have in common." Then he added, "How are your feet?"

"They hurt. I feel hot rubs on my toes and heels."

He nodded knowingly again.

"I saw a house up ahead," she said. "Do you think they will let us take a break there?"

Kelton shrugged, "Maybe. It's Braxton Greene's house."

She sat up, "The guitar player?"

Kelton looked at her suspiciously, "I think he said he was a plumber."

"It has to be him. I know him. Help me up," she said extending her arms upward.

Kelton grabbed them and pulled Baylee Ann to her feet before donning his pack. He wasn't so sure about getting any help from Braxton Greene. The only time he'd met the man, he'd been with Buck who had been a real dick. But they didn't have much in the way of options. It had taken them twice as long to get here as it had taken Kelton to walk back with Azrael that day, and he'd stuck to the road rather than saving a lot of steps cutting cross-country. Baylee Ann was a rider, not a walker.

Kelton followed behind, letting her take the lead. They couldn't see the truck on account of the overgrown landscaping until right upon it, but there in the driveway it was. She plodded to the freshly repaired door, and from her shifting gait he could tell her feet were really hurting her. He wished he had a pair of fresh socks to offer her, but his were much too large. Baylee Ann pounded on the door.

"Braxton! It's Baylee Ann. Get up, Honey!" she said as loudly as she could and still keep a sweet tone.

The door opened wide, him standing there in a pair of cutoffs and flip-flops. In his arms he held a clear glass mixing bowl from which he was eating macaroni and cheese. When he saw her his jaw hung loose and he dropped the fork.

"Are you going to invite me in, Sweetie?" she smiled.

"Ah," he said sticking his head out and looking around, "I guess so."

Kelton gave a small friendly wave, standing politely back. Azrael sat at his side in the heel position with bright eyes that seemed to say, "Hello again."

"And he and the dog can come in, too," Braxton said before walking back inside with the door ajar behind him.

Baylee Ann looked back at Kelton with a smile, shrugged, and walked inside leaving the door wide open. Kelton and Azrael were quite a few strides behind, but they hurried to catch up. Braxton had sat down in the middle of the brown tattered couch, but Baylee Ann didn't let that stop her from sitting next to him. Kelton sat on the adjacent recliner, Azrael laying down at his feet.

The two furniture pieces made a rough ell around a dingy shag rug. It exuded odors, mainly marijuana smoke and old beer. Across from the couch was a television set, a new flat screen digital model, on a stand containing a tired looking VHS player. The walls were the brown paneling with the black vertical grooves popular in decades past. A wood beaded entryway led to a kitchenette and breakfast table. A hallway the other direction led to what was most likely a bathroom and a couple of bedrooms. There were a few family photos, some shifted slightly on their hangers to reveal years of sun fading on the paneling. A dusty gun cabinet in the corner with a cracked glass pane held a rifle and a couple of shotguns. The coffee table was covered in sheet music.

"That's a good looking TV set," commented Kelton.

"Buck broke my old one. Sometimes I like to play along with the bands on old shows. There's not been much work recently, and that bastard Shep keeps taking my tips. Never paid me for the pipework in his kitchen neither. Hate him. I got a job coming up though. Seems Mrs. Mertle's family wants to sell her home over on Smallwood Street and the pipes aren't up to code."

"Speaking of Shep's place," interjected Baylee Ann, "Have you seen Bambi?"

"She's with Shep. I saw her last night."

"Was Rebel there, too?"

Braxton blinked a few times as if trying to recall, and then his eyes lit up a little.

"Yeah, Rebel was there. Talking to Shep. They were both in chairs at the front of Shep's desk, trembling something fierce. Things had a really tense feel in there, like they'd been doing some hard negotiating. I don't know what about."

Baylee Ann dismissed that, "I don't care what about. I just care about my friend, Bambi. I need to go get her, and it's a really long walk. Will you give us a ride?"

"I don't want no trouble with Shep. I hate him, but his thugs will bury me alive."

"No trouble, Braxton. I just want to make sure my girl is making her own choices. Everyone should be able to make their own choices, right?"

Braxton nodded, "That's right."

"If you don't want to go, can we borrow your truck? I know you don't want to be hours early for your gig tonight. And I just want to get Bambi. Then the two of us will come and see you. Would you like that?"

"Yeah. That would be okay," he nodded.

"Can I have the keys then, Baby? Bambi and I will be really grateful," her head and shoulders swayed gently from side to side while she talked with the exaggerated southern drawl.

Braxton leaned back on the couch to squeeze his hand into the pockets of the shorts. He squirmed a bit from side to side, but Kelton could hear the soft sound of metal on metal as Braxton's hand closed about the keyring. A second later, Baylee Ann leaned in to plant a kiss on his cheek. Kelton felt the old guy seemed exceptionally mellow.

Minutes later, Kelton, Azrael and Baylee Ann were outside firing up the two-tone pickup. Despite being adorned with the proud dents and scratches of a working truck, it started smoothly for Kelton. He put it in gear, and carefully returned his hands to ten and two o'clock on the steering wheel before taking his foot off the brake. They sat three across, the dog sitting up proudly in the middle to block the rearview mirror. As a result, Kelton looked over his shoulder and creeped slowly out onto the road.

"You drive like a grandmother," declared Baylee Ann.

"Quiet, please. I'm trying to concentrate," pleaded Kelton.

He turned the wheel as he backed into the road, and after stopping put the truck all the way into "park" before slowly moving the selector three clicks to "drive". A little bit of gas, and they were rolling down the road at close to 40 miles per hour. Kelton grinned.

"The speed limit is 55, but there aren't much in the way of cops out here," advised Baylee Ann.

It bought her another five miles per hour. Kelton leaned forward to peer through the windshield, both hands firmly gripping the wheel. Baylee Ann stared at him a little bit, and then sat back heavily and sighed.

CHAPTER—24

Rebel sat on the back of a bike riding like a bitch, and hating every moment of it. He hid his face in the back of the guy's jacket, much like how an ostrich sticks their head in the ground to avoid the image of something unpleasant. The pack of riders surrounding him kept making faces and rude hand gestures at him. But he also had to admit to himself he needed rescuing. His smashed nose throbbed, and his neck and back screamed with whiplash every time they hit a small bump. And this biker seemed to love to steer out of his way to get every little suspension jolt he could. The shotgun pellets, or car door fragments, were still in his hind end and maybe his arm causing numbness and swelling. Finally, the briars had torn at his face and hands leaving streaks of blood and embedded thorns.

He tried to keep his mind off all of that and concentrate on the money. Rebel had known someone would pick him up, sooner or later. He looked too much like he needed help for even the most selfish passerby to ignore. That Shep had sent his boys to look for him was a blessing. Legitimate Samaritans would likely have called the authorities, resulting in his eventual incarceration. He would be unable to resist in his current state; one phone call and he was done for. So he had stashed the plastic bag of cash. It was sealed and would resist the elements just fine. His biggest worry was forgetting where it was and being unable to find it again. Good landmarks were a little iffy and so was his memory. The only thing worse than being on the run looking for a complete fresh start, was having to do it penniless. Sure, he had some money in the bank but that would probably be frozen by the time he could reach an ATM.

Being picked up by Shep was a mixed blessing with its own set of issues. Police scrutiny of the Lowland Outlaws was going to bring a shit-storm to Shep's front door and he would hold him accountable for that. Like buried twenty feet down using a backhoe from some rider's construction day job, forgetting to kill him first kind of accountable. No one would ever find him. That might happen anyway, but that was the game to be played. Rebel was okay with gambling between freedom and death, versus assured imprisonment. Go for broke. All or nothing. It was the way he'd driven on the track.

Bambi wasn't a bargaining chip anymore. Rebel was under no illusion that Shep would give her back, or accept her as sufficient compensation for the damage Rebel's shortcomings had done to Shep's enterprise. Shep owned her now. Nor would Baylee Ann change the equation. She might be good to throw in as a deal sweetener, like if Shep was on the edge of agreement, but the woman was in real rough shape. The only leverage he had was the money and its location. Could it save him from summarily being executed?

Rebel felt the only thing the money bought was a delay in his demise. The biker gang leader knew if Rebel was penniless and on the run, his chances of making it were slim. Which meant getting nabbed, and trying to negotiate his sentence down by singing on Shep. After all, while breaking into Sheriff Fouche's car was a second offense after his old domestic violence conviction, it still was just attempted auto-theft. They'd done no violence. It wouldn't be hard for a prosecutor to rationalize some leeway for him with the juicy prize of a huge conspiracy. Shep would certainly kill him to squash that possibility, once he had his hands on the cash. Rebel felt his best play would be to lead Shep's men to it, but along the way somehow make a run for it and slip away. Maybe with the money, maybe not.

The lousy forty-five g's that was supposed to be in the package wasn't going to buy him that. Shep Primrose wasn't going to risk harboring him for such a paltry sum. Money like that probably passed through his saloon every few months. But if the cash bundle were in hundreds instead of mostly twenties, that would put the satchel's value more around a quarter of a million. That might get Shep to give him some wiggle room. But would Shep really believe that he had managed so big of a score? He'd find out soon, he thought, as they took the off-ramp for Azalea Estates Lane.

There was a half dozen bikes in the parking lot and their posse would double that. The lunch crowd was gone, and those that remained were Shep's men who would hang out until given orders. A few cars and light trucks were around the side of the old barn away from the road. Rusty beaters all, those vehicles would belong to the saloon staff doing cleanup. Rebel looked up at the square window with the sign that hung in the middle as they entered the gravel lot, and wondered if Shep was watching their approach. Of course, he was watching. Game time, he thought. Green flag.

Rebel struggled to get his wounded leg over the seat, but the guy didn't give him a hard time and held the bike steady. While the other riders dismounted and spread out to an informal perimeter behind him, Rebel made a beeline toward the front doors. Trying to run away on foot, while injured, from six guys was not going to work. He pushed through the doors with chest out and head high.

The man standing at the host stand cocked his head toward the stairway door to Rebel's right. Another thug resting heavily in a chair struggled to his feet and opened the door with a leer. Rebel went through to grasp the handrails on each side, pulling himself up each stair. He heard the door close before he'd made the third step, but he didn't look back. Instead he concentrated his effort to get up each step, exhaling like a weightlifter with each effort.

At the top of the stairs, another guy lounged and shook his head at Rebel's slow advance. He waited until Rebel was within a couple of steps of the top before raising a gloved fist and giving a single sharp rap on Shep's office door without getting up. Rebel stood for a moment at the top, taking a few deep breaths, and the doorman nodded. Rebel twisted the knob and staggered inside. Shep looked over at him from his desk. There was a large dark garbage bag next to his chair, the type used to line metal drums, standing up by everything stuffed inside.

"Sit down before you fall down," said Shep in an eerily calm voice.

Rebel moved back the left chair and plopped down heavily. Sweat dripped from his forehead and temples making the angry red scratches crisscrossing his cheeks burn. His tired shoulders slumped forward and he kept his eyes lowered. He waited for Shep to take the lead noting the revolver next to the knife and a cellphone with blue electrical tape on it. Quite a few seconds went by.

Bambi came out of the bathroom with a damp cloth and a glass of water. Rebel took it, not caring how dirty it was, and wiped away the grime and blood as she sat on the bed. He sucked down the water is a few gulps. Shep regarded him again as he put down the empty glass on the corner of the desk. Rebel continued to hold the rag, rubbing and twisting it in his hands.

"Did you get it?" asked Shep in flat conversational tone. His gaze was unwavering.

"Yes, I got it. Had to stash it. Didn't know who would be around to pick me up. Burt and Ripper, they died in the wreck. I'm sorry," said Rebel.

Shep acknowledged the apology with a shrug, but remained quiet.

"I should cut you in. It's quite a package. My guy, my dealer in Richmond, been behind and just made good. That's why I wanted the extra muscle when I hired Jesse. Need to pay you back for getting me out of the woods."

"If you stashed things, there's no hurry. The money is safe. Let's get you safe. What do you have at your garage that the police would take an interest in?"

Rebel froze. He hadn't considered that before embarking on this endeavor. He didn't think it would come to this.

"There's some papers in my office. Production records of the meth I cooked, supplies on hand so I knew what I could commit to making, accounting of what I had shipped and what I had been paid for. It's not in plain view, but if they tear the place apart they'll find it."

"Go get it. Burn it. You are the primary suspect and the only reason they haven't torn it apart already is that they are working two scenes and only got Bucky the Pig. Hurry."

"I need a ride, Shep. I wrecked my truck."

"Which is why they will be showing at your garage. I'm not sending any of my guys with you. I want to be far away from you and wish you would have taken Burt and Ripper's colors. But I can't move my building. I'm stuck to this spot so you're the one that needs to go away. Outside is a red Ford Ranger truck," Shep opened his middle desk drawer and took out a set of keys and slid them across to him. "Get your papers, and then get the fuck out. There's a thousand dollars in the glove box and the tank is full. Don't come back for your package for at least six months. And don't stop in and see me then, either. Just get back out. I don't need any warrants being served on me. You getting me?"

"Yes, Shep," his hands closed around the keys. "Thank you."

He staggered toward the door while Shep resumed sorting papers from his desk and filing cabinet and discarding into the garbage bag. Going down the stairs was much easier than going up. Both doormen glared at him with narrow eyes and twisted lips, disappointed to see him emerge seemingly in no worse shape than before he went in. Rebel concentrated on getting the longest and quickest stride out of his tortured body, to get back to his garage as soon as he could.

The red Ford Ranger wasn't a bad truck. Older to be sure, but it had recently been washed and there was good tread on the tires. Even the interior was wiped clean, and smelled of Windex. A sealed envelope containing the cash was in the glove box, as well as a signed title with someone's name he'd never heard of before. Rebel brightened somewhat, despite his body aches. It was a much better deal than he'd expected he'd be given. But then he thought about it from Shep's point of view. Cash and truck, maybe $2500 bucks all told, was a cheap way to make a really big potential problem go away and maintain plausible deniability of involvement. It took a couple of cranks to start. He'd work on that later. Purge papers and grab some tools.

Rebel knew he was in a hurry, so he merely slowed for a quick look as he left the parking lot for Azalea to time his exit with a crowded looking blue and white S10 cruising down the interstate off ramp. The driver was slow so Rebel gunned it out in front of him to turn right and east toward Lowland Road. He made one last glance into the rearview as he hit the accelerator. Rebel caught a flicker of movement, like a big arm gesture, from its passenger side and the truck fell in behind him rather than turning into the saloon or garage across the street.

He sped up some, and it kept pace, causing him to study it some more. He ran the stop sign at Thigpen Road and kept going straight. The other driver nearly stopped, but then came on strong to catch up. There were no side streets on rural roads to "box," to go around the block to see if you were being followed. The sun, high in the sky, caused some glare on its windshield but the trees drooping over the road allowed him an occasional glimpse of the occupants. Driving seemed to be a man in a cowboy hat with a wolf sitting next to him. A slightly husky lady leaned against the passenger side door. Rebel raised his foot off the gas and coasted a little, slowing without break lights warning the trailing driver, and letting the Chevy come up on his rear bumper. The next shadow they passed through gave him a clearer view.

"Baylee Ann!" he yelled to himself. "Fuck!"

How did she get out? Buck must already be turning on him. He was the only one who knew. Rebel considered making a run for it now, and not purging his garage. The cops knew it was him already and he was going to have to start a new identity somewhere anyway. So what if they added drug trafficking to the warrant for Rebel Tarwick? It was best to get a head start at slipping away.

But as the immediate panic subsided, Rebel reasoned that Buck turning on him didn't make sense. The deputy didn't want to be ensnarled by the investigation either, and the evidence was going to pass through a lot more hands than just his. Buck must be cleaning up for him, and would want him gone before the technicians crawled all over the place. Just like Shep. And Rebel felt an obligation, with all of Shep's help, to make sure to burn incriminating papers that might point at the Lowland Outlaws before jumping town. And he really wanted his tools anyway. He could make a living with his tools.

Rebel pulled the seatbelt tight, and made a couple of fine mirror adjustments as he leaned back into his racing posture. He alternated giving his palms a final wipe as he grasped the wheel with both hands; the truck was an automatic. Then his right foot stomped it, and the little engine screamed.

The acceleration was painfully slow, the little four cylinder nowhere near the horsepower of the big V-8's of performance vehicles. But racing on rural roads with light trucks wasn't all about quick acceleration when facing off against the same class of vehicle. It was about maintaining speed in the winding turns, and not letting the truck's high center of gravity flip you. He settled his painful hind end deeper into the bench seat, feeling the vibrations and using them to be acutely aware of the truck's roll and balance. Rebel had a gift for that.

His eyes looked far down the road, to the top of every rise which blocked his further vision, occasionally darting for a quick glance at the yellow diamond signs which told him how the pavement would curve. The asphalt immediately under the tires was old news, Rebel using his memory and peripheral vision for the needed tiny adjustments of the steering wheel.

He never checked his speedometer. It was useless to him. It was merely a number. The engine strained, and he kept it straining to its limits when he could, backing off only with the black snaking weaves of the road threatened to flip him. Through each he picked his line, not constrained by the double yellow stripes of staying in his lane, for maximum speed and centrifugal forces just shy of lifting his inside wheels from the pavement. The gap between him and the Chevy rapidly grew.

And kept growing. Within minutes, it had faded from sight. Even in the long straightaways. By the time he reached Lowland Road, he'd given up on thoughts of laying a false trail and doubling back. He turned to the north, on the beeline to his garage, with more focus in the rearview than on the road ahead. Nothing. Not even a flash in the distance of sun off the windshield. He started backing down from the edge of the envelope. Still way over any legal speed, but letting the churning pistons and crankshaft return to the upper limits of the normal operating range. He'd a long way to go and quickly. Pausing to fix a blown head gasket did not fall under the category of quickly.

Shortly thereafter he was in the outer fringes of the imaginary zone he considered his neighborhood. Even with slowing down, there'd been no sign of the pursuit. His mind began shifting toward how to make the stop at his garage in "pit stop precision and efficiency". He'd turn around first to back up to the middle bay. He had to turn around before leaving anyway, and doing it first would save steps loading the heavy tools into the back. He'd also grab one case of oil and radiator fluid in case this truck wasn't all of what he hoped it was. Rebel would then grab a can of something volatile, acetone or some other accelerant and take it back to his office. That'd be the only trip he'd make to grab clothes and such. There was a lighter by his bedroll from when he smoked meth. He'd light the papers on his way out. That would be far quicker than any sorting. Bringing firemen in addition to the cops already on their way to his place had no downside, and maybe an up one if they inadvertently damaged evidence.

His pine trees, showing glimpses of the junkyard, came into view and he braked hard by the mailbox. No use bending a tie rod or a rim going down the washed out driveway too fast. He scanned left and right, looking for anything that was out of place. Something that told him to bolt and run. With Baylee Ann on the loose he knew someone had already been here. A trap was what concerned him now.

When the building itself came into view, the shattered office window and ajar door on the left caught his attention right away. But the building looked dark and quiet, and he aimed for the far right corner to have space to turn around and park backed up to the left bay door. It was when making this turn that he looked over and saw Buck's patrol car. The blue flashing lights came on.

It had been nestled in like a tick, back behind the Gray Ghost and facing the drive. Rebel stopped the truck, askew in front of the bay door, and then slowly put it into park and sat back. The cruiser's door opened, and Buck emerged behind it with a drawn gun. Rebel struck the wheel in frustration. He was too late after all.

CHAPTER—25

Kelton Jager suffered Baylee Ann's complaints, "Your dog can drive better than you!"

The truck Rebel was driving had long vanished from view. Kelton took his foot off the accelerator and coasted, pulling over on the side of the road and wiping his palms on the front of his pants. He was breathing hard, leaning forward to eye the speedometer needle to make sure it hovered at zero, regardless of his booted foot pinning the brake pedal to the floorboard like the throat of a vanquished foe.

"You let him get away? What the hell is wrong with you?" she chided.

He sat back and swallowed, feeling his heart begin to slow, and closed his eyes for a few seconds. Azrael panted next to him in the middle of the bench seat, providing a shield against Baylee Ann's glares of angry disappointment.

"What are you doing? What's the deal?" Baylee Ann pressed him.

"I," paused Kelton trying to find the right words, "don't drive much."

"Well I figured that out. You're not even trying very hard, but then he didn't rape your ass, did he?" she shook her head in disgust.

"I'm not out here for revenge," he snapped back at her. "Dr. Fairborn will send your rape kit away for DNA testing. Mr. Redigan will prosecute. They'll take care of the justice end of things. If I chase after Rebel, all I will do is wreck and Azrael doesn't have a seatbelt.

I'm here to help you find your friend, Bambi. Braxton said she was at the saloon back there. Let's go get her. Make sure she's safe."

Baylee Ann softened, "You're right. Let's go find Bambi." But it was a voice with undertones of scorn, and of the type of disappointment which was used to disappointment.

He put it in drive, carefully counting the three clicks as he moved the selector, and made a methodical three-point turn. Cruising back east toward the saloon and the interstate only took five minutes, much longer than when they'd raced the other direction, which made Kelton wonder that perhaps he had given up the chase too early. But then he shook his head to himself. No way you were going to win that one, buddy. Don't risk your dog lightly, said the old K-9 mantra, and there are many ways to risk your dog. It's hard to admit your limitations, but a man knows what they are and acts accordingly.

The long side of the saloon faced the road, board siding with windows above to let in the south facing light to the old milking stalls. Across the street, a garage bay was open and a man rolled a worn-out tire to join the stack at the side of the building. Kelton turned left into the bar and grill's parking lot and scanned back and forth as they entered. Braxton Greene's name adorned the marquee.

Chrome sparkled in the sun of midafternoon. Black leather fringe fluttered from saddlebags and seat tops. Glossy fuel tanks gleamed with their wax polishes. Even a casual observer would note that it wasn't just a collection of motorcycles parked around the rutted gravel. These were the machines that made these people who they were. And they were proud of who they were.

"You sure about this?" asked Kelton.

"Come on," said Baylee Ann. "These are my people. Just don't touch the patch on the back of anyone's jacket. They consider that disrespect."

"I don't want to touch any part of them. Even with gloves and hand sanitizer," said Kelton rolling his eyes.

"Park over there," she instructed indicating the back of the lot even though there were plenty of spots near the building.

Kelton didn't mind at first. It would give him more of a chance to size things up. He also didn't like leaving his pack in the bed unsecured. Better to park where no one would have a need to go toward the vehicle and avoid the causal passersby to note anything worth taking. But Kelton, a dog trainer, wondered if it was a missed opportunity when it came to body language. Playing by their rules diminished him. It was always best to negotiate from a position of strength. Especially since it was just the three of them. And as Sun Tzu said, make the enemy think you are strong when you are weak.

He turned the wheel hard, gravel coming off the tires.

"Hey, what the hell?" she protested.

He drove right at the front entrance, turning off the ignition in the middle of the main thoroughfare. Anyone entering or exiting, would have to walk around the truck. They piled out. He didn't bother to leash Azrael, relying on the heel instead. Kelton looked up with an expressionless face and noted the dark window above divided by the sign, trying to pierce its depths, but the sun behind the building made it hopeless even with his sunglasses on.

"Shouldn't we leave Azrael in the truck?" she suggested.

He turned toward her, cold at the suggestion, "Not on your life."

He slammed the truck's door. Kelton could smell the tobacco coming from under the added-on porch as figures murmured in its shadow. They looked at him, eyes burrowing into him and his dog, as if they might arise and surround them in a display of intimidation or maybe vengeance. But then they had all heard the story of the bridge and could see the butt of the large automatic with its six-inch barrel and reflex sight swinging easy on his right thigh with every stride. He kept those strides in a steady confident rhythm. And the spoils of that fight walked next to him, putting in a gleeful skip as they approached the door.

Inside, Baylee Ann took the lead as he removed his sunglasses. Kelton eyed the bald guy to his right sitting by the stairwell door adjourned with a black and brass tag reading "Private". It was very much like an old barn, with a hoof worn concrete floor and rough bare timbers. It was a little long and narrow, but the conversion had been tactfully done with a degree of pride akin to the maintenance of the motorcycles outside.

"We want to see Shep," Baylee Ann told the man leaning on the host station, ignoring the weathered lady who'd just picked up a pair of menus.

His round red face began to say something negative, maybe even something unpleasant, but before the words could get out his head cocked to the side at the pair of hard distinct thuds from the ceiling above him.

"Please eat," he said standing up straight, "and I'll come get you when Shep is ready for you."

"Follow me, please," said the hostess who smiled despite her broken teeth. She must have gotten the job because she was too scraggly for anyone to want to pull her into the parking lot for a quickie.

Baylee Ann turned to Kelton, smiled, and swung her arms out in front of herself as she strode ahead after the hostess. Azrael took his cue from Kelton, following wearily and sizing up both the establishment and inside clientele as they made their way to the row of booths on the left. The Outlaw Saloon had the trappings of a legitimate roadside bar and grill if you had the balls to walk in and order something. Décor was dominated by Harley branding or motocross sporting paraphernalia. The lunch rush was over, and there was plenty of room for the dozen lingering patrons to be spread out from each other.

Kelton had figured everyone would go quiet and stare as he made his entrance, but that didn't happen. Customers drinking beer in small groups may not have noticed him. But the servers and the henchmen had to notice. It was their job to notice. And they all pretended a dog coming in was perfectly normal, and that the figure in coyote brown fatigues and a floppy hat was dressed in an acceptable equivalent to denim and black leather. Kelton decided to play upon that a little.

When they reached the empty booth, Kelton let Azrael climb onto the bench before him and sit down at his side. He put his menu down in front of the dog.

"We'll need one more," he said flatly, like he was pointing out that the hostess was too dumb to count.

She scurried back toward the hostess station.

"So, you can be a jerk," Baylee Ann smiled.

Azrael leaned his nose in slightly over the table at her.

"If there's three of us, she should have brought three menus. What type of places do you and Bambi hang out in, anyway?" he said with a wink.

Then she got serious, "Shep is no one to be trifled with. He's spent his entire life ruling over guys like these. Don't show weakness. But know that you won't be able to intimidate him. Make a straight up deal. And keep it. That's your best bet.'"

"Okay, what can I get you people?" croaked the waitress. She was squat thing, who's widening hips had turned a once toothpick figure into more of a square. Her lungs rumbled as she breathed after a lifetime of cigarettes. The hostess came running up behind her with the third menu and Kelton took it. The tabletop looked grease stained, but at least the service so far was quick. They ordered cheeseburgers, and Baylee Ann seemed happy, like a princess returned to court.

"Is this place normally like this?" asked Kelton. "I mean is this usually how you are treated here?"

Baylee Ann almost sang out with a glow of warmth rising in her eyes, before her face iced over and she considered.

"No. This is how I always wanted to be treated," she replied in careful measured words. "But usually it's more like the cafeteria in middle school."

"How do you mean?"

She shrugged, "There are cliques. They jockey for respect and dominance, trying to gain favor with Shep for the best jobs. The bottom cliques pick on isolated new people, forcing them to find and join a group or go away."

"You mean Shep's men?"

"Yeah, the Outlaws. The Lowland Outlaws. Everyone else always keeps their eyes from wandering to other people's business. And if you try and come in with another patch, Shep's men are quick to approach and suggest you take it off."

"Any idea why we aren't being picked on? Why no one is trying to prove themselves by knocking off the guy who killed five of them less than a week ago? Who continue to ignore and treat as normal a dog eating at the dinner table?"

Baylee Ann's lively energy extinguished and her shoulders sagged as her face became solemn. Then their food came, and she applied ketchup liberally over her fries. Kelton sliced a patty into pieces and fed them one at a time to his dog using his fork. Azrael bit gently to avoid rasping his teeth on the steel.

"Shep must have told everyone to chill out. Why would he do that?" she reasoned.

"He's worried about something. I'd guess things aren't going his way right now. But you know him, know this culture. I don't."

"Well, I guess we'll know real soon," she said, indicating with a toss of her chin that the man with the red round face was weaving through the tables toward them.

The lackey approached their table with a commanded stride and announced, "Shep will see you now."

Baylee Ann began to rise, but Kelton held her in place with, "I'm still enjoying my fries."

The man stuttered with eyes flashing wide. Through the tensing shoulders and bulging veins, physical violence was clearly his default response to disobedience or insolence. But with that option not available to him, he seemed at a loss. His eyes fell, and feet shuffled side to side, as he did some heavy thinking. Then he raised his arm with a pointed finger inches from Kelton's face.

"I said now, AGhhh!"

Azrael had leaped from his seat over the table like a lightning bolt, exploding off of compressed haunches that could easily spring him over a six-foot fence. He took the arm deep into his mouth before clamping down with his crushing rear molars, fangs effortlessly penetrating the thin soft leather. The thug had put some force into his pointing gesture, an over commitment of balance for the sake of emphasis, that hadn't considered the addition of a fast moving seventy-five pounds suddenly clamping on to his extremity. His rigid arm became a lever, and Azrael's momentum easily spun him to the ground with red flowing streaks gushing from the dog's muzzle down his sleeve.

"Get him off me! Get him off me!" he cried as Azrael splayed his feet and shook his head wildly without relenting in his jaw's vicelike grip.

Kelton slowly stood as others came rushing up, but they stopped short not wanting to suffer the same fate and formed a semi-circle around the row of booths some eight feet away. Baylee Ann partially stood in her seat to get a good view, but stayed back from the action. The thug slapped at the dog with his free hand, but had no leverage flailing about on the floor to get his bodyweight into the blows. All he managed to do was knock over some chairs at adjacent tables. Azrael easily jerked side to side, never softening with his teeth and keeping up a lively growl. He'd been conditioned to that, dodging and taking soft whacks with a bamboo stick in training, while holding his grip on a bite sleeve.

"Aus," said Kelton in a normal tone of voice. Sounded like Ows. Out. Drop it. Let go.

Azrael released and ran to take a heel position at Kelton's side. The dog's black mask and face didn't show much gore, but there was no mistaking the red splatter on the tan colored hairs of the side of his head and neck. He also panted in happy contentment, with eyes that begged to have another go.

The man gripped his savaged arm, blood oozing between the weathered fingers and soaking the torn fabric of his shirt.

"Motherfucker!" he cried, the voice much too high pitched in crying suffering to have any threatening credibility while writhing on the floor. Two of the Lowland Outlaws reached down to help him up. The other witnesses, three people deep as patrons, staff, and Shep's henchmen mixed together, whispered to themselves.

"That's enough of that crap. You people go back to what you were doing," it was an edgy voice, with a hint of disappointment in it, that bellowed down from a balcony above the entrance. A tall figure there, leaning heavily on the half wall with his palms gazed down on the scene with disgust on his face. He caught Kelton's eye.

"You two get up here. With the damn dog," he clarified before turning his back and stepping into the mezzanine office. The shutters closed.

Baylee Ann jumped to her feet, while Kelton reached over toward his plate and crammed his fries into his mouth and raising a finger in a "wait a moment" gesture at a couple of other patch wearers that ventured a few steps closer. They looked at each other briefly with their best "this guy has got to be kidding" looks while Kelton washed his mouthful down and wiped his greasy fingers on a paper napkin. Then Kelton made a lead the way gesture with his hand, and followed them with Azrael and Baylee Ann right behind. He didn't bother paying.

"Up the stairs," one instructed while holding open the door marked "Private".

The steps were narrow, so Kelton kept to the outside of the circle where they were the widest with his eyes scanning above. Baylee Ann huffed after below. The upstairs doorman rose as Azrael's bloody face came into view heeling alongside Kelton and he made his single rap on Shep's office door and stepped to the side pressed up against the wall. Kelton went straight in, not waiting for the man to nod. Shep stood by his desk chair.

"Bambi!" Baylee Ann rushed passed Kelton toward the small blond woman sitting on the bed in the corner. They grappled with each other, voices spewing simultaneous mutterings and whispers before Shep snapped at them in irritation.

"Shup up, Bitches," turning back toward Kelton and his dog. "You can sit."

"I'm not sure I want to," said Kelton staying where he was with Azrael sitting at his side.

Shep's desk was a mess of papers, cups, cellphones, a wadded up rag and a knife stabbed into the top.

The same couple of riders who led them from the dining room below came in the door and stood easy on either side of it. The doorman in the hallway reached in to grasp the knob and pull it shut with shuffling steps. The pair were younger guys, who's stomachs hadn't yet surrendered to years of beer, fatty foods and sitting. The taller one had stubbly cheeks that were red along the jaw line from periodic hacking away with cheap razors.

"You're not the type of person who frequents my establishment. What the hell are you doing here?" demanded Shep.

"I've come for Bambi," replied Kelton simply.

The girls looked up from where they were sitting on the bed, arms wrapped about each other.

"She's not yours. She's mine," Shep stated with raised chin.

"She's her own. Who can come and go as she pleases," declared Kelton with a slight headshake.

"No, she has a debt to work off for the two men I lost," he smiled. "Unless you pay it for her?"

"I'm not so inclined. And your men don't want to fight me again."

The cocking pistol made Kelton's head jerk around. The thug held it, not three yards away. Kelton's hand hovered over his pistol, but again he heard the old policeman's words in his head about how you can't outdraw an already drawn gun. Azrael omitted a soft growl and Shep held up his hand to his men.

"I don't want to fight you. But if I do, you die here. Maybe a lot of us die here. And absolutely no one will come looking. Lowland County doesn't have a whole lot of caring, and they aren't going to spend it on us."

"Then what do you recommend?" said Kelton, not taking his eye off the man with the revolver. He weighed his chances. It was a snubby, with a small site radius, and he held it one handed leaning into it off balanced. Clearly, he wasn't a shooter. A leap to the side and he may very well miss, even at that close range. Even if he hit, it was a small caliber. Maybe a .32 Smith and Wesson. But what concerned him more was Baylee Ann and Bambi sitting behind him in the cone of fire.

"A man named Rebel Tarwick lost a package running away from Bucky in the woods. I picked him up, and rescued his sad self, but I care more about that package than I do about him. I'll have my boys take you to where I picked him up. Find the package he stashed and bring it back to me, and I'll let the girls go where they want to go."

"What's in it? How big is it?"

"It's cash money. Drug money, belonging to no one legitimate. It's a sealed plastic pouch, and weighs about five pounds. Tear the pouch, and the deal is off."

Kelton looked over at where the girls huddled together. Bambi's eyes shivered under her bangs, but Baylee Ann gave him a slight nod, and he turned back toward Shep.

"And how do I know you will keep up your end?" challenged Kelton.

"When you come back for the swap, I'll let the girls go first," Shep smiled and sat down.

"Okay then, deal. But I need a scent item of this Rebel guy for the dog."

CHAPTER—26

Braxton Greene drove his truck, following a pair of Lowland Outlaws on their choppers up Thigpen Road, while Baylee Ann rode shotgun. In the bed of the truck sat Kelton Jager with his back against the cab and left arm tightly about his dog. Azrael sat beside him, turning his nose into the rushing wind to enjoy the smells and the visual sensation of rapidly moving scenery.

The ride gave Kelton a chance to suffer buyer's remorse over the deal. A deal made him involved, and Shep Primrose was not someone he wished to be involved with. The easiest solution would be to just track to the bag of cash, scoop it up, and run away. Or just wander away. He'd been wanting to leave this town for a few days and had no need for a bundle of cash. His account held plenty for his immediate needs after four years of combat pay and no real way to have spent it during his tours. But when he saw Bambi's trembling eyes under her gold bangs, and how small and vulnerable she looked embracing Baylee Ann, he couldn't stand it.

The road had many gentle ups and downs over creeks and snaking turns about little hills since engineers of long ago had lacked the budget to force a straight line upon mother nature. Trees were thick on both sides, testifying to the rural remoteness. Kelton began to worry about how much light there was left in the day to perform the task at hand, but the truck began to slow and he looked over his shoulder so he could see up the road. The bikers had drifted over to the oncoming shoulder and were now going slow enough to use their feet on the ground to keep their balance. Braxton had slowed in kind to maintain his trailing position without venturing from his lane. Then they stopped all together.

One of the bikers dismounted and dropped his kickstand before walking over to the truck. He didn't bother to stop at Braxton Greene's window, coming straight around to the bed. They hadn't been introduced, so Kelton thought of the guy with the stubble and razor burn as Rash.

"We picked up Rebel just up here. I'll show you exactly where," Rash yelled, hard to understand over the other bike's roaring engine.

"Okay," said Kelton with a thumb's up gesture and used the pipe rack to climb over the side of the truck.

Azrael opted to leap, irritating Kelton who worried about him developing arthritis in his shoulders in future years. Then the other biker finally shut down, and things were quiet enough to talk without raised voices. This guy was a little shorter and stockier, so Kelton dubbed him Squat. Kelton took the time to turn toward Braxton while Azrael raised his leg on a nearby pine.

"Have a good set tonight. Thanks for the ride," he wished him.

Braxton nodded back and after a quick sideways glance added in a whisper, "Don't trust these guys."

"Good luck, Kelton," waved Baylee Ann, leaning forward to smile at him around Braxton. She still wore the same jeans, but the pink Browning shirt had been replaced with a black Harley tank top. They began to turn around. Moments later they were heading back south toward St. Albans. He watched them go, and saw Baylee Ann shifting more toward the middle of the front seat.

"Hey, Dog-Boy. We going to do this, or what?" chided Squat.

"Yeah, I'm coming. How do you know this is the spot?"

"He came out by that fallen tree over there," he gestured at the dull weathered trunk choked in vines.

Kelton put Azrael on a tracking lead, essentially a super long leash to allow the dog the freedom to work ahead and side to side without control being lost, and then walked over to the tree while staying on the pavement. The roadside weeds and brush had clearly been recently disturbed, and Kelton even noted a small circle of dried blood on a piece of gravel.

"We'll follow you," said Rash. The kid with the razor burn kept his right hand in his jacket pocket, probably tight on the small revolver he'd brandished back in Shep's office.

They made no attempt to hide their bikes, and left their helmets on the seats. Kelton reckoned they didn't care about their brains so much, but rather being hassled by the State Police. Kelton noted they were leaving their heavy leather chaps on. He figured they weren't expecting a very long trip into the woods, or were really concerned about briars and poison ivy.

Kelton kneeled by Azrael, and put on his doggles and mutt-muffs.

"Ain't you making it harder for him to track?" asked Squat.

"It uses its nose to track, dumb ass," said Rash.

Kelton interjected in a helpful explanatory tone, "Covering the eyes and ears to limit those senses helps the dog concentrate more on its nose."

Kelton nodded his head for positive emphasis, trying to cover up that he expected gunfire in the near future.

"That's cool. Let's find the money," said Squat while Rash pretended he'd known this technique all along.

Because people smell better too when they cover their eyes, right? Not the brightest bulb? Not the sharpest tool? Kelton thought it might be fun to google a list of ways to express stupid the next time things were slow.

Kelton took the wash rag from his hip pocket. A plastic bag would have been better, but it looked to be a pretty solid scent article. He turned, so that when he kneeled to let Azrael sniff the article, his left side was to the bikers. This allowed him to unfasten the retaining strap on his holster without being noticed.

"Such," commanded Kelton, and Azrael's nose went to ground, circling and darting back and forth a couple of times. It sounded like "Zook" and meant search. The dog trotted into the woods, the long tracking lead playing out before him. It was an easy trail, with time enough for the scent to evaporate and be readily detected, yet shaded in the woods against boiling off. Which meant Azrael moved out quickly. The line was only half played out from the coil in his hand when Kelton bolted forward to disappear into the brush.

"Wait for us," scolded Rash who'd been watching the loops of leash and was taken by surprise.

The two bikers sounded like elephants breaking branches as they lumbered forward clumsily in their heavy boots and leathers. Kelton wondered what their instructions were. Clearly, they had been detailed as he watched their briefing from the truck back at the Outlaw Saloon's parking lot before driving to Braxton Greene's. Shep was too far away to be heard, but his hand gestures in front of the entire crew displayed passion. There'd been some questions as well. Kelton guessed there was a couple of possibilities.

First, was shoot him in the back after he found the money. It would be easy to do with them behind him. His body might be there for a few months, or longer since no one would be looking for him. The best chance for discovery wouldn't be until hunting season in the fall.

Second, was the possibility Shep might not be that attached to the cash after all, or at least not need him for it. If he'd picked up that Rebel guy they were now backtracking, then couldn't he lead them back to the cash? Which meant these boys might move on him as soon as they were off the road. Not worrying about their bikes and keeping on the heavy legwear seemed to lean toward that possibility. This could be Shep's simple way to eliminate him without a messy gunfight in his establishment. Which is why Kelton had suddenly sprinted off the starting blocks, after putting them asleep with slowly letting out the line then rushing forward while many coils were still in hand.

Kelton didn't try and outrun them right away. They would quit chasing too near the road, and rapidly find themselves back to Shep. That wouldn't help him rescue the two women. Instead he opted for a lively pace, that kept him too far in front to set up the sure shot in the back that Rash likely wanted, but one where they wouldn't lose him and return to their bikes.

"Come on guys, keep up!" he encouraged them.

Rash and Squat, smokers and dressed in heavy leggings, were taxed by Kelton's lively pace. While not at all hot, especially compared to the southern summer months that would follow, it was humid in the woods. That kind of thick humidity built from moist shaded soil which never dries out or is carried away on a breeze, that spikes with the approach of evening and the fading sun. Air so saturated, it surrounded them all like a sheet of plastic so that their perspiration couldn't evaporate. Not a quarter of an hour passed, and the bikers were both red faced, heaving and dehydrated. It ground them to a doubled-over halt and a plea for mercy.

"Wait up a bit," yelled Squat.

"Motherfucker," said Rash in a low gasping voice.

Kelton noted the lack of crackling branches and knew they had slowed or stopped. In truth, behind him was where his attention was focused. It was an easy trail, and he didn't need to help Azrael do his thing. And finding the money was secondary to him to being back in control.

"Come on you two. The dog's almost there. His nose is down on the ground," encouraged Kelton.

Which really only meant that Azrael was tracking with full attention. Kelton had no idea how long the trail would go. But the words spurred the exhausted men to action again to rob them of the last of their energy reserves. The sound of breaking twigs and roaring breaths resumed behind him. Then Kelton heard voices to the front.

"Platz," he whispered and Azrael went flat to his tummy. Kelton kneeled beside him and peered forward. Azrael's body went rigid as his nose stretched out, and then Kelton saw them too. A pair of men approaching. He lay still with his dog, trying to see and hear more. He wanted to call out to the guys behind to freeze, but worried he would be overheard by the strangers ahead.

Instead he began to stealthily crawl around to the right, relying on his brown clothes to blend into the forest floor. The bikers stumbled forward hurriedly, worried they might have lost him. They weren't looking down for him, but rather their eyes were up and straining ahead. They didn't pause to listen, and couldn't hear much over the sound of themselves rattling branches and snapping twigs. The two groups of men were on a collision course. Kelton silently drew his gun, and then slipped on his own electronic ear muffs. He had time. It wasn't urgent to shoot.

But shoot someone did. Kelton thought it might have been Rash, but wasn't sure. Electronic ear muffs block damaging noise, and amplify small sounds, but don't give the user much of an audible sense of direction. He continued lying flat, scanning back and forth trying to catch a glimpse of legs to locate everyone and make sense of the situation.

A louder gun, perhaps a .357 magnum, replied to the initial shot. There was yelling, and then several quick shots from an automatic. Kelton slipped off his pack and rolled over to a stouter tree. He took one last scan at ground level, but couldn't see much in the undergrowth. He rose to a kneeling position, using the tree for cover as he extended the Glock, while Azrael maintained his last command of down. Not seeing much again, he stood, still using the tree for cover and holding his gun at the ready.

There were four of them, including the two bikers, and all were gophering. They would pop up above the brush, fire a shot, and then duck back down only to do it again a few seconds later. Kelton decided to concentrate on the unknown new comers, staying up in a steady shooting position and hovering the glowing green triangle of his reflex sight where one of them had been popping up. He was rewarded a couple of seconds later, pulling the trigger smoothly, and watched the figure jerk backward as he fell.

Before the gun came down out of recoil, he was already pivoting toward the second man who rose to run. Kelton placed the triangle on the target's back and pressed the trigger again, sending him tumbling forward. Just as quickly, in the time it took him to let his trigger finger forward so the sear reset, he brought the gun back to the left.

The bikers rose in a victory roar, charging forward with their guns spewing a celebratory volley over where the opposition had been. Squat ran his .380 auto dry, spraying rounds in his excitement until the slide locked back. Rash canted his wrist as the revolver's hammer fell without the recoil of a report. Kelton instantly shot Squat, and then Rash a fifth of a second later. The woods were suddenly eerily quiet, the thick blueish smoke wafting in the thick air. Kelton's gun still held eleven rounds, but he used the pause to change to a fresh magazine anyway while still behind the cover of the large tree.

He continued to wait but heard nothing but the bugs, resuming their spring songs after being stunned into silence by the gunfire. There must be a marshy stream nearby thought Kelton. He reached down and removed the tracking lead, but decided to leave Azrael there and make his way around to the unknowns to the right first. The first man, wearing overalls and who had tried to run for it, had been hit between the shoulder blades. Kelton rolled him over and saw the bloody stomach on the oil stained denim. The man's nose was swollen, and his face was covered in small scratches. Red streaks trickled from his bearded mouth and his eyes were glassy. He didn't seem to have a gun, or at least not that Kelton saw.

The second was dressed in ill-fitting navy dungarees, also stained, with a white circle name patch on the front reading "Rebel." But the man wasn't Rebel, for the simple reason he was Buck Garner. Buck lay on his back, hand above the oddly cocked head holding his service revolver. The Glock's 10mm bullet had torn into the voice box area before ripping out the side of the neck, puncturing cardioid and juggler, letting his vitality empty. His protective vest would have barely come up high enough to help him, but whether it was trying to make the change of clothes work or he had been concerned about the uncomfortable hike ahead, Buck had made the ill-fated decision to leave standard police equipment behind.

Of the bikers, Rash was also gone from a round that entered below his sternum and deflected enough to miss the spine as it exited his back. Squat however lay paralyzed, with eyes following Kelton's cautious approach. The man's bloody chest quivered in rapid micro breaths. Squat's automatic, slide locked back on the empty magazine's follower, lay upon the mat of brown leaves nearby. Clutched tightly in his left hand was a second magazine, fresh rounds that had been awaiting their turn.

"Can you speak?" demanded Kelton.

The man's lips trembled slightly but there was nothing but a soft whistling sound. Kelton holstered and rolled him on to his right shoulder by lifting his left. There was no exit wound evident. He let him go, Squat collapsing onto his back again with a thud. Kelton walked back to his dog, removed doggles and muffs, and lay down with elevated feet to consider things. Azrael put his paws on his chest.

In the quarter hour it took for the shakes to rattle him about and his body begin to recover, it was rapidly growing dark. The temperature was beginning to drop, too. It put pressure on him to decide. To call or not call. To try and stay legitimate and explain oneself, or to slip away with no one realizing he was here.

He couldn't call. Kelton was no innocent this time. This hadn't been self-defense, but a fight he could have easily retreated from. A fight, not to prevent harm to himself, but over a bundle of cash. And that meant trying to cover up that he'd ever been here. And he had a cellphone in his pocket. It was currently off, but that didn't mean Apple didn't know he was here. Hopefully no one would suspect him enough to ask the question.

Kelton decided to try and find his brass first. He took out the marosnacks so Azrael knew he was really serious. Then he stood where he had shot from, which wasn't hard to find since he'd lay down there when he returned to his dog. He un-holstered his pistol, locked the slide to the rear and presented the ejection port to the shepherd's nose.

"Such," he said, watching with his tactical flashlight on its low setting.

Azrael started sniffing about, but there was no trail to pick up. When he strayed beyond the reasonable ejection distance, Kelton encouraged him back in. After a few minutes, Azrael looked at him with narrow eyes and a single ear cocked back.

"Yeah this is for real. Find it," he encouraged, "closer to me. Good boy,"

Then his dog lay down. Kelton stepped forward, really just three long strides, and under the glow of the tactical light was a shiny brass 10mm Auto casing.

"Yes!" he proclaimed and promptly forked over two of the snacks.

It took twenty minutes to find two more, but the fourth and final casing eluded them. After an hour, his dog was tired and losing interest. Maybe it landed up high in the nook of a tree branch, thought Kelton. Maybe he'd accidentally stepped on it when he went to examine the bodies, pushing it deep into the forest floor. There was no telling. His only hope was that if he couldn't find it, that no one else did either. But their search would be hours long, in the daylight, with many people. It didn't leave him with a good feeling.

The other task was much more unpleasant, but also had to be done. His bullet was in Squat somewhere. He didn't have an exit wound like the others. Rigor would be starting soon, so he needed to get to it. Kelton pulled off the jacket and then turned him over and lifted up the shirt to examine Squat's back along the spine and opposite the entry wound. It wasn't too hard to find, a protrusion just off of center. He dug in with his knife, flaying the shattered vertebrae to free the jacketed bullet. Arteries along the spine, severed from his effort, seeped blood. There was no doubt in his mind he'd gotten it everywhere, even without the man's heart pumping to spray it.

He considered replacing the man's jacket, and then decided to take it with instead. His hands were covered in blood. He might leave a finger print that survived the elements for several days, or longer if his skin secretions scorched some pattern into the leather. No forensic examiner would likely overlook the body had been tampered with. The best he could do was put him back like he had died, and hope Mother Nature was his friend.

Which left the money. Decision time again, Kelton Jager. Are you going or staying? The money had to be close, else they wouldn't have converged upon each other. With a deputy sheriff missing, a search would be mounted soon. And when the bodies were discovered, they would comb the area in meticulous precision and find the cash too. It would provide plenty of motive, a motive that he wasn't attached to like Shep, Rebel and Buck.

But Baylee Ann and Bambi were hostage. Or were they, really? This was the life they chose. Or was it? Remember those trembling eyes, Kelton, he told himself. They were weak and to be protected. Kelton didn't know how that would all go down when he returned to Shep. But somehow, someway, the cash would be a factor.

"Azrael," he said holding out the rag again with his bloody hands, "such."

Azrael was dutiful, although Kelton could tell he'd had his fill of nose work for the day. They had one false start, when Azrael ran over toward Rebel's body. After this, Kelton took him back to their trail coming in, having to put his tactical light on high to do so. But they found success, Azrael tracking to a fallen Birch tree which had been taken down by a storm. Under the root ball, covered superficially with leaves was the plastic bundle.

"Good job, Buddy. We better get the hell out of here."

CHAPTER—27

Shep Primrose fretted at his chipped up desk, staring at the burner and willing it to ring. He gripped the knife, and let go again not wanting to do further damage to the furniture. What had started as a macho nervous habit had become destructive. His instructions to his crew had been specific: if Dog-Boy wanted to run off, with or without the money, to let him go. Other than a chance at a bundle of cash, there was nothing to be gained from him sticking around. There was a chance, Shep had told them, that Rebel would return. If there was a fight between Dog-Boy and Rebel over the cash, don't take sides and run away. If Rebel won, he was leaving. If Dog-Boy won, he might leave after being in another shooting. And in all those cases, he should have heard back from his boys by now.

"Stop worrying. It will work out fine," advised Baylee Ann from the bed in the corner, where she lay on her side holding a sheet over her naked form. Bambi was downstairs helping out in the kitchen again.

It was possible, Shep supposed without conviction, that his boys had done in Dog-Boy when the money was found and took off themselves. It wasn't enough cash for Shep to want to risk his establishment by having to go on the run, or gain the unwanted attention of various health and safety authorities that could cripple his side business if government investigators of any sort wound up asking questions on his doorstep. But it would be a lot of money to a pair of younger guys, a big score worth betraying allegiance for and driving off for new adventures. And frankly, if that's what happened, Shep was perfectly okay with that too. He began to relax, slouching in his chair and stole a glance toward Baylee Ann in acknowledgment that she was right.

In the corner of his eye, he saw the headlights on the off ramp out his office window. Not bike headlights, but a car. That wasn't unheard of, but it definitely wasn't normal. It certainly wasn't one of the garage wreckers or a farm truck. Sometimes, even though there were no blue services signs on the interstate, a driver looking to turn around would spot them and consider stopping in even though they didn't belong. In those cases, his men would gently but assertively suggest to the driver that he would have a better experience up the road at Ed's or to wait until in North Carolina. He rose from his chair and walked over to the metal plated light switch by the stairs.

"Who's that?" said Baylee Ann getting up and peering out over the parking lot. She didn't bother to take the sheet with her.

He turned off the lights so the reflection didn't interfere with their observations and joined her at the window. There weren't many cars that came down Azalea Estates Lane, especially this direction at this time of night. But then Shep remembered he'd seen the same car at about the same time yesterday evening. Perhaps someone new had moved into the area or had found a new job and this would be their routine. He was turning away from the window when he saw the car actually turn in to his parking lot.

"Did someone hitch a ride to do laundry or some shopping?" asked Shep.

Baylee Ann crouched lower at the window, her nose leaving a smudge on the glass like a kid outside a toy store window. But despite the intensive peering, the darkness and on-coming lights didn't allow them to see any more than it was a dark colored four-door sedan. It circled once, and then retreated turning right to the east. This in itself was peculiar, as someone pulling in to turn around would have turned left to head back the way they'd come.

"Did someone just try and check us out?" asked Baylee Ann excitedly with a sly smile.

It annoyed him that she was turning on the charm so thick, like she could care less whether that Kelton character returned for her and Bambi or not. That she wanted him to confide in her, like she was a partner to his enterprises. But he was under no illusions. She wanted to be taken care of, and her loyalty would rapidly shift to any who was willing to do it. And no one wanted to take care of her for more than a few days at a time. Including him. It was time to trade them both to the next band passing through with their own pair of bitches to trade. He would even throw in some drugs.

"Why don't you go give Bambi a hand? I've some paperwork to look over," he shrugged.

Her shoulders and smiling cheeks fell in unison and she rubbed her tongue over the front of her teeth with a closed mouth. But then she found her jeans and new shirt and dressed quickly. She then walked gracefully to the door, the stout timbers of the floor thudding sharply with each step of her shoe's heels. After the door closed he opened the inside shutters and walked out to his perch over the floor below. A moment later Baylee Ann sauntered below him toward the kitchen, her voice lost in the murmurs of the crowd. He noted a mud dauber wasp working hard on a new nest on one of the rafters, too far away for him to squash without venturing out onto the timbers.

It wasn't a bad crowd, a mix of transient bikers and his own, buying burgers and beer from the company store. He was proud of how the business had developed over the years, even if it wasn't real. It allowed him to play at being real. It gave a rallying point for his gang. It allowed him to pretend that he could have been a business man. But it was the money from moving drugs and cash up the interstate that kept them going. Someday though, he'd like to go completely legit.

And if the law abiding came sniffing around, things would rapidly fall apart. There was no business license, or license for selling beer. There wasn't any health certificate, or fire inspection. His grill and bar had no certifications or inspections of any kind. They didn't pay business taxes, paid no employment taxes for their waitresses, cook, and dishwashers. With employment of some real dedicated staff to help out, things had grown too far from a local biker clubhouse to stay under the radar much longer. At least he'd purged incriminating papers, but he would still be in for a thrashing if the authorities poured over him.

But he couldn't lay low and still keep control over his men. Two were missing and they would want to go out and search. Loyalty had to be paid for in this way. Shep really felt the most likely explanation was they'd ran off with the money. But that meant Rattler, their crew leader, would have to admit their disloyalty, and that wasn't going to happen. So they'd sortie out again, and hopefully nothing would happen, or none of the knuckleheads would do something stupid that would drag him down.

He heard a phone ringing in his office and turned toward his desk with relief. They were a little late, but that was okay. He heard the phone again, but his desk was dark. Shep stumbled over to the side of the room again and groped for the light switch. He felt the cold metallic tubing housing the wires first, and followed it down to the switch. Again the phone range, but the burner on his desk lay still with no lights or vibration. His eyes then widened suddenly and Shep leapt for the upper right drawer. Inside, the phone with the green tape buzzed again. He ripped off the tape and flipped it open, hoping it hadn't gone to voice mail.

"Yes, I'm here," he said into it in a harsh desperate whisper.

The other voice started with an annoyed edge which calmed as the words came, "I must have the satchel you told me about that was in Sheriff Fouche's car."

"I don't have it. But I gave Rebel the red truck like you asked to help him get away."

"And the truck hasn't moved in hours. He didn't leave town. I know that from the GPS I put on it and from putting my own eyes on it. He never came out of the woods from his little stop.

That means this case eventually gets solved and Fouche looks like a hero. You don't want that, as he's got it bad for your people. He's coming for you eventually if you give me nothing to undermine him. Something that will make him look corrupt."

Shep thought hard a second.

"If I don't have the package, I don't have the package. But there might be another way to make him look bad besides being corrupt. What about some general mayhem? Like he's lost control of any sense of law and order? People afraid to go outside type of thing? If we can't make him corrupt, can we make him incompetent?"

There was a long pause on the other end, and Shep felt he might had gone too far. But then the voice came back, "If it goes far enough to make state or national news, everything will be scrutinized in the resulting backlash. There will be no place to hide. And that red truck was one I'd been keeping for you."

"Okay, I understand. I know where I picked up Rebel. I'll send my boys to troll around there for a bit," fibbed Shep. "If after a few hours, I haven't come up with him or the money, we'll do some small stuff."

Shep saw no reason to tell him everything.

"Keep it to bashing some mailboxes and starting a couple of dumpster fires. Maybe some bricks through some business owner's front windows. No one gets hurt and no serious property damage. Just enough to get everyone talking. I'd recommend making a list of what you will do, and assigning specific individual instructions to each man on what he is to do so you stay in control instead of your thugs freelancing. It will be far better to under do it, and do it again in a few days, than to overdo it. Understand?"

Shep swallowed, "I understand."

"Go purple," the voice said and hung up.

Shep first used the desk knife to pop the green marked phone apart and break its sim card in two like he'd been instructed. He'd send one of his guys with it, a paper sack, and a large rock to throw it off the bridge into the river. A plastic bag might float and wash up somewhere. It was beginning to be routine. Then Shep opened the side drawer again, pushed aside the orange, white and pink to grab a burner marked in purple electrical tape that had slipped under his county map. He plugged it in to begin charging.

There was a lot to do because he didn't want to be going to jail for murder and desertion from decades ago. He'd been a different person then, young and fit with an unchecked temper. He'd been fresh out of air force basic training and starting vehicle mechanic school at Sheppard Air Force Base, only to end up in a lethal bar fight. That young man didn't exist anymore, and Shep sure as hell didn't want to be the one to now pay for his sins. But it's what the man on the phone held over his head since the day the cardboard box full of twenty-dollar disposable phones had showed up UPS with one ringing inside shortly after.

He considered taking off, but he was too old to want to be bumming on the open road again. All his money was wrapped up in the barn. It had been his attempt to settle down. Kind of a drug runner retirement plan. Something to transition to so he wasn't always looking over his shoulder or playing tribal politics to stay ahead of his band of savages. Getting the property had taken all his saving from working in garages and running drugs, and he'd hopefully awaited the area's development to make a killing flipping it. He was still waiting. He'd stopped saving money, investing funds into the building instead hoping to go legitimate. And there wasn't a sucker to quickly pass it off on before fleeing out west. If you can't run, you hide he thought.

"Jingles!" he called.

The door opened and Shep looked at the bandage on the man's arm spanning from wrist to elbow. It was thick enough he couldn't pull the sleeve of his jacket over it, so he'd cut them away into a vest so he wouldn't have to forgo showing the patch. His eyes were determined and he walked holding himself upright. Telling them to hide colors was not going to be popular.

"Tell Rattler to get the other chiefs up here," he ordered.

Jingles nodded and closed the door again.

Rattler understood Jingles was conveying his instructions and would act accordingly. Shard and Frog would see Jingles as merely Jingles and give him a hard time. That was a conversation for another time. But no one fucked with Rattler more than once. It took a few minutes, but the three of them made it to his office with beer on their breath and no inhibitions about a belch or a fart. Shep stared them down until they settled and were ready to pay attention. He didn't want to have to hash through things any more times than necessary.

"We got boys missing, and we got to go look for them. That's the code," began Shep.

The three of them nodded. Shard tried to discretely pick something in his nose while still making eye contact.

"But we also got a lot of heat. So we need to do some things different."

Frog shook his head, "We can make barbeque of Bucky the Pig," he bragged with a snigger.

Shard smiled and Rattler gave a slow nod to show he agreed with the sentiment.

"No. Not this time. Another time. We've pushed them too hard and we don't want the state police or the DEA wiping us out. We need to back off a little. Just a little. This fight is about the long haul, so for now we got to lay low. The Lowland Outlaws are going to win the war, even if we avoid a battle now and then.

But there are things we need to do like check on our boys. So when we go out, go out in pairs. No big groups, to get the county all stirred up. And," he said with a deeper breath than he had intended, "have the guys turn their jackets inside out."

Rattler leaned forward, the muscles around his jaw suddenly slack in confusion, while the others made stone hard fists.

"We ain't scared," said Shard.

You also have nothing to lose, thought Shep. But he played it the other way, "You look like a scared pussy to me. Not man enough to stand on your own? Not so tough without being surrounded by your big brothers?"

Shard and Frog bristled, while Rattler picked at his teeth with a dirty fingernail, and freed a piece of gristle. Deciding it was too big to flick away, he licked it from his finger and swallowed. Then Rattler spoke.

"Shep wants us to hide the colors," said Rattler in a matter of fact tone, "then we hide the colors."

Both Rattler's arms came up and with a flick of his hands harshly tapped them both on the back of the head.

"Think of it as a special operation," said Shep.

Shep knew that the macho image would play well with their pride and help them to get over going incognito.

"There's three things we need to do tonight, and we need every rider we have with the colors hidden. And not just hidden, but only two guys riding together at a time. Don't let everyone leave and come back at the same time either or they'll bunch up out there and seem like a gang again. That's what we're trying to avoid.

First, we got to go check up on Rattler's boys. I've a bad feeling about them cause no one's called. But we'll check where they picked up Rebel, and run some local roads around there in case they're on foot.

Second, just because we don't want the pigs burning our barn down, doesn't mean we need to let the people in this county feel like they own it. I want to do some mayhem tonight, very targeted. We'll work that out on the map next.

And finally, we need to tie up loose ends. The waitresses and cooks don't know shit. But the bitches, got loose lips."

"You talking about their upstairs lips or their downstairs lips?" asked Rattler with a leer while he pushed Frog.

Frog slapped at the back of Shard's head like Rattler had earlier, but Shard turned away and it was soft thump.

"They know too much, and aren't going to stand silent with your brothers. When the boys are out on their missions, and all the outsiders have gone home, snuff them out. You can toss them off the bridge with the used burner before the sun comes up. No one will be out then."

The three nodded obediently with a new appreciation of how serious Shep was and how much was at stake. He spread out the county map on the desk, and they started working the details.

CHAPTER—28

Chandler Fouche drove home with the boys to a house crowded with vehicles and a semicircle of four milling parents along with his wife, Evelyn, and little Latoyia. Their presence was expected, as little fishermen needed to make their way home. What wasn't expected was Jim and Lauryn Redigan in his driveway. The Commonwealth's Attorney gestured with his hands, capturing their awl so completely that no one seemed to notice Chandler's Buick as he turned in from Caisson Road.

"Who's that, Grandpa?"

"Someone I know from the office," replied Chandler with no enthusiasm.

Another asked, "One of your deputies?"

"No. When I arrest someone, this guy tells the judge how bad they've been. It's who they call the prosecutor."

"What's he doing here?"

"I don't know…" trailed off Chandler.

As he came up the drive, he could see clustered around the side of the house the older sedans, kept running for years in the salt-free southern climate. Similar to his wife's worn Buick, they were the cars he'd expect to see with his people of child raising ages. Mr. Redigan's giant truck stood out, its shiny late model lines a relative extravagance compared with the others. But what wasn't there, a pride and joy afforded his position, was his Dodge Durango sheriff's vehicle. Only his wife caught his expression of disbelief through the windshield, her head cocking to the side with slightly pouting lips of sympathy. Everyone went quiet as he opened his door.

"What happened?" he said looking around.

They looked at each other, knowing and wanting to share, but also sensing that it wasn't their place to break the news. The tension didn't last long, as excited boys exited behind him to share their adventures.

"Dad, I caught a big one!"

"Mine wasn't as big, but it was a bass."

Jim Redigan fell in behind Chandler's wife as they both made their way forward through the hugs and excited hands stretched a bit too far apart to denote the length of any fishes that didn't come from the deep sea and a commercial charter.

"Some bad people came to visit us the night you left, Chandler. Had to use the shotgun. They wanted to steal your truck something bad," Evelyn declared with narrow eyes and a slight sideways jerking of her mouth.

He looked at her with wide eyes, lips moving and wanting to say something, but the mind failing to find the proper words with honed and carefully selected connotations to accurately express what he wanted to convey.

"Yeah, we all fine," Evelyn declared, eyes burning at him. "Even Latoyia was a trooper and held her stuff together."

James Redigan stepped in, "Three men broke into your vehicle last night in the small hours. Your lady laid it down on them pretty good and they drove off in such a rush they crashed a few miles up the road. Lauryn found the wreck and called it in this morning. Two men of the Lowland Outlaws were dead at that scene. Always wear your seatbelt. Main suspect is Rebel Tarwick, who owned the crashed truck and is thought to be the third perpetrator. Buck is out looking for him now."

The boys were still jabbering to their parents, but the parents weren't listening. Instead they focused on the two county leaders, a glimpse into the real life version of what they only ever got to see on television.

"Did you bring in the State Police to help while I was gone?" asked Chandler turning to look at Redigan a little sideways.

"Just the crime scene technicians per our county support agreement with their forensics lab. They expedited and cleaned things up here as a courtesy to you. Your truck's impounded in their evidence yard. I thought about getting the State Police going, but with two dead and Buck saying he knew the other and was confident to pick him up shortly," he shrugged, "I guess I thought I'd let our long serving elected sheriff make the call if he needed help when he returned."

You mean make me the one to cry for help, he thought, and look bad in front of the county supervisor.

"Nice of you to stop by and tell me yourself," dismissed Chandler.

"Okay, Chandler. You and Evelyn please let Lauryn and me know if there is anything we can do for you," James Redigan said with a pat on his shoulder as he walked to his truck.

A moment later the prosecutor and his wife were gone, and the family broods rapidly followed to include little Latoyia. The sheriff and his wife ate dinner, pork chops, and she had wine. To soothe her nerves in the aftermath, he gathered. She didn't usually drink, and her animated gesturing hands causally threw her glass about, somehow without spilling a drop. Her mouth spewed out words like a runaway typewriter, every now and then a twisted phrase implying that he was somehow at fault for no other reason than he was the man and hadn't been there. And then the moment came he had been waiting for; she hit the wall. A sleepless night followed by alcohol, and suddenly she was out in mid-sentence on the couch just shy of nine o'clock.

Chandler Fouche took a quick shower, and changed into his uniform. He opened the revolver, checking for any grit or corrosion on the cartridge cases, and made sure the cylinder spun freely. He gripped the butt tightly, using a one-handed sideways jerking motion to flip the cylinder back home. Lowland Outlaws daring to come to his house, in the middle of the night when he wasn't there. He'd show those cockroaches. Enough was enough. He forgot all about careful investigative plans dreamed up while fishing.

Downstairs he paused to throw a red and brown yarn afghan on Evelyn that she'd crocheted back when they'd first been married. She snored soundly, the empty bottle of burgundy a testament to one hell of a headache come morning. Then he strode outside to the Buick. A few minutes later he was heading south on I-85 toward the Outlaw Saloon.

Once on the interstate with its long straight lines, he turned on his cellphone. The juice was low, but it was still working. He dialed Buck's number. There were several rings, and then it went to voice mail. He disconnected instead of using up power leaving a message. The fact that he had called was all the message he needed to leave to be expected to be called back. But it didn't keep from trying again a few minutes later when that call back didn't come. Again there were several rings, and then to voice mail. He hung up in disgust.

He tried the alarm room next.

"St. Albans Emergency Center, this is Mr. Kissel. How may I assist you?" came Brett's familiar voice.

"It's Chandler, Brett. Do they ever give you a day off?"

Brett chuckled, "The overtime is good and it's better than sitting at home with the old lady. Sorry you had to come home to a mess, Sheriff."

"That's alright. Evelyn knows how to handle herself just fine. You have a twenty on Buck?"

There was a pause, and even his old ears could hear the flipping of pages in a logbook.

"Last annotation I have for Deputy Garner is leaving the accident scene to go after that Tarwick guy. He may have just forgot to call out at the end of his shift. It's been a big day. Do you want me to try his place?"

"No, that's okay. I'm near it anyway. I can drive by. Thanks," said Chandler before hanging up.

He took the St. Albans' exit, making a left at the bottom of the ramp to go away from town toward Buck's house. Chandler had never been invited over before, but he patrolled as well as his deputy and that meant he drove by sometimes. And it would be foolish not to do a drive by being so close. But it didn't tell him much. Buck's house was dark, with no car in the driveway. Chandler pulled in to turn around and headed back toward the interstate. Was it worth checking Dixie's he thought? Or the holding cells? If his deputy got Rebel, that's where he would be. And he was contemplating kicking Shep's door in. It would be better to have more than a six-shooter. Despite the boiling blood of his temper, it seemed the right call.

He scanned the parking lot of Ed's as he drove by, but didn't spot Buck's patrol car. Nor was it in front of Dixie's house, or in the city parking lot out front of their building. He grabbed the phone from the passenger side seat and went inside.

The lights were off and the air inside tasted stale. He flipped on the fluorescents, which blinked as they lit up, and started by plugging in his phone. Then he grabbed the keys to the equipment locker. Like all departments, there had been Department of Homeland Security grants for gear that wouldn't normally have been in the budget. Therefore, he was able to dress in a military grade flak jacket and Kevlar helmet. He put a handful of cable ties into his pockets for use as extra handcuffs. He also found a ram, a steel bar with handles used to break down a door like some medieval siege assault.

And he grabbed a nine ball machine, a Remington 870 pump shotgun. It had an 18" barrel, tactical light, and reflex sight. It held six shells of three-inch magnum in its tube-shaped magazine and was a law enforcement classic with various models in production since 1951. This gun was much more modern, but the design was proven, reliable, and powerful. He racked the pump slide, and then inserted another shell to replace the one just drawn into the chamber from the magazine to top it off. Chandler made sure it was on safe. On the stock was an elastic nylon shell holder he loaded up, and then put extra loose shells in his pockets.

He strode down the front hall, checking out his reflection in the glass office door. The helmet and armored vest were black, with "Sheriff" in bold yellow letters. Chandler felt the blood serge in his biceps as he hefted the short shotgun. Bad boys, I'm coming for you. Fucking with my town. Fucking with my home. Fucking with my truck. Yeah, bad ass, he said to himself stepping toward the door to exit. His urgent bladder made him do a quick about face to run to the men's room before driving off.

Chandler put the ram in the back and threw the shotgun on the passenger side seat, aiming the barrel down at the floorboards. He was already back to Ed's and the southbound onramp before he realized he'd forgotten to check if Rebel was in a cell. Or check on Dog-Boy for that matter. Well, no worries. This wasn't about Rebel and a couple of dead bikers. This was about the motherfuckers who sent them. He sped south toward the exit for Azalea Estates Lane.

His blood cooled some on the five-minute ride down the interstate. From the off ramp he could see the motorcycles under the glow of a security lamp swarmed with moths. There must have been nearly two-dozen of them. The old barn itself didn't appear to be rocking, but the lights were still on. He pulled in the lot, cursing himself for not checking the cells for Rebel. A pair of big men, crossed armed under the front door's awning eyed him suspiciously. Chandler knew he needed backup, knew he needed to get with Buck and determine the score. Track down the man who actually did it. That was the better play. He circled in the lot, and exited to go east on Azalea Estates Lane.

It would hit Lowland Road, where he could turn right and north to stop by Rebel Tarwick's garage. He knew the address, having apprehended the Dog-Boy vigilante on his way there. It was where Buck was likely to have gone, and it was a good logical next step for him too. He might not have been a fancy detective like in some New York City cop show his wife was always watching, but he knew how to get things done in his town.

When he arrived and drove down the driveway, things were dark and felt forlorn and lonely. Under his headlights the garage office's broken window drew his immediate focus, but old habits made him stop short. He grabbed the shotgun, and crouching behind the Buick's door he used the tactical light to make a slow scan. Off to the left, Buck's patrol car made him instantly relieved, which soon drained away to worry.

He approached and looked through the driver's side window. Neatly folded on the front seat was Buck's uniform and utility belt of equipment. Despite the large number of accouterments such as handcuffs, radio, night stick, etc., there was no missing the empty holster. Chandler lifted up the clothes with the end of the shotgun, not wanting to touch them for fear of interfering with forensic testing. It was only his uniform shirt and trousers. There were no shoes or underwear.

Chandler turned toward the quiet garage, the shotgun's intense tactical light easily overpowering the Buick's high beams. He pointed it through the broken window.

"Sheriff Fouche. Come on out," he yelled. The running Buick in the driveway dispelled any notion of trying to sneak around.

But the old building felt still. He found the office door unlocked and slightly ajar, and he pushed through with the shotgun out before him. The light reflecting off the close white walls hurt his eyes and made him squint. He reached out to the light with his left hand, never taking his right from the trigger, and adjusted the beam to its low setting. A quick walk through the back and the garage bays confirmed no one was home.

Okay, thought Chandler to himself. Doris sent Mr. Jager here when Dixie was missing. Buck was here. The owner of here was driving the truck which paid his home a visit. There must be something here to tie it all together. Something that would show the county he wasn't ready for pasture, that Sheriff Fouche was a serious lawman.

The papers on the desk didn't tell him anything. Work orders for various cars, trucks and tractors were in various stacks itemizing materials, fees and labor rates. Catalogues of parts and vendors, complete with diagrams of how things went together were stained with black oily fingerprints.

He turned toward the waste paper basket, brimming with small brown paper sacks. The size of bag they'd give you if you bought more than one roll of lifesavers, crumpled up and thrown away. Chandler reached for one and smoothed it out. He looked inside, finding nothing but a receipt left in the bag. The top of the receipt was for Ed's Truck Stop, denoting a total paid in cash for one item of just over six dollars.

Chandler grabbed another bag, and found a similar receipt. And then another. Sometimes the item total varied, but the one six-dollar item was always present. Like he got his usual purchase, but added a drink or snack to it. He pushed the desk from the center of the room to make space and emptied out the trash can. Then he found the overhead light switch, and dropped to his hands and knees to begin arranging what he had.

He used the dates to place them in order. There were over three dozen such receipts, the oldest from only two weeks ago. Receipts having multiple items were spread out over every couple of days, but everyday had at least a few and some had several. What was Rebel buying he thought? That was purchased one at a time, regardless of how many trips were made, even to the tune of multiple times a day? Doris didn't deal in auto parts.

But, thought Chandler, whatever it was came in packaging and all that was here was the sack and receipt. He grabbed the gun and left the office, going right around the building. His still running Buick lit the front and side well enough, but he resumed using the nine-ball machine's weapon light when he reached the back. There were several black trash bags in a pile. Rural addresses never had pickup. You had to take it yourself, and some went a long time between trips.

He slung the shotgun over his shoulder and grabbed a couple of bags by their topknots to drag into the garage bays. There was good overhead lighting, and lots of room on the concrete floor. Chandler made several trips dragging bags. He used his pocket knife to slash them open, contents tumbling out as he gave the bag a wild shake. There was a shop broom in the corner he used to spread the little mounds.

The trash smelled, but not near as badly as one would expect. There was little food waste, mainly crumbs of crackers or pork rinds left behind in foil or plastic bags. Certainly no rotting banana peels to contend with. A few soda pop bottles here and there, or the bloody Styrofoam of a tray of burgers. Some moldy bread. Most of it was paper waste, paper towels or carbon copies of old work order forms.

But then, he hit the jack pot. Tumbling out from the garbage bag came small cardboard boxes of cold medicine, and their accompanying empty foil blister packs. His lips and teeth made a wet howling sound as he suddenly sucked in a breath and assuredly gripped his shotgun.

CHAPTER—29

Dixie Johnson sat with her mom, Doris, and father, Ed, at their kitchen table in the small weathered apartment over the truck stop diner's kitchen. Exhaust fans shared some of the same ductwork. The apartment was built to the same standard as the motel, but didn't suffer from the same indifference. Her mom had tried to make it a home, separate from the business. Doris took the time to clean and display remembrances, and Dixie recalled many family meals here before the teenage years started.

The apartment's kitchen was just inside the door at the top of the outside stairs which led down to the diner's back entrance and where they parked the family car. It had an avocado green table in the middle, a color popular once upon a time and never updated since visitors weren't invited inside the Johnson's retreat. Dixie was graduating from high school before realizing the table was really a painted wooden wire spool, surplus from the power company, with a circle of plywood screwed on top. The checkered plastic tablecloth had been replaced a few times over the years, but her mom always stuck with the classic country style. Overall it was a poultry décor, with a wooden rooster napkin holder, rooster and hen salt and pepper shakers and the like. Even the clock showed a red topped hen pointing white feathery wings to show that it was a bit before midnight. Opposite the door was an entryway to a small living room before a bedroom and bath beyond to round out the home.

"Mom, I can't believe you let it come to this. There has to be a way."

"We'll just work harder," interjected her dad. He smiled and nodded vigorously to drive home his point.

Doris rolled her eyes quickly and ignored him, "I've run the numbers, Dixie. We're just not selling enough and if we don't make some needed repairs we're going to be fined out of business."

"Well, for starters we need to sell my house. If I can't pay for it out of my own job, then I can't have it. I'll move back to a motel room until we get things sorted out."

"That's not going to be enough, Dixie. The diner's not making money. The labor costs are too high."

"I can take a couple of hours each day at the register," pledged Ed with a shrug of reluctance.

"We need to get out of the open twenty-four hours' business. There aren't enough patrons at those hours. Most people who stop in then just want gas and a cup of coffee. We don't need to be paying for a waitress and cook in addition to the cashier."

Ed's face tightened, "We can't do that. This is what will put St. Albans on the map. Always open. We'll grow into a traveler's oasis.

And them cooks and dishwashers have families, too."

Dixie continued, "And I'd like to understand what really are the requirements with the fuel system update. What's a must do now and what are things we can plan for later? Is anything grandfathered? Does it apply to automotive pumping or just commercial tractor trailers? All those details."

Ed piped in again, "The man who did the inspection said he could fix it all for $50,000. We should go with him. He's already looked at it and it's a fair price."

"Let's have a couple of others take a look and get their bids," proposed Dixie. "Someone who is truly in the business and knows the inspectors, what they are looking for and the most recent regulations. I'm not convinced we need to pay that much without even knowing what it is we are supposed to have done and whether or not it is really needed all at once."

"Good work costs money. If you plan to run this place on the cheap, you can count me out," protested Ed.

Doris talked over him in the middle of his sentence, "It's been quite a while since we looked real hard at that. I told the county inspector we'd address their concerns but then I got too busy with your Dad's medical appointments and then the bills started coming. I kind of wanted to let that sleeping dog lay and just never got back around to it.

I think what you're proposing may get ends meeting month to month. But we'll never start banking money for the upgrades unless we find some other efficiencies."

Dixie nodded, "Okay. It's a good first step anyway. Maybe we can look at the numbers tomorrow and see how close we come. And make sure our prices are up to date with our costs. Seems to me a cup of coffee is the same price as it was when I was in middle school. Then, let's make some calls so we truly know what we need for the future."

Doris nodded while Ed talked about selling the car, but no one was listening. Instead the two women tilted their heads as they heard the steps outside ring with pounding footsteps. A moment later the door flew inward with a wood splintering crash, only the bottom hinge remaining attached to the frame so the door didn't fall completely on the floor.

"Sheriff's Office!" came the voice at almost the same time. The tall figure in military body armor dropped the metal ram, and slid a slung shotgun off his shoulder. He entered the room in a couple of steps, swiftly kicking aside debris.

"I've a warrant for Ed and Doris Johnson," he screamed. "Keep your hands where I can see them!"

Doris screamed into the blinding tactical light at the end of the shotgun with wide eyes while Ed started to rise, and then fell back down grasping at his chest.

Dixie screamed at Sheriff Chandler Fouche, "What the hell are you doing?"

"Don't interfere with the serving of a warrant. All of you, keep your hands where I can see them," Chandler loudly decreed.

"Hands, dammit!" Chandler reiterated with a stabbing motion of the shotgun.

Doris and Dixie looked at each other in confusion, their hands plainly visible with outstretched palms. Then they glanced toward Ed, who clutched at the front of his shirt with a bowed head while leaning forward over the table.

"Daddy!" said Dixie rising, but Chandler shoved her with the side of the shotgun and caused her to lose her balance. She fell out of the chair and backward, the dainty legs of the ladder-back chair coming apart.

Doris reached Ed first, Chandler powerless to stop both of them, and gently pulled his chair backward to lower him on to his back while Dixie scrambled to get back up. Her Mom wasn't strong enough to give him a soft landing.

"I said to freeze. What's the matter with you people?"

Chandler strode around the table toward Doris, and then saw the sweat pouring from Ed's face as he gasped for breath. His hand came up pressed against his jaw, as Doris pulled him free from the chair to lay flat.

Dixie screamed at him, "Daddy is having a heart attack. Call an ambulance!"

"I've got a warrant," said Chandler confused for a moment, "I need to…"

"Call an ambulance!" ordered Dixie again.

Chandler took his grip off the shotgun's slide and keyed his mike, "Control, it's Chandler. Need medic one at Ed's, possible heart attack. Come around the back of the diner."

Doris held his hand and cried as Ed's breaths became quick and shallow. Chandler stood in the doorway, mouth agape, the shotgun gripped only by the neck of the stock and pointing at the floor. Dixie sprang around the table to her father and kneeled at his side opposite her mother. The old man's face was beginning to discolor with tiny spider webs of purple and they both noticed his chest had stopped moving. Doris looked upward and began to wail.

Dixie put her fingers where her father's rib cage came together to find the center of his chest. She could hear the siren out on Main Street, even over her Mom's sobs. Chandler's radio crackled that they were turning onto Thigpen Road from Smallwood Street. Placing one hand over the other she started chest compressions.

The Fire Department's annual training last fall seemed forever ago, but the simple basics had stuck with her. Quick compressions, faster than one per second. Her technique was good. She had been well coached in the mechanics, and the dummy had given her a good feel. But they'd never made her keep going for a realistic amount of time.

She was only a light smoker, but hardly an exerciser. Even then, no one exercised like this. The fast speed of the compressions led her to starting out holding her breath, and soon the lack of oxygen clawed at her will to continue. Her shoulders and forearms burned. Dixie began to figure out how to force herself to breathe while compressing, but by then her body was behind. She gasped, choking a helpless sob. A hand pushed her away to sprawl on the floor.

Dixie looked over to see Chandler now on his knees spelling her. He was fit, but he was also an old man. He'd shed his helmet, but the armored vest forced him to lean in at an awkward angle. She counted the compressions, and noted their pace rapidly slowing. The old sheriff didn't have it in him, but he was going for it for all he was worth. Minutes later, the medics came storming up the stairs with a stretcher.

They were quick. Dixie knew them, or at least knew most of their faces. But never did she think she'd share a moment of her family with them in quite this way. There were shouts at each other as her dad was loaded on the stretcher, no time to be lost with a mechanical gurney on the stairs. Her dad's weight required all of them, rescue men biceps pumping, her mother desperately screaming and trying to hang on as he was led away. Chandler pried her hands free, and then pulled her back out of the kitchen where he fumbled with his handcuffs. Dixie's last glance at her dad was in the back of the ambulance with an oxygen mask on his face and his shirt being cut away for the cardio paddles. Within seconds of the back doors closing, they were racing from the parking lot with red emergency lights blazing.

Dixie slowly turned from the savaged doorway, to see Chandler pushing her mom before him with her hands bound tightly behind her back. He guided her around the hen clock on the floor, the battery compartment's cover missing and the Duracell lost under the table somewhere.

"You're still taking her in after all this?" Dixie asked incredulously.

"I am sworn to execute the warrants of the Commonwealth," stated Chandler in his solemn duty voice he used on television.

He knelt to retrieve the shotgun he'd tossed aside before starting CPR, and turned off its light. He also found his helmet, and put it on for no other reason probably than to free up a hand. Then Chandler leaned over a final time retrieving the ram. Dixie met her mother's teary eyes while the equipment was being gathered.

"Dixie, you just forget about me and Dad. We made our choices. This is your place now. Sorry it's such a mess. Don't waste your future on us," the final word cut short as he pushed her in the back toward the stairs.

"Was that really necessary?" challenged Dixie.

"You are requested not to interfere with law enforcement while they are performing their official duties," said Chandler in passing. "Please stay out of the apartment until investigators release it. Interfering with an active investigation or destroying evidence is a serious matter and carries criminal penalties. Do I make myself clear?"

Dixie stepped out onto the landing, and watched as he guided Mom in the handcuffs through the backdoor to be paraded amongst the kitchen staff and customers. She thought the sheriff was gone, but he reappeared back through the diner's rear door a few minutes later when blue flashing lights reflected off the asphalt and the motel's white siding. The state police cruiser had "Crime Scene" on its front fender. She darted down the steps without looking further at either and entered the diner's kitchen.

All the time around the sheriff's office and the fire department taught her that immediate leadership in time of crisis was essential. You didn't have to be perfect, but you had to show up.

"Rachel? Jesus? Carlos?" Dixie called out for waitress, cook and dishwasher.

They gathered around and after validating there were only a couple of patrons at this late hour and Rachel could be spared a few minutes, Dixie rapidly got down to business.

"Mom and Dad were arrested a little bit ago. I'm sure you saw," began Dixie. "My dad was taken away in an ambulance. That's all I know. I don't know what the charges are and I haven't talked to a doctor yet. But I will keep you posted as I learn more. I'm hiding nothing."

Rachel's eyes teared up, and Jesus and Carlos stared impassively.

"First, I want you to know I'm running things and we are open. Everyone's shifts are to proceed as scheduled," she nodded her head slightly for emphasis.

Jesus and Carlos both looked at each other and exhaled. Jobs weren't an easy thing to come by in Lowland County.

"Second, there will have to be some changes. I don't know what they are yet, but we have to be better to stay in business. I'll be appreciative of your ideas if you have any."

Jesus raised a hand slightly and Dixie nodded. His accent was a little thick so Dixie had to concentrate hard on his words to understand him.

"Well, it's just that everyone has a different shorthand or a way of saying things. Some say eggs over easy, some say over light. They abbreviate differently. Some write really small. Sometimes I misread what they say and I got to do the order over."

Dixie nodded for him to continue.

"My niece, she put together this check form with all the things we make. If the ladies can use that, I won't mess up as often. The form is kind of big. Comes off her computer at school. You would need a clip board. But if it works we can maybe make it smaller and get better at it."

Dixie thought a moment and said, "We have some clipboards we use when we're doing inventory. Rachel, what do you think?"

"I'm not wild about carrying anything bigger than my pad. But tips are sure a lot better when their order is right. I'm willing to try it. I think the other girls will too."

"Just for two weeks," promised Dixie, "and then we can all decide whether we keep doing it or make some improvement to it. What else?"

Rachel jumped in, "I've got one. Those drivers at the back of the lot," she said shifting her eyes for emphasis. "They often stop here for other things and don't make it inside. Either the walk is too long or they're embarrassed. But we don't get a sale. My boyfriend fixes up old vending machines. What if we put some back there with those little low liquid energy drink bottles and slim jims? Neither of those needs refrigeration, the drivers love 'em, and he's got some machines in the warehouse that don't need electricity."

"Tell him to think about a test proposal we can try out for a month. Any other?" she asked looking around. "Okay, we'll talk more about it later and we're going to talk on it regularly. We won't be able to try everything, but I want to keep a dialogue going. And with that, I think I'm going to order something to eat in my own diner. I sure as hell can't sleep."

They all gave her supportive smiles as she made her way out front to sit in one of the booths. But as she got out there, she changed her mind and grabbed a small pad of paper from behind the counter instead. It had been quite a while since she had eaten in her own diner. Eaten as a customer instead of an owner, anyway. Dixie walked out the front door with her pad and stood a moment to clear her mind. I'm going to look at everything with a fresh set of eyes she told herself, and write it all down so I don't forget.

Then she turned back around as a customer.

CHAPTER—30

Kelton shivered and violently exhaled through his nose to try and clear the drowning mucous away. It wasn't a terribly cold spring night, according to the thermometer anyway, but his clothes were wet and his stomach was empty. He knew most cases of hypothermia, where the body was losing heat faster than it could produce it leading to a lethal result, didn't actually happen in harsh wintry weather. They generally occurred when temperatures were in the forties, sneaking up on unsuspecting people over the course of hours. His years of training wouldn't allow it to sneak up on him. Kelton could see it coming, even before the tremors began in his body. The question was more, practically, could he do anything about it?

He'd gotten blood on himself everywhere while recovering his bullet stuck in the biker's spine. The worst had been along his hands and forearms, a thick red painting that rapidly became sticky. Everything he touched spread the evidence, from the bag of money, his knife, to the backpack he didn't dare leave behind at the scene while he cleaned himself up. Even a small drop, if he was apprehended, would seal his fate and that of his dog's.

The best he could do was find a stream and plunge in. Doris had made it clear she wouldn't rent a room to him, and even if she would he couldn't check-in covered in gore like a horror movie extra to spread DNA all over the floor and walls. There simply wasn't a hot shower and laundromat option. So plunge in he did, laying prone to completely submerge himself in the chilly running water to clean his body as well as his clothes and equipment. He grabbed handfuls of sandy pebbles using them to scour until he felt clean enough to open a backpack pocket for the laundry soap, baking soda and his washcloth.

He reckoned it was far from sufficient. A detailed cleaning would have to wait until he had light to see, hot water, and the time to scrub every nook and cranny. But it was a vast improvement, albeit at a high cost. Nothing he owned remained dry, the wet fabric rubbing his thighs, his shoulders under the pack's straps, and his hips as he made hasty strides back toward town.

Kelton considered stopping and making a small fire. A hot drink would go a long way to restoring his constitution. Dicing up green pine needles and adding to boiling water made tea rich in vitamin C. But there wasn't time for that. Azalea Estates Lane must be nearly twenty miles from where the cash had been stashed he thought. And he had to cover that distance carrying equipment and in the dark. Shep wasn't a man to be kept waiting. Deals were time bound, and things were working out very differently than what they had talked about. So he pressed on rather than stop for his comfort.

He didn't make bad time, all things considered. The roads pretty much went the way he needed to go, there being no advantage to fighting through briars or climbing over cattle fences cutting cross country. The hour was also late on the rural roads, and he didn't have to jump to the side much to hide from potential witnesses. Kelton knew that with a dead deputy amongst the bodies, the search net would be cast wide and with fervor. He didn't want to be this unusual man seen with a backpack walking his dog. The sheriff would put that one together.

Kelton never considered making his way back to the abandoned motorcycles. Azrael couldn't ride on one, and he didn't have the faintest idea how to drive one. He could barely ride a child's bicycle. Backtracking Buck and Rebel may have led to a car or truck, but there was a good chance it was the deputy's patrol car. He certainly wouldn't be able to keep a low profile in that and would have wound up going west when he wanted to go south for nothing. So he walked the dark roads at the ranger quick step, trying to fight his chills with activity.

The protein bars went quickly. With his weight and the pack, hiking on the rolling road, he was burning nearly 800 calories per hour. The bars were under 200 calories apiece. He'd had that burger at Shep's for a late lunch before they left, but that was getting to be a long time and a long walk ago even before the gun battle had happened. His stomach gurgled and he tightened the waist belt of his pack.

By the time Thigpen Road led him to the outskirts of St. Albans it was well after midnight. Maybe just a few hours until dawn. He rested his hands on his hips breathing hard and peered up at the flashing red light hanging on its cable over the road. Even Azrael lay down with the pause, his chest heaving, but the dog's eyes were bright and his ears were up. Damned Belgian Malinois, he thought. March them into the ground and they're like, hey can we do it again tomorrow, Dad? Please, huh, huh, huh?

His head turned toward town, looking down Main Street, but Kelton couldn't distinguish individual shops from that distance. It was a good example of an artist's one-point perspective where the buildings on each side of the street seem to shrink and converge into a single spot. Dixie's house, Mr. Butler's shop, etc. were indistinguishable. But it didn't matter because all were dark. There was no money for hot food commerce to be had in that direction until morning.

Kelton looked at the truck stop, its bright lights forming an arching orange halo that made the stars overhead disappear. They taunted him, his mind recalling Doris and her righteousness. He'd just assume take his business elsewhere. She had certainly done him no favors despite his best efforts to help her daughter. But there was nowhere else. At least not for several more hours and he couldn't wait. He didn't just need to get to the Outlaw Saloon. He needed to get there prepared to fight in case the deal with Shep wasn't still amendable. And Doris would likely be sleeping this time of night, giving him a chance to slip in and out unnoticed. Kelton decided to go for it.

He cut diagonally across the intersection. He'd already shot a law enforcement officer so what was a little jay-walking? A few big trucks were parked, dark and quiet, drivers either taking a snooze or getting a meal. A rusty El Camino pulled out from the gas pumps and headed toward the interstate. Kelton looked through the glass windows of the diner and saw patrons were sparse with no sign of Doris. Then he saw Dixie, alone at a booth way back by the soda coolers. She was looking at papers on the table intently.

It made him hesitate in reconsideration, but he needed hot food. Baylee Ann and Bambi needed him. He'd make the Johnson's tell him no again. He didn't try a stealth entrance, slipping in quietly and taking the first booth so Azrael could sneak underneath. What was the use? His dirty clothes and backpack, as well as notoriety the last couple of days, made that pointless. Kelton swung the door wide, marched down the tile floor with his dog at the heel, and sat down opposite a wide-eyed Dixie and her open notebook.

"What the hell happened to you?" she said with twisted lips.

Her makeup was far from flawless, he saw. He couldn't help but notice the abrasions, runny mascara, smudges and redness surrounding her eyes. Hard, determined eyes, which had a special spark to them, glowing like a coal fire's embers. Kelton took a few seconds to take it in.

"Let's maybe start with you instead," he offered.

She didn't hesitate at all, with a voice clear and forceful.

"This is my place now. Daddy's dead and Mom's arrested," explained Dixie and then yelled toward Rachel, "Hey Girl, get this man our farmer's breakfast!"

Rachel didn't bother them with the usual questions about how things should be cooked and adding cheese; she remembered him. Kelton fed his dog soggy kibble beside the table in the single bowl he carried. He felt bad about that, but it was what it was. Dixie then told him about Sheriff Fouche breaking the door of the family apartment down with a no knock warrant and dragging her parents away.

"So it's my place now, and I'm going to run it the best I can, unburdened by medical bills or a mortgage on Main Street."

"How are you holding up with your mom's predicament?" he asked with some sympathy in his voice while pouring syrup over his steaming pancakes.

"I'm fine and I hate her," Dixie declared.

Kelton slammed his head back against the booth.

"People make mistakes, but I know she loved you. It wasn't the epitome of selfishness and evil. You should consider forgiving her," Kelton encouraged as he put down his fork in surrender to the hash browns and bacon.

"It will take a lot of time for that. And even as crazy as it's all been, I never thought that you'd be back here in the mix. And so disheveled, too. Like a drowned rat that Patsy dragged in. What's kept you in little St. Albans and Lowland County?"

"Your friends from the pit are in trouble again, although I'm not sure you really care. After you were freed and before I got there, Rebel gave Bambi to this bad biker dude named Shep Primrose."

"I know who he is. He worked down at the track when I was in middle school. Doing emergency motorbike repairs and such."

"Well anyway, Baylee Ann went down to Shep's place to get her friend, and he decided to take her too. I want to try and help them out."

"Actually, I do care. I don't hate my mom for winding up in jail. I forgive her for taking part in the drugs. I hate that she whored me out," said Dixie who covered her face with her hands for a moment to hide a sniffle. "Growing up, she was always telling me how I was different and better than those girls out there," she said gesturing to the back of the lot. "How she'd look down her noses at them like this truck stop was high society.

I carried that attitude with me all through life. I left those two girls down in that pit when Buck picked me up. Didn't say a word, because they were nothing but used up lot lizards who reaped what they sowed. I was the one who didn't belong down there. I was better than they were.

Then my own mother treated me like a prostitute. Sent me to your room. It wasn't all her fault. I'm not thirteen anymore. I knew what I was doing. She wasn't some pimp, giving me a black eye. But she was the one who suggested it and I went with it. I'm not any different from them. I was just lucky enough to be born to parents who owned a business instead of a pair of alcoholics.

Those teen girls out there, they got to own their choices. But I can give them some choices to make. I need cleaners and dishwashers. I need waitresses. Maybe I can get some social program grants to support it. Perhaps I can get donation boxes for people to help out. But somehow I'm going to make that work.

Bambi was good to me in the pit, and I let her and Baylee Ann down. I'm not letting them down again. What do you need from me?"

She looked intently at him, with pleading eyes seeking atonement. Kelton felt something for her, regretting turning her down back in the motel room. But then, that hadn't been the same girl who was now sitting in front of him. Dixie was far from perfect, but had been blessed with an epiphany that put her on a whole new path with life.

"I need a ride. I've covered a lot of miles today, but I need to get down to Azalea Estates Lane. Drop me off, and then get clear. I don't want you involved or getting hurt in some way. It's likely to be an ugly scene."

She nodded, "My car's around back. What direction do you want to arrive from?"

Kelton thought about that for a few hard seconds, remembering Shep's office and looking out the window at the interstate.

"Let's take Thigpen Road down. It's not as fast, but they won't see us coming. Good question, Miss Dixie."

Out back, Kelton saw the yellow and black police line tape on the stairs awaiting detectives in the morning. It wasn't just the door hanging on the single hinge astounding him; the whole door frame had crumpled under the blow to lose its rectangular shape. They got in the car, Azrael entering first and squeezing between the bucket seats to the back. Kelton noted the clean interior despite the car's age, and felt bad for the ever shedding dog hairs floating in Azrael's wake.

"Do you want to drive?" said Dixie extending the keys.

He shook his head as his body cringed like a vampire exposed to crucifix, "No, that's okay. It's your car."

"Buck always had to drive. He's an asshole. I hope I never see him again," she declared fastening her seatbelt.

Kelton decided it was best to hold his tongue on Buck. He didn't want to be accused of lying or holding out later, but it wasn't relevant right now. And being sidetracked by emotional drama was not going to help anyone. And, Dixie was right. The guy had been an asshole who shot at his dog.

In a few minutes they were barreling south on Thigpen Road. Dixie had been a race fan in school, and no one in this town was ever going to give her a ticket.

"Hey, pull in at that house!" said Kelton as he pointed across the dash.

Kelton frantically grabbed for Azrael as Dixie applied the brake and everyone flew forward against their restraints.

"Sorry, forgot about Azrael. Do you know them?"

Kelton looked at the truck in the driveway and knew Braxton Greene was home.

"Yeah. Lay on the horn as you pull in."

She didn't hesitate. The quiet country fields echoed with the bold honking as she let the car come to a stop just behind the beat up truck. Dixie went to her parking lights, but continued to announce their presence by blaring the horn. Kelton climbed out, and closed his door before his dog could follow. He walked around to the driver's side and leaned against the hood. Dixie stopped honking to lower her window.

"Are you sure he's here?"

"He's here. Keep honking," he said.

It took another minute, but he saw a light come on inside. He was thankful, for he'd started to have his doubts. That something might have happened to him. But when the door opened, it was the same old Braxton in cutoff shorts and shirt that wasn't quite all the way buttoned. The old plumber guitarist rubbed his eyes and craned his neck forward to size them up.

"What the hell you doing here?" his tone was curious rather than annoyed.

Kelton shrugged, "I took your advice and was careful. You were right. They tried to move on me."

Braxton nodded, "There's something weird afoot. It's Saturday night and they always want me to play. Even came to my house once and dragged me there when I didn't show. Beat me over it. Been months and it still hurts inside when I shit. When I got back with Baylee Ann, she went up to see Shep and I went to the cans before starting my set. After a joint I walked out to my truck for my guitar. Rattler met me in the parking lot. Told me to take the night off. Wouldn't let me take back Baylee Ann. Never made it back inside. Saw some visiting bikes in the lot. They weren't forcing people out right away, but if you weren't a patch wearer of the Lowland Outlaws they weren't letting you inside."

"Any idea what it means?"

Braxton nodded his head, "Always really bad when he's clearing outsider witnesses from the mix."

"I've only seen the front of the barn and Shep's office. What's at the other end of the building?"

"The far end is the cans. You got to go outside and walk around the building to get to them though. There's a side entrance about halfway down the building, opposite the road. Sometimes people will go back there for a cigarette and a chat they want no one else to hear. Then it's just the kitchen."

Kelton nodded, "Okay, thanks. Sorry to wake you."

"Ain't no thing. Sunday tomorrow. What can I do to help? Baylee Ann's the best thing that's happened to me in a long time," said Braxton.

Kelton stared at the ground a second and then called back toward the car, "Dixie, come out here a second. I think I have a plan and we don't have much time."

CHAPTER—31

Bambi was washing dishes and watching Baylee Ann while she mopped. The kitchen was in the old milk room which had already been piped and wired for frequent cleanup. Baylee Ann was humming as she squeezed the gray water and disinfectant from the head using the strainer built into the wheeled bucket. Then she rolled the bucket aside and did another section of the worn concrete. By the end of the night Bambi's knees and back ached from long hours of standing. It was, however, a well equipped kitchen with a galley table, shelves, and reefer units of stainless steel, all of commercial grade quality although bought on the second hand market. Things had come a long way from grills in the parking lot and paper plates when Shep had started.

Baylee Ann had come down earlier from Shep's room and asked if any help was needed. It'd been busy then with the dinner crowd, so the extra pair of hands had been most welcome. She couldn't cook worth a damn, but it took pressure off the waitresses running out orders. And it gave Baylee Ann a chance to flirt with everyone without really having anything to fuck up.

But not an hour later, the dinner crowd just dried up. Candi had stood by the grill with her spatula and knitted eyebrows.

"Wasn't Braxton supposed to play tonight?" Candi croaked out.

"I thought so," Baylee Ann replied. "He's not sick or nothing. Just gave me a ride."

Another half hour later, Rattler had come back to the kitchen.

"Not much is going on tonight, so Shep wants to let you girls go home early," he said smiling like he'd just made a generous offer.

Never mind that the staff was paid by the hour, thought Bambi.

"Some of us already are home, you know?" replied Baylee Ann.

"Not you two Bitches. Candi and the staff. You two dumb broads can clean all this shit up," said Rattler shaking his head as he walked out.

Candi had then begun to ready her meal tickets for Shep's closing time audit. She divided them into piles by waitress on the countertop next to the sink, and then began to tally up on an adding machine. Bambi slowly scraped a plate over a garbage can watching her work. Candi punched the keys unhurriedly, and then did things a second time to be sure. When she'd watched her in past nights, her fingers had flown over the keys.

Fifteen minutes later Rattler stuck his head in the kitchen doorway and challenged, "I thought I told you to go the fuck home?"

"Shep wants to do this new money check with the waitresses every time we close," explained Candi, showing no signs of being intimidated by his bluster.

But the man known as Rattler would have none it, shoving himself off the doorframe to reach her sooner and striding into the kitchen. But when he drew close to the old lady he softened some. Everyone liked Candi. Even him.

Rattler said in a low voice, "Not tonight he doesn't. The waitresses have already all gone home. I'll walk you out," and turning toward Bambi and Baylee Ann with more force and volume, "Get to work cleaning this shit up!"

Candi let Rattler take her gently by the arm, and she made small steps as she rolled her eyes back toward Bambi and Baylee Ann.

After they'd gone, Bambi put down the plate and turned toward her friend.

"What's going on?"

"I don't know," said Baylee Ann. "Some car drove by and checked the place out earlier. Maybe Shep is just being cautious. I'm sure he'll tell us later what's up."

"Do you think the guy with the dog will be coming back?"

Baylee Ann stared fixed toward the sink for a while and then shrugged, "I don't think so. Kelton was nice and all. But he's not one of us. We're with our people now and we can let him go on to his."

Bambi crept to the kitchen's doorway and snuck a look about the corner. All the patch wearers were assembling quietly at tables and no visitors were present. A couple of them were summoned with a wave from Shep's balcony, and they quietly rose and made their way to the stairs up front. Baylee Ann picked up a greasy napkin from the bus cart by pinching it between her thumb and index finger, and wrinkled her nose as she dropped it in the garbage can.

Bambi whispered back toward Baylee Ann, "They've gotten rid of everyone who isn't a gang member except us."

"We're members," said Baylee Ann. "They love us!"

"Baylee Ann, I love you. And I love how you are always upbeat and nothing ever keeps you down. And I know you think we belong here, and that everyone has been real nice to us recently. Daddy was always real nice, too, just before he hit Momma and me. It's like they feel guilty and start making up for it before they do it. I can feel it coming. We need to hide. Stay out of sight. Sneak away if we can," advised Bambi.

Baylee Ann furloughed her brow and then smirked at her, "Things will be fine."

Bambi sighed. Baylee Ann had been in her memories since learning that ducks like to eat bread and fireflies don't last long in a jar. She wouldn't abandon her, but Bambi knew she couldn't help her getting beat or worse beside her. That had happened too many times over the years whether it was bikers, truckers, and once upon a time drunken football players.

"Okay, why don't you start organizing things in here to make the cleanup easier while I take some of this trash out of our way," said Bambi.

"Good idea. And I'll turn the fryer back on, too, in case our boys need a snack later."

Bambi nodded with her meek eyes that she hid behind and tied the drawstrings of the garbage bag. It wasn't too heavy to lift from the gray Rubbermaid garbage can as it held mostly butcher's paper from premade burger paddies and plastic wrap. She took a deep breath and dragged it out the kitchen doorway.

She didn't want to go out into the dining room, but it was the only exit. The other was blocked by a large stainless steel reefer unit leading to what was now the bathrooms. Ductwork for the ventilation hoods had filled in what had been the only window.

"Hey, get back inside there, Bitch," snarled Jingles pointing with his bandaged arm.

Several men who'd been quietly sitting turned their heads toward her.

She looked down at the floor, "I'm just cleaning up like Rattler said to do."

Bambi rounded her shoulders forward, giving her very practiced meek and submissive look.

"Burrito will take that to the dumpster. Get back in that kitchen," he ordered.

She dropped the bag and turned to slowly walk back toward the kitchen. She'd gotten less than a half dozen steps. Bambi sensed him watching her, keeping his focus on her, until she was back where they wanted her. There were murmurs from the other men, but absolutely nothing she could hear over a couple of choppers outside, the rumbles growing faint as they sped away into the night.

Baylee Ann smiled at her from in front of the dishwashing station as she walked back in. Bambi gave a quick smile back, but her stomach was churning. They had to find another way out. She cocked her head as she heard another pair of motorcycles revving from the parking lot.

"Can you help me move that reefer forward?"

"What the hell we need to do that for?" replied Baylee Ann.

"I just want to see if anyone's cleaned behind it. Since things have shut down early, it seems a good time to take advantage," Bambi explained, her eyes shifting sideways.

It was a commercial unit, wedged between some wire shelving units containing dried goods, pots and pans. There was no gap on the bottom, and no wheels. The design kept filth from collecting in places that were hard to clean, but it sure wasn't mobile. Not for these two women to move anyway, and the other equipment around it made it impossible to gain purchase. The old doorway behind, which they could escape through, was completely blocked.

"We can ask some of the boys to help us," suggested Baylee Ann.

"No, they look really busy out there. We should just clean the other parts of the kitchen, and take the time to be really thorough. We'll do that one another time."

If they couldn't escape, Bambi reasoned, their next best chance lay with being useful. No one out there wanted to clean the kitchen. Even to the low bar of their standards. They could slow roll it for a while until it became obvious. Then it would make them really angry.

She began to fill the sink with water, and added detergent to form foamy bubbles. Nearby were a pair of rubber gloves she pulled on. They were a bit too big for her gentle hands. Baylee Ann filled a mop bucket at a wall hydrant and added a disinfectant and degreaser. But after mopping about a third of the floor she turned and walked through the doorway. Bambi heard the angry shout as she crossed the threshold.

"How many times do we have to tell you Bitches? Stay in the kitchen!"

Baylee Ann's voice was scornful, "I have to piss. Don't have a cow."

"Then use the sink in the kitchen," he snarled and a moment later there was a thud and the shattering of glass.

Baylee Ann retreated back through the doorway.

"He even threw a beer bottle at me, the bastard."

"I told you," hissed Bambi. "Now get busy so they think we're useful."

Baylee Ann stared at the floor as she came to grips with what Bambi had been trying to tell her and then looked up with angry eyes, "We're prisoners, aren't we?"

"Duh. Why do you think I've been trying to keep our heads down?"

"I can't believe they're doing that to us. Bastards! We're not surrendering and going along with it," declared Baylee Ann.

"Well, there's no way out."

Baylee Ann nodded, looking at the big reefer unit blocking the backdoors to the bathrooms.

"Then let's barricade ourselves in."

"There's no door. And you know they'll eventually break down anything we pile up and be really mad when they get us."

"A lot can happen in that time. Shep wouldn't be cleaning house unless he's scared of something. That means someone's coming. I don't know if it's the sheriff or Kelton, or another gang. But no matter who they are, they're better for us than Rattler out there."

The stainless steel wire shelving units which flanked the reefer were on wheels. They were wider than the kitchen's doorway, having to be turned lengthwise to roll through. Baylee Ann rolled the first long ways across the doorway, and Bambi kneeled to lock the castors.

"What the hell are you doing in there?" came an ill-tempered challenge from the dining area.

"Just moving stuff around to clean and mop better," sang Bambi.

No one else said anything else or bothered to get up to come and look at what they were doing. Shep's order was they were to stay in the kitchen. As long as they stayed there, no one was apt to show further initiative.

It was a flimsy barrier that would fall over if pushed on. They rolled the second shelving unit behind the first, locking its casters as well. Bambi took a roll of plastic wrap for covering left overs and used a half roll of the clinging wrap to lash the posts of the shelving units together.

The galley table came next. It was too long to wedge between the shelves and the opposite wall so they had to turn it sideways like the shelves. Again they locked the casters, then grabbed all they could to fill the gap between the galley table and wall to pin everything in place. The mop bucket was a good start. So were racks of empty beer bottles. They emptied the reefer of sacks of frozen frying potatoes and hamburger patties, and then used the adjustable shelves inside. Glassware, bottles of cleaners, serving trays, even their purses piled into the gap between the galley table and the wall, to pin the shelves in place against the doorway. The trash cans wouldn't fit without compressing the top, but they did so to wedge them into place.

Baylee Ann reached for the fryer baskets to throw into the gap and yelped as her hand touched the hot metal, "Ouch that's hot."

She smelled the boiling cooking oil and then she looked at the pots on the shelves and said, "Grab me some of those."

Bambi also realized the value of a weapon for their desperate last stand to defend their makeshift wall. She found a pair of long pointed kitchen knives, and using the last of the cling wrap lashed them as tightly as she could to the end of the mop and the broom handles to form a pair of makeshift spears. They might be good for a single desperate thrust through the open shelving units. Some cleavers remained for when they breached the wall and it was close hand to hand.

She'd been a submissive all her life. But not this night. Bambi could feel the shaking starting in her arms and legs. But it was a different type of shaking. It wasn't the trembling bunny trying to lay perfectly still in the face of a predator. It was the relaxed trembling of a prize fighter pacing and dancing before the bell rang. The adrenaline of a competitor. She turned toward Baylee Ann.

Baylee Ann's face was set and determined, but loosened enough to display a look of shock when she met Bambi's gaze. Bambi didn't back down her hard stare. Baylee Ann recomposed herself in a second, nodded as she gripped the mop stick tightly, and faced the barricaded doorway. Game on, you dirty, greasy, pieces of crap, biker thugs. We don't need you anymore and you don't own us, thought Bambi.

They waited by the barricaded kitchen doorway and listened. Every few minutes they heard a couple of men rise and walk toward the front, their boots echoing on the wooden planks. Baylee Ann eventually climbed onto the galley table so she could squat over the suds in the wash sink and finally relieve herself. Bambi herself yawned and she rubbed her eyes. The adrenaline of anticipation had faded, and they felt tired.

Yells and flying gravel clearly audible over the roar of an engine, a car's engine, suddenly came from the front parking lot. It was followed by the crunching of steel. A second later there were gunshots.

Rattler's confident and commanding voice boomed through the barn, "Jingles and Burrito, watch the kitchen. The rest of you apes, come with me!"

The women heard the car's engine rev to a vibrating roar, like someone was flooring it in neutral. Another volley of shots popped over the mechanical thunder and Jingles leaned his head around the doorframe to peer inside the kitchen.

Bambi thrust with her spear between the shelves, arms extending and legs springing off the concrete floor. It caught Jingles above his right collar bone, just to the side of the voice box. With all her weight behind it, it sunk deeply with only the weakness of the plastic wrap splicing preventing the full transfer of momentum to penetrate out his back. When she drew back, the wrap gave way and she was left holding the broom handle as the blade remained embedded in his body.

Jingles stepped back from the shelves he had tried to fight through, his weathered face turning ashen. His eyes widened and his bandaged arm came up to grasp at the blade stuck in his body. He took his hand away, looking at his crimson fingers and returned to grasp the hilt. Burrito turned toward him, placing his hand over Jingles' to prevent him from trying to pull it out. As the light faded from Jingle's eyes and his knees buckled, Burrito helped him fall gracefully to the ground.

"Damn, couldn't get a shot on Burrito," complained Baylee Ann peering through the shelves with her mop spear, "but good one. You got Jingles."

Baylee Ann stood back from the doorway some, seeking a target through an opening where she could thrust as a loud rifle boom sounded outside. Bambi nodded at her, trading the broom for a large cleaver. She stood to the side of the doorway up against the wall, ready to slash at any prying hands or fingers that tried to remove their protective shield.

There would be regrets later. She'd killed someone and she would cry about it. But for now, she had a lifetime of rage waiting to get out and one simple kill would not slake it.

"Fucking Bitches! What did we ever do to you?" screamed Burrito through the shelves as more gunfire erupted in the parking lot.

Baylee Ann set the spear aside to quickly pick up a small paring knife and side armed it through the upper shelves at his face. It slashed his cheek just below his left eye and he rushed forward in rage to grab and shake the shelves like some frustrated prisoner on the bars of a jail cell. She was quick to pick up the spear, and he jumped back in just the nick of time. The large rifle boomed again, drowning out the smaller rapid pops of the pistols.

Then Burrito turned and ran toward the front knocking aside tables and chairs in his panicked strides, "Hey guys, we need some help with the bitches!"

Baylee Ann looked at Bambi and they exchanged smiles. Their eyes glowed with hope and adrenaline. Then they heard a sharp rapping sound as a bullet tore through thin sheet metal followed immediately by a rifle's roar. Superheated oil from the fryer gushed through the bullet hole in the drywall out onto the dining room floor. It also flooded onto the kitchen floor, pooling underneath the appliance and finding the heating element. Seconds later it ignited, and moments later flames licked at the dry seasoned timbers of the roof as thick black smoke poured from the kitchen's doorway.

CHAPTER—32

Kelton Jager crouched with his big Glock 40 behind the engine block of Dixie's old Mercury Cougar. Under the car's belly was a knocked down row of motorcycles, backed over until the car was aground on its oil pan and the suspended wheels spun uselessly. He'd bailed out the driver's side and took cover by the left front wheel as a hail of bullets rained from the porch and the barn's windows, sprinkling the car's passenger side with bare metal stars. He wanted to rise and make shots, but didn't dare with some half dozen barrels gunning for him. Normally he would have been forced to move immediately, even across the open parking lot, because if he didn't they would come around both sides of the car at the same time and have him. Except, there was Braxton Greene.

Braxton Greene wasn't a trained marksman, but he was southern country and owned a deer rifle. The off-ramp from the interstate was a great elevated platform to fire from, the rifle steadily rested on the guard rail with a good view into the front of Shep's establishment. Hardly anyone took the exit in the daytime, let along in the small hours of the morning so witnesses weren't an issue. It was a simple matter to place the crosshairs of the scope on the silhouettes backlit from the barn while sitting on the road's shoulder, and fire. The powerful .30-06 bullets pierced bodies and splintered barn timbers. He fired slowly, and deliberately, giving Kelton Jager the time he needed to slice the pie.

Kelton crept to the front of the car still using the engine block for cover until he could just see one of the bikers. As the green triangle of the reflex site was placed over the man's chest, he fired. Then he inched around a little more, until he could see the next man and did the same. From a bird's eye view, one could draw a pair of lines making a wedge of what the shooter could see much like a slice of pie. This tactic allowed Kelton to engage targets mano a mano, rather than facing down multiple shooters at the same time. And with his skills, he was well equipped to win these one on one combats. Especially as he was acting, instead of reacting, toward a target coming into view. Action was always faster.

The bikers were tough men who didn't back down from a fight. Rather than fade back into the cover of the barn as their numbers slowly fell away, they rallied into a group that rushed forward. They weren't particularly quick or athletic, but they were determined. They were also backlit from the lights of the barn and easy pickings through the scope of Braxton's deer rifle. A couple of quick shots and two of them fell, mortally wounded. Another sharp crack of the rifle sounded as a bullet flew over the heads of those falling back.

Kelton didn't cut them any slack, popping up from cover to press home shots while he and Braxton had the initiative and emptied the last of his pistol's fifteen-round magazine at their fleeing backs. None of the bikers went down, but Kelton felt confident he'd scored several hits. He dropped back down under a few wild shots of return fire, loaded a fresh magazine and slipped the empty into his hip utility pocket.

The fight then settled down to him behind the car, and the bikers replying from the edges of the barn's doorway and over the sills of its flanking front windows. No one was able to maneuver to advantage for fear of being shot. Kelton began to feel trapped on the island of the car's cover in the openness of the parking lot. Only Braxton's rifle shots kept him from being overrun, but he also knew that would be coming to an end soon. Braxton only had a dozen rounds or so in the house, left over from a box of twenty from the last time he'd gone hunting several years ago. Kelton would soon be on his own.

Bambi and Baylee Ann flipped the makeshift spears in their hands and used the mop and broom to beat at the flames steadily spreading from the fryer in the kitchen. The ends absorbed the flaming oil and soon ignited, causing them to rush back to the water filled dish sink to extinguish them. In less than a minute the bellowing smoke, trapped against the kitchen's drop ceiling, began to blind and choke them. They dropped to the floor.

"Is there any way we can crawl out into the dining room?" yelled Baylee Ann.

Bambi slithered toward the doorway on her belly, flinching at the numerous gunshots audible over the roaring flames. Hugging the floor to have air, she reached toward the metal posts of the rolling shelves and used them to pull herself forward. Tiny abrasions formed on her stomach and forearms, but her senses were so overloaded she didn't feel the old concrete. The thick smoke really only let her see the legs of tables and chairs. But plenty of orange flames licked upward from the floorboards.

"It's no good. The room's filled with flame," shouted Bambi and then yelled for all she was worth to be heard over another volley of shooting. "Oil ran out through the hole in the wall. The beams are on fire overhead."

"We'll have to make a run for it anyway. Push through!" instructed Baylee Ann.

Bambi peered again at the inferno, wondering when the roof would collapse upon then. But her friend was right about one thing. Staying in the kitchen was about giving up. And she would never ever give up ever again. Bambi rolled on her side to squirm through the shelves, wondering how in the world Baylee Ann would ever fit behind her.

A deep thumping noise made her look backward. Unlike the distant shooting, this was nearby. At first she thought Baylee Ann must be clearing a path for herself, but her friend had rolled on her side to look back too.

"Someone is trying to get into the kitchen from the bathroom," said Baylee Ann in disbelief.

Bambi stared at the base of the reefer unit, and saw it vibrate in time with the thudding. Then she felt cool air rush by her face, sucked in by the raging flames and making a whistling sound around the edges of the door.

"Come on," said Bambi pushing herself out of the entanglement of the shelves and making her way back toward the reefer.

"We couldn't move it before," reminded Baylee Ann.

"But it was full and the shelves were in the way. And them are pushing to help," explained Bambi.

Bambi grasped with fingers behind the reefer and put her feet on the wall to push. It slid a little with the next thump of the door against its back. The cool air felt like a godsend at first, soothing her nose and lips with its clean crispness. But she also felt the temperature rising as the flames were fed.

"I'm stronger. Roll clear," demanded Baylee Ann.

Bambi did so, rolling over the discarded broom handle and bruising her hip. Baylee Ann took up her position and strained with her legs and hands, but the old chipped concrete made for hard going sliding the reefer and sweaty fingers slipped from the smooth stainless steel. Bambi wanted to stand over Baylee Ann and pull with her, but the arid choking smoke had forced them to the bottom of the floor. There wasn't room for her to get close enough to help. Or was there?

Bambi grasped the broom handle and thrust the wood behind the reefer under Baylee Ann's legs. Baylee Ann felt the stick and turned and looked.

"Great idea," she said. "Let's pull when they push."

The girls grasped the wood while lying flat on their backs and their feet on the wall. They heaved, and the reefer pivoted on its far corner. Then the door pushed into the back of the reefer and they redoubled their efforts. Cool wind rushed across them as the gap between the door and its frame became a few inches, and then a foot. Dull and lethargic flames at the base of the walls, fed by the rush of oxygen brightened and leapt with energy. Bambi felt the skin on her forehead blistering, but one last pull and the gap was a large enough for Baylee Ann to slither through.

"Give me your feet!" came Dixie's voice as a pair of soft pale hands grabbed Baylee Ann's ankles and drug her into the bathroom.

Bambi rolled and scampered through the gap, coughing and heaving at the wonderful air. Baylee Ann rested on her side for a moment, smiled and gave a thumb's up.

"Y'all okay?" asked Dixie.

They nodded, as thick black smoke billowed out the door and began to fill the bathroom. A wispy orange arm of light reached in and kissed the ceiling, leaving glowing fibers of wood where it touched.

"We're not safe yet," yelled Dixie. "Come on!"

Bambi took Dixie's outstretched arm and watched Baylee Ann take hold of the other one. They pushed themselves to their feet, and then fell in behind Dixie as they exited the barn through the west facing bathroom doors, hacking in the fresh air. From there it was a stumbling and clumsy lumber through the vines and drainage ditch to reach the road. They faltered here and there, picking up small cuts from the gravel and broken glass which always collected along rural roads, but they were clear.

Kelton saw the flickering flames inside the barn and the thick black smoke billowing out the top of the front doorway. It was just a bright background glow at first, but soon twisting and dancing orange fingers reached to the dry timbers of the rafters. He saw the men inside raising their heads, looking back at the inferno and where to possibly run for cover under fire in the parking lot. He engaged them as they appeared, trying to put pressure on some of them to stay inside so they didn't come out all at once. Kelton knew the heat would force them out.

He knelt and inserted a fresh magazine to top off his gun. Sixteen rounds were quickly at the ready. Kelton stopped firing and remained kneeling, waiting for the better quality opportunities to get hits that would soon follow. As a central section of the roof collapsed over the dining area, orange fireflies danced into the air. Combustion gases, that had been trapped by the shingles were suddenly released to create a sucking vacuum. It brought in fresh air to the flames through the doors and windows, starting a powerful updraft. Even out at the car, Kelton felt the rush of air through the barn doors and windows and saw the orange glow brighten like a blacksmith's forge with a breath from the bellows.

They scurried out as the heat became unbearable, jackets smoking from their backs, half blinded by the smoke, and coughing.

Aim and shoot thought Kelton. Release the trigger slightly as the gun recoils letting it settle with the glowing green triangle on the new aim point. A tiny squeeze to discharge the gun again, and repeat. Slow is smooth, and smooth is really fast.

Shot placement was perfect center of mass, the bullets punching through them into the barn's inferno. Seconds later, all that had run forth were down. Anything his bullets hadn't finished, the flames soon would.

Kelton could feel the intensity of the heat himself, and began to walk backward, scanning over his gun for other targets. Drifting embers landed among the upset bikes and car. Seconds later, they found gasoline spilled from the tanks. With a shaking whoosh, another set of flames reached up toward the night sky and he felt the small shockwave roll over his face. The pile of motorcycles and the car was burning. There was no more gunfire.

He felt he must have watched for a good couple of minutes, and then finally lowered his gun. Again he exchanged magazines so his gun was topped off, and after one last scan he returned it to holster. The whole building was now consumed, and as he jogged toward the road to get away he could see raging flames coming out the old stall windows down the entire side. With a crash, another section of roof gave way as its lost strength could no longer support its weight. Then the long wall on the south side, facing the road, began to tremble.

Kelton ran all the way across the street, the heat too intense for him to stand on the asphalt. He then made his way west, weaving through the scrub pines covering forested lots once cleared but never built upon. The cool night air soothed the skin of his face, Kelton not truly realizing how angry the painful intense heat had been until it was taken away. He made his way slowly, not wanting to trip and hurt himself, but anxious to get to the rally point and count noses. In a few minutes he saw three figures standing in the road, just outside the circle of light cast by the burning barn.

Instinctively, he reached for the butt of his gun but there were no mistaking women's curves and especially the wider hips of Baylee Ann. He stepped out into the roadway so they could readily see him. They all laughed, reached out their arms as they ran forward, and wrapped him into a large group hug. Then the adrenaline made them cry and shake, as their bodies twitched with leftover survival hormones.

"Everyone okay?" he asked.

They all nodded and then the four of them turned to watch as the walls of the barn fell in upon itself in a glowing roaring infernal of rubble.

CHAPTER—33

It was midmorning on Sunday, and Kelton Jager held Azrael's leash as they walked west on Main Street toward St. Albans from Dixie's Truck Stop. The air was cool and fresh, and it felt pleasant to have finally chased away the smell of ashes and soot from his nostrils so he could enjoy the dogwood blossoms. The morning rush of cars to church was over, and the town had returned to a sleepy look with most of the stores closed until Monday morning.

They'd all watched the barn completely collapse the other night, glowing embers wafting upon the fire wind. Braxton eventually pulled up in his truck. The fire had been so intense he didn't dare risk driving by it on Azalea Estates Lane. Instead, after gathering his spent brass and rifle, he'd driven down the exit ramp and right back up the onramp. The next exit was River Road, and he'd driven by the small fishing cabins and vacation homes until reaching Thigpen Road. A little trip north, and Braxton had been turning right back on to Azalea. In short, he'd simply gone around the block. But in the country, that was often a half-hour ordeal.

Baylee Ann and Bambi had sat up front with Braxton, which meant Kelton and Dixie had to ride in the bed with their backs against the cab. He hadn't minded, and didn't think she had either. Braxton had driven slowly, minimizing the bumps and the centrifugal effect of the rural road's twists and turns. The rush of the wind had been too much for them to talk, but the holding of hands and an arm over the shoulders said more than words ever would.

Braxton had stopped at his house, but left the little Chevy's lights and engine running. Kelton had leapt over the side of the truck and despite his exhausted legs ran up the concrete steps of the porch to turn the doorknob. Azrael had danced around, emitting barks skyward and circled about to collect his flock of one. Kelton scooped up his pack, retrieved his phone and put it back in his usual shirt pocket, and then they were in the back of the truck again and rolling toward the truck stop.

Dixie had gotten him a room key, but hadn't stayed. She had said she needed some things from her house, and to feed her cat Patsy, and had asked Braxton to drop her there. Kelton had been too tired to do anything more than nod.

In the little motel room, Kelton had done the best cleaning he could do. He'd stripped all his clothes in the tub and showered away over them, scrubbing furiously with the thin white washcloth despite the redness of his skin. When the water had drained after, he'd refilled the tub and added all his other clothes and odd possessions which could tolerate a long soaking. He'd added the last contents of his laundry soap bottle, and was fast asleep in no time at all.

It had been late morning on Saturday when he'd awoken, legs stiff and crampy from the long cold walk the evening before. He'd felt the mild burn on his face and rubbed away the sleep. Azrael had needed to go out, so he'd wrapped himself in the spare blanket to stand watch from the doorway. The soapy water in the tub had turned gray during the night and he drained it away to refill for rinsing. Then he'd hung things on the shower rod and towel bars to dry.

The knock on the door had surprised him, but Azrael hadn't appeared weary. He'd wrapped himself in the blanket again and opened to find Dixie standing on the room's stoop with a steaming tray of food.

"Room service?" she'd greeted with a sweet southern smile. "And you know," she had said playfully while nodding her head in time to her words as she walked in, "we do have a dress code."

"Sorry. Everything I own is drying. Going to be damp for quite a while."

"Brought you my dad's robe. I've an old fan in the maid's closet I'll bring you in a few minutes to help your stuff dry, too. How are you feeling?"

"I'm okay. Just worn out. Did you get the car reported stolen okay?"

It wasn't about insurance. It was about having deniability of being at the scene. He hadn't planned to get her car stuck making the distraction, but as they said in the army, "No plan survives contact with the enemy." At least the part where she snuck in the back when there was a distraction had worked out fine.

She'd nodded and hadn't stayed long, and was back for just a moment a few minutes later to drop off the box fan. The weekend brunch crowd was busy time, and there were new shifts of employees she'd wanted to bring up to date on current events. So he'd lounged and tended to his gear.

His gun had definitely needed attention. There'd been a lot of shooting and exposure to the elements. He'd also removed all the remaining cartridges from the magazines and given them a careful wipe and inspection. At the first opportunity he would replace them all, but for now they would serve. And while he doubted meaningful forensics would survive the fire, as soon as he had a shipping address to order new parts he thought it would be worth a couple hundred bucks to replace the barrel, firing pin and extractor.

Dixie had come back to him midafternoon and said she was exhausted as she flopped down on the bed. She probably really was with getting through the morning shift after the night they'd had, and she had wanted to talk to the evening workers as well. He had been definitely feeling low key himself. So they had sat against the headboard and turned on the television. When he'd looked over, she was asleep on his shoulder.

He'd decided to try and nap as well, but couldn't. It had nothing to do with having slept so late. His body had been plenty tired, but his conscience was unsettled. He'd killed more men home in America in one week than he'd killed in four years on the battlefield. He'd decided he was okay with that. It wasn't about how many. They'd all been violent thugs, keeping women against their will.

Deputy Garner was the one that bothered him. Dixie had lay sleeping beside him, having no idea he killed her boyfriend. Sure, she'd declared her loathing for Buck. But he reckoned if he confessed to her, she'd not react favorably. So he'd not talked about it.

A cop. That bothered him. Supposedly a good guy. Who'd shot at his dog. Chandler hadn't condemned Buck for that, even after Azrael had done the sheriff a service. It was why Kelton had done what he'd done. But it had also branded him a criminal. A nasty label with grave consequences. He'd be pursued with vigor and he would run for all he was worth. But he couldn't run from himself. It was like he had this subconscious desire for someone to tell him that what he'd done was okay. But there was no one to tell him, even if they would tell him such a thing, because his mother and Mr. Hesp were dead. Telling it to himself had been the only option, and self-doubt thrived under the weight of the issues.

He'd become tormented and restless that evening. Unable to rest further, he'd gone with her to the diner for a few hours. His outer clothes, not fast drying synthetic, had still been slightly damp. Braxton and the other ladies had come in as well. Dixie had pitched her idea of intervening with the young girls at the back of the truck lot, and the two alumni, looking for new direction and purpose in life, latched on. When the three disappeared into the kitchen for a tour, Kelton and Braxton had time to exchange their respects.

Sitting quiet and listening to the locals had also given him the vibe of the town. Everyone had been abuzz with the spate of broken windows and dumpster fires. In addition, the deputy had been formally declared missing and search parties were underway. Put simply, the one-man sheriff's office had its hands full without worrying about an old barn that had burned down that no one had bothered to report.

As far as either of them knew, no authorities had been to investigate the scene yet. Braxton had done a drive by, and told him not much had stood. The black ashes were still smoking, and only some steel appliances had any semblance of form. He'd mentioned some bikers had been in the parking lot walking over the scene, but then had mounted up and driven away. But they both knew it was only a matter of time before Sheriff Fouche came poking around and that meant Kelton would do well to move along. Especially before Buck's body was discovered.

The final moment of truth for Kelton came later, back again in the tiny worn motel room. Azrael had been restless after being cooped up for a couple of days. Dixie had come to him, tired but still very much determined to make the business work. If he had stayed, and it would have been far from wise to do so, this is what life would be and it wasn't the life for him or his dog. Even if he could live with hiding his secret guilt. And she'd known it wasn't the life for him. And he'd known she'd known it so he wound up not making a move on her, even though she would have most likely acquiesced. The time for that had just somehow seemed past.

Kelton had given her the bundle of cash. It would have been too heavy for him to carry anyway. She'd sacrificed her car and he'd known she was strapped for some of the upgrades that the old fueling station would need. And even though it was drug money, he'd felt she was both entitled to it for the price her family had paid, and besides was trying to do something good with it. She'd kissed him in thanks, and then had talked excitedly about her evolving vision. Baylee Ann and Bambi would start work and they were going to give Braxton's live music a try on the weekends when he didn't have construction jobs. He sincerely hoped they made it.

And so, with one last leisurely breakfast, he and Azrael had gotten underway as Dixie and Baylee Ann argued in the kitchen about serving fried fish for breakfast. The doughnut shop was open, but despite the smells of fresh glazes the large meal of steak and eggs in him kept him going on by once again. He was sad to see sheets of plywood covering Mr. Butler's barbershop window, but encouraged by the red spray painted sign "Re-opening Soon." The small dumpster by the loading dock of the hardware store was blackened with soot and the plastic lid was warped and melted.

He took a right on Lowland Road to go north by the town square. Across the street, city hall was dark for the weekend. But he noted a small crowd in front of the church, including some media. Standing in the middle of the circle was Sheriff Fouche, his uniform immaculate, and his wife in a crimson dress with white lace and matching hat. Kelton paused to listen, as the sheriff's voice carried across the street.

"Doris Johnson was a predator in our community. I am proud to have brought her to justice and save our citizens from the dangerous drugs she pushed upon our children," he said with his back straight and shoulders back.

A reporter thrust a microphone forward, interrupting Chandler's rehearsed remarks, "Isn't it true you took vacation in the middle of our county's wave of violence?"

"Vacation is an entitlement. Negroes aren't slaves no more. If you are going to interrupt my report of public service with racist questions, my time will be better spent in God's house. Please excuse me," said the old sheriff as he turned to climb the steps with his wife on his arm looking indignant.

Other reporters called after him in a flurry of indiscernible questions, but Chandler and his wife didn't break stride. Kelton shook his head and kept on walking up to Smallwood Street. But instead of turning right toward the rescue station and the clinic, he turned left toward the railroad tracks. He was ready for a new direction, somewhere he hadn't been before. After crossing the rails, the road meandered to the north northwest. Maybe tonight he would turn on his phone for a look at the map.

Within fifteen minutes he was well out of St. Albans and traffic continued to be a rare event. He knelt to let Azrael off his lead, and then began stroking his head and ears. Azrael looked up at him with expectant eyes, wondering what was next.

"Azrael, I need to tell you something. Mr. Bacharach said when you were a puppy that you only have about a hundred vocabulary words so I shouldn't confuse you with idle talk like this. But the thing is, I respect you too much not to share with you what I'm thinking because you keep standing by me. That you've no idea what I'm saying really isn't the important part. It's just eating at me, and I need to get it off my chest.

What it is, is that I need to apologize again. My actions left you out on your own and me powerless inside a cage. I was taught once upon a time to respect authority in terms of black and white. To be loyal and obedient, and obey lawful orders. That's what was good and right. I'm a hypocrite maybe because it's what I demand of you.

But I don't see things that way anymore. People seem to have their own agenda and its mostly for power or money. They take idealism and try to manipulate it for their own ends. They try and coerce people by arguing it's for the common good, even though it's really just their own agenda. They could care less about me and you. I'm done with that. Their gleaming white panache is soiled.

I'm tired of being duped. I don't care if they are a sheriff, a deputy, or a store keeper. A general, or a president. If someone tries to lock either of us up again for any reason whatsoever, I'll shoot them dead. No hesitations or regrets. I've made my peace with that.

The authorities won't put up with that, will send men prepared to do violence to try and make us conform. They will try and tell us where we can go or what we can do. Rather than living to be old, it probably means a lot shorter lifespan for me. But Azrael, if I only live as long as you, it's plenty long enough for me."

And with that he petted Azrael's head once more, getting his wrist licked by a darting tongue in the process and rose to his feet. The muscles in his legs still ached so he'd take it easy today. There wasn't any reason to press hard to get anywhere. He just wanted to be underway again. Free as a couple of outlaws.

ABOUT THE AUTHOR

Charles Wendt is a former United States Air Force Civil Engineering officer, who lives with his wife on a farm in central Virginia. He enjoys horseback riding, dog training and shooting. When not busy providing process engineering consulting services, he is working on Kelton's and Azrael's next adventure. Please visit him on Facebook: https://www.facebook.com/Charles-Wendt-1073232879427462/?ref=bookmarks

If you enjoyed this book, please consider leaving a review. Your kind words are what keep independent authors going.

DID YOU KNOW that you don't need a Kindle to read eBooks? Amazon's free App can be downloaded to computers, tablets, and phones. So, if you are wanting to please read *By Dog Alone* (Book 2), but aren't ready to make the commitment to a Kindle reader, you can still enjoy the continuing story.

CPSIA information can be obtained
at www.ICGtesting.com
Printed in the USA
LVHW092339140519
617892LV00001B/173/P